Aphrodisiac for an Angel

Aphrodisiac for an Angel

Thomas Timmins

Zoëtown Media
Haydenville, Massachusetts

ZOËTOWN MEDIA

Aphrodisiac for an Angel

Copyright © 2016 by Thomas Timmins

www.thomastimmins.com

Cover design: Oona Hart

www.dandoprojects.com

ISBN: 978-0-9893283-8-8

Library of Congress Control Number: 2015943302

1. Fiction – Coming of age
2. Fiction – Love story
3. Fiction – Environmental thriller

Printed in the United States of America

This book is dedicated to
Rick, Barb, Joe, Betty
who know saints and angels.

Bent with worry,
God paused to smile.
And look, there were many holy angels
with bodies of the radiance
he had given them,
some with enormous wings
and others without any,
which is why I weep so much
because even more than God himself,
I love his fair angels.

Marina Tsvetaeva
Tr. Elaine Feinstein

You are my special angel
Right from paradise
I know you're an angel
Heaven is in your eyes

Jimmy Duncan
Sung by Bobby Vinton

A few years from now ...

LITTLE LIMBO

One

EHAWEE

Zoë perched on the edge of the bed, holding a pink nasal syringe in the sleeping woman's parched, withered lips. With her other hand, she propped up the old lady's chin. Mrs. Spalding's narrow jaw had dropped and begun to lock, her mouth's silent cry of "O" signaling death's imminent approach.

"Hurry," Zoë said, her fingers poised to squeeze the bulb at the moment of old lady's death. She'd draw Mrs. Spalding's soul into the syringe, adding it to the jug of souls she'd collected to lift her up, body and soul, straight to her mother Ruthie in Heaven.

If she could ever gather enough souls. If Mrs. Spalding would cooperate and let go of her shrunken life, right now, on Zoë's shift.

Zoë's ears perked up. The supervisor's shoes squeaked down the hall on her nightly rounds. Zoë snatched the syringe out of the old lady's mouth and buried it in her pocket. With the tip of her thumb, she smoothed the faint worry tracks on the ninety-nine-year-old's silky forehead.

Soon, no matter how tired her body, how stubborn her will-to-live, how deep her life force, Mrs. Spalding would sigh, and in a tender burst of energy, release her immortal, Heaven-bound soul into Zoë's Soul Bubble.

Just hope she's not waiting around till she's a hundred, Zoë thought.

Humming, Zoë stepped into the room's shadows and backed into the closet, leaving the door cracked wide enough to watch. A half dozen cricket chirps bleated out of her coat. Shrugging her shoulders to jiggle the leather bomber jacket hanging like a parka on her small frame, she whispered "Shhhh, shhhh" to her flock of bugs.

Weaving her way between soft print farmlady dresses Mrs. Spalding would never touch again, Zoë withdrew into the closet dusk, the peppery odor of mothballs tickling her nose.

Mrs. Spalding's room door opened and Nurse Margie Franklin, the night boss, stepped in, elbowing the rheostat on the wall. The ceiling light soared up, spreading a creamy sheen across pale lime walls.

From the dresser top, a glint flashed off the photo of Mrs. Spalding's four daughters and twelve grandchildren and seven great-grandchildren, one of them pregnant. The glass frame reflected a narrow beam of ceiling light through the crack in the closet doorway into Zoë's eyes.

For the first time, it dawned on Zoë that no husbands' or fathers' faces were perched behind the women and children in the photo. Could all of her men's souls have departed already? Where were the women? Maybe Mrs. Spalding wasn't really dying.

The nurse went to the bedside and picked up the old lady's gnarled hand. She fingered the pulse and bent over close to her face. She glanced at her watch and set down the arm and tightened and folded the sheet under Mrs. Spalding's chin. "Still breathing," Nurse Franklin said.

Straightening up the teddy bear flopped on the dresser, the nurse looked around the room as if seeking another way to comfort the sleeping woman in her final hours.

Turning away from the bed to the large dresser on the wall opposite the closet, the nurse paused and squinted into the mirror, then she plucked a few daisies from the wild bouquet Zoë had brought in earlier that day and tossed the wilted flowers into the trash can. She picked up the tablet from the dresser, snapped a photo of Mrs. Spalding, looked at it, and tapped a few strokes, pocketed it, then dimmed the room light, leaving the door open.

Good, Zoë thought, old Prairie Dog forgot me.

Zoë waited until she heard the nurse's shoes squeak away on the waxed linoleum. She tiptoed out of the closet into the glow reflecting off the walls.

Sitting down beside the old lady, Zoë dug into her pocket and retrieved her Soul Bubble, one of the two tools she used to catch and keep souls. At one end, the Bubble had a long pink nipple and at the other, a soft squeeze bulb the size of a tennis ball. She'd borrowed the nasal syringe from the supply closet when she first came to work at Prairie View Nursing Home.

She'd borrowed three of them from the supply closet, just in case she had a big day. She used one syringe per soul catch, boiling it every time after she was done. Her step-mom Bonnie had taught her how to keep herself and all her clothes and tools cleaner than just clean – sparkling clean. It was a good habit now that she lived mostly on the land under the open sky, exposed to the constant seethe of South Dakota topsoil blown into every crease on a person's body.

Roaming on foot or bushwhacking on her bicycle in the arid foothills beyond the town, Zoë often found herself miles from water of any kind until just before she had to rush to work. Then, taking advantage of the Home's facilities, she shook out her hair and jacket and scrubbed off the grainy film of dirt in the 'Terminal Wing' mop sink.

A year ago, her tidiness and enthusiasm for the aged had landed her the job as nurse's aide at The Home. That, and her willingness to stay awake all night.

In exchange for always smiling while she cleaned up after the fragile and the bedridden, the Home had already provided Zoë between twenty-six or forty-two souls.

She wished she knew the exact number but she had to be realistic. She couldn't always tell if she caught the soul or if its angel had snatched it off to Heaven before Zoë trapped and stuffed it into Little Limbo, her Soul Keeper travel mug, the other tool of her trade.

With all the experience she'd gained in the last year as a nurse's aide, Zoë had expected scrawny Mrs. Spalding to leave this world by midnight, but the old lady hung on and on.

Whoever's the saint of stubbornness must be Mrs. Spalding's friend, Zoë thought.

The banana yellow color of her skin had darkened toward a flat mustard until, during the last week, opaque amber had bloomed all over her face. Liver failure, Zoë knew. Mrs. Spalding's chest barely rose and she lay on the bed like a bronzed statue.

Except for her eyes. She'd fooled Zoë with her eyes. Popped her lids back, rolled her eyeballs, then blinked before Zoë could zoom in with her own soul-meeting gaze. Usually, the old people welcomed death – a rare few struggled at the last. They opened eager eyes and stared into Zoë's encouraging gaze, beseeching her, wanting assurance or maybe trying to give her a last message for someone.

Peeking out of watery eyeballs between drooping lids and deep wrinkles, they always showed Zoë innocent infant's eyes. Zoë realized that people's baby eyes never changed, they only hid in grown-up faces until it didn't matter any more who peered into their souls.

If a dying person smiled at her, Zoë grinned and nodded her head, encouraging the intrepid soul on her way.

"Don't worry, brave one. I'll take care of your soul. Won't be long, we'll all be up there together."

When Zoë drew an unsuspecting smiler's soul into the Bubble, guilt sometimes gnawed at her stomach, but only for an instant. The poor old souls were so eager to go to their reward and now they had to spend the next year in the Thermos bottle socializing with the other souls Zoë had been lucky enough to snag.

Zoë rationalized that when the little community of souls she carted around in her Soul Keeper finally reached Heaven, they'd thank her for the introductions to new friends. Going new places alone was scary for people who spent all their lives in Shannon County, a place past the Badlands even everyone in South Dakota called "the middle of nowhere."

Mrs. Spalding took tiny breaths into her pinched nostrils but clenched her teeth. Despite the old lady's soft cheeks and smooth skin, Zoë recognized resolution in her bite.

Maybe she's mad, Zoë thought. She didn't get to do something she wanted to. Maybe upset with her husband for dying before her. Could be she's telling somebody off in a dream. Maybe she's fighting off the devil!

The yellow skin at the edges of the old woman's eyes wrinkled and smoothed, wrinkled and smoothed. Her lips spread and she sniggered.

Private joke.

Mrs. Spalding cackled and snorted, hauling her jaw back from her tongue like an ax rising over a chunk of firewood. Watching the emotions flutter across the crone's face, Zoë guessed that it might take days before the cords in her neck softened and let her jaw relax again, before her tongue unfurled and stretched forward in salute to her soul's imminent departure.

Still, despite Mrs. Spalding's stiff jaw, something in the air jostled Zoë's mind. She knew she'd make a soul catch tonight – somehow she always knew when it would happen – but if she didn't practice patience, her fervor might frighten all the old people into backing away from death.

Zoë noticed the tidied-up flowers in the canning jar. When the old folks made it onto the Death Watch charts, Zoë always brought gifts, usually wild flowers, to the people who might soon join her fleet of souls in Little Limbo.

She hoped the wildflowers made it easier for the soul to leave the body because there was teaching in the flowers Zoë wanted to remind the diers of – wildflowers sagged within a few hours, telling the dying person that every living thing wilts in time and it's all right.

Besides, no matter how much people pretended to be safe and domestic, like dogs and chickens, Zoë knew every single soul was wild and free. Only they didn't know it must be why they didn't act like it. If they did behave even a little bit different, other people treated them like they were strange. The way people treated Zoë. Except Old Prairie Dog. She understood Zoë would never be a tame kitty or a cow in a barn. Never.

Zoë figured that's why most people die – so they could become their own true free selves. As for her, she would never die because she didn't need to.

Her weight barely denting the mattress, Zoë sat close to Mrs. Spalding, smelling the sour breath, holding the bony hand with its transparent webs between the fingers, waiting for her to twitch or spring her eyes open again.

Zoë's vocation required fortitude as well as sleight-of-hand. If she was to catch souls who were buoyant with release from gravity before they whirred off into the sphere of effortless spirit, she had to stay alert, sometimes for hours without moving. The way she'd seen cats wait for mice and moles.

Yawning, Zoë patted a pocket of her jacket three times and said, "Sing now. Keep it soft."

A gentle chorus of cricket chirps tolled like miniature bells, its percussion with lingering chimes keeping Zoë sharp for the fleeting moment she would nab the soul.

She nodded a bit but caught herself and sat up, slapping her cheek, ready to pluck the soul quick before the old lady's speedy guardian angel snatched it, stalling Zoë's own plans for her living, wide-awake ascent, body and soul, and crickets, into Heaven. Her mother up there could wait because time didn't exist in Heaven, but Zoë on Earth had no time for patience.

Mrs. Spalding dug her heels into the mattress pad, as if by her will, stanching the flow of not only dribbles of pee and saliva, but clutching the invisible life force Zoë depended on catching.

If everything worked the way it should, Zoë would be only the second virgin ever to ascend deathless to Heaven. And the first to plan it and make it happen of her own desire and guile, without a son or a Heavenly father to haul her up off the Earth. She'd do it on her own. Well, with help from Ink'p'du'da and her crickets.

Time passing nagged at Zoë. Only three months – ninety four days actually – until her sixteenth birthday. She had to ascend while she was still fifteen, and a virgin, the same age as Kateri Tekakwitha, the girl saint. The only girl saint she'd ever actually met.

Zoë had found a photo of Kateri one afternoon while browsing in the St. Joseph's parish library, right there in Spring Creek. She'd filched the book and stared at the grainy drawing for hours, recognizing her soul's sister in the beautiful young Iroquois who was tortured and killed because she refused to give up her virginity to the white trappers.

One night, after weeks of talking over everything with Kateri, not concerned at all that the spirit never spoke aloud, Kateri came to Zoë. Silent as ever, standing across the campfire, wearing fringed and beaded leathers, her kindly face aglow with the same sweetness as in the photo.

Never one to waste time, Zoë said, "I only have one problem with you." She was comfortable speaking straight to the holy apparition because she'd imagined seeing her so many times. Braids now. A darker face, but that could be the shadow. The saint raised her eyebrows and cocked her head.

"They tortured you and murdered you. That's not for me. I have to rise up just like I am. Zoë Rarefield, a regular South Dakota country girl."

Kateri agreed. No dying. She couldn't guarantee no torture.

"All right. If it has to hurt." Zoë didn't mind pain. Better than snoring away like most people, missing life. "No scars."

Kateri shook her head in firm, wide arcs, allaying Zoë's fears of men's knives and sticks wielded with malice.

"My mother wouldn't like scars on me. I'm going to see her, you know. I really love it here, but...."

Kateri's mysterious smile widened into a grin, and she sat down, crossing her legs under her skirt, and nodded at Zoë over the low orange campfire flames. They gazed into each other's eyes until Zoë fell asleep.

When she woke, it was white dawn. She lay happy beside warm embers, watching a chipmunk nip at a cookie she'd dropped when Kateri had surprised her.

From then on, Kateri was Zoë's protector and her ally in her journey to Blissville, the town up in Paradise where Ruthie Rarefield waited, ten years gone now and eager to see and hold her baby girl.

Unlike Kateri, Zoë planned to return to Earth after ascending. She'd keep her soul firmly planted inside her body and come back whenever she wanted.

But first, she had to hang out with her mom, who was stuck in Heaven without a body – this Zoë knew for sure. She touched one of her mom's bones in her pocket right now. But even if Heaven had all the beautiful singing and flying it was supposed to, Zoë couldn't bear leaving the Earth forever.

She loved her stepbrother Devan too much and her stepparents Bonnie and Royal most of the time and her best friend Annie and even Old Prairie Dog.

She even loved George One Cloud a little bit, more than a brother, that's for sure. For his thick, soft lips. And the way she felt with him that first time they found themselves alone in the back room of the Golden Turnip Health Food Shoppe.

Zoë promised herself that she wouldn't abandon any of them. She didn't know how, but once she arrived in the Eternal Realm, she was sure she could reverse her journey, the same way she took the round-trip airplane flight from Rapid City to Denver five years ago with Devan.

Mrs. Spalding's eyelashes fluttered, her nostrils wiggled, tiny muscles displaying their appetite for air.

She's stubborn, like me. She's not going anywhere tonight, I guess. Her people must know or they'd be here already.

Zoë nodded to the old lady, deciding to let her hang on all by herself. She tweaked the old lady's cheek and tugged at her jaw. It felt as rigid as a pony's horseshoe. Zoë caressed the chalk-white hair haloing the bilious face and left the old lady to her snuffling.

On her way out of the room, she looked into the mirror, seeing all the way to the bottom of her thigh-length leather coat. She smiled at herself, combing her long crimson, blue and gold-tipped hair with her fingers, pulling it forward to hang over her collar down below her throat onto her T-shirt.

Flipping her head, she draped a veil of hair over one eye, across a freckled cheek. She smiled at herself and, as usual, her mother, Ruthie, smiled back from the mirror. Then she shrugged her jacket off her shoulders, catching it on her elbows and exposing her T-shirted front.

Jutting her chest out, she pulled her coat back and she tugged her shirt tight. Her nipples showed through the cotton shirt round and wide as lifesavers perched on her ice-cream scoop breasts. Her breasts hadn't grown any bigger this year, but they felt softer and Zoë didn't mind when certain boys brushed against her when they passed her in a store, or at a football game. In public places.

Fluorescence from the hallway cast a dull glow on her hair, darkening the blue and yellow tips she'd carefully colored last night. Shifting her jacket into place, she made a face, pulling the flesh back from her temples and flattening her nose.

I'm a green-eyed jack o'lantern.

Checking the trash can, she spied a dozen perfectly fresh bluettes the nurse had mistaken for wilted. She curled them over her ear, securing them under a wave of hair.

Blue diamonds in a red sunrise, she thought. Glancing at Mrs. Spalding, she turned and skipped down the hall. She stopped at the nurse's station and peeked over the counter, resting her chin on its glossy surface.

Old Prairie Dog looked up from her magazine, grinned, and said, "There you are, Ehawee. Pretty flowers. Where've you been? Sleeping in the laundry room?"

Old Prairie Dog gave everybody a Lakota name. She had at least three names herself. Besides Margaret Franklin and Speaking Woman, she'd told Zoë she could call her Wachiwi – Dancer – when they were alone.

Zoë liked Ehawee because it meant Laughing Girl and she told her boss that she could call her Ehawee any time, any place, just don't call her Zoë Marie Kent Rarefield, her long, boring birth name.

Taking her cue from Wachiwi, Zoë blinked and sighed, as if she were barely awake. "Sheets're folded and stacked," she said, giggling.

"Did I ever tell you how sweet your voice is? When you laugh like that, I hear pianos tinkling. You sure you don't want to come with me to church choir? Lotta cute boys...."

Zoë blushed. She liked to sing, but she preferred listening to Heavenly choirs. Besides, on Earth, nobody sang prettier than her crickets.

Cute boys? She didn't need church to find cute boys. She grinned at Old Prairie Dog. "Sounds fun, but I don't like church." The only time she'd ever step inside a church again, somebody she loved would be dead.

The boss frowned, her jowls ticking. "How're you gonna save your soul, young lady? You can't be a wild mustang roaming around the Black Hills all your life. It's time you started growing up."

"If you die, I'll go to your funeral. Otherwise, no way."

"You want me to die?"

Frustrated, Zoë sighed. "Nobody around here's dying tonight, that's for sure."

Old Prairie Dog's eyebrows lifted.

Zoë hoped she wasn't too disrespectful.

"What did you do with your hair? It looks like a rainy street with neon lights on it."

Zoë tossed her head back, flipping her long hair with her hand. "It's fresh. I did it myself." She grinned and swung her head back and forth. A few strands tickled her nose and she sneezed.

The nurse scrunched up her nose and leaned back in her chair with her hands behind her head. Her ample bosom about to pop the buttons on her greens. "How's Mrs. Spalding?"

Uh oh. She's mad. Did Old Prairie Dog know I was in the closet? Naw. Zoë giggled, holding her laugh in her throat the way she did when she was nervous. "Hmmm. Same."

"You always have a smile on your face, Ehawee. I never know if you're happy or guilty. You're not like the other kids, drinkin', doin' meth. Please, never do meth."

No way she'd do meth. It had made her old best friend Candy crazy. First her face turned into a scab farm, then her teeth fell out. Last she'd heard of her, she'd gone to Rapid City. She was probably dead by now. At fifteen, like Zoë.

"My mother used to smoke cigarettes," Zoë said. "I never did."

Old Prairie Dog blinked and held her eyes shut for a moment, then opened them, her fleshy lips tucked into each other.

"You do take somethin', don't you?" She absently touched the medicine cabinet key that hung from a hook on the side of the desk. "Sneak something? Everybody tries to."

Zoë rubbed her palm across her lips and flattened the upturned corners of her mouth. She lowered her eyebrows and everted her lower lip, pasting hurt onto her face. Some boys had died from taking something like morphine powder they stole from a drugstore, she'd heard. Old Prairie Dog was looking out for her.

Sitting up, the nurse inclined her forehead. She stared back from under penciled eyebrows until Zoë crossed her eyes and stuck out her tongue. The boss laughed and tilted her round body back in the wide leather chair.

"Ah, that's my sweet little Ehawee."

Old Prairie Dog resumed reading her magazine, the way she always did when she was really thinking about giving Zoë some new chore.

While Zoë waited for orders, she fiddled with the pencils Old Prairie Dog had arranged like dried flowers in a heavy blue mug labeled 'SoftMove for Seniors,' the pills the other aides sometimes force-fed their patients. That felt cruel to Zoë so she always hid the bottle from the other aides. Besideas, not one of them ever had a nice thing to say to Zoë when they came in while she was leaving. Not one "Good morning" or "Thanks" or even a "Have a nice day, Zoë." Zoë called them the "Poop Patrol."

Old Prairie dog opened her yap like Zoë expected.

"Zoë, go sit with Mr. Johannson. We took him off support this morning. Doctor says two or three days. Family lives up by Anpetu Mountain. They'll be here a little after breakfast."

Zoë grinned. Maybe it was him she'd catch tonight. "Remember: no water. He's on a DNR order, too. You'll call me if anything happens, right?"

"How about ice chips?" Zoë said, biting her upper lip and raising her eyebrows to let Prairie Dog know she was joking.

Serious now, the boss wagged her finger and showed her tiny teeth. "You know better."

Zoë laughed out loud and sauntered away down the hall, skidding her rubber heels in rude squawks on the linoleum.

"Zoë. No ice chips!"

Ice chips. That's the last thing I'd give him, Zoë thought. If he's ready to go, he won't need to take a thing with him.

Two

SOUL SNATCHER

Zoë sat down next to an old man who looked healthy as a working carpenter. Ruddy face, fat hands crossed on a bulky chest.

She licked a finger and smoothed out his tangled eyebrows.

A crumpled and weary helium balloon saying 'Happy Birthday' sagged a foot above the headboard. Its silvery skin was striped with chartreuse reflections of the wall and crinkled at the bottom like the mouths of all the old men and women sawing away in their little rooms.

Zoë checked the clock on the bedside table. With ornery Mrs. Spalding snorting like a young heifer and fat Mr. Johannson sticking around till who knew when, it didn't look like she would catch any souls tonight, after all. Another boring wasted shift.

The hump of the old man's belly rose under the sheet and triple chins circled his thick neck like sausages. Zoë speculated that he was so big, he might be carrying a great soul inside all that blubber.

During a lifetime, some souls inflated barely an inch beyond the skin. For great ones – Zoë could never tell who was great or who was normal or little until they died – their souls ballooned out and soared over a whole county, taking in a conversation in a coffee shop, a new colt being born, a thunder and lightning storm, all at once.

She knew, when the body dies, the soul contracts into itself, the same way stars do on their way to becoming black holes. Prudent in planning for her voyage out of the atmosphere into Heaven's realms, Zoë had studied novas and black holes, just in case she got an angel who flew too close to a black hole – that would be the end. Zoë wouldn't allow that.

Most likely, the angels who would fly her up probably had maps of the universe in their brains - they were as smart as God, just not as old and powerful. She'd never heard of an angel who could make light. But maybe one could trip on some dark matter and lose his balance on the lip of a black hole.

Zoë shuddered at the thought.

Once a soul condensed itself to the size of a grain of dust, it deposited itself near the person's heart. More precisely, Zoë had noticed that at the moment before death, the soul perched in the dier's throat, right below the root of the tongue, the soul's runway.

She reasoned why the soul flew out of the mouth on the first leg of its trip to Heaven: because it was the person's last word.

In the beginning was the word: when the baby cries to let everybody know she's here. So, at the end comes the last word, same as when you're born except now the soul is soaked with life and life loads it down with the heavy chains of being like everyone else and too many memories until it pulls the body all the way down into a grave.

That's why it was easier to catch an old person's sluggish, burdened soul than a baby's fleet wild soul.

Mr. J's sour breath swirled into Zoë's nose. She flinched. Some old people's breath stank like the runoff from a cattle yard. This puzzled Zoë. Was it only her keen sense of smell or was the body itself giving the soul an excuse to leave? Who could bear living in that stench?

Ever the scientist, Zoë deduced the smell's purpose: the first stage of spoilage, alerting the soul that the flesh had given up, unable to hold off the rot of years any longer.

That stench was the next-to-last stage of dying. Shortly before the aged body died, flowery or fruity fragrances seeped out, signaling the soul's final passage beyond the lungs' zest for life, through life's final strictures in the throat, into the soul-birthing cave of the mouth.

Those last perfumed breaths made Zoë wish more than anything she could see souls. She imagined the lilac-scented as queens, the rosy ones dancing girls, the peach blossoms cowgirls. Cinnamony applesauce was cowboys. The ripe banana smells had to be Heaven's sweaty highway patrol.

A moldy apple odor still lingered on the lip of Little Limbo from the soul of a retired state policeman she'd snagged almost a year ago.

Now, a vile gout of breath poured off Mr. J's face. Zoë glanced around the room for the can of air freshener Old Prairie Dog put in the rooms when she stopped letting people drink water. Must have forgot.

With the collar of her T-shirt pulled up over her nose, she sat with the old man, practicing her great blue heron pose. Mr. J would know she was there and think she was his granddaughter or his wife. If he opened his eyes, when he saw Zoë's veil, maybe he'd think he woke up in Islam Heaven.

She traced the line across the middle of Mr. J's forehead where his sunburn met the oatmealy skin his hat had shaded from the sun. When she narrowed her eyes and looked through the veil of her eyelashes, his bald head resembled the foot-wide Christmas ornament, bottom-red, top-white, that the Home manager hung like the Star of Bethlehem from the solarium ceiling and kept up all year round.

The thick white eyebrow stalks and the soft gray weeds sprouting out of his ears were the only hairs growing on Mr. J's head. Each time Zoë swabbed an eyebrow down with a licked finger, it sprung back, defiant as a poplar sapling.

At this sign of Mr. J's vitality, she decided to escape his foul breath and continue her rounds or take a nap in the laundry room. But like many dying she'd known, Mr. J read her mind. With his eyes shut, he raised his pale arm with its thick palm and stubby fingers facing her, motioning stop, or gesturing hello.

Zoë went still, her hearing tuned for the sound of wings whirring. If it was soft, his guardian angel was in the room, warming up. Loud, his death was imminent and she'd have to dash into soul-snagging position.

Soft, and getting louder.

She had a few minutes.

She took time to prepare herself for what she realized might be her final soul-snatch.

After what she discovered yesterday afternoon ... she'd found a faster passage for herself than this endless catching of souls ... but she might be wrong, she'd not had time to examine the new idea, but if it worked ....

The reality of her job set in and she dismissed the thought and concentrated on bagging Mr. J's essence.

Zoë sniffed a few times, then inhaled deeply. She didn't smell any flowers yet, or fresh fruit.

She fingered her syringe and extracted Little Limbo from the big pocket in her coat. She fiddled with the canister, a stainless steel thirty-two ounce Thermos travel mug she'd filched from the Rapid City WalMart.

A lucky find, Little Limbo confined the souls until she'd collected as many as she'd need to haul her all the way up to Blissville. She thought of the souls as her Heavenly reindeer of herself as a big basket and the souls as unpoppable balloons that would buoy her up beyond the stars.

She twisted Little Limbo, running her fingers around the rim, and shook it, waking up the souls inside to get them ready for a new neighbor. She set it on the bedside table, just in case, and sat down on the bed, focused on the old man's face, the Soul Bubble in her damp palm.

In a few seconds, Mr. J's eyelids flipped open. His watery blue eyes wobbled, searching the room, scanning the edges of her face. They lingered on her hair and when they met her gaze, his eyes nearly bulged out of his face.

She laughed and took his gourd of a hand in both of hers. The calluses had softened into mushy lumps, and she prodded them with her fingertips.

"Don't be scared, Mr. J. Just because my hair's red don't mean I'm a devil."

Last night, out at Devan's trailer where she kept her things and stayed during bad weather, she'd tinted her hair the color of flame. She bleached out her natural brown, then drenched the hair in sunrise crimson dye, except for the last two inches. She applied an iridescent blue to most of the hair below the red, leaving a halo of bleached yellow on the tips. When she shook her head, she wanted her face to shine out of a burning bush.

Giggling, she flipped her hair back and forth. "It's just me, Mr. J. Take a good look. My windows are wide open."

She sought to show him compassion, but who knows? He might be expecting Saint Peter and he sees a girl with her head aflame, and he thinks he blew it.

Mr. J gawked, then the corners of his mouth turned up a fraction and he grunted, trying to clear his throat. Unable to raise his head off the pillow, he tipped his chin back, and groaned a few notes, his eyes falling shut.

"Pretty," Zoë said, patting his arm. "You sing real nice." He settled back and she relaxed. She let go of his hand but grasped his pinkie, so thick it fit into her palm like the grip of her bicycle handlebars.

Soul-catching was tricky, but with trained reflexes faster than most angels', Zoë could trap a soul before its guardian angel swooped in. She raised the Bubble and worked the firm tip between his pulpy lips, propping apart his square, yellow teeth just enough to lodge it in his bite. He sucked on the soft nipple, then tried to push it out with his tongue.

Zoë heard wings thrashing in the invisible ether on the other side of the air. She tensed, holding the syringe gently in his mouth. She squeezed Mr. J's little finger, encouraging him. "Come on. You're ready."

Mr. J nipped the rubber nipple between his teeth, then settled into rhythmic sucking, his puffy cheeks indenting, his floppy lips pulling. Thirsty, he swallowed and sucked and swallowed again and kept sucking. A drop of saliva emerged at the corner of his mouth.

With Zoë's Soul Bubble in their mouths, dying bodies couldn't resist sucking. Zoë wasn't a nurse's aid, but a midwife of souls, helping them get born out of tired Earth into fresh, juicy eternity. The Bubble was a little womb and Little Limbo was a stop on the way to forever.

Mr. J's lips released the nipple. His mouth opened and he tried to suck all the air out of the room into his lungs. "Uuuuuuuhhhhhhh." He held the breath for so long, as if hoping his lungs would bear him up like life preservers, out of the bed, and float him back to his ranch.

Zoë watched the old man Adam's apple swell and stiffen while he choked himself free of his useless body. Then he exhaled a pungent but fresh gas that Zoë couldn't identify at first. In a while, he inhaled a deeper draught of his own dilute floral breath, "Uuuuuuuuuuhhhhhh."

Zoë inhaled with him, locking her breath behind sealed lips, mimicking his lungs' determined two-step with death. Perfect timing was everything.

Her fingers taut on the syringe, Zoë exhaled and focused her eyes on the tip of his nose. Mr. J's agonic death-breathing tensed her, because he could stop breathing on the inhalation and die right then.

His soul could sneak right past the syringe. He could exhale and be dead before he inhaled again and his soul might vanish into a sneaky angel's arms and Zoë could wait till sundown, her Bubble full of nothing new but stale air.

Mr. J finally exhaled. Rich herbal fragrance billowed up, almost visible, almost mauve.

"Geraniums." Zoë perked up. "You're my first geranium." He took another bottomless breath, deep enough to vacuum all the air out of the county. His belly and chest bulged with his lungs' final attempt to sustain him. His finger prickled Zoë's palm and his Adam's apple twitched and softened, sinking down under the damp rolls of skin of his neck.

Zoë squeezed the bulb once, twice, then pushed the nipple deeper, to his uvula. When she felt the tip nudge the hard lump, she pulled it back and compressed it again.

The bulb filled up and punched into her hand. It stung like a hard-pitched baseball and she knew then that Mr. J was a great soul. So huge that when it shrunk to its microscopic core, it rebounded, blasting out of his body with the energy only a great soul could discharge.

"A geranium soul. That's a mighty flower." Zoë had seen old geraniums as almost as big as hydrangea bushes.

Zoë eased back the sipping latch on Little Limbo. She jammed the nipple into the slot and squeezed, clamping the bulb between both palms. She stoppered the canister and tucked it deep into a pocket. She wiped the syringe off with a tissue and dropped it into her pocket.

Caressing the dead man's cheek with her knuckle, she bussed his warty forehead. Containing her excitement, she opened her jacket and spoke into the pocket.

"You make some new friends in there, Mr. Johannson. Everything's all right now."

Goosebumps peppered the backs of Zoë's thighs and arms. She shivered and shook her shoulders then twirled around the room. Her arms raised and flailing, she danced between the pill stand and the dresser with nothing on it but a *People*.

She jumped up on the chair by the bed and hopped back down, rocked the empty IV drip hanger, standing there now useless as a winter peach tree.

Zoë exulted, happier than she'd been since her last soul catch. After a moment, calmer now, she jerked the chain above Mr. J's head three times, listening to the merry Code Blue ring-buzz at Old Prairie Dog's desk.

The bell brought the boss squeaking down the hall in a few seconds. She stalked over to the bed, peered at the body, and shrugged, looking through Zoë.

"I'm sick of that bell," she muttered to Zoë. "Doctor wrong again, huh, Ehawee?"

Zoë was finished here and besides, nurses pulled the sheets over dead faces. As Old Prairie Dog confirmed the absence of pulse – no soul, no pulse – Zoë slipped out the door and bounded to Mrs. Spalding's room.

Little Limbo vibrated against her thigh. Mr. J's soul was excited all right; he bounced around, exhilarated to be free, thrilled to meet his new neighbors. Zoë imagined his confusion, thinking Little Limbo was Heaven or hell.

Touching the cap of the soul cage – that's really what Little Limbo was and that bothered her, but only now and then – Zoë paced back and forth beside Mrs. Spalding, listening for a death whistle in the depth of her wheezes.

The sun was on the horizon, shining through the window. Zoë's head ached from so much concentration. The crickets who lived in her jacket chirped. They needed their dawn meander and feed in the cool grass. They loved these early June mornings best, next to warm September nights.

Mrs. Spalding's airless room closed around Zoë. Her body had to get outside to breathe and move, but she was dutiful, despite her headache and Mr. J's soul flopping around in her pocket.

"I have to do one little thing, Mrs. Spalding," she whispered, as she flipped the sheet away from the old lady's feet.

Zoë knelt on the floor. With one hand, she retrieved a toenail clipper from a pocket, with the other, she raised Mrs. Spalding's foot.

"Silky skin," she said, "like a baby girl's. You should see my soles – tire treads. Calluses so thick you'd think I was part coyote."

Fondling the crooked bony toes, Zoë inserted the point of the clippers along the big toenail and snipped. She pared all ten toenails and spilled them from her palm into a baggie she stuffed into her small pocket with a zipper.

Covering the feet and pulling a blanket over the immobile body and tucking it under her stony chin, Zoë said, "Good night, Mrs. Spalding. Thanks for the toenails."

She glanced into the mirror at the flowers in her hair. Plucking the bluettes out, she tossed them in the can with the other flowers.

Zoë's mother's eyes stared back at her out of the mirror until they grew moist and crinkly at the corners and Zoë's sight blurred. Her mother's eyes blinked and disappeared, leaving Zoë sniffling. She wept a little, not out of sadness, but in sweet anticipation of seeing the real Ruthie soon.

Nearly ten years since she lost her mom, and Zoë still missed Ruthie every day. She felt her loneliness in an ache behind her belly button where she used to be part of her mother. She missed her mother's skinny arms holding her on her lap, whispering in her deep, smoky voice, "My little bluebird. My little custard pie. My little kissy kiss."

Taking one last peek at the old lady, Zoë said, "I might be back but don't wait if you decide to go. I'll see you up there."

Rubbing Little Limbo's cap in gentle circles to calm down Mr. J, she shouted back down the hall to Old Prairie Dog, "Hey, boss. I'm going. G'bye."

She punched out a few minutes early. Who cared? Old Prairie Dog was busy with Mr. J's body and Zoë didn't want to see the other aides coming in to work. With the new great soul ricocheting in Little Limbo, cricket song bubbling out of her jacket, Zoë bounded out into a lavender dawn.

From the porch, she looked off into the distance, over the parking lot fence, beyond the long grass swirling and ruffled like a green lake, toward the Black Hills. The playful morning breeze tangled in her hair, huffing sweet nothings into her ears.

Miles away on the horizon, the golden towers of Anpetu Mountain glowed like a second sun, its spires and turrets calling her as if toward the very entrance to Heaven.

A sudden gust of wind whipped around the corner of the Home. Gripping her with the force of a large hand, it pushed Zoë forward into the day. She bounded down the concrete stairs, barely able to keep her feet on the ground.

Three

EARTHLY JOY

Zoë dashed across the parking lot and skipped over the shallow ditch, racing past the Meyers' farmhouse and barns. On the far side of the house, she collided with a dense current of fragrance from the ranch yard's cluster of late-blooming lilacs.

She stopped and inhaled, immersing her whole body in the purple air, recalling all the delicate spring-scented souls she'd made herself custodian of.

Then, gripping Little Limbo through the leather jacket, she jumped over rows of corn shoots and sprinted with the wind at her back across the meadow to "Wolf," the giant cottonwood tree ruling the pasture.

Ancient as the mountains, Wolf grew in an abandoned pasture, surrounded by a sapphire and pink carpet of blooming Dames Rockets. Dew crystals sparkled on the petals like constellations of morning stars beaming up from the Earth itself.

Collapsing at the foot of the tree, Zoë crawled into her safe seat in the wide notch between two arching roots. She scooted back against the rough but soothing bark and hugged her knees, muscles trembling and flushed skin itching.

With the great soul of Mr. J. pulsing in the bottle, Zoë now felt so wide awake and prickly she couldn't relax. Her pulse raced and she nearly hyperventilated.

Little Limbo vibrated, the new soul boiling, the Thermos steel scorching her thigh. Heat flowed through the sides of the jug down her leg and across her hip and rose into her chest. Once the wave of heat reached her neck and the back of her head, on its own, her body rocked sideways, arcing back and forth, seeking balance.

She looked up into the ragged morning shadows wavering in the cottonwood branches and said a prayer of thanks to Ink'p'du'da, her spirit coach for her ascension.

"Thank you, Inky. A few more souls, I'll be up there with you."

She fell silent, listening for a reply. He didn't speak but a wave of heat poured up her legs from the soles of her feet all the way to her face. Instead of Ink'p'du'da's face, she saw herself dancing with passionate souls, heard drums beating, sage smoke licking at her ears.

Zoë tingled with ardor. She unbuttoned her jeans and slowly unzipped them. Pulling her jacket back and snuggling into the arms of the tree, her fingers slid under her panties and she opened her legs and settled her fingers in her pubic hair – since she'd colored it flaming red last night, it felt silkier and thicker.

Keeping her palm flat against her belly, her fingertips inched lower and lower into the moist field between her legs, into the simmering, where they finally touched down.

In the snug arms of the tree, Zoë let herself disappear into her body's comfort and pleasure. The instant her fingers met her damp lips, she trembled, caressing herself until she felt the swelling rise. A deep tremor raised her hips, her whole body floating in an aching warm wave. A stream of liquid seeped out, drenching her hand and thighs. She shook and moaned and lifted her fingers until her body stilled and she drifted into a foamy dreaminess.

She didn't know how long she lay there with her eyes closed, watching a flock of smiling angels swimming in the warm lake of her body.

She drowsed with both hands inside her jeans, then woke, sneezing and chilled. Her crickets had abandoned the jacket and were trilling from somewhere in the field.

Opening her eyes, she drew her arms out and tugged her jacket over her as she gazed into the branches overhead. Light wind tickled the cottonwood leaves, shaking loose flocks of snowy seed puffs. The seeds hung in the air, slithering among sunbeams and shadows, reluctant to fall to the ground too close to the mother trees.

Zoë relished the calm. A few hours before, her anxious vigil over Mrs. Spalding and the tense race with Mr. J's angel had driven truth and its companion, peace, from her mind. In the distraction of the hunt, she'd forgotten that every soul's body was made of love, and when the flesh body died, all that love fountained out, showering the atmosphere with joy for anyone who wanted to feel it.

The deeply grooved tree trunk rose behind Zoë, a titanic column supporting the canopy of a nave of sky. Agitated by the incessant wind, the shiny leaves swished and branches creaked. She sat up and strummed her fingers across the gray ridges of bark and watched a colony of ants scurry up and down the deep grooves.

That bark reminds me of the Badlands tipped sideways, she thought. All ridges and erosion. Not that it matters to ants.

The ants drew Zoë's gaze higher, up toward fragile sprouts with a few leaves that had emerged from the trunk, well below the main branching. In the glancing light, she noticed a spider web swaying between trunk and leaves.

"It's the Badlands of spiders," she said aloud.

Wind whisked across the moist insides of her thighs. She shivered.

I should wear a diaper when I do that, she thought, chuckling silently, her own best audience.

She stood up and pulled her boots off and stripped out of her panties, taking a minute to hang them over an exposed root. A rising breeze drilled goose bumps down the backs of her legs.

Dropping her coat and peeling off her sweatshirt and the clammy T-shirt under it, Zoë found a low stream of breeze tumbling along the ground. She stood in it, grinning to herself as the cool current washed over her. In private, if the temperature was warm enough, and in summer it usually was, Zoë took off her clothes. She was a nudist.

She adored the word nudist. It was the only word in the dictionary that described who she was all the time. Even when she wore clothes, which was almost always during the days, she was a nudist, inside her shirt and pants and her beloved leather coat. Second best to wearing nothing was to go barefoot in the grass along the lakeshore wearing only her coat.

I love my body. I love it. It feels every tickle of wind teasing me. The sky is inside me and I'm inside the sky. The clouds float inside my stomach and make me laugh. I see trees' blood running in their branches and hear leaves singing their wispy words.

She laughed and hugged herself. On soul-catching days, any happy thing could happen. Today was a wonder of days, she not only caught a great soul, but Devan was due home from California.

Bringing his new girlfriend … Lulu? Laurie? Lolly? Whatever it was, it was a sucky name. Boring.

Zoë dug into the wide pocket at the back of her coat and pulled out fresh clothes. A couple of tampons spilled onto the ground. She picked them up and dropped them into another pocket, smiling.

Won't need those for a few days.

Walking away from the tree to the edge of a wild raspberry thicket, she squatted and peed. As she dressed, a gust skimmed a fine spit of topsoil onto her bare skin. She brushed at it and hurried into her clothes.

The morning would warm up in an hour or two. She slipped into her cozy leather coat and lay down again, against the cottonwood. The coat quintupled as coat, knapsack, blanket, pillow, and mobile home for crickets and girl.

When the right hour of the day came, just before dawn in spring, but anytime after dusk in the summer and early fall, Zoë unzipped her pockets and flapped out the remaining crickets, watching them hop into the field wherever she chose to camp that night.

Usually then, before sunrise, they, or their replacements wandered back into her pockets, miniature dark stars settling into a retreat inside the friendly cosmos of Zoë's coat.

A pungent and sweet taste of geranium and lilac in her mouth, Zoë rested, restoring herself for the final few days of her life on old Earth.

Zoë wiggled herself between the roots of the cottonwood and let her mind wander. Poked her index finger at the clouds, waving it around as if spooning cookie batter out of a bowl. The sweetness of possessing Mr. J's great soul percolated in her body while the heat of her self-love had cooled down to a yummy hot chocolate temperature.

"Mmmm. It's a sugar donut day." She wished she had a glass of milk.

Four

"AN APHRODISIAC FOR YOUR ANGEL"

For the first time since yesterday afternoon, when she'd sniffed a Prairie View death in the air and hurried to her shift, she had time to reflect on the discovery she'd made in Devan's cookbook – a recipe that could change her whole life. Forever. For all eternity.

Zoë had found the recipe because Devaa n had a sweet tooth and she always baked special treats for him when he came home from California. The last time, she'd baked a rhubarb pie and two dozen chocolate chip cookies. This time, he'd be with his new lady friend. He always had a lady friend. They never lasted.

Yesterday morning, Zoë thumbed through Devan's cookbooks, looking for bang-up dessert. She doubted the new girlfriend could cook anything even half as tasty as her simple butter and sugar cookies.

Devan had only a few cookbooks. The one she liked was called "Cooking with Herbs." Zoë remembered a TV show about a goofy guy named Herb so she thought she might find a funny recipe in a cookbook named after him.

Devan loved it when she joked around with him. Once she baked him a cow pie with meringue frosting and he howled. Still talked about how he dug his fork into it and raised it to his lips. Almost took a bite before he burst out laughing.

Yesterday, she didn't find any silly recipes in the cookbook, but she discovered something almost unbelievable.

The recipe said that all she needed to do was gather up a dozen ingredients, mix them together with water, stir them up on a hot flame, and she'd have a miracle: a special angel to take her up and out of here.

Zoë dug into her breast pocket for the crumpled page she'd ripped out of Herb's cookbook. She stretched the paper across her knees and read.

An Aphrodisiac for Your Angel

This is Gramma Esther's most powerful recipe. She swears that she used this potion with Grandpa Harold, her own angel from paradise, from age seventeen until he left the Earth seventy-seven years later.

His last words were "Honey, if Heaven's half the fun we had, I'll be happy forever."

Grandma says: "Use this libation with care. Give it only to your real angel, the one who you know you want to soar with in infinite joy, the one you trust with your soul for all eternity. Keep this recipe a secret. It's too powerful for just anybody to have it."

Ingredients

Fresh root hairs of wild leeks
Pinch of dried mint leaves
2 ground red jalapeño peppers
Clippings from all ten toenails of a mature woman
Ash from more than a hundred cottonwood seed puffs
1/2 cup virgin's urine
2 handfuls of crushed crawfish claws or chicken wing
       bones or any little bones
One apple mashed
1 cup pure spring water, boiling (real hot is fine)
For a male angel: 10 finely ground yohimbe pills
For a female angel: 10 finely ground damiana pills
A tear of happiness
A deep breath of longing

Directions

*Collect your ingredients and place them in bowls. Mix dry
ingredients in a bowl, liquid ingredients in a saucepan.
Gradually stir dry ingredients into the liquids, bring to
a near boil. Sing or hum your favorite love song. Strain
everything through a cotton cloth. The strained liquid is
the love punch. Add your tear and your deepest breath of
longing. Believe me, this packs a wallop. One small glass
down the hatch and your beloved Angel will swoop you
into his arms and away you'll soar to Heavenly Glory.*

Reading the recipe again made her sweat. Zoë threw open her
jacket, peered all around, as if she might see an angel dive out of the
cottonwood branches into her lap. She craned her neck scanning the
cloud-strewn sky. Elephants rode dragons and three-headed dancers
climbed ballooning trees of cumulus.

If I could find one angel...one beautiful angel who I loved...we
could soar!

She sat up, then sank down on her heels, and bowed her head,
honing her mind and heart in on Ink'p'du'da, her spirit friend. She'd
called him often lately, and he hadn't heard her, or if he did, he
ignored here. But today of all days, within seconds, she saw him step
out of the gray and white moon, first in her mind, then in front of
her.

Gratitude blossomed in her heart. She hadn't seen him for weeks
and, this blessing of days, he came as soon as she asked.

She cherished the image of his wide dark face with the acne scars
scattered like birthday confetti across his cheeks and his black eyes
smiling at her from between eyelashes as long as a pony's. The way
the tip of his bent nose wiggled when he talked always made Zoë
giggle. As usual, he kept his mouth closed over his broken teeth until
Zoë spoke.

Moving her lips, speaking with respect, she said, "Inky, Ink'p'du'da,
I'm so happy you're back."

His answering smile sent chills down Zoë's neck. He was happy to
see her, too. She knew it. He was busy before and besides, she hadn't
had anything new to talk to him about until now. "Inky, are you my
angel?"

"Well...." His voice echoed from far away.

"Why don't we go see Ruthie right now?"

"I'm not an angel, Zoë. I don't have a body is all, like most angels."

"Angel's don't have bodies, Inky. They're spirits."

"You'd be surprised," he said. "Angels can have bodies, if they need them. Some of them are so fat they can barely fly."

Ink'p'du'da's image thinned. Seeking clearer reception, Zoë moved over to sit on a boulder a few feet from the tree, concentrating on his eyes.

"I never heard of that," she said.

His image sharpened. "Angels can have any kind of body they want. Horses, dogs, even crows. A beam of light. Any being who moves through space and time."

"Could I be an angel?"

"Sure. You'd trade in your human body for an angel body. Then the angel would pour itself into your body. The new Zoë would be the angel Zoë."

This possibility astounded Zoë. She'd already traded old clothes at the Wabe Sabe Used Stuff store for new ones and she felt different as soon as she dressed in the new ones. Maybe all she had to do was find an angel to trade bodies.

"What happens to the old Zoë who traded places with the angel?"

Ink'p'du'da's body solidified and thickened as he squatted beside her. She looked up into his face. She'd never noticed how yellow his eyeballs were. Honey gold, she thought, like a halo inside his head.

"The old Zoë has to find her way to Heaven by herself. If she makes the trip on her own, she joins the angel choir. If not, well ... she gets lost somewhere and there's nobody to rescue her."

Zoë frowned and pursed her lips. "No way I'm gonna get lost. I can name a hundred constellations."

Inky moved closer and touched her shoulder. She almost felt his fingertips. "Only crazy souls want to jump from planet to planet without a guide."

With her feet on the ground, Zoë could find her bearings no matter how deep she trekked into the backcountry. But when it came to outer space, Zoë was a practical girl. She knew her limits.

Dismissing the body-body trading idea, Inky said, "You need a strong angel, one who already traded for a flesh and bones body. One who can carry it a trillion billion miles. Who won't drop you and let you drift like a star falling through the universe."

"I never knew that."

"That's why I told you to capture so many souls. But I've been thinking about that. I'm not sure even a million regular angels would be strong enough to carry your body without you slipping out of their arms."

"A million?" Zoë calculated the number of souls she had snagged and sealed up in Little Limbo. Twenty-six? Forty three? She was a patient woman, but she didn't want to spend the rest of her days on Earth getting old and sinful while she collected souls for angels who might drop her and let her drift in the dark forever.

She said, "One strong angel, with a body, is better than a million regular angels?"

"That's right."

"Can't my guardian angel help?"

Inky shook his head. Pursed his lips. "You don't get to meet her until your dying day."

Annoyed, she snapped, "That's one angel I'll never meet. I'm never dying."

Ink'p'du'da chuckled. "Your guardian angel promised me she'd stay out of your sight. But she'll watch over you. If something bad is going to happen to you, she can stop it."

"I don't care. I never want to see her."

If I see her, she thought, I'll never get my body to Heaven. Remembering her manners, Zoë said, "Tell her thank you. I'm not mad at her or anything."

Inky's voice rumbled. "Your angel talks to Ruthie almost every day. Ruthie asked her to take special care of you."

Zoë gasped. "My mom and an angel ... talking about me?" She'd never had a day like today. Well, maybe when the crickets showed up and healed her legs when she was little. Now, Zoë knew exactly what to do – get to Ruthie right away, while her luck held.

"Inky, I found a recipe. It says if I make it and give it to an angel, we'll soar off to Heavenly Glory."

Inky smiled and nodded, as if he'd expected her to find the way, eventually.

Excited by the coincidence of the recipe and Inky's new information about one strong angel, she said, "I'll find my strong angel and get out of here before you know it."

Zoë breathed a silent prayer to the great God that she didn't have to spend the rest of her life sweeping up souls in the Home.

"Inky, thank you. You make me feel – "

Ink'p'du'da interrupted. "It doesn't have to be a man angel. But it can be."

"If it's a man, I know who he is: Devan!" She leapt up off her seat and threw her arms out. "Devan! Devan!"

Ink'p'du'da faded into murky clouds where she could barely see his sand-colored pupils.

"Inky, wait. What's wrong?" Zoë stopped and crouched, then sat cross-legged on the ground. She couldn't see his face. She should know better: when she got excited and giddy, he always went away. She couldn't stop tears from bubbling up from her throat, through her cheeks, flowing out of the corners of her eyes.

Then, Inky spoke from the darkness, almost whispering, as if he were a dream talker and not real. She held her breath and listened.

"Devan's not your angel. He's just a man. But he's your good luck. Stay with him. Go with him. He'll lead you to your angel. It's the only way, unless you want to search for years and years."

"Go where? How will I know who my angel is? How will I meet...?"

Of course, Devan was her luck, the best luck a girl could have. He'd saved her life when she was six and and his parents adopted her and he'd loved her ever since. If he wasn't an angel, he should be. Inky didn't know everything.

Sensing Inky's invisible presence still with her, Zoë called, "What about the recipe? Should I use it? Does it work?"

She listened hard, peering into the twilight behind her eyelids, seeking the glints of Inky's golden eyes, but Ink'p'du'da had withdrawn to the other world.

Hoping he was still listening, Zoë said, "What am I supposed to do with my souls, Inky? I can't just let them go." She waited, squeezing her eyelids and clenching her jaw, scanning the gloomy Inky-less dark.

Just like him. As usual, he left her to figure out all the details by herself.

She opened her eyes and glanced around at the leafy young alfalfa glinting gold in the morning sun, then slipped her hand into her jacket and found the souls. She patted Little Limbo, reassuring the souls, because they could hear everything she and Inky had said. "Don't worry, little ones. 'Specially you, Mr. J. I'll take care of you. We'll fly up together. My angel will be strong enough to carry all of us."

Zoë unfolded the recipe and read the ingredients again, racking her brain, wondering where she would find them.

She had seventy-three dollars and some change, and a lot more in the bank. Still, health food cost a lot of money, but she didn't worry. George One Cloud worked in the health food store. A couple of years older, he gave Zoë vitamin pills or leftover sandwiches or dried fruit when she asked him. She would ask George to get her some yohimbe and damiana for her Angel recipe.

The first time George took her into the health food storeroom where nobody could see them, except the cat, they sat on a stack of fifty-pound brown rice bags while they kissed. The room smelled like corn and dust but his kisses tasted like cloves mixed with buttered popcorn. Usually, he only put his hands under her sweatshirt. When his fingertips grazed her nipples, they tickled her like the peony petals she brushed her body with in the spring. George made her shiver the same way the wind did when she came out of the lake after a long swim.

The next time they were alone in the store, he locked the front door, flipped the *Closed* sign, and with the sweetest smile on his face, took her arm and turned her toward the back room. He asked her to play with his willy. At first she said "No," until he said all she had to do was touch it. He wouldn't even take his clothes off or touch her if she didn't want him to.

So, always game for something new – besides she trusted George never to hurt her – she said "Why not?" and unzipped his pants for him. His pretty brown willy felt like a warm candle in her palm. He moaned, and soon as she squeezed it a few times, he lurched and the tip of his candle spurted thick juice like warm yogurt all over. She'd known George's willy would burst, but he seemed surprised.

After that, whenever she stopped into the store for leftover food, George begged her to do it to him again, but she said no. If she touched him like that she knew, before long, he'd want to put his willy inside her. She'd thought about that too much. It would feel really good, she knew for sure, but no way way she'd miss her chance at being with Ruthie.

She had six months to go of still being a virgin, six more months to rise up before she was sixteen, all innocent in like a baby's body, only with some hair in the personal places like even the Virgin Mary had to have, since all women have it, unless they shave like silly Patricia Dove, who bragged about it to everybody.

Zoë agreed to be George's good friend and kiss him and let him touch her nipples, but that's all. She'd heard that George had a girl-friend now so she hoped she wouldn't have to offer to cuddle his willy in exchange for the yohimbe and damiana. She could collect all the other ingredients easy, especially the virgin's urine and the cottonwood puffs.

Zoë brought the wrinkled page close to her nose to read the smaller print at the bottom of the page.

DON'T FOOL WITH DANGER!

Give your special angel only a few sips of this potion! The effect lasts a long time. Bury the mash where animals can't get it. If they drink it, your whole area will be over-run by the horny descendants of the Angel Aphrodisiac. Store leftover potion in the freezer, in a sealed jar. Frozen, it retains its potency for weeks. If your Angel gets too ex-cited and you have to neutralize the drink, give him a shot of whiskey. A glass of beer works all right, too. The booze cools his love-heat and lets you rest. Everybody needs to rest, even from love.

Zoë had heard of aphrodisiacs. Some kind of drink old people used to party with. Carrie Green Fingers' grandmother sold aphrodi-siacs for love and money and to help people stop drinking. She grew special plants and crunched up bird bones and seeds. Carrie called them "Poshents."

If this Grandma Esther recipe really was a love "Poshent" for an Angel, pretty soon Zoë would be on the holy express bus, flying faster than a sundowner wind past Rapid City, further than yesterday's clouds, beyond even Sioux Falls, straight up to the last stop: Ruthie's lap in Blissville.

Five

INK'P'DU'DA

In the spring after she turned thirteen, Zoë had moved out of Bonnie and Arthur's and into the fields and mountains during most days and nights and into Devan's trailer when she needed shelter from rain or snow, or when she wanted to take a hot bath and sleep in a bed. Devan was never there but he kept the lights and heat turned on just for her, in case she stayed over.

She told Bonnie and Arthur school was too boring and she'd learn more on her own without all the distractions of the kids texting and sexting and talking all the time in class. Nobody included her in their texts or stupid tweets anyway and Zoë didn't care. She had Inky and Kateri and Devan and her best friend Carrie, so she didn't need school friends who didn't care about anything she cared about.

She liked her phone and tablet but hardly ever used them except to call Bonnie and say hi or watch a movie sometimes when she'd sit outside the library or the Buck's Coffee and Tavern and use their WiFi. When Bonnie said Zoë needed to be in school so she could go to college, Zoë said homeschooling was what all the smart kids everywhere in the whole U.S. were doing.

"I'm joining the Homeschool of the Universe," she said to her scowling stepmother. Her friend Danny, who was so smart he could fix every computer and virtual reality gadget and the giant combine Melvin Peters drove for the farmers, told her he was a Hackschooler. Public school was for lazy people, he said. Go. Sit there. Do nothing.

A year before she left home, Bonnie took Zoë shopping at Clara's Clutter Closet in Rapid City. There, she found the leather coat she now wore everywhere – an extra-large man's coat, a dusty, scuffed, walnut brown bomber jacket slung half-off a rack in the darkest corner of the store. The bomber jack became her home on the road, her rucksack, and her cricket saddlebags.

When she slipped her arms into sleeves that seemed to have no end, the thick leather bearing down on her shoulders with the weight of a life lived full-bore, Zoë's spirit soared.

Modeling for Bonnie in front of the floor-length mirror, she said, "I could be a fancy dancer in this." She twirled and the coat billowed out, its bottom edge spinning out from the middle of her thighs like a hula hoop.

"Sure could. Just sew on a few red and blue feathers and some bells and beads."

"Crickets will love these pockets."

"They'll love more than that. They'll eat the lining and gnaw on the leather." Bonnie thumbed the leather and brushed against the nap on the sleeve, showing Zoë how it shined lemony under the bare overhead bulb.

"I can sew everything in leather. Be warmer that way."

"The coat already weighs a lot. Let's look for a girl's jacket?"

"No way." Zoë stood up on her toes. The coat hung to her knees, the cuffs dangling below her hips. Bonnie bought the coat for eighty-seven dollars and fifty cents and Zoë wore it home. She'd worn it almost every day since then. Even when it was too hot, she kept it close, using it for a pillow when she camped out on sultry July nights.

It took her a year, but she tailored the coat into a High Plains anorak, without a hood. She replaced the torn silk lining with maroon suede and patched in an extra dozen pockets and pouches, stitching them tight with thin mule twine she'd found in an abandoned horse stall.

When she pulled her baseball cap down to her ears and pedaled her bike into the wind with the coat flying out behind, she fancied herself a two-wheeled cowgirl, protected by her coat from dust, heat, rain, and chill.

A prayer circulated through Zoë's mind throughout the early days of her new solitary life. Always some form of supplication. "Ruthie, I want to talk to you. God, let Ruthie and me talk. Ruthie, I know you can hear me. Talk to me. God, let me see Ruthie. God. Ruthie."

More than one night, she'd wakened in one of the aspen groves she favored for camping hearing Ruthie whispering her name.

"Zoë, baby. You little rapscallion. Zoë snookie...."

She squeezed her eyes shut and stopped breathing. It had to be Ruthie. Nobody else ever called her that. Who but her mother could ever think up such a term of an endearment?

She listened until she had to take a breath, but the aspen leaves brushing together in the night zephyrs drowned out Ruthie's delicate voice.

The dreams kept Zoë's faith alive in her prayers. They became an easy mental habit, a word stream that flowed under all of her thoughts and ideas. Even when she spoke to a friend or read a book, if she listened down inside, she heard the prayer stream bubbling along, heading nowhere but one place: to Heaven and Ruthie.

One Saturday afternoon in the late summer of her first solo season – Zoë skipped school almost every day, she loved learning so much – she wandered into the dusty parish library of St. Moriah's on Pine Ridge. The reservation library was nothing like the high-ceilinged, leather-chaired St. Joseph's library where she'd found the picture and the story of Kateri Tekakwitha, her soul friend and role model.

From the outside, the library looked like a farm shed built of scalloped and dented sheet metal. Always curious and a great reader when the mood struck, Zoë stepped into a hollow gloom illuminated by hazy beams of sunshine struggling through the dingy windows.

She shut the door and settled herself at a table, her ears popping in the absence of prairie breeze. Wind creaked the casements and rattled the metal outer walls, stirring up a fine cloud of dust inside the drafty building.

The walls sported posters of Lakota culture and art: costumes and headdresses, fine leathers embellished with complicated beadwork, powerful horses. The windowless rear wall was postered with the sorrowful sights of frozen Lakota swamped by the snowdrifts at the Pine Ridge Massacre.

Zoë blinked hard, then let the tears stream down, as they did when she had first witnessed the terrible photos. On the wall, above the blowups, a stained wooden Jesus lolled on a crooked cross, as if he was ready to pitch forward into the snow with the other victims.

No wonder nobody's here. How can they stand to look at their murdered relatives day after day?

In one corner of the room, a mural depicted contemporary Lakota life in colorful but childish images: the brown grocery store fronted by a huge red Coca Cola machine surrounded by half a dozen stick people; a basketball game in a gymnasium jammed with people under 'Champs' signs; a girl feeding a horse; boys standing beside a herd of cows. A bottle of Budweiser beer tipped over.

Once her eyes adjusted to the murky light, she thumbed through dog-eared and torn magazines lying on the tables.

Turning away from the wall art to the shelves and strolling between the tall stacks, she ran her fingertips across the books, clearing narrow trails in the dust on the spines. Her fingers stopped at *Heathens Saved, Heaven's Saints.*

Working the book off the shelf, she took it into the light and sat down on a sagging black leather couch with split armrests. Flipping through the pages of dense print, she came to a section of sepia photos of old Lakota villages. In most of them, people gathered around a priest who was baptizing children and some adults.

About to close the book, she glanced at the last photo: a scowling Lakota dressed in what seemed dirty buckskins glared at the camera.

The story under the picture read *The warrior, Ink'p'du'da, once heartless marauder and remorseless killer of innocent settlers, found redemption. Two years after Father Gaspar le Fleur poured the holy waters of salvation over Ink'p'du'da's forehead, purifying him for his entry into the Communion of Saints, he sacrificed his life while saving five girls from death in a burning house.*

Zoë sighed at the obvious conclusion. *If anyone deserves to become the first male Native American saint, Ink'p'du'da passes all the tests: remorse, self-sacrifice, devotion.*

Zoë stared at the photo, lost in the Lakota's deep eyes. He looked angry, but Zoë identified his soul's pain as the source of the frown.

He's definitely in Heaven already. All he needs is a few miracles and they'll call him a saint, she thought. She looked at the date of his death. Only one hundred forty nine years ago. She was quick at math.

The closer and longer she stared, the more his eyes began to twinkle. She thought she saw him wink. His glowering eyebrows smoothed and smile wrinkles showed at the corners of his eyes.

She hustled the book to the front door, opening it wide to examine Ink'p'du'da's smile in full sunlight. A harsh blast almost tore the book from her hands, forcing her to turn her back to protect the photo. Tiny beads of dust peppered her neck.

She felt the Lakota's smile inside the scowl. Other people might see him pouting or fierce. She saw his expression as a communication from how it was in the way old days – this man had given his life for young girls.

Ink'p'du'da's face also glowered, as if he couldn't bear the pain of his life. And he smiled, sharing a secret with one living person who understood him – that person was Zoë.

She peeled the picture out of the book, folded it carefully to not crease his face, and inserted it into her inner chest pocket. That night, for the first time, she prayed to Ink'p'du'da to help her rise up body and soul to Ruthie's side.

After that, Zoë said Ink'p'du'da's name every night as she fell asleep in the orchard or on the lakeshore. She said it first thing when she woke up and she said it while she ate.

"Ink-pa-doo-da, Ink-pa-doo-da." His name flowed like a shining wave through the streambed of thought that Zoë's prayers had carved into her mind over the years of praying to her mother.

After she'd said his name and chanted it a million times, Ink'p'du'da finally answered in a dream that was more real than most everything in her life, except the crickets.

He stood on a rock above a lake with one hand holding a canoe paddle over his shoulder, the other straight out, palm up toward her. He wore a dark shirt and buckskin pants, like in the picture. And new shiny boots and a silver buckle, not like in the photo. He'd cut his hair, too.

He said, "Be patient. Gather souls to lift your body with them up as they speed home to Heaven."

Zoë's eye's popped open in the middle of that dream. Amazed at the vividness of his image and confused by his message, she couldn't sleep the rest of the night.

From then on, she called to him every chance she had: every night and some days when she rested against a tree or a boulder. One afternoon, as she lay on the shore of the lake, from behind her closed eyelids she heard, "Call me Ink'p'du'da."

Always alert, she responded without thinking. "I'm Zoë." She waited, then opened her eyes.

There stood Ink'p'du'da, a few feet away, tall and lit by the afternoon sun, smiling, his eyes in shadow under thick eyebrows, real as a living man. She scrambled to her feet, awed that the saint would come to her in broad daylight. Her first time meeting a saint in person. Shocked that he'd come at all, that her prayers had so much power.

They watched each other in silence, the man smiling and glaring, then Zoë stepped toward him, her hand outstretched.

Ink'p'du'da didn't move. His sharp outline in the exact shape of a man surprised her with how dense and real it looked. He stood on the ground, his solid frame pasted onto the air, set down into the middle of the world, appearing ripe and shining.

Zoë took another step forward, wondering if she could touch him. She examined his face and his clothes. She watched his hair, expecting it to resist the wind of this world and hang flat against his head and neck. When a gust came up, whipping her hair across her nose, his hair also flipped and swung across his face. Long strands rippled across his cheek and swept up under his chin.

Inky – she hoped it was right to call him that – was a miracle, emerged from the spirit world, alive in a real body. Proven by wind.

"Zoë, you're a little one. The perfect size."

She stepped closer and he offered a broad hand, as if in invitation to lift her into his arms and transport her with him back to Heaven. She'd seen plenty of Transporters on the SyFy channel, so she was ready for a painless disappearance and resurfacing in Heaven.

Grasping for his hand, she clasped her two hands together through his, feeling only her sweaty palms against each other. Surprised, more even than at his appearance, she clutched at his wrist, both of her hands passing right through. She lay her hands, palm down, on top of where he held the hairy back of his hand. His wrist rotated to take her hand in his palm, his bony fingers curling around hers.

"I can't feel you." She raised her eyes, her pulse slowing, she sniffed for other clues to his existence. She saw him. Heard him. Maybe she'd learn to feel him.

All I smell is the usual – dust with a tinge of old hay on it, she thought. I always expected spirits to smell like incense, or sage smoke, at least.

She inhaled one more time, this time a blend of the sweet perfume of a newborn foal's breath and the sharp musk like a man at the end of a workday. Their eyes met and she staggered, almost collapsing against him in a fog of devotion.

He didn't move when she flailed, her arms windmilling through his stomach. She fell forward trying to catch hold of his belt.

"Let your body be a sleigh being pulled by souls up into the sky." His voice sounded muffled.

"What?"

She got her feet under her and looked up. He'd disappeared. She'd fallen through him. She twisted around and faced his broad back. Brightness obliterated his head and shoulders. The flat cardboard cutout of his torso and legs dangled from a halo as blinding as the sun.

Ducking her eyes down, away from the light, she started around Ink'p'du'da's body, then changed her mind and backed up. She closed her eyes, spread her arms wide, and walked straight ahead, expecting her cheeks and face to cool off from contact with him, wondering if the temperature inside his body would be colder than on his skin.

Four steps and her forehead felt warm as she stepped into a strong sunbeam cutting between spread boughs on the tree. Spinning around again, she faced him, five feet in front of her. He hadn't moved.

Ink'p'du'da's image wavered a little. She had to keep him talking.

"What? What do you mean by a sleigh?"

"Gather your own flock of souls. They'll be your Heavenly reindeer and your body will be the sleigh."

"My own souls? How?" Dying people would be in a hurry to get to their rewards, why would they volunteer to hang around and let her use them as reindeer?

The Lakota's eyes focused on the horizon behind her. She looked back. No one. Concentrating on his meaning, she thought, dawdlers. Some people are late for everything. Souls might hang around their bodies for a while before they decided to jump into their guardian angels' arms for the ride. How would she find dawdlers?

"Guardian angels are fast as lightning. You have to get there before they do."

"I'm fast. I beat Amanda Long Felton in the fifty yard dash." How could she beat one if she couldn't even see her?

"You're smart. Tricky. But nobody's faster than an angel." You could be a heyoka." Ink'p'du'da's eyes twinkled. "A heyoka is smarter and trickier than anybody."

Zoë said, "Ink'p'du'da...I...can I call you Inky? Ink'p'du'da's really pretty but if we're friends...."

The reflections on his buckskins and cheeks dulled as if a cloud slipped between them and the sun.

"Yes. Inky is a good name. Especially when you say it."

Zoë called to his fluttering image, "How will I find enough souls? How will I find one?"

Inky's frame wobbled and he shuffled his head and shoulders back and forth sideways as if peering around an obstacle for a better view of something in the distance. Then he vanished without raising a hand to say good-bye.

"Come back. Wait." She ran a few steps in the dream and stopped. Shouted across the field, "Inky! Ink'p'du'da!"

He disappeared into the wispy stratus clouds arching from west to east, a hiss of prairie grasses and shallow waves brushing the shore the only sounds in the empty day.

"Did Ruthie send you? I know she did. Tell Ruthie I love her!"

Zoë dashed back to her tree and threw her body down against it and shut her eyes, squinting, searching the dim light between the inside of her eyeballs and the sunshine, straining to see beyond the darkness into the dream world where she'd always found him before.

Desperate minutes spent whipping "Ink'p'du'da" furiously off her tongue until she slowed down and let the word chug out of her throat, combusting in the air in a rough beat she accompanied by pounding her fist in the dust.

"Ink pa du da. Ink pa du da. Ink pa du da."

Eventually, her voice slipped into whispering, then mouthing and pleading in silent longing. Moaning the syllables of his name, she flicked them into the breeze as off the sensitive tip of a fly rod, playing his name out into the world where this one and the next merged. Not a nibble.

After a while, she opened her eyes and shrugged. She replayed her exchange with the spirit, obviously a saint though nobody had ever heard of "Saint Ink'p'du'da."

She laid her head back against the tree and considered the meaning of his visitation – a guy from Heaven, the man she'd prayed to, had popped right into her life. She talked with a spirit and he talked back. He called her "Zoë."

Chills runneled up and down her back. She'd prayed for Ruthie, and she got Ink'p'du'da. Ruthie had sent her a helper. Her whole life was changed now. For the first time since Ruthie died, Zoë felt absolutely sure she and Ruthie would soon be in each other's arms again.

Oh thank you, Ruthie.

She leapt up out of her sleeping bag and shot her arms straight over her head to open her body to the sky like a lightning rod for spirits. A golden violet channel of light coursed down into her fingertips and through her head and her whole body and out her soles into the ground.

Zoë's body shuddered and hard tears racked her as she fought to stay standing with her arms aimed up. Her skin was hot and stinging as if she'd stepped into a honeybee nest, but inside, starting in her chest and flowing into her stomach and lower and rising up inside her head behind her eyes, a cool river flowed under he skin and gentled her.

The same eternal cool she'd felt when she and Inky had almost touched fingers.

Zoë posed stiff as a lightning rod until the shadow of the tree crept up her back and she felt the sundowner wind gust across her neck, causing a normal shiver to snipe at her shoulders and behind her ears, waking her out of her communion with Inky.

She flopped down flat on the hard earth, her muscles turned to cotton fluff. As she lay staring into the lilac sky, the crickets blurted their salutations to the night and crawled out of her coat, swarming across her neck and shoulders, jumping off to meander through the grass.

Giggling from the familiar tickles of the crickets' toes, Zoë closed her eyes, and before the stuttering rain of cricket song could drizzle into her ears, she slept.

The next morning, as she turned over to lie on her hands before she got up, her fingertips felt stickiness on her thigh. She sat up and peered at her panties. At last. She was thirteen and every other girl she knew already had her period. A pink stain across the crotch led to a pink smear on her leg. She rubbed it between her thumb and finger, tasting it. Meaty and sweet-salty at the same time.

This is my blood, she said. This is the blood of my body. I'm a woman.

Zoë stared up into the branches of her sleeping arbor. "I'm a woman now. Like you, Ruthie." Her throat seized and a few tears slipped down her cheeks.

Bluejays squawked and nuthatches sang from the cottonwoods, as if this were any old day. The cool morning winds swooped low, drying Zoë's sleeping bag and chilling her legs. With spread legs, she watched her bloodstain begin to change color, from pink to maroon to brown.

She stripped off the panties and washed herself. Then she rummaged in her jacket for the tampons Bonnie had sent with her when she moved out.

Zoë probed her lower belly and pinched her inner thighs, wondering where the pains were that all her friends said tortured them every time they bled.

She would tell Bonnie the next time she saw her. All Carrie would say was "'bout time." And she'd insist Zoë take some of her condoms. Carrie had offered them before but when Zoë explained the last thing she worried about was getting pregnant since she'd never had a period, she said, "Lucky you. Soon as you do, you better tell me."

This time, as vulnerable to pregnancy as any woman, Zoë would accept the condoms, but really only out of friendship. They were the last things she needed to drag around in her coat pockets.

The coincidence of getting her period the very night Ink'p'du'da made his first appearance confirmed Zoë's hunch that Ruthie had sent him. It was a woman's sign.

Beneath the massive cottonwood, Zoë buried her first period-stained panties in the lidded plastic bucket along with her mother's dress and her jewelry. A faint scent of mildew annoyed Zoë. She'd washed the dress only a few weeks ago. Maybe she hadn't let it dry completely.

She replaced the bucket and covered it with moss and branches and walked over to her bike to see how it felt to pedal with that cotton tube inside her.

Six

EXPERIMENTS

The memorable morning she became a woman at thirteen, the gray sky stayed shut and Inky stayed in Heaven without even showing himself or whispering her name in a dream. Zoë accepted his disappearance and silence as another message: Inky had told her to gather souls and now it was up to her.

Thinking hard, she pedaled across the back roads of Shannon County through summer's blown silt, wearing a bandana across her face. To follow Inky's instructions, Zoë concocted a plan that would send her to Heaven like a rocket ship. She'd call down a whole flock of angels to carry her up, their wings tucked back as they aimed Heavenward, speeding her into Ruthie's arms.

Inky's encouragement gave her no concrete guidance on the details of her assumption – it would be an 'assumption' just like Mary because she wouldn't be able to rise up, to ascend, on her own power – instead angels and souls would carry her up.

In her private mind, the one she never really shared with anyone, Zoë clung to the idea that she was going to ascend to Heaven. It might not be under her *own* power, but it was her idea. She had to make the plans and come up with the inventions she'd no doubt need and do the work to get ready for the angels to haul her out of here.

So, she explained to herself, technically she was 'being assumed' into Heaven, but not like God sending down his elevator. If she was 'assumed,' she'd owe somebody – God, yes, but she didn't want to owe God – he owed her, when it came right down to it. He took her mother – he had no right. God wasn't the cool dude the old ladies claimed. She knew it better than anybody.

No, Zoë would 'ascend,' with a little help from a bunch of souls and angels. She would ascend and descend whenever she wanted, back to Earth using whatever tricks she could come up with. Didn't Inky call her a heyoka? A magic girl who did everything in her own way.

Khalsi, a Mexican-Tibetan friend of hers who hated school as much as she did, told her that her people knew more about dying and the next life than anybody on Earth. He showed Zoë his mother's book about dying that said souls left their dying bodies through the nose and mouth, with their last exhales.

She'd seen a cow, a cat, and a snake die, besides millions of insects, but she didn't notice if they died and then stopped breathing or vice versa. She'd seen dead cattle, dead horses, dead dogs, dead prairie dogs all over the roads – she'd probably killed mice and chipmunks by accident when she rode her bike blindfolded and hit little bumps.

Zoë gave Khalsi the benefit of the doubt, but scientific and practical as she was, she wanted to see for herself if she could spot a soul leaving through a nose.

If it *was* true, all she had to do was catch someone's dying breath and she'd have a soul. She set out to watch dying.

She turned to the TV. Thousands of people kicked the bucket on TV movies and shows and seeing dead people on TV news was easy, but because the camera panned so fast, it was impossible to notice any breathing. Newspapers in the libary files showed pictures of hundreds of dead. She googled "death" on the library computers, and got 689,000,00 results – boring. She googled "life" and got 768,000,00 citings – boring.

Not quite as popular as life, naturally, nobody really wanted to believe they would die. Still, death showed up everywhere – all you had to do was notice the trillions of plants that died in the fall – so why did everyone keep the actual happening such a secret?

One night, Zoë chanced on a raccoon snatching a careless hen behind a barn she was sleeping in. The hen squawked a few times, but the raccoon ran off with the bird before she could watch it die.

Rats flattened under traps, her friend Carrie's little brother's pet gerbil, fish floating in the river downstream from the slaughterhouse: all were still, stiff, breathless.

Frustrated that she couldn't find animals or real people to watch when they died, Zoë heard about the Humane Society where she volunteered and sat with the dogs while Doc Raymond gave them euthanasia.

The dogs died with dignity, falling asleep in her arms, breathing so shallow Zoë had to put her nose up to theirs while she held her hand on their hearts, comparing the last heartbeat with the last breath. After holding about three dozen dogs as they passed on, she couldn't prove it, but she noticed that their heartbeats usually stopped a good half a minute after they sighed their last breaths.

For nearly two years, with the zeal of a visionary and the confidence of a missionary, Zoë roamed the arid countryside of Shannon County searching for human souls.

She snitched plastic vegetable bags from the Hy-Vee supermarket and invented the Soul Sack, her original, clumsy soul-catching technique. She practiced Soul Sacking a couple of barn cats, befriending them with offerings of canned tuna. When they finished, she slipped the sacks over the cats' faces. They immediately ripped the plastic to shreds and clawed Zoë's hands and arms bloody.

Convinced that her Soul Sack would work if she found the right subject, she tried it on Hector, the russet Weimeramer her stepmom Bonnie spoiled like a baby. Once she'd placed the bag over his long nose, he wiggled his hot dog body and jerked his head around, snapping his jaws at the bag. He raised up on his stubby rear legs and cried into the bag.

When his eyes bugged out and he started gasping, Zoë whipped the bag off his face and gave up on Hector. She loved him and couldn't bear his painful whining. He was too young for a euthanasia. Besides, she needed cooperative subjects.

Cows. What about cows? They just stand around chewing their cuds and blinking at the sky. Perfect.

She biked out to Bar Tri Bar ranch's farthest pasture where the new mothers grazed with their calves. The cows cooperated but the Soul Sack system revealed its fatal flaws.

Zoë held the bag into the breeze. As soon as the air inflated it, she pushed the open end down the cow's nose and held it. Once the cow deflated the bag with an inhale, drawing the plastic into her nostrils, Zoë pinched the bag and tied it off with a wide rubber band just under the cow's eyes.

Within minutes, the bags split under the pressure of cow's jaws opening and closing, as she mistook the thin plastic for grass and tried to chew it into cud. Zoë tried double-bagging, then triple-bagging, but whatever she did, she couldn't manage to secure the bags against the hard bone and rough hid of the cow's face.

Desperate to seal the leaks, Zoë duct-taped a triple-bag to the face of a fat Holstein with bulging udders. She planned to seal the breath in for good with the tape. The cow rotated her jaws and breathed, filling the bag, then sucking it empty, drawing plastic deep into the twin barrels of her nostrils. She exhaled, filling the bag so full Zoë could read the green letters on the bag: "HyVee, Your Fresh Choice."

The cow inhaled and exhaled a dozen times. Satisfied she'd found the right system, Zoë reached for the tape. She lay her hand on the cow's forehead just as the black and white milker's knees buckled.

The cow reeled and crumpled onto the grass, her legs stiffened and splayed straight out. Zoë ripped open the bag and peeled it back from the cow's nose.

The cow inhaled and a quiver passed through its thick torso. Zoë tore open the bag but the cow lay on the ground for five minutes before she opened her eyes and staggered to her feet. Relieved, Zoë tugged the duct tape off. The cow shook her head and lowered her face to the grass.

Cows're too big, she thought. Too stupid. I have to try it on people.

But human death came to Spring Creek only every few weeks or months, not because the townspeople possessed any secret of longevity, but few people lived and died anywhere in the empty territory south of the Black Hills.

The search for a final human breath seemed an impossible task. Its difficulty almost guaranteed that if she could actually do it, before long, she'd be standing on the ramparts of Heaven.

Zoë believed good luck favored someone who knows what she wants and pays attention to all the possible ways she might get it and good luck found its way to her.

One night, while wandering the aisles at Borman's Gas and Convenience Store, Zoë heard a harsh staticky voice calling "Car Number Three, Car Number Three." Silence followed for a few seconds, then "Roger, Dispatch. Car Three here."

She stopped beside the bread rack, cocking her ears to a garbled dialogue coming from near the cigarettes and jerky beside the cash register. Between the "Do you read me's" and the "Ten Four's" and the sirens warbling over the voices, Zoë concluded that she was listening to the story of a police car chasing an ambulance to an accident on Country Highway 212.

Eventually, one of the voices mumbled in a soft voice, "Got two potential DOA's. Car smells like a brewery. Probably didn't feel a thing."

With a package of Hockhead baloney in one pocket and a Zingo lemonade in another, Zoë turned to Steve, the night manager, wearing her most disarming smile. When she shopped and he was on duty, they played a game.

If he named the brand of the product she'd lifted, in one guess, she'd put it back. He was sharp, and she didn't like to upset him by pilfering too much stuff, so she rarely took the same food or drink twice, usually skipping out of the store when he was distracted. That way, he didn't have to catch her if he didn't want to play.

One thing she could pinch right under his nose was Tampax. She'd pick up a box, hold it to the light, juggle it between her hands, balance it on her head. He'd turn away, never say a word. His modesty endeared him to Zoë more than his tolerance of her payless shopping.

That night, her curiosity about the police voices forced her to take the risk that he'd catch her that night with the baloney or the tea.

"Get a new TV?" she asked.

"Naw. Larry would never spend that kind of money."

"Well, is it a police show on the radio?"

Steve glared at Zoë, pursing his lips, then licking his bottom lip. The tip of his tongue crept out further and curled up, caressing the tips of his sparse mustache hairs, first to the left, then to the right. Finished, his tongue withdrew and he said "You mean the short wave?"

A smile lay plastered under Zoë's nose, but she watched his narrowing gaze as he examined her coat for strange bumps. Her pockets always bulged, but Steve had memorized those bulges.

"I bring it in from home," Steve said. "Tune into the county Emergency Frequency. You know, the police band?"

Zoë didn't know, but she shook her head.

"It's real. Whenever there's an accident or fire. Shit, you know, like a blizzard – they have to call out the cops or the staties. It's all on the radio."

"It's real?" Zoë sensed a new way to energize her soul catching.

"Real as that Zingo," Steve said, grinning and looking out the window.

"What?" Her jaw dropped in mock surprise. He couldn't have seen me snitch that bottle, Zoë thought as she pivoted to replace the bottle in the cooler.

Most nights and some afternoons after that, Zoë hung around the store, listening to the county Emergency Band. When she heard the Emergency Voice dispatch a patrol car, Zoë biked away at top speed, often arriving at car accident sites and barroom brawls while the blood was still fresh.

But she was never fast enough or lucky enough to find bodies dawdling at death's door waiting for her to throw a plastic bag over their heads.

The one time she beat the ambulance to an accident, the EMT's thought she was one of the victims. She'd crawled into the overturned car and had just slid a double-bagged Soul Sack over the upside down head of the driver, a wrinkled blond woman who smelled of alcohol and rose perfume. The woman's body shivered and her blue eyes stared through the plastic at Zoë.

An EMT shouted, "One's alive. A kid. I'll get him."

Zoë felt hands grip her ankles and pull. She lost her grip on the bag as the EMT drew her out of the car.

"Take it easy, girl. You'll be all right." He picked Zoë up and wrapped a blanket around her and carried her to the ambulance. He lay her on a gurney and said, "Oxygen. Check her neck," then he turned back to the wreck.

"Holy shit, Don," he called. "She musta been a glue head! You gotta see this."

Zoë's EMT snapped an oxygen mask over her face and ran back to the wreck. Zoë threw off the mask and blanket and dived into the drainage ditch on the other side of the road. Keeping her head down, she sprinted away from the ambulance until she came to a culvert under the road. She crawled in and waited, trembling.

Inky, she thought, I don't know. What if the lady wasn't dead when I put the bags on her head? If somebody sees me when I'm catching souls, they'll think I'm a monster. Inky, Inky. I need your help.

A week later, she saw the ad for the Nurses' Aid job at Mountain View Nursing Home.

With an unsurprised but grateful nod to Inky, she applied for the job. She'd just turned fifteen, old enough to work, but the man said she looked twelve. Once Bonnie and Arthur vouched for her, and she volunteered for the graveyard shift, the Home took her on.

"Conditional," the manager said.

"Don't worry," Zoë said, looking him straight in his bloodshot blue eyes, "I like old people."

Instead of the extra pay for night work, she negotiated with her supervisor to let her wear her bomber jacket over her nurse's aid clothes. She couldn't abandon her crickets, just because she had a job. She also promised her boss that she would wear a fresh clean uniform every night: blue jeans and a short-sleeved T-shirt with the green picture of the Home printed on the front.

The Home was a reservoir of death, a catch-basin where fragile old bodies flopped into the beds, lay around cooling down, then gasped their souls free to flutter Heavenward like butterflies.

Old people were far more cooperative than animals or accident victims. Sleepy and trusting, they offered her the chance to realize her dream.

During the first week of aiding the nurses, she found everything she needed to collect her souls.

Once she discovered the nasal syringe, the travel mug that became Little Limbo jumped off the WalMart shelf into her pocket. The fourth night in the Home, she sat with Bert Mineola while he mumbled and snorted and gave up his soul to her syringe.

But instead of glorying in the power of her invention, she became cautious. She didn't take every soul that left its body behind in Mountain View. She knew the nurses watched dying people real close and if Zoë was with every single one who of them when they died, the nurses might ask questions.

The Home job became the focus of her life. Days, she still biked everywhere, wandering the county roads and the front country trails in the mountains, always daydreaming of the day she finally would have enough souls.

The moment she was ready to take off, she'd unscrew the lid of Little Limbo and release the souls. Eager to rise up, but needing help, the souls would hang around with her like a crowd waiting at the bus stop for their guardian angels.

Then, when all the angels gathered to retrieve the souls they'd lost to Zoë's trap, she would open her arms, and glide off with the choir of guardian seraphim and cherubim and powers and archangels. It was a sketchy plan, she knew, and it was the best she could do. She counted on Inky to herd the angels together and instruct them to heist Zoë all the way up to Ruthie, like celestial shoplifters snitching a present for Zoë's mom.

But today, after nearly two years of experiments, after diligent studying the countless ways of dying, after months of hanging out all night with wrinkly, dying people in the Home, after she'd gathered Mr. Johannson's soul, Ink'p'du'da told her it would take about a million years to capture enough souls.

She felt like the stupidest girl in America, concocting a silly fantasy with no possible way of working out. She should have put the idea to some real scientific tests, only she was not a scientist. The cats and dogs and cows proved that.

But why didn't Inky tell her this a long time ago? Maybe he didn't know as much about life and death and souls as she thought he did. He wasn't a saint yet – if he was, wouldn't he be in Heaven? So he probably still had dumb ideas like living people did. Try this, try that. Hope something works. Good thing she'd found Grandma Esther's recipe. She was one lucky girl.

Why did Inky tell her to collect souls? He loved her so much he'd never lie to her or trick her. It had to be a test. A test of her patience. Or an exercise to prepare her for the miracle she was sure to experience.

Folding and unfolding the poshent recipe in her damp fingers, she barely believed how easy this new plan would be, compared to soul-catching.

Zoë didn't mind the work – she loved to work, everyone knew that. Besides, she was proving her worthiness for Heaven.

Zoë decided she'd head out to Devan's to sit in the cottonwood grove and think.

Her friend Carrie and she often talked about Heaven and angels and boys – Zoë wasn't really interested in boys but she liked talking about them with her girlfriends. They all agreed angels could dive down into human bodies if they needed to. Otherwise, Khalsi argued, how could one boy – like her crush, Samuel Blue Rock Williams – be so good looking, smart, kind, and the best ball player anywhere?

Zoë needed a full-grown, strong angel with a body. Where could she find one? No man she knew was anything like an angel, no way she'd want any of them to put their arms around her even to bear her up.

Maybe she should collect all the ingredients and mix up the poshent first then find the angel. Or the other way around, find the angel then make the poshent? How did it work? She needed Inky, every speck of luck waiting out there for her, and the poshent better do what Gramma said it would.

She only had a few months before her sixteenth birthday and no time left for dumb schemes.

She'd left her bike out at Devan's trailer and she never minded walking. The sound of one foot scuffing down and grinding the chunks of gravel followed by the other foot scuffing and scrunching always put her in a thinking mood.

Little Limbo bounced against her thigh keeping time with her steps. She gripped the lid and shook it gently to comfort the souls.

What would become of them? Could she really take Little Limbo with her while she blasted through outer space? Should she release them and let them find their own way to their guardian angels? Maybe she should wait until All Souls Day when everyone prayed for souls. They could ride the prayers up. But All Souls Day was in November. It was only June now and Zoë would be in Heaven long before then.

The sun beat down on her out of a white sky as she walked and she started to feel sleepy. Zoë had planned to walk all the way to Devan's trailer before she rested, but the euphoria Mr. J had brought her had drifted away in the morning light. Now she wanted a nap.

She glanced behind her. Puffs of dust from her boots trailed behind her like a flock of ghost lambs forming and trotting away under the strict hand of the wind.

She noticed Hepzibiah Simpson's dilapidated barn tucked against some young oaks. She headed for it, to lie down in the shade. She didn't see a salt lick or smell any fresh horse biscuits, not that that smell bothered her.

For now, she was grateful to find a private place to nap. By the time she got to the barn and lay down in its shade, she was groggy.

The responsibility of carrying around old Mr. J's great soul wore her out, especially now that she didn't need it for her own purpose.

She was tempted to unscrew Little Limbo's cap and watch the souls pour up into the clouds. She'd often imagined that when she opened the cup's lid, a flock of iridescent butterflies the size of geese would flutter up, casting rainbows over her as they began their journey to Heaven. She would step into the rainbows, tie a few around her waist, and sail up with the soul butterflies. Like parachuting in reverse.

Zoë put her hand on the mug and sighed. She'd lived long enough to know that her plans didn't always work out. Just look: Inky changed his mind after all these years. The angel poshent idea now seemed perfect – it might be the only one that she could use to rise up before she turned sixteen – but you never knew. Always better to have backup plans.

Besides, she loved her souls and owed them something in exchange for the hope they'd given her.

As she drifted off, she imagined the ways she could attract the angel. She'd mix up the poshent and dab it on her throat and behind her ears like perfume. The fragrance would drift into the solar wind that blows across the galaxies where angels hang around watching over people. Her angel would smell her poshent perfume and slide into a powerful body and come to find her right away.

He'd say, "How nice you smell."

She'd say, "It tastes even better than it smells," and she'd offer him a drink. He'd gulp down the poshent, and time would stop.

Angel would gather her into his strong arms, rise up on his toes, and *fooosh*, off they'd fly, climbing higher and higher until they heard the first strains of Heavenly song.

The next thing Zoë would see was Ruthie waving to her from the emerald hillside while Ink'p'du'da and his pals laughed and drummed and sang with the angels and saints when they threw her a Heaven-warming party.

Since she'd never heard of God apologizing for anything he did – and he did about as much wrong as he did right, a lot more wrong in South Dakota with no water, so many drunks who had to get water from beer – Zoë didn't expect God to show up at the party. If Ruthie invited him, and he came, that would be fine with Zoë, but it was up to Ruthie because as far as Zoë knew, God was not too smart, and cruel.

How could anybody imagine letting his son die on a cross like that was anything like love. More like hate, if you asked her.

Seven

DEVAN'S CALL

Zoë woke up refreshed and thirsty, one hand in her pocket clutching the poshent recipe, the other shading her eyes from the piercing sun. Shaking out her hair, she brushed off the grit that had settled into her clothes, and set out to fetch the poshent ingredients.

She needed chicken bones or crawfish and if they were the same thing as crawdaddies, jillions of them lived under the rocks by the shore of Center Lake. She liked to boil them and strip the meat from their tails with her teeth.

Center Lake was down a rutted path a mile before Devan's. At the lake, she slugged down a quart of water from her food and drink stash, then pulled her canoe out from under the shrub where she'd tied it. As she paddled into a tiny breeze, she splashed water on her hands and face. She landed her canoe in the sheltered center of a small cove.

A fruity odor blew down from the apple orchard and its scant blossoms on the knoll above the shore. A stand of young aspens Zoë had named "the chatty girls" whispered and rasped.

Today was washday. She loved washing her clothes in the skimpy stream still dribbling into the lake. She got the idea from TV when she saw some women washing clothes in a river in the sun, their kids splashing nearby. When she'd washed her clothes and lay them out to dry on the boulders, she could think at the lake as well as she could in Devan's cottonwood grove.

She didn't hang them up because she'd lost too many shirts and pants to sudden blasts of wind. Once she found a pair of her under-pants five miles away, hanging from the rusted exhaust pipe of an abandoned tractor. After that, she always placed rocks on her clothes while they dried.

She had only two days of work clothes to wash, so she finished quickly and sat down on a rock.

With her feet in the cool water, Zoë perched on her sitting rock and relished her lunch of chips and jerky and strawberry juice.

Wading out a few feet into the water, she turned over the rocks where crawdaddies hid during the day, her fingers flashing faster than a duck's bill. She picked up the juicy lake bugs by their tails and dropped them into a plastic bag.

She stood up straight, listened. She sensed Devan approaching Spring Creek from out in California – she could always tell when he was close – and changed her mind about spending the night in her tent at the lake. She'd stay at the trailer and put the crawdaddies in the fridge so they wouldn't die before she could boil them up and use them in the poshent.

Peeling an orange she claimed from her food cave, munching on the juicy slices, she glanced at the sun peaking in the center of the sky and mused on Devan's arrival. She loved him more than anybody and he loved her just as much. The red Z with purple wings tattooed on his biceps proved it. When she was eleven, he came home from California wearing the tattoo like it was a special prize.

She knew it was for her but her stomach flipped when he said, "Z for Zoë. Who else?" Devan picked her up and swung her around. "Someday, when I get the money, I'll have them draw a heart around the Z."

She giggled and kissed the Z over and over, her lips smacking loud against his smooth skin.

"Hey, stop it," he said. "It's poison if you lick it."

Horrified, she stopped. Her lips trembled until he said, laughing, "Just a joke, Zoë. Don't cry."

She kicked him and said, "You wait and see if I get a *D* tattooed on my arm. If I do, it won't mean Devan. It'll mean Dumb."

He tickled her and they laughed together.

Every year she planned to get the *D* tattoo on her arm or leg, maybe near her heart. A lot of people she knew had hearts and dragons or roses inked on their backsides. One day, Zoë walked into Spring Creek Tattoo Parlor but the smell made her gag. She liked rings and things, but the tattoo artist wore so many silver and gold and steel rings and pins and nails dangling from his eyebrows and nose and mouth, his face looked liked a hardware display at Reveneau's Hardware.

His words clicking against his teeth, he said, "I've been waiting for you." Turned off the TV and pushed himself out of his deep leather chair and started toward her.

"I changed my mind," she said. "I'll come back later." She sped down the steps and hopped on her bike just as he reached the door.

"Check it out," he said, his mouth clattering. "I got a special devil I'm saving for you."

"I don't believe in the devil," Zoë shouted and rode off.

A few days later, she and Carrie Fingers were fooling around in Carrie's mom's beauty parlor. "I can tattoo you just as good as Eric," Carrie said, lifting her blouse. "I did myself. Two days ago."

Zoë touched the crusty cross embossed on her friend's stomach. "Did it hurt?"

"Yea-ah."

Caressing Carrie's scab, Zoë grinned. "It's beautiful."

Zoë shrugged out of her coat and sat down in one of the hair-dresser chairs. She pushed her sleeve up to her armpit. "Give me *D*."

When she showed it to Devan last summer, he said, "It's pretty." He stretched it between his thumbs to sharpen the blurry edges. "Ran a bit, didn't it."

He must have noticed the tears forming because he let go of her arm and rolled up his sleeve. "Don't worry. It's not as bad as my first one." He inverted his forearm and revealed a black, oblong, dime-sized stain floating between his veins.

Sniffling, Zoë said, "What's that?"

"A knife."

"A knife?" She shook her head. "It looks like a grease spot. At least you can tell mine's a *D*." She raised her arm in front of his face and grinned. "Just don't lick it," she said. "You'll get poison."

Zoë chuckled to herself at that memory. That was about the last time she saw Devan in person. He didn't come home at Christmas any more and she couldn't wait to see him.

A breeze spun off the water and ruffled her hair. Despite the sun, a chill trickled down her shoulders, inside her coat. In her imagination she reached out to Devan. Normally, his crinkley eyes flashed in her mind and his body shined, surrounded by blue and gold colors, but now thick smoke obscured his face and body.

In her mind, she leapt over the smoke, looking for him on the other side. Fear struck Zoë when the smoke thickened and she heard muffled crying. She'd never heard him crying before. The sound of his weeping diminished while his image merged into the smoke and evaporated.

Zoë opened her eyes onto the rippling lake water. A cloud had settled above the lake, darkening the silver water to steely gray.

Devan was her luck and she was his luck. Was he in danger? Sad? Did her vision mean that he would lead her to a sad angel? All she needed was a strong angel and a strong angel didn't have to be a happy angel.

After folding her clothes, she lay on the grassy shore and, shielding her eyes from the golden sundogs cavorting all over the water, she sent a request to Kateri. Inky told Zoë things and taught her about Heaven and Earth, but Kateri did things for her.

If Devan is sad, she prayed, make him happy. If he needs luck, tell him to remember, I'm his good luck. Like the time he took me with him to look for motorcycles and we found the green one. Or the time I sent him a red tail hawk feather and he got the role-playing an Apache in the TV movie.

Her phone chimed. She'd fixed the ringer to sound like a cricket chirping "Happy Birthday To You."

Zoë usually kept the phone turned off and stored in the pockets her crickets lived in. She didn't want to scare them when it rang. She never knew which cricket had a birthday today, but once she estimated that in a year, maybe a million crickets lived in her jacket. So every day a bunch of them had a birthday to celebrate.

Today, she'd kept the phone on since Devan would probably call her just before he came down the lane to his trailer.

It could only be Bonnie or Devan. If it was him, she would tell him her good news about the poshent to cheer him up.

The phone's face said "D."

"Hi Devan."

"Zoë, hey, you're there. Great!"

She looked around, grinning. Her dream must have been wrong. His cheery voice made her happy.

"When are you coming home?"

"Tonight. I'm close. We're at Anpetu."

"See the castles on top, all gold and everything?"

"Yeah, Anpetu's old skull's shiny as ever."

Anpetu, the radiant one. Zoë loved camping in the woods around Anpetu more than anyplace she'd ever camped. In the morning, Anpetu's bare granite cliffs cast a glow over the valley and by after-noon, its towers glowed plum as the day waxed into night.

"It's the closest place to Heaven in the Black Hills," Zoë said.

"We'll go together sometime."

"Sometime? No sooner?"

Devan ignored her question. "Where are you sleeping now, Zoë?"

"Mostly in the old orchard. I like to sleep under the gnarly trees. I pick one that still has blossoms and when I wake up, I have flowers on my face."

"Still blossoming?"

"Late-blooming Johnnies. Hurry up and come home."

"Fast as I can."

A thrill of joy bubbled under her chin. She stood up and paced. "I better hurry with my baking." Tucking the phone under her chin, "You want chocolate chip or oatmeal?"

Devan laughed. "Whatever you make. How about chocolate chip oatmeal – no cow pies!" He laughed.

When Devan laughed, even over the phone, every muscle in Zoë's face softened. "No cow pies ... but maybe something else?"

"You better not, you little fox. By the way, Laurel loves cookies. She can't wait to meet you."

Zoë thought a moment. "Laurel. Well, I guess I want to meet her." Holding her breath, she said, "You better hurry up and get here. I'm getting ready to take off."

"Don't give me that."

"If you don't hurry, I'll – "

"You wait – "

" – eat all the cookies I baked you." She laughed. "Tricked you."

"No taking off." Devan sounded mad.

Serious, now, she said, "I found a faster way –"

"We've been driving for five days and I'm wasted. Don't make me worry."

He's not mad, he's upset about something. "I have to wait for you," she told him. "You're my luck."

"Promise?"

"Cross my heart and kiss Tekakwitha's toe."

"Who's Tek…wita?"

"Tekakwitha. My saint." Zoë whimpered. "How could you forget?" Devan should know. She'd told him fifty times about Kateri, how she makes things happen for her, like right now, Devan being happy.

"I'm sorry. I guess I forgot."

How could he forget? Zoë almost punched the red hang up button.

"You'll love Laurel," Devan said, relaxing his tone. "She might even make up a song for you."

"Can she sing with my crickets?" Zoë never liked Devan's girl-friends, but this time, she'd only have to put up with her for a few days.

"If anybody can, she can," he said. "I told you she got a job singing at Full House Casino in Deadwood?"

Zoë watched a vulture riding the thermal drafts up into a silvery swath of sky. "You know who my favorite singer is?"

"Who?"

"Suli Tanaka."

Devan laughed. "Laurel's better then her."

Another vulture followed the first in lazy circles. They distracted Zoë, thinking about the meal the birds would make from some animal's bad luck. Nobody sings prettier than Suli.

Devan broke into Zoë's silence. "Guess what? We picked up an old Hunkpapa man. Hitchhiking in from the Tetons."

"One of my friends is Hunkpapa," Zoë said. "She's the smartest girl I know. She never went to school." Still thrilled to feel his voice swirling in her ear, she felt herself beginning to babble.

Devan went on. "Says he's from Jackson Hole. He's taking us to his parents' graves inside Anpetu."

Zoë's radar perked up. "My friend Bobby's mother told us Indian graves have curses on them. If you touch them, bad medicine gets under your skin and melts your bones from the inside."

Devan laughed again. "That can't be true. Every adult you know has touched a dead person. If they melted, they'd be a bunch of goopy jelly donuts rolling along the street."

"That's gross."

"Don't worry, little fox. You know I respect the dead."

He called her 'little fox' when he was serious. 'Little fox' meant, Remember, I found you when you were staggering around in the alfalfa like a hurt little fox the day your mother died in the crash.

Ever since then, Devan had been Zoë's guardian protector, her Earth angel. He loved her so much she understood why he didn't want her to leave him for Heaven. If she could only convince him that she'd come back even better than she was now. If only he could speak with Inky, or some other spirit.

"I respect the dead, too, Devan. I just don't want to be one." She dropped her voice to the most serious alto notes she could reach in her throat. "Guess what?" She paused half a beat. "I captured a new soul this morning. A great one."

"Still trapping souls for your big trip?"

"Yeah," she said, excited. "But this is my last one. I found a new way to get there real fast. Inky said I should do it."

"Inky did?"

"He said you're my luck. I'm supposed to stay close to you and you'll help me find an angel."

"You're my luck too. You know what? I found my angel."

"You did?" Zoë didn't know he was looking. This was good news.

"Yeah. Laurel. Who's your angel?"

"Oh." Disappointed. "It's still a secret." She paused. "Devan, hurry up," she said, "cuz if you don't, I'll have to take one of your shirts for my luck."

"Whoa. What're you talking about? You have to collect a lot of angels."

"Not angels. Souls."

"I mean souls – "

"Don't need them now. They would take a million years."

"Zoë Rarefield." Devan's voice snapped in her ear. She held the phone away and looked at it. He sounded just like Bonnie, his mother, when she tried to discipline Zoë.

"Who's that?" she snapped into the phone in her palm.

"Zoë, do you hear me?" The phone jabbered.

"Devan. You sound like the auctioneer at the horse barn."

His tone hardening, he said, "Listen. We haven't seen each other for what, a year? I miss you. You stay right there."

Zoë didn't respond.

He lowered his voice the way he did when she sat on his lap. "You owe me those cookies."

Zoë considered this. "I miss you, Devan. I miss you a lot. So hurry up."

"We'll be at the trailer in a few hours."

Brightening, she said, "I'll make you one more batch of cookies. Save the best for last. One for the road – to Heaven." She giggled.

"Zoë, don't talk like that."

"I gotta go." Zoë wanted to see him, but right now, he put her in a bad mood. "Call me when you're almost here. I love you."

Devan said, "I want you to see me in the Passion Play this summer. It's the best gig I've had since *The Bad Times of White Bear.* You better be there."

If she hadn't found her angel by then …. She blurted, "I saw you caught in dark smoke. Be careful."

"Dark smoke?"

"I saw you. It means trouble all around you."

Devan paused. He muttered something Zoë didn't understand. Probably talking to his girlfriend.

"I'll be fine," he said.

"Kateri will bring you home safe. Bye."

Devan can be so obnoxious, she thought, stuffing the phone into her pocket. All he thinks about is cookies and acting and his new girlfriend.At least he'll be happy for me when he learns about the poshent.

A sharp gust caught Zoë from behind, rocking her forward onto her toes. She lurched a few steps sideways and leapt up, spinning around to face the wind. The gust passed by, leaving gentle fingertips of breeze caressing her cheeks. Like Devan did when he took her head in his hands.

Zoë touched her face with both hands, sliding them around her skull under her hair. Yes, she thought, still a cantaloupe.

Devan called her 'little fox' when he was serious, but when they played, he called her 'my cantaloupe, my loopy lope.'

That was from when he rescued her from the hayfield after Ruthie's crash. She could almost remember it, ten years ago when she was almost six but, they say, no bigger than a three-year old, him holding her head in his hands saying "Your head feels like a cantaloupe. It smells all sweet and milky."

She asked him why he said that and he said, "I didn't say that. I only thought it."

That was the first and only time Zoë had ever heard somebody's thoughts. She'd lost that gift, but it it didn't matter. She'd rather talk to a spirit like Inky than listen to the million boring things that buzzed around in people's heads.

She giggled again at the image of her cantaloupe head. "Must have been a bloody cantaloupe," she'd told Devan, because he had to rush her to the doctor for stitches.

Well, the joke was, the 'doctor' was a veterinarian, Doc Raymond, who sewed up the gash on her head and splinted her broken arm before he sent Devan racing her to the hospital. Old Doc, still fixing horses and cows in Shannon County, got a birthday card from Zoë every year on her birthday.

She never forgot her time in the hospital. Devan visited her every day, bringing her Snickers and Starburst and once, a bouquet of flowers he bought at the HyVee. When she learned that her mother had died, she cried all night and wanted to die.

Devan brought his mother and father over to see her and eat ice cream and play games on an iPad they gave her. She didn't have any other visitors except the nurses and a gray old preacher and a couple of old ladies who smelled like rotten lilacs, but Devan and Bonnie and Arthur made her forget about Ruthie, until they left her alone in her room.

Zoë prayed to Ruthie to come get her right then, steal her from the smelly hospital bed, and take her right to Heaven. If she knew how, she'd have died herself before Devan told her she was coming to live with him and his parents. She didn't know where else she'd live, unless it was with that stinky drunk Ralph Scoosher, who wrecked the car that killed Ruthie. Who killed Ruthie.

Ruthie loved Ralph. Anyway, Zoë thought she did. Why else would she take her baby and ride in a death car with him?

After the hospital, Zoë went to live with Devan and Bonnie and Arthur. A little while later, when they said "We want to adopt you," Zoë shrugged. "We don't care if you talk or not." When they said that, Zoë grinned.

When Bonnie found her reading the iPad one night, she called all her friends and they had a big party that Saturday. Zoë had to show everybody how she could find the Shannon County News online and read out loud the headlines and the local people's ranting and raving about the schools and the churches and the president and the advertisements. She refused to read the sports pages or the business section with cattle prices, but nobody cared.

After she revealed to them that she could read, everyone was so happy that Zoë expected some reporter to come and tell their story. When she was thirteen, Zoë got sick of being indoors and going to school all the time.

About the time, Devan had moved to California to act on TV shows and commercials and YouTube and webisodes, Bonnie was getting uptight about Zoë's staying out all night whenever she felt like it. Arthur told he she could move out if she promised to stay in Devan's trailer and always keep her cell phone on. She agreed, even if sometimes she 'forgot' to keep her phone on.

Bonnie wanted to corral Zoë in her little room until she was sixteen. No way. Zoë felt sad about Bonnie, but Bonnie would never understand her. Nobody but Devan understood her, except lately even he didn't get her. Maybe because they hadn't hugged or snuggled for so long. A whole year of not seeing him.

Almost ever since she started gathering souls he sounded like he forgot who she was: his loving little sister. Step-sister. Adopted sister. Whatever. Soul sister. Sister.

Zoë picked up her sun-dried nurse's aide clothes, absently wondering if she'd ever wear them again.

Little Limbo bounced against her hip again, reminding her of her responsibility. She'd hidden the souls from their guardian angels for a long time. It was selfish, but the souls were sort of like a holy vaccination for her, keeping her healthy for her flight to infinity. When she got there, she sure didn't want a reputation with the saints in Heaven as a soul jailer. She'd ask Inky to tell her what to do with her purloined souls.

That's what they were – purring lions of God. She had to take care of them.

"Don't worry, any of you," she said aloud, caressing Little Limbo's stainless steel skin. "I promise, I'll take you with me. My angel will be so strong, he can carry you on his pinky." She would carry them, rather than depending on them to drag her along on the way up. What a treat that would be, fair pay for her keeping them in Little Limbo.

Now it was time to visit George One Cloud at Mimi's Health Food Store to gather more ingredients for the poshent. She'd pick up the yohimbe pills and damiana, maybe some two day-old hummus sandwiches before he recycled them to his pigs.

Since Devan wouldn't be home until late, maybe she would camp out at the lake after all and invite him and his new girlfriend over tomorrow – she had to at least give her a chance since this was probably the last time she'd see him or her until she came back from the beyond.

Tonight, she'd stay up late, gazing through apple wood smoke from the campfire she'd make, nibbling chocolate she was sure George would stick in her pocket. As the fire died down, she'd stare at the sky, watching the invisible web the stars spun among themselves.

Before long, if she decided not to sleep in Devan's trailer, she'd crawl into her tent through the bead curtain that protected her from strange people and animals. She loved lying on her sheepskin cuddled into her sleeping bag, listening to owls hoot fair warnings to mice and moles.

No telling when she'd be back to sleep outside on the ground again.

In her dream, she flew underground through a warm, velvet tunnel, gentle wind washing over her hair and cheeks. Her hand rested in a large invisible hand pulling her along. As they flew deeper – she felt their descent – she sensed the tunnel walls a few feet away from her body, just out of reach.

In the dream, they'd plunged miles past glowing walls that changed colors as they descended. The walls became black then gray and pink, and finally, gold. The hand released her and she landed in silky dark. She walked on and on until she emerged into a pale sunrise.

MANY PATHS

Eight

THE MANY PATHS TO THE GODDESS WITHIN

Normally clear by mid-morning, Roy Kassup's eyes surprised him. Squinting back at him from the office bathroom mirror, his lids wanted to stretch wide, a muscle gesture he usually saved for listening to customers bitching and moaning when they wanted to cut his price. He had little sympathy for anyone but himself, but he could act as well as anyone.

Touching up his silver and turquoise bola with his cuff, Roy grinned at himself. Depite his bloodshot eyes, he liked his looks. His jaw was strong – no double chin – and his shallow wrinkles and even tan attested to his self respect at keeping himself in decent shape. He'd had to trim his once gorgeous shoulder-length surfer-blonde hair first for his preacher work and then even shorter for his Sales Manager job at Really Organic, Inc. Short hair suited him now that gray had started to mow a swath across his crown, not to mention how handsome his rising forehead looked.

If someone asked his ex-wife what he did for a living, she would say, "He used to sell fertilizer but now he's a preacher who sells water. Sells Jesus at that church he started out west of town."

Roy saw no problem with being a preacher and his regular evening drinking, especially when he was traveling for R.O.I., the "most vital, forward-looking company in Shannon County, South Dakota," as he repeated to all of his customers.

His drinking was simple evidence of his common, flawed humanity. "We're all sinners," he told his congregation again and again, "that includes me. So, let's get on with the hard work of forgiveness and don't stick our noses into the private business between Jesus and his weak little lambs."

If a new woman asked Roy what he did, especially if he'd met her in a bar, Roy would say, "The Truth?"

And the inquirer, carelessly joining his game, would say, "Sure."

"O.K."Roy would reply, leaning forward, gazing into his listener's eyes for five intense seconds, he would admit with a shrug, "I'm a professional actor. There's only three differences between me and George Clooney...."

Roy paused while his listener registered mock disbelief. Then Roy would laugh, "Well, maybe a few more than that. But we're both handsome. Funny. Wise. We've been around, you know. Maybe I'm a little more weathered, but what do you expect if you live your life in cowboy country, not Hollywood or some Riviera."

His prey would nod at the clear truth of his statement. After all, she'd lived her life on the unforgiving High Plains, too.

At that point, Roy would smile and gently touch the side of his nose. Thank god, he'd had good insurance after that Zoë Rarefield cunt had bit off the tip of his nose in his church that Sunday morning three years ago. Then she fried it on the hood of his car. He'd like to pitch her over the altar and give her what she had coming.

Lucky he found an Omaha plastic surgeon who specialized in nose jobs. He left a barely visible seam above his nostrils, arcing below the bridge of his nose no more visible than a shadow of a spider's midnight thread, faint enough so you couldn't see it from a few feet, and if someone got closer, Roy had told his believable story with him playing a hero's role.

After that humiliating episode in front of his entire congregation, Roy decided to let the church go and use the Internet to get rich. The weather had driven those farmers deep into poverty anyway and he'd never make decent money off them.

Still, he'd learned a lot about how to pick out people's fears and make them feel he was their best and only shot at a happy life in this sorry world, never mind the next. Only a few of the old women believed in the afterlife, anyway. Everybody else wanted what they could get as soon as they could get it.

Like the women he would dally with in a bar.

"You know," he'd say, leaning toward a woman with his finger six inches away from his nose, pointing, "my surgeon was the best in the West. You can barely see the scar."

She'd always say, "I can't see a thing. What happened?"

"Frostbite. A few years ago I was up in Fargo one January. Thirty below. Car in front of me skidded off the road in a blizzard."

When he said that, Roy loved how her eyebrows would rise and her eyes open wide. She was taking the bait.

"I called 9-1-1 but the snow was so heavy the Highway Patrol was busy with a bunch of other wrecks and the EMTs were tied up, too. By the time I got the old folks out of the car and into mine, my nose and toes got frostbite. My toes thawed all right, but the tip of my nose didn't."

His smile would sag, inviting her sympathy as she compared his graying head, shining eyes and strong – he was built to work – but stocky body threatening flab, with the heroic picture he was painting.

"It looks normal," she'd always say, whether she meant it or not.

"Yeah, really natural, don't you think?"

He'd tighten his lips and shake his head, a faraway look in his eyes. "A little bit of flesh to save the lives of two people?"

"Wow," she'd say. "They're okay?"

"Fit as a fiddle. I get a Christmas card every year."

"I never met a hero before." She'd smile and lean toward him, finally flirting, even a tiny bit.

"Not a big deal." Roy would sit back in the booth or stretch his legs if they were at the bar. "You know what I say about my surgeon?"

Absorbed in his story, she'd say, "What?"

"He gives great nose job!" Roy would chortle and a smile would emerge on the woman's face until Roy laughed out loud. If she joined in the laugh, he was on his way to a fine and dandy night.

Roy would keep talking and revert to his self-comparison to George Clooney. "I imagine George would have done the same thing." Roy counted on a favorable identification with the actor.

"I hope so," the woman of the evening would say.

"Still, George and I have a few differences."

"Sure," she'd say, and if he'd told a convincing story, with his visual aids and all, she might say, "He ain't no real life hero."

"Three difference." Roy would shake his head and go on, ignoring her compliment. "One's obvious. He has press agents. I never got, never wanted any publicity about that snowy day."

She'd nod, curious.

"Two. I write my own scripts. Three. I never take a day off, or a night for that matter," he'd laugh and wink.

"What about right now?" the listener asks, intentionally brushing her voice with cynicism since she had caught him in a patent lie about never taking time off.

"That's a good question," would come Roy's response, having worked her into a conversational corner, all about him. Then follows Roy's favorite line, "Wha'd'you think?"

That moment made all the years of lost sales and rejections by insipid buyers and hundreds of thousands of miles he'd driven over the years worth every bit of effort. Here he practiced his sales profession to its peak attainment: Getting into a new woman's pants and by invitation only.

Roy tried to choose the classiest woman available on any given night, and if sometimes he chose someone faded or as familiar in her style and responses as a joke he'd told too many times, or like home plate in the Rapid City Rush baseball park, the most scored on spot in the city, he'd still picked the finest woman in sight that night.

After he got her interested with his nose story, he started the woman talking about herself, especially about her sufferings. He listened with his big eyes rounded like moons rising into his eyebrows and his lips parted in innocence.

Roy had perfected his seduction mask during twenty years of practice since his first success with a girl – really a woman – whose influence led him not only to his deepest insights but to his dual vocation as a salesman and church preacher.

One of his teachers at the North Woods Christian Fellowship Summer of Sacrifice and Joy Camp outside of Hibbing, Minnesota, changed him from a socially backward, morally rigid seventeen-year-old boy into a lusting, altruistic, dedicated lover of women, deep thinker and compassionate preacher.

His teacher at the camp, Barbara Moffitt, revealed to young Roy her tale of the loss of her baby, her husband, and her mother to the berserk protester dressed in a cowled black monk's robe swinging a scythe and reaping random shoppers strolling the Mall of America.

Roy's organs of compassion swelled as he touched her delicate fingertips sprawled vulnerably, miserably, on the bare knee she exposed at the hem of her plaid Bermuda shorts. She persuaded him it was not only his duty, but his higher mission in Fellowship to comfort her.

Barbara taught him her preferred techniques of comforting. She named them *The Many Paths to God Within.* A few years after that unforgettable summer of comforting and Pathfinding, he realized what a popular and fitting self-help line she'd come up with. He began to use it, especially with younger, idealistic women.

Lately, the women, even South Dakota women over 40, demanded something new from Roy, if he wanted to pursue his avocation into his midlife.

He told none of the women about his Sunday occupation: preacher, minister, pastor, whatever, at his little country church. Roy loved watching the dewy eyes of the women in the congregation when he told his fabricated redemption stories, and the forced smiles from the dour men in their work clothes whose wives had dragged them in for services.

Roy always surprised his flock with his praise for the transcendence the imperfect human animals could find in "joyful unity" with each other. "Transcendence" and "Oneness" showed up in all his sermons. The adults knew what he meant – grins tugged at their cheeks whenever he said it.

Since the "joyful unity" was the only real pleasure any of them found in their arid, arduous lives, they recognized Roy as one of them, unlike all the other preachers they'd tried out who raged against any bodily pleasure. Roy knew how to keep a congregation coming back Sunday after Sunday, with his tolerant, realistic, spiritual teachings.

Roy never harangued or admonished his congregation. Instead, he spoke to the ranchers and clerks and livestock truck drivers and their wives of "Divine Abundance" and "Jesus's Flesh" and "The Sweet Meat of Infinity."

His faithful requested one particular homily every April when weather and their animals and their hopes inspired optimism for a month or so. He called it "Soul and Body," with its core message being, "Please the body, please the soul, please the Lord."

His self-improvement studies naturally blended into this preaching and his seductions.

Roy had sensed his seduction rate decreasing over the last ten years. For the year after losing the damn tip of his nose, his success curve took a "nose-dive" – the private joke he soothed himself with – and he had to work his tail off to get back in the game. His best move was to update the title of his persuasion technique to "The Many Paths to The Goddess Within."

He had some data but not have enough yet to conclude whether this small change improved his results radically. In his data collections, Roy had disciplined himself to be painstaking. Conscientiousness paid off.

In his gut, which had grown into a prosperous bulge, he sensed the subtle power his "mature" approach offered him.

Still, Roy owed profound thanks and his lifelong gratitude to his mentoress Barbara. Not only had he borrowed her my-tongue-in-your-cheek phrase to name his seduction strategy, but without his Techniques, his life would feel boring, maybe even empty. In fact, from his relentless nocturnal efforts and occasionally noteworthy successes with women, Roy developed an exciting, trademarkable sales program: *The Many Paths*.

At the same time, Roy renamed his church *The Church of the Many Paths to Heaven*. The new name with its implied tolerance of diverse cultures, diverse tastes, diverse beliefs, expanded his congregation. He lost the staunch Bible ranters who had barely supported the old *Cowboy Church of Christ*, and good riddance. He gained dozens of practical people whose desperation overrode accepted South Dakota beliefs and opened them to ideas and dreams that elsewhere in America in the twenty-first century were conventional morality.

Once his new congregation confirmed his dream that people would really wanted what he offered them, he imagined making videos for YouTube and setting up a website and selling an video series and licensing it to Learning Strategies and the you-can-get-anything-you-want-for-nothing sites.

Roy planned to shed his country preacher venue to tour the nation teaching the Many Paths, showing everyone how to sell whatever, whenever you want and enjoy the grand buffet of life, a feast far beyond what you got at Chang's Mandarin Buffet in Spring Creek.

When he'd saved up enough money from the hefty commissions he expected to make selling R.O.I.'s water to the parched lips of the West, Roy would would be on the road, on the internet, on the air, he and his electronic self would be everywhere. Roy intended to teach his clients how to buy only exactly what you want. He'd give the most successful TED talk of all time.

Soon, Roy would have an impeccable reputation as the modest, the brilliant, the humble guru of *The Many Paths*. And he'd be rich.

Church preaching, with its tiny collection basket take, was only his opening act. He'd salt away vaults of money from his upcoming Vegas-quality performances would bear.

"Because it all starts with the sale," Roy repeated daily to himself and anyone who'd listen. And, his second favorite motto, "Everybody's selling something all the time."

Roy understood that the sweetest, most singular sex happened when his client used his own techniques on him.

When he learned to reverse his momentum from seducer to seducee, he discovered something every salesman depended on: the Unique Selling Point of *The Many Paths*. "When you're selling, be the buyer." And its corollary: "If you can't be it, act like it. Nobody will know the difference."

These words guided him in everything he thought, said, or sold. Or almost everything. He kept a small collection of maxims he referred to when he needed to keep his emotional gyroscope stable, balancing his thoughts and feelings.

When the office bathroom door swung open interrupting his reflections, Roy bent over to wash his hands for the seventeen seconds needed to scrub off all the bacteria.

"Hello, Roy," muttered Harold, Really Organic, Inc.'s new salesman. "Mr. Lockhart's looking for you. He says the meeting's starting now."

"All right, I'm coming, you young order taker," Roy said with mock affection. "The boss will be there when I am."

To himself he concluded, As soon as I get the right face on. He looked at his nose for the hundredth time that day, and he had to hand it to that Omaha doc. He did give good nose.

Roy loved his wit and couldn't help snickering to himself at his tired joke.

Pushing against the swinging door en route to Winston's office, he continued mentally priming himself for the day. As a matter of fact, he thought, my face is starting to look better now that my hair is receding. I really am looking like a baby face. What woman in her right mind would ever turn down such an innocent, soulful look?

Nine

OUR TAJ IS THE REAL TAJ

Roy shadowed Winston, his six foot six boss and owner of Really Organic, Inc., into the conference room.

Dragging his bulk on stiff legs, Winston paced back and forth in front of several large photographs of turbulent black water boiling and spraying in forced abandon under the relentless storm of a towering, broad waterfall.

An oil painting of a gleaming ivory structure built into a hillside hung at the end of the row of photos, framed in a hand-carved Baroque gilt frame. The building glowed and gloated over its own image which lay luxuriate in a reflecting pool. A wavering image of an emerald green "R.O.I." rippled in the water like an algae bloom.

"Look at this baby, Roy," Winston pointed toward the luscious painted image of Really Organic, Inc.'s new corporate headquarters. His wrinkled shirt hung over his belt. He leaned tiredly against the wheat-colored conference room wall while he growled at Roy.

Roy fawned. "Winston, she's more beautiful than the real Taj Mahal in India."

"Roy, this *is* the real Taj," Winston retorted, hefting his bulk away from the wall. "That other one was a gimmick put up by a shabby king who wanted to impress his enemies with his money. Our Taj is pure art: the spiritual married to the practical."

"And to the expensive," Roy added, assuming that Winston's wife had given him the bullshit about the spiritual and the practical.

"You're right, Roy. But it's only money. That fact that four men died, even if they were Mexicans and Indians, is what makes it expensive. Life's priceless," he lectured. "It's like that old peasant custom. If you want something that doesn't breathe to grow, treat it like a god. Make a little sacrifice. They do it in front of the cross at St. Mary's every day. Did you ever think of that, Roy? When you're kneeling there worrying about your mortal sins?"

Winston snorted, his nostrils quivering. "Between you and me, Roy, I'm glad we poured a few quarts of blood into Our Taj's foundation. Blood makes the concrete harder."

Winston paused, looking for the right transition into what he wanted to get out of Roy.

"Just like that wrinkled old hose you've got hanging between your legs. Right, Roy?" He snorted again, coughing and pounding the table to help recover his breath.

"Funny, Winston," Roy said.

Winston's jolly act worried Roy. Winston rarely acted and when he tried, he alerted everyone in the room to his obvious machinations. Roy felt more comfortable with Winston when he played his customary, cruel, gruff, intimidating persona.

Roy led Winston on, wondering what he wanted from him. "It's true. A lot of people die when someone builds an architectural masterpiece."

By now, Roy realized that the meeting had nothing to do with sales quotas or new product introductions.

"Like the Sears Tower," replied Winston, pleased to hear Roy placing 'Our Taj' among his favorite design and construction feats. "How many do you think croaked building that beast?"

"Or like the Freedom Tow," Roy added.

"Roy, that's right. Sacred country now in New York. Seen it yet?" Winston raised his voice. "I'd almost give my nuts to bleed every raghead I could, and they're still sliming the good parts of the world. Let it alone. Just think about our sacrifice." Winston's eyes glittered, whether with dewy compassion or with gleaming sadistic pleasure, Roy assumed the latter.

"Our sacrifice was great, Winston. Everyone knows that," Roy acknowledged, implying his compassion more for Winston than for the dead builders or their families. What did he care about the dead workers? He couldn't do anything about it. South Dakota either killed you or made you tough. He told his parishioners that at every year on Good Friday.

"What about the Grand Coulee Dam, Roy. We've got something here that's going to change the way the world is run the same way the Grand Coulee did. Everybody's going to want in on our new way of running things."

"You're right, Winston," Roy said with a false restraint in his voice. When Roy fudged, he made sure that he had data and statistics at hand to prove himself right if anyone questioned him. For now, he chose to play it safe and walk the Path of the Humble Servant Acknowledging the Wisdom of His Superior. He taught that to his parishioners who joined him in his versions of holy rites on Sundays.

"I don't have all the facts about Grand Coulee," he said, "but you're the expert. About the only great architectural structure I know anything about is the Hanging Gardens of Babylon."

Winston sat down heavily at the conference tale, slumping into his leather padded oak chair the staff called *The Throne*.

"Tell me about those gardens, Roy," Winston sighed. "I've been thinking maybe Our Taj needs more trees and bushes. Maybe some flowers. I've already spent the Denver mint on landscaping. Now she's grown so goddam gorgeous, maybe we want to doll her up even more with necklaces and bracelets of roses and things."

Winston looked exhausted to Roy. His instinct warned him to distrust Winston's weariness as another act. If he's consistent at anything, Roy thought, he's sly. What did I do? Why does he want a story? Well, if I'm good at anything, it's telling a story.

Ten

ROY CHOOSES AN UNPREDICTABLE PATH

"Back in the days of Babylon," Roy began, standing up, deepening his voice the way he did in the pulpit. He would soothe the old man with a fairy tale, a nice calming bedtime story. "All the kings grew weak as caged rabbits because of all the mother and sister fuckin' the royal family engaged in. Probably quite a bit of disgusting brother fuckin', too."

Winston grimaced. Roy felt encouragement and heard inaudible applause leaching out of the lines etched around his boss's mouth.

"They didn't trust any one outside their own bloodlines with the money and the power. So they bred themselves into weak hearts, idiotic minds, and crippled bodies. If it wasn't for some clever queens, who got pregnant by their smartest, strongest slaves, the old kingdom would have disappeared before it became famous as the center of world commerce and culture."

"What does that have to do with the gardens?" Winston asked, still seeming tired but typically impatient.

"The kings," Roy explained, "in their stupidity and weakness, became so sensitive to their priests and so refined by their riches that when they executed somebody, they did it in the cruelest way they could think of. They hung their criminals in a garden. Stabbed them while they dangled. Gory as shit, blood dripping on flowers."

"I've seen plenty of 'gory' executions, Roy," Winston divulged, sitting up straighter until his jowly chin was almost even with Roy's square one. "Never developed a taste for them."

Winston's somber admission contradicted Roy's assumption about Winston's sadistic tastes. "Nobody's a saint in war," Winston explained.

Roy misinterpreted Winston's wry smile as praise for the farflung story he started.

"The Babylonians developed their 'Terraces of Justice' that circled the castle and became famed and feared throughout the world. Eventually the flowers in the different gardens became nicknames for all types of criminals around the Mediterranean.

"Spies were called Starflowers. They worked under the cover of night. Burglars were Men of Ivy. They climbed and clung to walls. When you needed a murderer, you asked around for a Thorned Beauty." Roy paused, waiting for Winston to encourage him or tell him to sit down.

Finally Lockhart spoke. "Where did you get this shit, Roy?" Winston grinned, condescending.

"I didn't make it up," Roy claimed. "I took a course down at State when I was in college called Horticulture Through History. I thought it was about hookers in different cultures and eras. The stuff about the Hanging Gardens is all I can remember."

Winston glared at Roy, pretending disbelief and frustration in the entire Hanging Gardens story. Then he smiled and opened his arms warmly, pointing with one open palm toward a chair across from him. Roy laughed, relieved.

"It's probably all you remember from college, period. Sit down, Roy."

Roy sat.

"I amaze myself, Roy. I had the insight to hire the biggest bullshitter in South Dakota. You could talk the tail off a cougar."

Right. Just give me the chance. And a 30.30 in my hands. Roy felt ready now. Telling the story had loosened his shoulders and sharpened his tongue. Whatever Winston threw at him, he could handle.

"We have a little trouble with Our Taj's water supply." Winston's sudden directness spiked Roy's eardrums with fresh apprehension.

"What's the problem, Winston?" Roy asked with a hoarse voice, anxiety torquing in his solar plexus. Winston's familiar, confidential tone flustered him and his palms seeped sweat.

"Roy, you sneaky son of a bitch, I'll tell you as soon as you give me that disposable camera you've stuck in your pocket."

"I paid good money for that, Winston. It's not disposable," he said, pouting as he removed the pen and handed it over.

"It is now," Winston said, pitching the pen into a trashcan. Then he drove his size fourteen ebony Angus leather boot into the can, crushing the pen with his polished toes.

"Jesus, Winston, did you have to do that?" Roy groaned as Winston mangled the plastic.

"Roy, I'm glad I didn't hire you for your brains."

With his boot still in the trashcan, Winston stared at Roy. "Don't pretend you've got that camera to record your sales. I should fire you for attempted blackmail."

"What? What do you mean?"

Winston twisted his boot in the can again, then lifted his foot out, shaking it as if trying to rid it of mud, or manure.

The stunt refreshed Winston. His normal resounding vocal timbre returned, matching the bully size of his body. "I'd worry about myself if I ever trusted you, Roy. You know you could never do me any damage with one of your videos, not in Shannon County or anywhere else. Just do whatever I say. Nothing else. Got it?"

Roy struggled to slow his breathing. "Why me, Winston? R.O.I.'s got plenty of young guys who are quicker than me. They've got more guts, too." Roy realized if he didn't downplay his effectiveness for Winston, he could end up in deeper shit than a feedlot lagoon. "They'd do anything for R.O.I. I know. I trained them," he concluded, inserting a last note of self-preserving self-promotion.

"Roy, shut up," Winston huffed, "until I tell you what you're going to do. Then you can ask me how soon you can get to work."

Winston has a powerful sales technique, too, Roy thought, now breathing deeply, the portal to all of his paths. You wouldn't need to make it into a YouTube series. It's the oldest means of persuasion in history: Big Man with Big Stick. You could give it a catchy name, though. The B.M. with the B.S. He chuckled sub-vocally, using *The Path of Waiting Until You Have a Chance.*

"One more thing, Roy," Winston snarled, jabbing his manicured paw into Roy's briefcase. He withdrew the video camera and the remote microphone he'd supplied Roy as company sales manager. "Take hold of the microphone here, Roy."

Roy did.

"Now pull," he commanded.

Roy obeyed. The wire popped out of the video pack with a flat thud like the sound of a can of soup dropped on the floor.

"I'm going to smash the camera now. I know how well you use it for the Tech Advantage when you sell for R.O.I, but never try to use it on me." His voice rose. "In Jalalabad...."

Roy blinked.

"You know," Winston growled. "Afghanistan."

Roy didn't know but he nodded.

"More than once," Winston continued, "I heard eyes pop out with the same sound you heard when you pulled that wire out."

"Winston, you know me," Roy said, trying to maintain a steady tone, but his wobbling larynx betrayed his stiffened lips. "I was just practicing one of my most highly refined Paths."

"Sure, Roy," Winston said. "What's the Path's name? *The Path of Self-Destruction?*"

Roy acquiesced before Winston's mean streak surged into rage. More than once in the past few months, Winston had turned an oak conference table over into the laps of trembling employees.

"Sure, Winston." Roy inhaled. "Just what is it I can do for you?"

"Thanks, Roy," Winston said, relaxing. "It took you long enough to get the message." He sat down. "Here's the problem we're going to solve. We're not getting enough flow through the underground river below Our Taj. We need a million gallons an hour into our reservoir to run the turbines." He sat up and hammered the table. "We're getting fucking 250,000. We can barely run the lights in the basement on 250,000."

"What do the engineers say?"

"What the engineers say," replied Winston, his voice edging into a snarl, "is there's an underground lake bigger than Lake Oahe at the head of the river and the passage we planted our turbines in is wide enough for three million gallons an hour to flow through right down into the Oglalla Acquifer. In a flood, it will take five and a half million. In fact, their records show that, five years ago, three million gallons per hour flowed through the channel like a walk in the park. Exactly where we installed our turbines – four hundred fifty feet straight down."

Winston glared at the floor. "If those goddam frackers don't drain it first."

Roy followed his gaze. The navy blue carpet revealed nothing except a white paper dot someone forgot to sweep up after using the table to punch holes in notepaper.

Both men stared at the dot in silence.

"The only reason we built Our Taj seventeen miles out of Spring Creek is because we're sitting downstream from the natural reservoir that holds two billion gallons, enough to run 'Our Taj' full bore forever."

Roy nodded in agreement, bouncing his neck like a bobble head doll. "You told me that when you hired me."

"Oahe dam cost the feds half a billion to build. Did I tell you what we spent?"

The wrinkle between Lockhart's eyebrows reminded Roy of his tenth-grade math teacher's threatening stare whenever Roy couldn't answer a question, which was most of the time.

"You should know all this, Roy," Winston admonished his sales chief.

"I do."

"How much then?"

"Hundred billion?"

"Jeezus, Roy. Where would I get a hundred billion? That's oil money."

"Okay, how much?"

"Didn't cost me nothin', Roy." Lockart's eyes glittered and a grin swelled into his cheeks.

Roy stared at him, far out of his league.

"I'm leasin' it, Roy. I'm sharing the patents with the Department of Energy and the Department of Defense and Bictone, used t'be a division of Bechtel. You heard'a them?"

"Of course. Who ain't?" Roy had seen Bechtel logos on equipment outside of Kabul when he took his obligatory nine-month tour of Afghanistan.

Lockhart leaned back in his chair. "Roy, here's the facts of business. I know it's over your head, but there's one way to get rich in this world."

"I know that." Roy paused, pretending to think. "You gotta sell stuff and keep sellin' it."

"True," Lockhart said. "Except it'll take you a lifetime, unless you're selling bank securities and insurance shit. I wouldn't touch that."

"Don't keep me waiting, Winston. How do you get rich?"

"You know, Roy. Everybody knows. You get the taxpayer to transfer dollars into your bank account."

"Sure. Let's see. There's unemployment. There's food stamps. There's Section 8 housing. There's living on the Rez."

"Too bad you think like that, Roy. Poor people will never climb the ladder." Winston slapped the table. "They don't have the brains. Are you like them, Roy?"

"No, no, no. I'm like you, Winston, just not lucky enough yet. Give me the big picture."

"It ain't luck, Roy," Winston said, slinging his arm back toward the photo of Our Taj. "The bank and the town put up the building, the Army Corps of Engineers under the finger of the Department of Defense taps the lake. Big companies like Siemens, Bechtel, whoever, I'm not saying it's them – they install the turbines. Senator Johnson, he brings me in as the private business to get the PPP deal going – you up on Public Private Partnerships?"

Roy shrugged.

"And guess what? All I gotta do is bottle some water, maintain the turbines, and let the lake flow." Winston paused, then said, "Of course, I'm keeping the whole deal a secret. That's part of the package."

"Cool. I see how you can get rich on things like that."

"By the way, did I tell you my name for the lake?"

Roy shook his head.

"I call it Satan's Pond. Y'know why?"

Roy shrugged.

"There was a guy named Dante – you never heard of him? – he was Italian. Wrote a book about Hell. *Inferno.*"

"Yeah, I saw the movie."

"No, you didn't." Winston shook his head in disgust. "I'm talking about the original *Inferno*, not some Hollywood crap. At the bottom was an iced-up lake where the worst sinners stand with ice up to their waists and the rest of them is on fire."

Winston was starting to alarm Roy, but maybe there was something he could use in his preaching. He said, "Never heard of that. Wha'did those guys do?"

Lockhart leaned toward Roy and growled, "The worst sin of all. They betrayed their friends."

Squirming, Roy said in as strong a voice as he could manage, "You don't think...you know me, Winston. I'd never betray you. Never. You know that."

Lockhart squinted and frowned, paralyzing Roy in his seat.

"You got me locked up with that non-compete, non-talk, non-everything agreement."

"Right, Roy. You remember how you gave us permission to confiscate everything you owned if we ever caught you speaking out of turn or doing anything to jeopardize R.O.I.?" Lockhart stood and leaned his long arms on the conference table, his head between the ceiling light and Roy, his face a shadow dropping over Roy's face.

Roy squeaked, "You know I'm your man. All I care about is making R.O.I. a success."

"I believe you, Roy. I also believe you are a weak, sniveling liar who can't resist his own stories. That's why if you break your non-compete, you'll follow your Path right down to the Sioux Falls House of Correction." A malicious smile crossed his face. "Think you need some correcting, Roy? They got guys there who can fix up anybody – to just the size they like."

Roy took another deep breath. Winston was out of control, as ridiculous as Roy had ever seen him. Something deadly was on his mind. "Where's this going, Winston?"

Roy couldn't stop his head from bobbing in time to the churning beat of his heart, his teeth sticking to his lips as he tried to smile. Fake it, man. Be cool. Breathe. He'll come around. Winston needs my hundred percent total agreement with his opinion of himself as the company's true master salesman, so give it to him.

Lockhart sat down, his heavy body shuddering into the chair. He sat for a moment, then said, a whine stealing into his voice. "Roy, we're ready to open the warehouse and the bottling plant. We've got the Grand Opening of Our Taj scheduled. Press releases out to all the media. Have you checked our website lately? An invitation to every important person in our six-state region. And to governors across the West."

Roy had heard countless complaints from Lockhart, usually with disgust, or anger. They didn't bother Roy, but when he whined, Roy cringed. He'd heard the whine before Lockhart fired his chief financial guy. The whine was the last thing Roy heard the day Winston upended the conference table into the laps of Roy and his sales team. Roy clenched his teeth.

"We've got a schedule to keep. We opened our sluices last week for the test. Everything looked good. We ran the reservoir down to its operating level." Lockhart glared at Roy. "Then guess what happened?"

Roy kept quiet.

Winston steepled his finges, enunciating, "We got a lousy trickle." Fuming now. "I could piss more water than the goddam river has given me since last week."

Tiny white bubbles of saliva emerged from the corners of Winston's lips. To himself, Roy admired the control and rhythm Winston used to glue his rant together with.

Winston inhaled. From a condential whisper he built to a messianic crescendo. "Here we have the most energy efficient, legal, private power generation facility in the Unites States of America, probably in the whole world. We plugged it right into the deepest, quietest, coldest sub-basement of the largest, most profitable, state-of-the-art pure water bottling company in all of history." Huffing. Righteous. "Jesus, Roy, a rat pup would drool more flow than we get from the mightiest underground river the U.S. Army Corps of Engineers has ever measured."

Roy heard practice and measure in Winston's passionate outburst. He probably said the same thing to his lawyer, his banker, his architect, his engineer, his accountant, his vice-presidents, his wife, his kids, and anyone else he cornered into listening to his tale of woe, Roy thought.

"The water's there, Roy. The Ogallala Acquifer. It's the New York City of underground dams, the Amazon of undeveloped resources, the Tokyo Stock Exchange of water power. And it ain't gonna last forever the way those damn Kansas farmers are suckin' at it."

Winston stopped. "Even them fuckin' frackers don't bother me like the idiot farmers using my water to turn a desert into an oasis. Christ." His hypothalamic eyes bulged, daring disagreement.

"Goddammit, Roy. Something's stuck in the river, blocking my goddam water, keeping my goddam Cal Tech Minus Zero resistance turbines quiet as a morgue."

The boss paused, shaking his head up and down, smiling, confirming an ugly secret Roy needed to know, but feared knowing.

"Roy." Winston paused and frowned. "Roy," he murmured. "We're gonna make you a hero."

Horror clutched Roy's neck. He felt the blood drain from his face.

"Why me, Winston? I know bupkus about dams."

Winston stared at the ceiling over Roy's head.

Roy gulped. "Hydroelcetrics. Hydromatics. Except my Uncle Paul's classic Olds 98." Roy let his fear frenzy his thoughts. "He paid me to wash it once. I used laundry soap on the wax finish. When the English racing green color turned yellow, I told him that a lemon was just a ripe lime."

Winston, ignoring Roy's babble, tipped The Throne back, stretching his long legs, gazing at his boots. He brushed a piece of plastic from Roy's crushed pen off the tip of his sole.

"Or hydroencephalics. I saw a TV show about kids born in China with water on their brains. They treated them with acupuncture for a few years. The kids all grew up to be great wonton soup chefs."

Winston looked up and grinned at a humorous image only he could see painted into the ceiling plaster.

Roy had nearly exhausted his nervous rambling. He was about to give up. A last desperate idea came to him.

"Or hydroponics," he said, hoping to offer Winston a new business idea to distract him from the awful assignment Roy saw coming.

"Hey, here's the solution, Winston. Grow lettuce and beansprouts down there, just like they do in the basement farms in Chinatowns in big cities." Deep breath. "You only need a sprinkle of water and a few chemicals to grow that stuff. You have plenty of water for that and the lights. Hey, you can't beat the profit margins on stuff that's 99% water!"

Roy stopped. His panicked banter couldn't loosen the boss up to free him from whatever scheme of doom Winston planned to launch him into.

"Roy, we're never going to forget what you did for us." Winston promised Roy, his soft voice now frightening him further. "Your portrait will go up on this conference room wall right next to the painting of Our Taj."

Roy wheezed. "What did I do for us?"

"Roy. You blew that sonofabitchin boulder jam that's stuck in my river! You made Our Taj turbines turn!" Winston threw his arms up, exulting.

"Winston," Roy complained, straining indifference to Winston's threats, "I was in the Guard. The infantry. I don't know shit about bombs. I'm claustrophobic. I can't go into a fuckin cave!"

"Roy, my friend, you *used to be* afraid of caves." Winston's smooth assurance lanced terror in Roy's belly. Winston rhapsodized. "Like every hero, you overcame your fears and weaknesses. You'll be the gold in the heart of Black Hills spelunking legends."

Roy's fear stank around his sweating body. "I quit," Roy said without conviction, his eyes focused on the table.

"And, of course, Roy," confided Winston as he laid the final brick in the mausoleum of Roy's old life as a small time salesman, "after you do this job for me, I'll set you up with the money and manpower you need for your *Many Paths* thing."

Roy gulped, stunned at the cruelty and hope in Winston's bribe. In his deepest heart, though, he doubted Winston would follow through. Unless he held cards Winston feared.

"No strings attached?" Roy's heart skipped until he felt giddy. "All the capital I need?"

Winston nodded yesses to all of Roy's dumbfounded questions.

"Let me think about it," Roy said, holding out the delay ploy to negotiate easier terms for himself. He felt trapped, unable to move inside the MRI tube of Winston's will.

Winston stood up and sauntered along the gallery wall, brushing his fingers around the frames of the photos, polishing the glass with his silk cuffs.

"Sure, Roy. Take your time."

An irresistible Unpredictable Path had presented itself to Roy. And he had no choice.

"Just answer me one question."

Winston nodded assent.

"Why me?"

Grinning, Winston said, "Welcome aboard the Rescue Mission. I knew you'd grasp the essential advantages to Roy Kassup and his dreams. We'll give you everything you need to get the job done down there. Wink Lamb will go with you. He'll take care of the details."

"Lamb? That ex-FBI guy or assassin or whatever who runs your security firm?" Roy's fear sensors climbed to a new level. "Lamb's got a bad rep around here. You seen those two kids who'll never walk again just because they tried to liberate something from his car? Open window and everything." Roy began to hyperventilate. "Lamb can take care of this by himself. Let him do it. I'm old. I'd slow him down. I suck...I ain't young enough to play caveman." *Christ almighty. Lamb's temper is worse than Winston's. Everybody in Spring Creek knows he kills people for looking at him cross-eyed.*

"No, no. You're important, Roy," the boss insisted. "You're the non-negotiable absolutely necessary linchpin to the whole operation. You're the perfect age. Lamb wants you. We believe in you – you being a preacher gives us the perfect cover." Winston laughed. "You *The Man!*"

"That scares the shit out of me."

He gripped the arm of his chair, restraining himself from getting up and charging out the door. His best chance to get out of this would be to appeal to Winston's rational mind. "Even if I did go along, and I'm not saying I will, that lake and river flow somewhere under Cascade Mountain National Wilderness, right? Anpetu Mountain?"

"Everybody knows that."

"What if we blow up the whole fuckin mountain or they catch us? What will I tell my congregation? They need me."

"I'm proud of you, Roy. You already figured out why I want you for this job. Wink will take care of the demolition – like you say, he's a pro. You'll take care of the public, if there's any problem. You can count on your preacher reputation. Your church will be so crowded you'll have to use garbage cans for collection baskets." Winston chortled then stared hard at Roy. "I'm sure there won't be any problem, but – let's be transparent, here, Roy – you're our fallback plan."

"I still don't get it. Why me, Winston?"

"Because you're the best goddam liar I've ever met. And I've met hundreds. If you get caught you can talk your way out like you talked your way out of that jam with the Indian girl the Spring Creek cop found drunk in the back seat of your car over in Pierre last month."

"How did you know about that?"

"That was stupid thing you did. Who do you think handled that for you? I couldn't let one of my most valuable employees get locked up, could I? Besides," Winston's tone turned sarcastic, "your faithful flock would've lynched you."

Roy sighed. It had to be Lamb. He must have every cop in the county in his pocket.

"You know what?" Winston said, a glint of false kindness falling from his words. "Why don't you submit the receipts for those spy toys of yours on your next expense form. You used them and lost them while on company duty. Go back to your desk and file those expenses now because as of noon today, you're fired."

Roy slumped on the desk, bewildered by Winston's reversal.

Winston stood up and headed for the door, his grin exposing broad teeth gleaming in the fluorescent light like polished freshwater clamshells.

"Transparency here, Roy," he snorted. "Just in case. You might say firing you is my 'Path of Covering All My Bases'."

Eleven

MINISTER KETCHUP

In The Good Foods Store, Zoë placed the bottles of damiana and yohimbe beside the cash register and, with her front teeth pinching down on her lower lip, she tilted her head, flirting with George as she always did when she needed a sandwich or a juice.

George frowned. "Too expensive. Mimi will know I let somebody swipe them."

Zoë smiled to herself. I knew it, he's bargaining. He's a good businessman.

While George waited on the only other customer, Zoë wandered over to the herb shelf and accidentally knocked a bottle of yohimbine onto the floor. The white plastic jar didn't break, so she accidentally stomped on it. When it cracked under her heel, she picked it up and said, "Oh, I'm so sorry. I knocked one of your bottles on the floor. It broke."

George laughed and said, "At least you can get the broom and sweep up."

When she left the store with a mound of black yohimbine and brown damiana pills in her pocket, she kissed George on the lips but he pulled back. "Somebody might see and tell Margie, my new girl-friend. Come in the back room."

Zoë said thanks but no, kissed his cheek and skipped down the street. She passed Halvacek's feed store, the last building on the street before the *Come On Back Spring Creek Wants To See You Again* sign.

Her attention focused on finding more poshent ingredients, she didn't hear the SUV approach until gravel crunched behind her and a man's voice said, "Howdy, Zoë. Kinda hot today. Need a ride?"

At the sound of the voice, she started jogging, ignoring the man. It was Minister Ketchup. He was the last person she wanted to see. She could already smell him.

Devan's was less than two miles away. If she had to, she'd take off into the hills. Ketchup would never catch up to her.

"Why so quiet?"

She jogged, veering toward the shoulder. Ahead, a muddy irrigation ditch passed beside the road. If she had to, she'd slide down into it. If he tried to follow, he'd crash his ugly red truck.

"Hey, Zoë. Take it easy. Nice to see you out here. All is forgiven. Wouldn't be Christian if I didn't give you a chance to repent. Need a ride? Like my new truck? We could take a spin up to Rapid City." His laugh sounded like a sick coyote trying to bark.

Zoë picked up her pace while the truck stayed with her. He pulled close, so close when he spoke she could smell his cigar breath.

"I see you're still feisty as ever," Roy said. "They say you're autistic or something. I know better. You're just a cute girl who takes care of herself by pretending to be retarded. I don't blame you."

Zoë stopped and stared at him with cold eyes.

"The young guys at the church got a joke about you. They say you've got the Ass Burger Sin Drome." Cackling, Ketchup brushed the tip of his nose with the back of his hand. "Bad joke, I know. I told them they're being unkind but, y'know, it's really true. Just like you're the only who can bite off my nose, I'm the only one can save you from your Sin Drome thing."

Ketchup. Ketchup. He never stops talking. He still wants to baptize me on his church altar.

"You know I'm more than just a preacher now," he said. "Working for R.O.I. I'm their Sales Manager. See? I'm dressed for success."

He was wearing his preacher clothes, blue and red tie and white shirt. Zoë stopped running, shrugged, backed away.

"That big water company up Route 71? I'm friends with the owner. He depends on me for everything."

She rolled her eyes. Ketchup's body odor seeped off him like a dead snail all the way to where she stood six feet away. He reeked so foul a crow wouldn't touch him if he was road kill.

"You're not to up on things, like usual," Roy said. "I make good money now. Still got my congregation, too. Thinking about building a new church. Hey, let's go take a look at the building lot."

The truck door lock clunked up like the sound of a Bible dropping on the wood floor in Ketchup's church. He opened his door a few inches.

Zoë turned and trotted the way she'd come. A hundred yards back, she'd noticed a steer path that led out to the trees. He'd never follow her there. She looked over her shoulder.

Ketchup reversed his truck, keeping pace with her. Zoë's lips pulled back in an attempt to smile to herself but her throat seized up. She put her palm on her stomach and coughed. It helped.

Ketchup shouted at her. "You have a soul, girl. Autistics have souls like every human. You're also real smart about some things. Don't let anybody tell you different."

Zoë looked over her shoulder.

"It's my job to save that little soul of yours," Ketchup laughed, his truck weaving back and forth across the dusty gravel as he drove in reverse. "We can spin over to Center Lake. Get you that baptism you need. Rapture you right up to bein' normal."

The word "baptism" shot into Zoë's muscles like a crack of thunder and she leapt off the road, bursting across the ditch. She bounced up and over the barbed-wire fence and sprung into the field. She ducked her head into the wind and, holding her arms close to her sides, kicked into a gallop. She looked back again. The truck was parked on the road, shimmering like a cherry fire.

She didn't see Ketchup in his truck, so he must be in one of the hollows behind her. When she looked for him over her other shoulder, her toe stubbed on a rock and she fell, sprawling on sharp stones. Sharp pains shot up both of her arms and her knees.

She lost her breath for a moment, regained it, and picked herself up. She tried to run, but her knee buckled.

Inky. Kateri. Help.

She stood up again. Now Ketchup was right beside her. She screamed then bit her lips before the wind could scoop up her fear and spread it over the foothills.

She backed away on wobbling legs. Ketchup was the same height as her, but he must have weighed as much as a hog. The scarred tip of his pointy nose gleamed hot and reddish black like an ember.

Zoë couldn't hold back a giggle when she thought of how she'd bitten the tip of his nose off in his church. "Hmmm-mmm-mmm." It was one of the craziest and funnest things she'd ever done. She couldn't wait to tell Ruthie in person.

"That's good. Don't be afraid, Zoë. We're outside, where you like it. I come to my people where they need me."

Breathing hard, Ketchup bent over, grunting and snuffling. He smiled, exposing yellow teeth. The gristly feeling of his nose in her mouth rose from her memory, gagging her.

When she was thirteen, just after she became a woman, halfway into her first year living on her own, her last year in school, Reverend Roy Kassup from the Spring Creek Church of the Many Paths convinced her to come to church to join a Rapture ceremony.

One afternoon, he approached Zoë and her friends outside Roker's, the store where middle school kids hung out after school. "Come on over to the Church," he said. "We got a big Rapture Healing, music, singing, lots of people you know. Every one of you's a sinner. You know that, right?"

Curious to learn about Rapture, Zoë accepted his invitation to join him in his next Sunday service. None of the others would come.

"He's crazy," one said. "So're you, if you go."

"Who isn't?" Zoë said.

One of the boys said, "My mother makes me go to Saint Paul's. Except when she and my dad get drinking on Saturday night and sleep in on Sunday. Why would you want to go to those Holy Rollers out in the country anyway?"

Everyone else agreed with him.

The minister's promise raised Zoë's hopes that he could teach her how the Rapture could get her to Heaven to be with Ruthie.

The idea had first come to her when she was ten, living with Bonnie and Arthur. One night just before she went to bed, the scan function on her radio stopped on a church station.

The preacher sobbed because, he said through his nose, "The Apocalypse is about to fall on the world."

The day before the Great Destruction, the Lord Jesus would come to Earth and gather True Believers, living and dead, and haul them up to Heaven. This was the first time Zoë had heard of this.

"The Rapture, children," the radio preacher growled, "the Rapture is the only Goal of your life. Not things of the world. No that new car, no. Not that big house, no. Not that vacation in Hawaii. No. No. No."

Zoë never cared about things or vacations. She'd rather shop at the thrift store for clothes than buy new things. New clothes always smelled like the insides of a laundromat.

Ten-year old Zoë leaned against her cool bedroom wall, entranced by the high-pitched radio voice.

"No," the preacher said, bitterness edging his words as they droned from the speakers. "No. No. You were born for one thing in this life: Trials and Tribulations."

Problems, he means. Zoë had a good vocabulary for a ten year old – she read as well as twelfth graders – and she had plenty of problems in her life. Her real daddy was drunk half the time, always trying to get her to come live with him. Mrs. Harkins, the school counselor, made her come see her once a week. Devan had left after high school for his actor life in California and he was never around to take her for drives anymore. Most of her crickets died in the winter. Not to mention the worst thing of all, Ruthie not being on Earth any more. Trials and Tribulations. Nice sounds. Ugly things. Plenty of problems.

Then, his voice swelling out of the speakers, the preacher raved. "If you don't leave this sorry vale of tears with the other Believers at the very moment of the Rapture, you're lost, lost...." Then his voice plunged and he said, almost whispering, "lost" and he paused. "My poor sad sheep."

Zoë waited, hunched up, imagining sheep wandering, bleating their confusion as they climbed hill after hill finding nobody. Finally, the preacher said, his voice a drum beating three times. "For-ev-er."

Forever? Always. For all time. Eternity. That's where Ruthie was. Eternity.

"Our Shepherd calls his millions of Lost Sheep to sup with him in his Celestial Castle. We soar faster than angels. Past the speed of light – gone from this universe, children, gone. We Rapture like lightning into Heaven. Here doing our moans and groans, now there, in the arms of Our Lord, praising and joying and laughing...cuz we made it, children. We left all our Trials, all our Trials, all our Tribulations down here in the vale of tears. Children, we made it. We. Made. It. By the – Rapture! Faster than lightning – right into the Lord's tender arms – forever!"

Lightning meant thunder, a storm tornadoing people up to Heaven. Zoë sat on her bed, imagining people getting sucked out of their houses and car windows and off their tractors, flying up in a flock. She saw bones and skeletons whirling up into the sky wearing big grins on their skulls and sick and dying old people sliding out of their wheelchairs as they drove into the middle of an electric storm.

At the rim of the people storm, the Lakota and the Minneconjou people floated up silently, their faces long, some riding horses, carrying babies in their arms. A few bison straggled behind the Indians.

She wondered about the animals. Would only bison and horses go? What about dogs and cats and sheep? Would crickets and spiders and fish Rapture up? No animals or bugs ever sinned, so wouldn't they join the backwards rain of souls?

With the memory of the radio preacher's description of the Rapture and refreshed by Minister Kassup's promise, thirteen-year old Zoë got up in the dark that Sunday morning, before Bonnie and Arthur woke up, gulped down a yogurt and slipped out the side door. Zoë left her bike at home, wanting to take her time, to enjoy the land and the trees in case this was her last morning on Earth.

So excited, Zoë almost danced all the way to the Little White Church, her toes bouncing, her heels lifting, floating her above the gravel road, like a taste of The Rapture.

Arriving at the wooden church building just after dawn, she read the sign painted with red letters: "Church of The Many Paths - All Sinners Invited."

The idea of sinning made Zoë's stomach growl. She couldn't sin until she was much older, sixteen. It's something Ruthie had taught her. She didn't remember all the things Ruthie taught her, but she'd never forget that.

A month before Ruthie died, Uncle Augie made Zoë go in his car with him to the drive-in and all she remembered was seeing him and his fat lips reflected in the chrome of the door hands. He was leaning over toward her and then she forgot everything. After that, her mother told her not to worry about whatever happened. Zoë was only six, way too young to sin. She never had to go with Augie anymore.

What happens to people when they grew up? Maybe things changed and they couldn't help themselves from sinning. When she was almost sixteen, would they change for her? She might even like sinning. Most everybody else seemed to laugh about it.

Zoë had to get to Heaven before she turned sixteen or even Inky might not be able to help her. She had to...before she gave in to temptation to sin and that always happened when everybody turned sixteen. They couldn't help it, so even if she tried as hard as she could, she'd start sinning. Getting up to Ruthie was all that mattered in her whole life and you had to have a pure soul to get into Heaven – no sins!

She entered the Church of the Many Paths. Everyone looked out of the pews and Minister Kassup shouted, "She's here. Our newest lamb!" The people applauded and one of the women offered Zoë a white gown. She pulled it on over her running clothes. It was so long the hem dragged on the shiny plank floor.

"Come on, little one. Up here." Reverend Kassup patted the altar and, grinning, Zoë hopped up and knelt on the altar, then the reverend directed her to lie back.

"Why?"

"This is the holiest place in Shannon County," he said. "We anointed it with blood these fine people here donated from their own hearts. We want to share it with you."

A pack of devoted worshippers surrounded her, caroling, flapping their arms in the air, whimpering as they caressed her cheeks and chin and tangled their fingers in her hair. An electric guitar howled in the background.

Zoë twisted her neck around to see who was playing the music when Minister Kassup took her head in his rough paws and whispered, "Now Spirit comes."

He climbed up on the altar and lay with his legs thrown over her calves. He had a soft belly and he got his legs caught in his gown. He brought his face next to her ear and mumbled, "Take my spirit into your body and soul. It is Jesus in me who wills you accept him and me."

The minister's chorus raised its pitch to the level of a country singer with a stomachache. The electric guitar clunked like someone pounding a car trunk with a stick.

Zoë sat up but the minister pushed her back down by the shoulders and swung his body up so he sat on her legs, his face bent, inches from hers. He stank. He started running his hands up and down her sides. Then he pushed them between her legs. Other hands started pulling at her waistband and tugging at the legs of her sweatpants.

Nobody had ever pinned Zoë down before and right now, she'd had enough of church. She shouted as loud as she could, wriggling her body and slapping the minister's back with hard, open palms.

"This ain't no Rapture! Let me up!" She screamed and punched and scratched at his neck. Bony hands gripped her arms and feet, pressing them down into the stone altar. She swung her head back and forth, angry and scared as she'd ever been.

The chorus wailed "Jesus, Jesus, Jesus, save her. Free her soul."

Minister Kassup locked her head between his hands. "Relax, honey. You need the Kiss of Freedom." He lowered his face to Zoë's, puffing clouds of putrified rat smell into her nostrils while he tried to kiss her.

Zoë clenched her teeth and compressed her lips, so the man slobbered all over her nose and chin. The other people's hands poked her in her stomach and yanked at her sweatshirt, and she gritted her teeth, madder than she'd ever been in her life.

Minister's eyes narrowed and a rumble came from his throat. His turkey beak nose chopped at her as she flipped her head back and forth. Keeping her eyes wide open, Zoë saw her chance. She relaxed her body and plumped up her lips.

In response to her sudden acquiescence, the preacher's eyes popped open and he smiled. He licked his lips and slowly lowered his head toward hers.

"All you need, little one, is one healing kiss of the Lord. Everybody here has received one. Join us now."

When Zoë sensed his lips about to touch hers, she grimaced, raised her head, opened her mouth wide, and clamped her front teeth together on the tip of Minister Kassup's nose and bit down.

Her teeth sliced through the soft flesh and he jerked his head up, leaving a bleeding hunk of nose in Zoë's mouth. The salty gob slid back on her tongue and lodged against her palate. She choked. Her stomach cramped as a gush of nausea rose into her jaws. With her teeth closed, she breathed through her mouth.

The wounded man screamed and stood up on the altar, blood leaking down his shirt, dripping onto Zoë's gown. He roared and tossed his head, spraying blood over his astounded congregation. The electric guitar twanged on, hammering out a driving beat.

In the instant Kassup sat up and the hands let go of her legs and arms, Zoë spun over and rolled off the altar, landing like a cat and springing away.

She dived through a line of flowered skirts and shiny black pants and shoved, scrambling across the slippery wood floor to the door. She turned the doorknob in her hand, but the door was locked.

As she turned around, scanning the room for another door or window, Kassup leapt off the altar and fell, crushing two of his congregants under him. While the crowd clustered around the fallen trio to pull them up, Zoë ran to a window, tried to raise it. Locked.

She twisted around and saw thick black books lying in the pews. She picked one up and threw it at the glass.

Kassup bellowed, "My nose. She's got my nose."

The window shattered and Zoë whipped off her blood-spattered baptismal gown, wrapped it around her wrist, and poked out the sharp peaks of glass along the bottom of the window frame.

She hoisted herself up and was about to kick her leg over the sill to freedom when someone grabbed her by the waist and dragged her back. Zoë lay on the floor panting as the crowd lunged toward her.

Kassup screamed, "My nose! My nose!"

"His nose! His nose!" The chorus assaulted her with a cry as full of longing and devotion as their earlier hymns meant to call the spirit of Jesus into Zoë.

Kassup bulled through his people, his face drained of color, the end of his nose shredded and slick with pink plasma leaking off his storn nostrils onto his lips and chin. "Gimme my nose you little...." He raised his fist.

She looked up at it, the fingers clenched and red, his hairy arm trembling.

For the first time since she'd bitten off his nose, she felt it lodged between her tongue and cheek like a hunk of chaw, bitter as the snuff she'd tasted once. Only once.

As she watched his hand raised above her, she saw it tremble. A peaceful feeling arose in her.

Even the terrorizing Minister and his ghastly minions didn't shake Zoë's calm. She'd faced angrier men in her life, not to mention her old daddy Bruce, and Augie, her idiot uncle who was still trying to touch her.

Zoë smiled with her mouth closed tight and blew a bubble of air into her cheek, rounding it outward to reveal the nose's sanctuary in her mouth and said, "Ow slolo id."

"Grab her," Kassup said.

Zoë flung her arms out at the flurry of stiff fingers and rough palms that groped from the crowd. "Ow slolo id I sled."

"What's she sayin?"

"Sounds like 'I'll swallow it'."

"Jesus," Kassup said. "I mean, Jesus Lord save us."

The minister raised his other hand and the goblin hands and arms of the crowd fell and silence settled over them.

"Reverend, you gotta get that tip back on you as fast as you can. Before the flesh dies."

"I know, Rhonda. The little creep won't give it up."

Zoë said one more time, "Ow slolo id. Lemme ko."

The reverend stepped close to Zoë, the gore suppurating a few inches from her eyes. "Now, Zoë, you give me that nose right now. If you don't, you might get hurt."

"Lemme ko ri now – er ow slalo id. Yu av den slecots."

"I'll get her, Rev. Take the nose and throw her out. I'll take her to my ranch. Nobody will miss her."

"No, Anthony. Don't be stupid. We have a future here." Turning to Zoë, Kassup held out his open palm. "We'll let you go. Spit my nose out right here."

"No. Ow go outsli an leab id there. Yu shtay heah." Zoë turned and angled her little shoulders between a man's bulging thigh and a swollen sundress beside it.

The man laid a callused hand on the top of Zoë's head, clenching it between bratwurst-sized fingers and pulling her head back. Kassup hissed, "Eugene, don't touch her. She might swallow it."

The way the blood ran down Kassup's chin, he looked like he'd dribbled ketchup on it from a greasy hamburger.

Zoë whirled and marched away tind waited at the door. One of the women rushed up with a key and unlocked it, pushed it open, and scurried back. Zoë bubbled her cheek out to show the minister she hadn't swallowed the nose, then she walked out into the sun and slammed the heavy door.

She ran through the parking lot until she came to a cherry SUV parked near the entrance. Looking back at the church, she squinted against the glossy sunlight reflecting off the building's white siding. Two men descended the steps and kicked up dust as they ran across the gravel.

Gagging, half-blinded by the scorching sun, she spit the chunk of preacher snout into her hand, and held it up, waving it like the prom queen hailing her subjects.

She laid the pulp on the scorching hood of the pickup and heard a sizzle. Wiping her hands on her jeans, she dashed across the road, into the empty field.

The crowd hollered at her and at each other. Kassup roared, "Bring it here." Zoë didn't look back or stop running for half a mile. She climbed a hill and crouched on the other side of its flat crest, concealing herself behind the buffalo grass.

Raising her eyes up and peering over the sparse growth of hay, she saw a trail shecould make through the field. If anybody wanted to track her, all they had to do was follow her in a truck and they'd catch her in minutes, but no one had followed.

A convoy of pickups and SUV's and vans and cars, led by the gleaming red truck, raced down the road toward Spring Creek. Before long, the dust rose around the caravan so thick, only the red pickup in the lead remained visible, leaving a brown cloud as fluffy as a squirrel's tail stretched over the caravan of followers.

The rotten tomato taste of Kassup's nose lingered even after she spit fifty times. She tore up some alfalfa stems and scoured her mouth out, flossing her teeth and chewing until her spit turned green.

Minister Kassup the baptist. Minister Cat Piss. Zoë giggled. Cat Piss. No, she didn't want the taste of cat piss in her mouth. Kappus. Krap us. Worse. Cat guts. Vile. Catsup. Catsup. Ketchup. Minister Ketchup Face. He'd never ketch up to her.

Exulting in her freedom under the immense blue sky, she loped across the fields to an empty horse trough. She levered its creaky pump handle up and down until the water rose hundreds of feet from underground darkness and gushed out of the spigot in a silvery ribbon and splashed into the aluminum trough, making muck of the dust in the bottom.

Pumping hard with both hands so water would flow without her having to push and pull the handle, she let go and lowered her head under the stream. She shuddered, icy claws scouring her neck and behind her ears. She flipped her hair back and forth and gulped an achy mouthful of water and gargled and spit it into the trough.

That's a real baptism, she thought, still gagging a little.

After chewing a handful of wild peppermint, she washed her mouth out five more times and gargled. She chewed cud after cud of wild mint until her mouth felt clean.

Ever since then, when she's spotted him around town, Zoë ducked around the corner or turned her back and skipped away. Now, nearly three years later, Minister Ketchup had caught up with her, not a mile from the safety of town. Her knees bruised, her palms bloody, Zoë tasted the ghost of Ketchup's foul nose in her mouth. Here he was, all red-faced and snotty as ever, oily lather dripping off his face, stinking up the wind, reaching for her.

He grabbed her by her coat collar and pulled her against him. Ketchup thrust his fingers into her hair and tugged.

"You got real pretty hair. That red really turns me on."

He grinned and opened his teeth so wide Zoë could see his uvula in his throat wobble, a tiny mottled broom brushing at the fuzz on his tongue.

"If I thought it would help me, I'd bite your little nose off right now. See how you like going around with a gray nose for the rest of your life."

He opened his mouth again, exposing the tip of tongue. He jammed Zoë's face toward his and bit down.

Zoë knew what to do if a man trapped you close to him. Bonnie had taught her and she'd practiced at the Home because Old Prairie Dog worried about her wandering the roads by herself.

"You're so pretty, Ehawee," she'd said. "So tiny. Some of the old guys in here don't know what they're doing and they might grab you when you're not looking. Out there," she pointed through the front door, "you're too cute for around here. You're a sitting duck, especially when they get drunk."

Zoë took a deep breath, looked Ketchup in the eyes and yelled "Kateri!" as she slammed her kneecap into his groin.

The perfect height to take the brunt of an intrepid fifteen-year old's athletic quadriceps whacking her patella into the only tenderest part of his entire being. Ketchup gasped and bawled "Oh, fuck."

He crumpled, landing on his side, rocking and moaning.

Zoë retreated. "You're not gonna make the Rapture, Ketchup. You're too stinky." The wind blew her words away.

"Is that any way to talk to an adult," he snarled. He stared at her. "What's this Ketchup crap?"

"You. Minister Ketchup. When I bit off your nose, you looked like a ketchup bottle spilled on your face."

"Don't call me Ketchup. You do, I'll make you bleed worse than I ever did. When I catch you...." The man whimpered and rocked, his hands buried in his crotch. "You Spawn of the Devil!"

"Sorry I bit your nose off, too. I didn't mean to."

The fallen man blinked at the girl. "What? You're sorry?"

"I shouldn't be. You were mean. Just like now."

"Help me up."

"No way."

Zoë pivoted and the knee she'd jabbed him with locked. She groaned and took a shuffling step with her other leg, dragging the painful one. She headed down a ravine and into a good hiding place behind some boulders. A blistering wave of wind slammed against her, nearly toppling her, turning her sideways.

Zoë stumbled across the field, halting every few steps to shake the pain out of her knee and breathe hot air into the molten anger blazing in her stomach. Finally, she approached the slope leading down into the canyon. If she made across the canyon to the ridge, she could lose herself where nobody but the coyotes could find her.

She shambled up, favoring the knee. Looking for a stick to lean on, she turned around. There he was, limping back to his truck. Tempted to scream at him, she opened her mouth to shout "Ketchup! You stink." But prudence prevailed and she clamped her lips together.

I'll never see him again, she thought. *If I do, I'll....* She knew what she wanted to do but she didn't know what she would do, except run. Like Bonnie told her, "Some people you just stay away from."

"You'll never see me again either," she muttered, her fury at Ketchup still burning in her stomach. "Never on this Earth. And," she screamed, "never in Heaven!"

She scrambled down the embankment, setting out for home in Devan's trailer.

Twelve

ANGEL HAIR

As she approached the trailer in the early twilight, Zoë noticed thousands of gauzy clusters of seeds sailing out of the cottonwood grove, drifting over the roof, trusting their future to the wind.

She felt Devan somewhere close, his strength and love moving toward her on the rising breeze.

Heartened, Zoë imagined Devan running out of the trailer and laughing and hollering the instant he saw her. He'd pick her up and throw her high up over his head. Then she'd climb up on his back and they would gallop around the yard, her flaming hair streaming out.

The wind picked up and Zoë caught her breath when millions of cottonwood puffs fanned out in a burst of leaf and branch percussion.

There's my next ingredient, she said to herself.

The puffs snowed over her, brushing her cheeks and palms. The winged seeds rose into the sunlight, gliding free.

Zoë giggled. "It's a seed-puff Rapture."

She kicked out and splashed into the drifts of the seed-puffs that lay in flimsy burls on the grass. They exploded against her calves, rebounding and spreading their gossamer tendrils into the wind.

Her knee felt relaxed and normal. Angel hair, Zoë mused, waving at the seed-puffs spluttering around like dense snowflakes.

It's sorta a miracle. Maybe that's why Grandma Esther put puffs in the recipe. They must make the angel feel even more floaty.

She scooped up handfuls of skittish cottonwood flyers with tiny black hearts and silky wings. Zoë flung them over her head, letting them flurry into her hair and eyelashes. Inhaling a ticklish puff, she sneezed and laughed in the dry snow.

Mr. J's great soul, still unsettled in Little Limbo, quivered against her hip. Feeling false, even deceitful, now that she'd crammed all her energy into cajoling one strong angel and keeping the souls as a back-up plan, Zoë patted Little Limbo. "How's everybody? You being good to Mr. J? Mr. J, you happy now?"

Stuffing seedpuffs into her pockets, she mumbled quietly to her cricket crew. "Don't worry, honeys. They're gonna help me get wings. They won't hurt. Maybe you can even eat some."

It's gonna work, she thought. For their size, they're the best floaters I've ever seen. I could stuff my coat with enough to lift me off the ground – in a tornado.

She laughed at her joke.

Zoë squinted into the canopy of cottonwoods on the far side of the trailer. Their branches rose into the stratosphere and their roots drilled into secret channels of water running deeper than welldiggers could reach.

Not only were they powerful, most nights the trees sang so loud Zoë heard them in her sleep. They accompanied each other with leaf cymbals, brushes, flutes, tamborines, harmonizing their branchy voices in an all night chorus conducted by the wind.

During several summers, on different nights, Zoë slept at the foot of each tree, paying attention to her dreams for messages, learning the trees' ways of survival by giving themselves away to the sun and the wind and the stars. She identified with the wind, changing shape and chanting – her words like leaves and branches – while hiding half of her true self in the dark underground.

And now, the trees offered her the gift for her future: the seed puffs.

She studied their crowns, singling out the trees she'd always counted on for their songs and wisdom. She thanked them for being her true aunts and uncles when all her blood relatives had abandoned her.

"Sky Anchor, thank you. You bring Heaven to Earth." She cried out the trees' names in a farewell litany. "Eagle Net! You captured my soul. Prairie Fist! Drive Ketchup away forever. Angel Hive! Let every starling in your branches chirp out to the seraphim. Sun's Root! Tell them Zoë's coming."

She stopped speaking, listened for the trees' replies. The outer branches tossed in the wind and the leaves played, smashing into each other like little boys play-fighting.

"Winter's Mercy! It's summer now. I hear your secret, Mountain's Whisper. Don't tell anyone else until I get back."

She raised her arms to the widest tree in the grove.

"T'sunke Witko, oh T'sunke. They call you Crazy Horse and you're not crazier than me. You're the only tree who's ever cried with me."

Between T'sunke's roots, Zoë had buried the most priceless treasure she possessed: Ruthie's skull. Nobody but the tree knew it was there, packed in a zinc-lined milk pail and wrapped in Zoë's blue-and-white checkered baby quilt. A tear slipped down her cheek.

Sliding her hand into her side pocket, Zoë fingered the postcard she'd taped Ruthie's picture to years ago. Her thumb rubbed the curled and shredded card that she'd taped over a dozen times. She took out Ruthie's faded image and squinted at it.

Pinpoints of yellow light shot out of Ruthie's wide eyes, thrilling Zoë as they always did. She kissed her mother's curvy raised eyebrows and her juicy puckered mouth, and sighed. Glancing at it once more, she shrugged. The cigarette drooping from Ruthie's lips always bothered Zoë but she'd accepted it as just her showing off how she was as beautiful as an old-fashioned movie star.

She didn't remember Ruthie smoking, and her mother always smelled like the gardenia fragrance of Paulette's Cosmetics and Lingerie in Spring Creek, not the sour smell that oozed from cigarette smokers.

Zoë lifted her face toward the vast cottonwood canopy again. She held up the photo and pondered.

Ruthie would look the same in Heaven, but Zoë had changed so much since she was six. Now, if she put a cigarette between her lips and looked askance at the mirror, Ruthie stared back. They could be sisters.

Pretty soon, when Ruthie spotted Zoë skipping across the celestial clouds, she'd think it was her own self, dancing toward her. Then they'd both laugh and laugh at how they looked like twins.

Scanning the branches overhead, Zoë spotted one squirrel's nest and the bough a tiny bard owl favored when he passed through.

"You know, T'sunke," she said aloud to the tree, "Pretty soon, I won't need Ruthie's skull. I'm going to the real woman. I won't need her bones. You can let them change into your bark and leaves. When they sing in the wind, I'll come back from Heaven to listen."

Turning, she lifted her eyes higher, to the tallest tree, its crown a shimmering fountain pouring dusky silver and green light over an ocean of shadowy grass.

Every spring since she could remember, she'd climbed this tree eighty feet into the sky to tie a fresh remnant of Ruthie's burial dress to the highest branch she could reach. Less than a month ago, she'd sent up this year's signal flags to her mother.

"Cloud Raker! My true father in this world. Protect all of us. Knock on Ruthie's door and tell her I'm on my way. She should get out her cookie pans and chocolate chips."

Scanning the grove's entire canopy, she almost missed seeing Kateri – Kateri there, hovering a few feet above her, robed in golden deerskin, her eyes twinkling. Kateri's long face glowing in the sunshine, her narrow nose and wide eyes set like a double-wicked candle. She spoke to Zoë through closed, full lips.

"Yes, yes." Zoë nodded her head in gulps of affirmation. "Devan is here. I knew it. Ruthie knows I'm coming. Thank you, Kateri."

Cottonwood branches swayed and pitched like ponies prancing and whinnying around a pasture, their bodies shuddering in the pleasure of wind.

Zoë said, "Thank you, everybody."

A gust rippled through the grass, sliding into Zoë's open jacket, flipping it back. Playful wind raised her sweatshirt and brushed her stomach, as if Kateri's fingers were tickling her, inviting her to rise up and join her on the thick bough of the tree. Zoë examined the trees, but Kateri had disapeared. That tricky saint who showed up when she felt like it, answering Zoë's prayers, and then, with no warning, she'd split.

Zoë scrambled up from the grass. In a few minutes, she'd be hugging Devan, her luck, who would lead her into the arms of her angel. She ran toward the side of the trailer, her hair rippling out like crimson feathers behind her ears.

Thirteen

The Five P's

Exhausted from his failed encounter earlier in the day with the creepy girl, Roy lay on his living room floor listening to some bluesy hims by Jesusboys. He liked the lyrics to "Now or ever" because he'd put it on his Many Paths CD program recommended for deep relaxation prior to visualization. He still had a slight ache in his groin from where the girl had kneed him.

Why he was attracted to that crazy girl with her clown hair, he didn't know. She'd bit the tip off his nose and he somehow he still wanted to fuck her. It had to be revenge, but he'd have to give that up. Negative feelings and thoughts had no place on the Many Paths. They'd bung everything up and he'd never get rich. Gotta be positive, even if his emotions got the best of him way too often.

His nose didn't look too bad anymore. Everybody said it was normal. He knew they were lying. If a gray tip was normal on a human being, well, let them think whatever they wanted.

Roy's stomach twinged and he wondered where his wife had gone because usually had supper ready about now. He rubbed his belly and in a moment, the hunger sensation passed. He had more consuming questions stamping their feet behind his eyebrows like impatient drinkers pounding the floor while they waited for the bands to start playing at the Acropolis Bar and Grill.

He couldn't concentrate, Jesusboys or no.

I'll go up to the Greeks and have a drink or two. Have to get set for tomorrow. Fearing the worst, he thought, We gotta get it done fast so I'm home tomorrow night in time for the Many Paths discussion at the church. Can't disappoint my first five customers...I mean 'students'....

Plan's in place...Plan's in place...Plan's in place.

The sound of his spontaneous mantra took the edge off for a moment.

Now, as the familiar bass guitar surged from his speakers, he let the beat settled his mind.

He breathed deeply, counting backwards from seven, letting his shoulder joints sag, his chest and arms flow away with his exhalations, his pelvis and stomach dissolve, his thighs and calves melt, his feet evaporate, his skull evanesce into the pure images he had programmed before he lay down.

All thought disappeared. Roy entered the only cave he ever spelunked in voluntarily, the enormous movie theater of his mind.

He watched himself standing in the spotlight while a disembodied voice sang his praises as discoverer and promoter of "The Many Paths," the transformational series that had improved the lives of thousands and, incidentally, but irrefutably, had made Roy one of the wealthiest men in South Dakota.

Cheering and whistles broke out of an invisible crowd. Wave after wave of chants of "Roy! Roy! Roy!" surged over him in praise of Roy's elevating the people into the rarified air of potential fulfilled and prosperity acquired.

Euphoria settled into Roy's muscles. He let his body sink into the carpet, his magic carpet. He'd flown hundreds of times on the rug in his self-hypnotic trance into his inevitable future of fame and riches.

Just by lying down on the same spot, halfwaybetween the coffee table and the TV, with his head facing south, the direction of abundance and fertility, he sensed the raw power of his imagination when he lay on the green shag.

His wife had pleaded with him to get rid the "...filthy raggy scrap of moldy dog bed..." and replace it with a wall-to-wall carpet from Home Depot.

That was the last thing he'd do. His old shag rug brought him more freedom than his wife ever had in their sixteen years of marriage. No matter how intensely he used his athletic imagination when she was around, he couldn't leave her limited existence.

Early in their marriage, he easily imagined she was a hundred different women. Lately she popped every dream balloon he tried to inflate around her. In her presence, he lost the ability to fantasize she was anyone other than who she was. By insisting on her own drab reality, she outmaneuvered Roy, neutralizing his imagination. She paralyzed him. Not even abject fear of Wink Lamb or Winston Lockhart held that power over him.

Roy noticed his negative thoughts about his wife dim the spotlight in his mental theater and muffle the chants. He struggled to regain lost focus on his imaginary screen when the phone rang.

"Got to be Wink Lamb," he muttered to himself. Jumping up, he shed euphoria like a quilt on a January morning, feeling this teeth begin to chatter. He said, ""Hello."

"Hey, Roy? Roy?" Lamb's cheery tenor voice exuded friendship as if the two shared a lifetime of victories and happy memories. "You working on the Paths? Those Many Paths to Wealth and Freedom?"

Roy's salesman's telepathy alerted him to a setup. He'd never mentioned the Many Paths to Lamb. He'd hardly ever talked with the guy. Wink Lamb, the diabolical owner of H.I.S.S.S. –

"Honest, Industrial Secret Security Systems." Roy'd heard Lamb had piloted drones over Pakistan and was trained as a Secret Security agent. Lamb was the last person Roy would trust with his personal security. Jeesus.

Winston must have revealed Roy's ambition to Lamb, maybe the whole deal they'd made. The few times he'd met with Lamb, he sweat the dank sweat of fear. Now those few words from the R.O.I. security chief chilled him. If he couldn't do what Winston had assigned him, Roy had no doubts that his boss would hand him over as a sacrifice to Lamb.

Roy breathed into his solar plexus, determined to have faith and follow his training, whether Lamb ridiculed it or not. He'd try the Deflecting a Thousand Pounds of Force with a Twitch of an Eyebrow.

Roy admitted to himself 'Deflecting' needed work, but just invoking it gave him confidence in his aggressive powers.

"Lamb? Wink Lamb. It's good to hear from you," Roy said, imitating Lamb's lightheartedness, following The Path of the Warrior's Mirror. "Winston said you might call."

"Who?" said Lamb. "I'm just calling to take you up on your offer of going with me on that fishing trip? Getting out of Dodge for a little moisture in the mountains."

"What fishing trip?" The words slipped out before Roy understood that they were speaking in code. Well, he thought, another possibility for a Path. I'll record Lamb's code and analyze it later. Roy recorded every call he received or made.

"The one we talked about at the Greek's the other night.

Hey, Roy, were you too drunk to remember it?"

Lamb retained his jovial tone, but Roy felt impatience in the voice verging on threat. He'd heard the government had forced Lamb out because his short fuse had caused some hideous damage to some higher-up's wife and children he was supposed to be guarding.

"Oh, yeah," Roy agreed. "The trip to Wahtaki Lake."

"I'm ready, Roy," said Lamb with false enthusiasm. "I called the camp. They said the pike will be jumping at dawn."

"At dawn?" Fear tinged Roy's voice with incredulity.

"You heard right. First thing. You know where my country place is over on the western side of Anpetu Mountain? Meet me there say, 5:30. We'll take my Blazer over to the lake."

"Christ, Lamb, I've got to get ready." Roy stalling, his knees weak.

"That's smart, Roy. Wear your Reserve boots and a heavy jacket. It still gets cold up there this time of year. We got some climin' ahead of us. That Devil's Backbone can be mighty rough. See you in the morning."

"Yeah. Okay," Roy said. What Devil's Backbone?

"You remember that management seminar, Roy?"

What's he talking about now, Roy thought. "Sure, sure, Wink. Yeah. It was a good one."

"Then you know the Five P's, right?"

"5 P's?" Was this a trap Lamb was laying for him? "You mean my Many Paths? There's a lot more than five."

"Take it easy, Roy. We use 'em all the time when we wanna get something done without complications. 'Proper Planning Prevents Poor Performance.'"

"Oh, that Five P's. Sure. I use it all the time."

"Good. We ain't gonna have no fuckups, Roy." Lamb hung up.

Relieved, Roy shook his head like a dog come out of water and did his rolling breaths half a dozen times, then lay back down on the rug and let his conscious mind slink down the stairs of his breath toward his mental theater. He gulped, the muscles in his thighs trembling. He couldn't master his breath or clear his mind.

Then, Roy imagined a giant hand wiping away his thoughts and his mind reached the landing in front of the Many Paths theater door. He opened the door to nothing but blackness. The chanting voices he strained to hear sounded like a river rushing against granite walls rather than gentle waves washing a beatific shore, endlessly grateful, singing his praise.

Another sound dulled the gushing of soothing water in his Many Paths daydream. A rustling, like a flock of birds or bats, scraped back and forth across the constellations painted in luminescent dots on the ceiling of his mental auditorium. He could almost feel guano dripping on his head.

Roy gave up trying to concentrate. Instead, he decided to pack for the trip. He'd stored away his hunting boots and jacket somewhere since the only hunting he did these days was for parishioners and "students." An anxious spasm twisted through his chest like the pleurisy he was prone to. To calm himself again, he repeated his favorite affirmation he'd long ago wired into his mind, the center of his teachings. "Seekandyoushallfind. Seekandyoushallfind."

When Roy needed anything, his boots, his jacket, a sandwich, courage – now he needed all of them – he charged his optimism with "Seekandyoushallfind."

Everyone who ever heard of the Bible can relate to that saying, Roy reminded himself, resuming the commentary he continually ran on his life and the Many Paths practices he followed. For most people, knowing what they seek is the main problem.

Right now all I need is the boots and the coat. The boots and the coat. I'll pick up a sandwich at the bar later.

Rummaging in the back closet for his cold weather gear, Roy noticed the stock of his .12 gauge shotgun propped in the corner behind his winter topcoat, hidden but accessible.

"O.K.," he agreed aloud with his unspoken suggestion. I'll take it and the .38. Lamb won't see the pistol if I stick it in the inside pocket. Reasoning furiously, he thought, I'll keep the .12 gauge in the trunk of my car. Most guys carry a thirty ought thirty or shotgun in their trunks.

Roy filled his quart flask with Dewars and stuffed it into his other inner coat pocket. Damn. I only got ten .12 guage shells left. Well, can't see why I'd need any more, he thought, picking up the box, his thoughts skittering, but with the gun in hand, Roy felt almost ready to face Lamb. Better take some hollow points for the pistol. Lamb's the right guy for the demolition job. No way I can trust him otherwise. Those military guys don't give a fuck about you if you get in their way. 'We ain't gonna have no fuckups, Roy.' Goddam right, Lamb.

In the garage, Roy lowered his car's trunk lid on his emergency ordnance, hoping he'd not need it, but who knew what Lamb was really up to. He inventoried everything again before he climbed in the driver's seat, clicked the garage door open, and backed his car out for his nightly drive to the Acropolis.

God, I better keep my mouth shut at the Greek's tonight.

Checking his rear view mirror, he thought, Winston's probably got a tail on me and a plant at the bar. One of those ferns or philodendrons the Greek's always cursing about, I bet. Roy chuckled out loud at his fine wit.

The drops of sweat Lamb's phone call had painted on his breastbone slid down onto his paunch like snow melting. Roy hoped one of the Greek's special beakers of ouzo and vodka would drain the chill pool of fear from his gut. If one doesn't work, he promised himself, two will.

SECRETS

Fourteen

DEVAN'S HOMECOMING

Zoë limped, running as fast as she could across the dry grass as she came up to Devan's trailer. She tilted her face up, absorbing the slanting sun on her face. Gusts of sweet alfalfa breeze tickled her cheeks, whisking up cottonwood wisps before dropping them back to the Earth. The puffs sailed toward the pasture as if somebody was towing them on invisible strings.

Zoë opened the door to the trailer and stepped into the narrow kitchen, hoping for signs of Devan.

Sunshine angled through the window illuminating the new orange flowery tablecloth she'd bought for Devan's homecoming. The ingredients she'd already collected for her poshent lay scattered across the table.

Her mortar and pestle sat on the counter under the open kitchen window Devan always closed if he was home. Zoë noted what she still needed while brushing Mrs. Spalding's toenails off her palm into the mélange.

"Devan. Devaaaaan!" She called into the hollow trailer. "Devan. Come out if you're here." Her voice echoed, stirring up dust motes that whirled and collided in the stuffy silence.

Willing him to be napping, Zoë dashed across the living room area and snatched back the accordion door to the bedroom. Her eyes adjusted to the faint light leaking in narrow stripes through the closed blinds.

Devan's white quilt with golden starflowers on it lay smooth and neat on the empty bed. Maybe her eyes needed more time to make out somebody sleeping in the dark.

Squeezing between the wall and the mattress, she edged around the foot of the bed. "Devan," she whispered. "Devan." The corners fit tight and the folded sheet snugged up against the pillows, same as the beds she made at work.

Zoë fiddled with the blinds, flipping the slats up. She blinked against the light, and held her eyes closed, saying silently, "Inky Devan Inky Devan."

When she opened her eyes, she saw her used hair dye system strewn across the vanity. She squinted into the dresser mirror. Running her fingers through her disheveled hair, she tossed it back, over her shoulders. She peered at her face.

Even with the dirt on her forehead and chin, she looked ghostly pale. Two days ago her cheekbones didn't cast shadow crescents beside her nose. Last time she looked, she didn't notice how white the crimson hair had made her skin look, as if all her blood had drained out.

Where was Devan? She could feel him close by. Zoë turned toward the bathroom.

Rivulets of moisture ran down the walls and the shower door and bath towels stained with muddy blotches filled the sink. A heap of dirty jeans and dark shirts and filthy white socks and Devan's boxer briefs and a pair of silky women's underpants lay on the floor.

Zoë reached down and picked up the panties. Who wore slippery green underpants?

The clothes stunk as if Devan and his girlfriend had worked in the fields all day. She inspected Devan's jeans, shaking a heap of fine gray dust onto the bath mat. The knees of both legs had ripped out and the rear pockets hung in shredded strings.

She checked the woman's jeans. Scuffed knees, no rips.

Zoë ran to the door. "Devan! Devan, I'm here." She pushed her forehead against the screen and saw Devan running up the knoll in front of the trailer. His girlfriend followed a few steps after him.

Devan sprinted toward Zoë, barechested and barefoot. His long blond hair sailed out like a palomino mane. In the orangey dusk, his front teeth shined. As he ran, he hopped, kicking one leg out in front and dragging the other stiff one behind, barely landing on it before the good leg shot ahead, as if his feet were hobbled with an invisible bond.

A few day's growth of whiskers covered his cheeks and jaw the russet color of Falstaff, his poor dead dog. She thought his beard would be blonde, too.

Maybe he dyed it like I did my hair.

The tall woman trailed close behind him wearing a long-sleeved purple shirt with big pink and yellow flowers, unbuttoned and flapping against her ribs. The woman's bare legs kicked high as if she knew how to run, but something was wrong with one of her arms. Or was it the evening shadows that obscured one hand as she pumped, one sleeve flapping over an empty wrist?

Her legs and arms and hair reminded Zoë of a whirligig spinning around the still center of her body. Was that a diamond in her belly button? It perched above lowrider shorts the same shiny black color as her shoulder-length hair.

The running woman looked almost naked. Zoë spotted her as a fellow nudist. Maybe a good sign.

Devan ripped the door open and filled the whole space between the jambs with his shoulders. "Zoë." He hugged her and kissed her on her nose and put his arms around her, pulling her against him.

"I missed you, Devan." Zoë burrowed her face into his bare chest and sneezed when the hair tickled her nose. Stretching on her tiptoes, Zoë kissed Devan on the lips and giggled. "Heh-heh-heh. Beards tickle."

She pulled back a few inches to see his whole body. The fingers of one hand dragged across his stomach. "Devan, you've got goose bumps. You're muddy! I know what you were doing!"

He arched away and winced, then held Zoë by the shoulders while he examined her face. His blue eyes ran down her body and narrow furrows creased his forehead. "Are you all right?"

"I'm happy now." She kissed the air between their faces. "We're going to find my angel."

He grinned and hugged her again. This time, she kept her eyes open a few inches from a mingle-mangle of scabs and welts on his ribs. She pulled back. "What happened?"

"I fell," he said. "I'm all right."

Zoë grinned and pretended to swoon. "My luck is back again."

She blinked her eyes open just as he dived toward her and scooped her up in his arms and swung her around, flinging her feet straight out.

They whirled around once, twice, until Zoë's hands slid from his neck and they tipped, Zoë squealing, Devan laughing, and started to collapse. Devan clutched her lapels and flipped her over to land on top of him. They bounced on the floor and hugged. Then, Devan groaned. The screen door slammed behind Laurel.

Zoë grabbed her jacket and tugged the Little Limbo pocket to the side so it wouldn't dig into them and slid off Devan's stomach.

"Uuuugh," he said. "My rib's don't like that." He rolled over and stood up. He held out his hands to Zoë and his girlfriend and they pulled him to his feet. He caught them and pulled them into his bare ribs, gently this time.

As they clung to each other and rocked, the sky in the east took on the violet tinge of night's approach,

Releasing them, Devan said, "Zoë, meet Laurel, the love of my life."

Zoë pursed her lips as she extended her hand and locked her elbow. She grimaced when the woman took it and squeezed it without shaking.

Zoë said to Devan, "I thought I was the love of your life."

Laurel said, "He means the lover of his life. You'll always be the love." Laurel's almond-shaped eyes twinkled above a streak of dust smeared across her nose.

A smile angling up one side of her face, Zoë said, "You can be his lover - he's had about a thousand, right, Dev?"

"You jealous, Zoë?" Devan said, touching her cheek.

"No," she said. She blushed and stopped smiling. "Only I'm a virgin and I'm gonna stay one until I get where I'm going anyway. Then I'll see."

"Zoë, I love you more than anybody, and I love Laurel more, too. Don't ever worry. Laurel's my woman. That's all."

Zoë glanced at Laurel and then she kissed Devan's hand. "Hi, Laurel." The top of her head came up to Laurel's breasts.

"Hi, Zoë. Devan told me all about you." Laurel's words undulated like a piano playing in a car that drove back and forth on Main Street. You could almost tell what the next note would be, but as the car passed, the note rose a little, then faded. "You're a pretty amazing girl."

"I know," Zoë said, relieved that Devan was here, even if he had this Laurel with him – at least she had a pretty name.

Devan had told her she'd meet a beautiful woman. Maybe he didn't send a picture because he didn't want anybody to know about her arm.

"I love your hair," Laurel said.

"I dyed it myself. Can you tell what it is?" Turning her back to Laurel, then suddenly whipping around, her hair flew straight out.

"Hmmm," Laurel said, peering closely at Zoë's head. "Crow's wing?"

Zoë shook her head.

"Mare's mane?"

"No way."

"Sun rising out of the night?"

"No. But close."

She waited for Laurel to guess again. When she stayed quiet, Zoë said, "It's the tip of a candle flame. Red, blue, gold – it's hot. Don't tough it, you'll get burned."

Zoë giggled. "You're tall," she said, bending back to stare Laurel in her wide brown eyes but really letting her own eyes scan Laurel's body. She might be a runner, but she definitely had no hand. Zoë decided not to say anything. She didn't need a distraction from Devan.

Devan groaned and sat on the floor.

"What's the matter?" Zoë said. "Your leg's hurt. And why do you have a beard?"

Devan ran his hand over his stubbly face. "For my part in a play. I'll shave at the end of the season." He glanced up at Laurel. "You can wait a couple of months, right?"

Laurel grinned and ran her fingers through his hair.

On her knees, Zoë stuck both of her hands in Devan's beard and turned his face back to her. "What part?"

"Judas. In the Passion Play. A tough guy Judas who would have saved Jesus's ass if he'd listened to me. I didn't hang myself, either. Or give back the thirty pieces of silver. It's a big part, Zoë. We haven't had a Passion Play in more than ten years. This could lead to a TV series."

"Wow." Zoë was impressed and knew he would be a star Judas. She'd seen Devan on soap operas and in one movie where he played a lazy California cowboy who lost a herd of cattle because all he wanted to do was kiss a Chumash girl while the padres tried to catch her and send her back to their farm. Devan had promised her a front row ticket to this summer's Passion Play revival. "You look, uh, kinda pretty anyway," she said, knowing how he liked to hear how handsome he was.

"Thanks, Zoë. They wanted me to shave my head."

"Yuk!"

"I told them they needed a heartthrob Judas. He'd be even more evil."

"You'll never be evil." Zoë kissed him on the forehead. "You don't know anything about it."

"You do?"

"Plenty."

Laurel sat down beside them, crossing her legs and displaying her empty wrist on her bare knee. "You're right, Zoë. Devan doesn't have an evil eyelash. But we found plenty of evil back there in Anpetu Mountain."

Ignoring the woman and her long legs and missing hand, Zoë eyed Devan's arm, her fingers tracing the vivid red and purple 'Z' tattoo. The artist had etched wings onto the letter so the 'Z' appeared to fly above his biceps, almost as if, when he raised his arm, it was the winged 'Z' that lifted it. The proof of his love moving her to tears, she asked in a wavery voice, "Does Judas have a tattoo?"

"This one does. He'll keep it, don't worry. The director will probably tell me to cover it with make-up, but we'll know, won't we?"

She pulled back to arm's length, but held on. "You could show the two little dots over my e and people would think they were moles." She paused a beat.

Devan's eyes flicked back and forth across Zoë's face. "I don't see any dots above your eyes."

"Oh, Devan," Zoë beamed. "You silly. Over my e. My e."

Devan made a face and looked down at her knees.

"No! The e in my name! Z ... O ... E!"

"Ah," he said, "Your e."

He still didn't understand. Hadn't she shown him this obvious fact about her identity those years back when she discovered it? Maybe not. She didn't brag about it or write her name with the sign, but anybody who was curious could figure it out, if they doodled a minute.

When Devan raised his eyebrows and tilted his head to the side, she said, "The dots over the e. They're circles. When they touch? They make the infinity sign. Zoë. My name, "Forever." Zoë means infinite life. See?"

"Oh, I know that." He fingered the tattoo.

"Zoë means I'll live forever," she whispered, disappointed about his lack of enthusiasm for the blessing the two dots imparted. She placed her finger now on his lips, a vertical bar to confine his words.

"Sure," he mumbled, a tired smile flickering on his lips.

She squeezed his finger and bent it and lay her mouth next to his ear. "Don't worry about anything. We'll see each other in Heaven."

She leaned back and shot a fierce glare into his eyes, intending him to understand. She'd tried fifty different ways to persuade him, to show him that she was only doing what she had to do.

Devan looked away. "Of course we will. I'll ride up on a unicorn and meet you." Softening his tone, he said. "Heaven's right here and now, if it's anywhere. That's all you can prove."

The same boring argument she ignored every time he said it.

"I see Inky and Kateri and a hundred other saints all the time. Look around," Zoë said. "Do you see them?"

He turned his head over his shoulder and started. "There's one," he said, pointing to the picture of a redwood tree on the wall. "Another one. Up there."

"Where? I don't see her."

"Over there, by the stove. Uh oh. There it goes, flying off."

"Devan, you're crazy. Saints don't fly around like that. You see angels." She giggled and slapped him on the arm.

"I see what I see, just like you do," he said. "Angels, saints, gremlins, whatever. It's all in the mind."

"You make me so happy. You see angels. I knew you could." She closed her eyes and bowed her head. Folding her hands together, her lower lip everting in concentration, she prayed. After a few seconds, she smiled and opened her eyes. "I know," she said. "You should ascend to Heaven with me. Catch an angel and ask him to take you. You're so big you might need two, maybe three angels. Four! Five!"

Devan stared at the exuberant girl, her eyes now pleading with him. "Ah, Zoë, I love your will power. But you believe in something that can't be." A film of moisture shined in his chocolate drop eyes.

"But Inky says –"

"Inky and all his kind haven't stopped one war, one death. Think about it: he couldn't even save his own people."

"He says not to worry. Things will look really bad and then...."

"They'll look worse?" Devan squeezed Zoë's hand and stood up.

"Laurel, can you see Devan's angels?" Zoë challenged the tall woman.

Laurel peered at Zoë. "You're the only angel I see."

Beetling her brows, Zoë said, "I'm no angel."

Zoë sat down on a chair, her head sagging onto her chest, as tired as when she worked all night at the Home after staying up all night and all day the day before. Her knee ached again.

She glanced at Laurel who crunched her eyebrows together and nibbled her top lip. Her lips were almost as plump as Zoë's.

"Devan, we better get organized," Laurel said.

"Yeah. Give me a few minutes. I just got home, baby." He glanced at Zoë. "What about those cookies?"

Zoë jumped up from the couch.

"I'm sorry, Devan. I didn't have time yet. I'll make 'em tonight. But what happened? How'd you get so dirty? You ripped your jeans. Did you have an accident?"

"Warm chocolate chip cookies – best medicine I can think of. Right now, I gotta rest," Devan said.

Laurel lay her head on Devan's shoulder, catching his biceps in her handless arm. "You're right. Let's both rest."

At the sink, Zoë filled three glasses with water.

Her concern must have shown because when she handed Devan a glass, he said, "I'm all right. Don't worry. Thanks."

Worrying about him wouldn't make him feel better. He was right – he needed rest and cookies. "I don't worry. I never have to worry. Right now especially. I'm taking off. I told you."

"Don't start that. I have too much on my mind right now." He shot a glance at Laurel.

Zoë asked, "What happened to your ribs?" This Devan was different than any other one she'd known. She backed away to observe him more carefully.

When he came home from California every other time, they always played for a week at least before he got serious, and then he only got serious about his acting. Like when he pretended he was Wild Bill Hickock playing poker and getting shot while he played poker. He claimed it was a serious job.

Fake guns, fake blood, fake dying. Every time she watched him stagger around the saloon, pretending he was dying, punching a little bag of colored water under his arm to spray the tourists with Wild Bill blood, Zoë couldn't stop laughing. The boss of the bar finally told her to stay outside when he performed. She didn't get why they didn't see how funny Devan was.

Devan's solemn face worried Zoë. Out at the lake she'd seen his bright blue light dim and fall into shadow in her mind. Something awful had happened.

"Devan, are you really all right?"

He scowled. "I never saw so many fracking pumps. They depress me."

"You mean the peckers?" Zoë said.

"Peckers?"

"Yeah," Zoë said, "We call 'em pecker. Pecker pokers."

Laurel raised her handless arm to Devan's side and Zoë wanted to know right then what happened to her. Maybe Laurel's missing hand made Devan sad. Zoë scooted close to Devan, taking his wrist. He winced again but smiled. The tips of his fingers were raw as if he'd used them as a shovel. He'd ripped off some of his nails.

"You're not okay," she said, her breath hot in her mouth.

He exhaled.

"I saw your light go dark."

"What?" he said, putting his arm around Zoë's shoulder.

"Out at the lake when I was washing my clothes. I looked up and you were there. When I see you in my mind, you're always royal blue but yesterday you were smoky gray."

Devan stared at Zoë, then exhaled. "Yeah, something weird happened." He turned to Laurel.

Her thick eyebrows pinched close together again, Laurel looked at Zoë. "What do you mean you looked and saw his light?"

"She means she has visions. I told you about her spirit guide Ink'p'du'da? Sometimes Zoë sees him, sometimes she sees me, my mom, people she loves. Guess it's a way she keeps in touch. Better than Skype, right, Zoë?"

"I don't need Skype to see Inky," Zoë said.

Laurel opened her eyes wide at Zoë and bit her lip. Then she rose and kissed Devan. "Prickly," she said. "You need a shave." She turned toward the door. "I'll go get my magic wands." The screen door banged shut behind her.

In silence, Zoë and Devan watched Laurel saunter toward the truck.

"You'll come to love her, Zoë. She's not the sweetest, uh, grown-up woman I've ever met. But she's fun."

"I know. She's beautiful. Her hair's thick as Rosemary Nightbird Pine's."

Devan shook his head, puzzled.

"The Lakota who won the beauty contest at the fair last year?"

"Oh. Too bad I didn't make that one."

"Laurel could win, even with only one hand. How did she lose it, Devan?"

"A long time ago. An accident when she was little. Wait till you see her bionic hand. She's got a kit of attachments. Scepters and wands she calls them." He pulled Zoë close under his arm. "You'll see, she's a magic princess all right. Almost as magic as you!"

At that, Devan barked a laugh and stood up. He grabbed Zoë's hands and picked her up, hoisting her into the air like a baby. She squealed and he heaved her higher. When she came down, she clamped her arms around his neck and held him. He coughed and she squeezed his mid-section with leg muscles made tensile from hundreds of miles of roaming the foothills and mountains.

"Not so hard," Devan laughed. He kissed her on the head and she released some pressure, still clinging.

Devan swayed. "Man, am I spaced."

Zoë slipped out of his arms. Devan's dark mood frightened her. "You have to tell me right now. You're all upset."

He sat down again. "Okay. Fifteen minutes. I need to rest. I have a lot of work to do tonight. Let me enjoy being home with you. It's the last time for a while."

"I know it. That's sad but it's happy, too."

He sighed. "Not for the reasons you think, Zoë."

"Fifteen minutes," she said. "Okay. C'mon, let me show you my poshent ingredients."

He said, "That's all right. Laurel and I ate a late lunch. I'm still full."

"It's not food," she said.

"What then?"

"You know. I got it out of your cookbook. It's a recipe. 'Love Potion Number 1?' When my angel shows up, I make a little hot soup with these things," she pointed to the paper bag and the crawdaddies. "He drinks it and off we soar."

"You never give up." Devan smiled and shook his head and retrieved the sports bag he'd left on the kitchen floor. "What about your souls? I thought they were in Little Limbo, waiting to fly you up?"

Squeezing the thermos at her side, Zoë said, "I don't know what to do about them."

Devan tipped the bag and shook off bits of leaves and powder that had blown off the table. He raised a pinch of poshent debris and sniffed. "Mint?"

"From out back," Zoë said. "I dried extra to make tea for you."

"I'll drink the tea, but don't give me any poshent. I'm not ready to go to Heaven. They probably wouldn't have me anyway."

"You can't have any. I thought you were my angel, but Inky said you're my luck. That's what I need. All I have to do is stick with you and zoo – my angel will find me."

She hugged Devan with the sports bag between them and he grunted, flopping backwards onto the couch.

"Sorry," Zoë said. She knelt down and took his hand. "Let me put some miracle cream on it. It works on my cuts. I get a lot of them, and they always clear up right away."

Zoë dug around in one of her pockets and pulled out a small jar with a stained, torn label that read 'Nivea.'

"Here, give me your fingers."

"Looks like the same cream Bonnie used to put on my hands after I'd been baling hay all day."

"I got the jar from her," she said, slathering his fingers and palms with the lemony goo. "Made the cream myself. I already put some on my leg I hurt a while ago and now I'm better than ever. George down at Good Foods says I should go into business, my cream's so good."

Fifteen

CHILDHOOD ACCIDENTS

Laurel came back into the trailer wearing a plain blue long-sleeved shirt buttoned and tucked into a flowery wraparound Mexican skirt. She wore red plastic fashion sandals with thick soles. In her hand, she gripped the handle of a scarred leather case, too long for a computer.

Laurel set it down and pulled Devan's phone from her skirt pocket, which she tossed and he let land on the couch next to him.

Taking a bundle of white cloth from under her arm, Laurel bunched it up and pitched it at Devan, striking him in the chest. He flinched, smiled, and sighed.

Zoë snatched it with her quick, soul-snagging fingers and held it out, away from her face.

"Pee-you. This shirt stinks. Your clothes in the bathroom smell rotten."

"From driving in this heat all day," he said. "You'd stink, too."

"That's not the only reason," Zoë said, grinning and raising her eyebrows. "I know what you guys were doing."

Laurel chuckled. Devan said, "How did you get so smart?"

"It's obvious," she said, inhaling loudly and wrinkling her nose. She held the shirt by the tips of her fingers and dropped it into his lap. "Moss stains on your knees. Laurel has muddy elbows."

"It's comfortable on the moss. We had to take a nap."

"I know. I know. A nice long nap." Winking at Devan, she said, "I've seen you down there before. Wasn't that Madeline Summers last time. Before that, I caught you with Jen – "

"Zoë. Forget it."

"Oh, really, Mr. Jamming." An edge crept into Laurel's voice. "You take all your girlfriends for a nap on the moss in your sacred grove. Is that it?"

Devan shrugged but scowled at Zoë.

Pleased to inform Laurel that she was just the latest in a long line of Devan's amours, Zoë was almost sorry she had to embarrass Devan.

Devan said, "Honey, that's all over. Zoë, you don't know what you're talking about, so give us a break."

Needing to change the subject fast, Zoë smiled and said to Laurel, "What's in the case?" She already knew: the bionic hand. "It's not a trumpet, is it?"

"You'll see in a minute."

Nodding her head, Zoë muttered, "Bionic hand. I've never seen one." Zoë stared at the empty end of Laurel's sleeve. "Where's your regular hand?" Zoë asked. "Devan didn't tell me you had only one hand."

"He didn't?" Laurel laughed. Looking down her nose at Devan, she said, "Yeah, no hand, but I have a dragon instead." Pushing her sleeve back, she revealed the head of a peacock blue dragon enveloped her forearm, a bold emerald muzzle emerging from the nubbin while beady scarlet eyes challenged the world. Laurel swooped the dragon in figure eights around Zoë's head.

Zoë dodged, batting at the air where Laurel's fingers should be. "He's not scary. He's pretty. Were you born with him that way?"

"No. I had an accident."

"I thought so," Zoë said, now holding Laurel's nubbin and caressing the dragon's nose like a cat's forehead. "I had a car accident with my mother when I was six. Devan saved me. Only my mom didn't make it. Who saved you?"

"My mother."

Zoë's chin trembled, then she said, "What happened?"

"I had a car accident, too. I was seven. My hand got crushed when the door slammed against my wrist. It was a Mercedes door, so heavy it tuned my poor little hand into pulp."

"That's gross. I'm sorry."

Laurel said, "Well, I guess we have a sad thing in common. But yours is sadder. I got this new hand I can do almost anything with. All I have to do is think or feel something and it acts by itself. Just like my other one, or your hands."

Zoë nodded, contemplating the information. Pausing a moment to examine Laurel's face, she changed the subject. "What tribe are you?"

Laurel put her index finger to her chin and thought. "The Japanese-Mexican tribe," she replied, glancing at Devan. "One of the new tribes."

"Oh. Do Japanese-Mexicans live on a reservation?"

Laurel moved close to Zoë, opened her arms. Zoë stepped back but Laurel wouldn't let her away.

"I doubt it," Laurel said. "I live off-rez."

Zoë let herself be hugged. She held her body stiff, but relished the arms around her. The tall woman smelled like roses and Zoë let herself melt against her.

Laurel's warm breath flowed over the back of Zoë's head, her arms burrowed into the folds of Zoë's bulky coat. Zoë closed her eyes and lay her head against Laurel's warm chest.

"I'm so happy you're here, Zoë. I couldn't wait to meet you."

I could wait to meet you, Zoë thought, keeping her lips shut.

Laurel rocked back and forth, humming a song Zoë didn't recognize. She wondered if Laurel would sing for her. She didn't care, jazz or country. Zoë didn't like either one, but even Laurel's speaking voice soothed her in the way that only her crickets and sunset breezes could.

Zoë backed out of Laurel's comforting arms, relieved and sad at the same time.

Devan opened the refrigerator and pulled out two cans of Coors, popped them, and handed one to Laurel. They sat at the counter and drank, their eyes on Zoë.

Devan drained his beer and got another one. "Where did you get these?"

"Your dad brought that over before they left," Zoë said. "Said you'd want them. Brought me a dozen juices, too."

Devan handed Zoë an apple juice bottle and opened a second beer for Laurel. "What do you think, baby?"

"Call your friend. We gotta get this over with."

"I'm going to."

Devan sat down on the couch and picked up his phone, then dropped it onto the cushion. "Zoë, come and sit with me. You, too, Laurel. I'll make the call and we'll fix supper."

Laurel squeezed between the couch's armrest and Devan, cuddling under his arm. Laying her head back and closing her eyes, she massaged his thigh with her nub.

Watching the smooth globe of flesh furrow Devan's jeans, Zoë asked, "Are you guys gonna get married?"

Devan shook his head and said, "Always count on Zoë to speak her mind."

Laurel sat up and smiled. "I'm definitely getting married…someday…to somebody. Maybe it'll be the big guy here, but…somebody has to ask first."

Devan said, "Tell you what. We make it through the next couple of days, we'll talk about a lot of things. A trip to Mars. Winning the lottery. Marriage."

Laughing, Laurel punched him in the shoulder.

"I mean it," Zoë said.

"We don't know, honey," Laurel said. "We're still getting to know each other."

"I'll never get married, that's for sure." Zoë's tone turned steely, then she said, almost whispering, "Well, maybe in Heaven…."

Devan inhaled and looking out the side window, he and growled. Zoë said, "Sorry."

"You'll meet somebody you love and then you'll want to get married," Laurel said. "I used to say I'd stay single all my life."

"Used to?" Devan said.

Laurel grinned and nodded. "I'm getting older," she said, a humorous note in her voice.

"I won't get married," Zoë chimed in, hearing her chance to explain the logic of her ascension. She wanted Devan to understand, even if he wouldn't believe. "I'm staying a virgin. Just like Mary."

"She got married," Devan said. "To Joseph."

"No way. If she did," Zoë argued, "she'd never be the Virgin Mary. You can't be married and be a virgin."

"Story goes, Mary got married and stayed a virgin," Laurel said. "Joseph was the father of Jesus."

"No, she didn't," Zoë said. "Joseph was step-father and they never got married. Don't believe everything you hear about virginity." Zoë knelt on the seat, facing Laurel and Devan. "Nobody who's married is a virgin. Soon as you say 'I do,' you lose it. All the girls in Spring Creek know that. Didn't they teach you that in San Francisco? If you're not married, you must be a virgin."

"It's all about sex," Devan said. "Once you have sex you lose your virginity. I hate to bring it up," he looked at Laurel, "you're not married and you haven't been a virgin...."

"Devan!" Laurel sat up, pretending to be shocked.

"Devan's smart about some things, but he still doesn't understand things any fifteen year old girl knows," Zoë said

"I can't win," Devan said.

"I'm not trying to fight you, Devan. You always tell me 'express yourself.'"

"That's right. We have to express ourselves, or die."

"That's what I'm saying - I'm not gonna die."

Zoë plopped down next to Devan and, her eyes rolling, she tickled his stomach.

"Stop it, Zoë. My ribs hurt. My whole body hurts."

Zoë's face fell. "I forgot."

Devan coughed. "Rolled down a rocky hill."

Zoë eased herself up and peered at his face. She lifted his hands and stared at the swollen, torn fingertips.

"Where did that happen? At the Hunkpapa grave?"

"Not exactly a grave. More like mausoleum."

"What's that?" Zoë sat down beside him, poked her face next to his and waited. If she didn't push, he'd talk.

"It's a grave above the ground. A place they keep the bones so they can visit them. Talk to them."

Confused, she asked, "Did you fall into the mausoleum?"

"Sort of. More like I fell out of it."

"Just tell me, Devan. I always tell you everything. Even if you don't like it."

Zoë widened her eyes, waiting. She could outbargain Devan. She'd read that fifteen-year-old girls had bigger brains than anybody. She might as well use it before adulthood shriveled it up like an apple stuck all winter on a tree. Another reason to get to Heaven quick – once you're there, you never get older.

Devan started to speak and Laurel interrupted. "It's a big mess, Zoë. Can't you see Devan's wasted?"

Zoë ignored Laurel's insult. Of course she saw Devan's exhaustion. He was usually as wired as a Lakota basketball player. Could run all day if he had to.

Shifting to get more comfortable, Devan said to Laurel, "It's okay, baby." To Zoë he said, "We were looking at the bones in a cave."

"On Anpetu?"

"Inside Anpetu."

"Inside? I wanna see those bones."

"You can't."

"I'll wait to take off if you'll show me the bones. My friend, Betty Three Deer, when she tells Lakota stories, she waves a bone around. She says it's her great-great-great grandfather's thigh bone."

Devan frowned. "In a minute. Right now, I don't want to think about it."

Zoë nodded, understanding. "Like I don't want to think about saying good-bye to everybody. But I have to and it's part of getting to Heaven."

A few crickets chirruped, then more, gaining momentum for the night's work. Soon, they hushed. No one spoke.

Laurel left Devan's side and wandered to the window and looked out. From behind, Zoë watched Laurel's pale reflection in the night-black glass.

"As long as we don't think about it, it's all right," Laurel said. "Pretend it's okay. Like everybody else."

Zoë decided to let the subject rest. When he was ready, he'd tell her. He loved to talk. Wouldn't be long.

"What about that phone call?" Laurel said.

"In a sec. Can't believe how good it feels to chill."

Zoë turned to the refrigerator. "We have ice for your bruises." She ran water into the sink, holding a full ice tray under it to loosen the cubes.

Laurel went over to Zoë. "Good idea, honey. We have some mud potion for his bruises, too." She tossed a small plastic bag filled with an amber substance onto the table.

Zoë dropped the ice into the stainless steel basin. "You have a poshent?"

"A sack of mud a Hunkpapa lady said would help heal Devan's sores real fast. Our friend Leo's sister."

Zoë frowned. "Leo?"

Devan said, "The hitchhiker. He's Hunkpapa. It was his parents in the mausoleum."

"Ah." Zoë leaned back against the counter. "Poshents work better than ice." Nudging the conversation back toward the Indian, she said, "Is it Lakota loam? That's the strongest."

His eyes still closed, Devan piped up, "Minneconjou. That's more powerful."

Zoë stuck her tongue out at Devan.

"Want to help me mix it up?" Laurel asked, reaching into the plastic bag. "We can spread it on Devan's ribs."

Zoë almost danced to the table. "You can teach me to make a poshent?"

"This is more like a balm, but it's fun," Laurel said, expertly unsealing the bag with one hand, setting it on the table, and sifting the earth between her fingers. "I'll show you how I use my bionic hand to stir. Get a mixing bowl."

Zoë's head swiveled between Devan and Laurel. A toothy grin on her face, she shook her head, her hair riffling like scarlet angora in the kitchen fluorescence. "Maybe you're both my luck," she said.

You don't have to like somebody for them to bring you luck, she said to herself. Zoë's crickets chirped again, random notes, then a series of rhythms.

"Wait a minute," Zoë said, spinning around. "My crickets have to go outside. They need fresh air."

Zoë opened the door into a still dusk. "Gonna storm tonight," she said. "Did you see those thunderclouds today?"

Without waiting for an answer, she stepped into the shadows and removed her jacket, laying it on the grass.

In a moment, hundreds of shiny black crickets shuffled out of the coat, invisible against the aged leather to anyone but Zoë. They loitered on the coat, then an eager few of them hopped off, scouting among the blades of grass.

The insect clan moved slowly, advancing from their day's seclusion. In a few minutes, their tweeting and peeping ballooned into a competition of ringing solos and passionate duets. As she did every night in the warm seasons, Zoë reveled in the cricket mating songs.

Beside her, arm in arm, Devan and Laurel stood on the concrete stoop, listening.

"You don't need many crickets to make a choir," Zoë said. "One handful's plenty."

Flitting and creeping, the bugs scouted the yard, intently fiddling their wings, seeking what crickets always seek in dewy grass – others to join their erotic harmony.

Sixteen

MUD PIE

Zoë filled a measuring cup with water and set it between Laurel's sack of Minneconjou dust and Devan's mixing bowl. She stepped up on the green stool Devan had built for her and boosted herself onto the counter.

Sitting on her hands, she watched Laurel lift her antique case. Zoë gawked at Laurel as she laid the case on the table and unsnapped the lock.

"Why so quiet?" Laurel said. "I'm just getting ready to mix up some mud pie."

Devan stood up and leaned on the counter, his arm around Zoë's shoulders. He laughed, wiping his forehead with the back of his hand.

"Go to it, ladies. It's so damn muggy right now, I'm gonna melt. I have to take a cool shower. I'll call Josh when I'm done. You whip me up a nice batch of magic goo."

He limped out of the kitchen as Laurel pushed the sleeve of her shirt up to the elbow above the empty wrist.

Zoë saw through the tattoo to the naked bud of flesh at the end of Laurel's empty wrist and a tender fillip rippled in Zoë's chest.

Folding back a narrow lip of skin, Laurel separated the dragon's nostrils on the nub of her left arm to reveal steel and copper links buried in the recess of flesh.

Zoë shivered.

Laurel reached into the case and searched around. Catching hold of an object, she pulled out a silvery steel device and held it by its black plastic cuff. "Meet Glinda, my prosthesis. She's my magic wand.

It's powerful. Does things flesh and bone hands can't. But if I want to do something delicate, like play the piano or, hey, if I want to sew or tickle Devan, I have another attachment – a magic hand."

"Can I see?"

Laurel smiled and lifted a blue velvet bag out of the case and extracted a translucent tan hand – dark finger and wrist bones overlaid with skin-like substance. Several colored strands of wire emerged from a cuff collapsed on the wrist. She laid it on the table, arranging the bent fingers around the palm. Zoë counted six fingers. No, one was a thumb with two joints and not quite as long as the fingers.

Zoë slid off the counter. Reaching out, she caressed the palm of the hand. The soft plastic with lifelines etched into it yielded to pressure from her fingers, then bloomed back to a smooth fleshy promise of sensitivity.

"If it had hair," Zoë said, "it'd be a tarantula."

Laurel snickered. "You got it. She's my spider paw."

"Put it on."

"Later, sweetie. I wear her when I play piano, but she's too delicate to wear every day. Go ahead. Pick her up."

Holding the false hand in both palms, Zoë cradled it against her chest. The long fingers dangled over her hands, leafless pink vines with smooth tips for exploring, while the connector wires hung down, roots seeking an airless place to burrow in.

"No fingernails?"

"Touch the tips. They're harder than the rest of the skin."

Zoë put the hand on the table, petting it and grinning. "I bet you play pretty piano with this on."

"Maybe I'll get the keyboard out later." Folding the fingers into each other under the thumb, she slipped it into its pouch and knotted the cord. She closed the cover of the case and picked up the other apparatus.

"When I put my hand on for you," Laurel said, "you can decide what color you want to see. I can make her glow in the dark, too."

"Let me see now," Zoë said.

"Later, honey. We have to mix up the healing mud."

The Glinda prosthesis resembled a tall silver beer can. A wide green stripe, nearly the same color as Laurel's dragon, inset with mother-of-pearl moons and stars and strange symbols circled the center of the slender cylinder.

Her lower lip slightly extended in concentration, Laurel hefted it in her palm. It was about the size of a three-pound silver bass Zoë caught when she camped out at the lake.

Twisting the cylinder against her stub, Laurel folded the empty skin back. Tipping the thick shaft back and forth, looking for the correct angle to fit it into its socket, Laurel said, "My bionic trinity – metal, flesh, plastic."

She tapped the prosthesis into place under the loose skin, and plunged it into the dragon's mouth, hitching steel to bone. Then, she velcroed a black leather sleeve onto her forearm, concealing the dragon's head, and said, "That's it. Glinda's home."

Disappointed that this fake "hand" was only a can, Zoë placed her small arm beside Laurel's, as if measuring the difference between the sizes of their arms. "It's a strange shape for a hand. I guess that makes it bionic."

Laurel chuckled and aimed her steel-capped stump of wrist at the ceiling while stepping close to Zoë. "Watch this." She pointed to a curved panel on the side of the hand and said, "Here, press."

Zoë jutted her jaw and narrowed her eyes. She tensed her shoulders as she pressed the panel with her index finger. The cylinder clicked and hummed, powering up. In a few seconds, two titanium rods slithered out, sleek and menacing. One had a sharp curved end, the other had a rounded, softer point.

"Watch Glinda's tricks."

Zoë couldn't do anything else.

Laurel pinched the rods together and separated them, slid and grazed them together, up and down. She absorbed the rounded one all the way back into the base. She extended the other until she sported a long fishhook at the end of her arm. The ceiling light seemed sunk into the matte finish on the rods.

Laurel aimed the hook down and with a faint whine, the rounded rod emerged from inside the Glinda while the hook receded out of sight. Bending her arm so the rods pointed up and flicking her elbow to the side, Laurel locked the rods into place.

"They look like sabre teeth," Zoë said.

With her electronic paw humming, Laurel demonstrated a flashlight, several screwdrivers, two knife blades, and a car key. "I can add on just about anything," she said. "I've got a canister of Mace, my phone. In the city I wear my garage door opener and my TV and CD remote."

Zoë steepled her fingers in front of her mouth and contemplated the futuristic appendage. All she could say was, "Awesome."

"Really, Zoë, watch." Laurel laughed, elongating the rods, then spinning them. "Just think of Glinda as a super electric toothbrush."

Zoë smirked. "Sure, if you're a robot."

Laurel laughed and attached a flat steel plate to the curved spike and withdrew it a few inches so the plate reached two inches beyond the blunt-tipped rod.

"Built-in spatula and spoon," she said. "Before I started singing, I thought about baking school. I love cooking, so Glinda comes in handy."

Laurel picked up the crumpled paper sack and dumped a fine dust into the bowl. She inserted her futuristic digits into the powder and said, "Pour."

Still awed, Zoë poured water, slowly, avoiding spatters.

"Hi Glinda," Zoë said. "Welcome to Spring Creek."

Laurel tapped another recessed button on the black cylinder that held the electronic hand works. The rods rotated in slow circles, blending the water into the dust. The machine hummed in a high pitch. "My very own Mix Master."

Zoë splashed out some water. "More?" she asked as she went to the sink and filled the beaker. She dribbled the last of the water onto the mud paste, washing sludge down Laurel's mixing rods while they folded the mud into soft swirls.

"Looks like gingerbread batter," Zoë said. "I made gingerbread people with my mother when she was alive."

Laurel slowed the spinning rods further and looked at Zoë, her eyes wide and liquid.

"Do you still have your real hand?" Zoë asked.

"No. I wanted to keep it in a bottle, but my mother took it away and burned it."

"I got burned once," Zoë said. "All over my legs. They hurt a long time, but I still have them." She bent over and pulled her jeans up to her knees. White burn scars ridged and marbled her pink shins and calves.

"Oh, honey, that must have been awful."

"You can touch my burns," Zoë said. "It doesn't hurt any more." She lifted both legs of her jeans up to her knees.

Holding her prosthesis overhead like a torch of mud, Laurel knelt and caressed Zoë's legs with her natural hand, first one leg, from ankle to knee, then the other. "How did this happen?"

"My stupid uncle."

"Your uncle?"

"My step-uncle. Augie. He said he wanted to show me his cattle, how fat they were. I said okay."

Laurel stood up. "Do you want to tell me about it?"

"Maybe." Zoë knit her brows and nodded, thinking.

After a while, she said, "What happened to Devan?" As if she didn't really want to know, Zoë peered into the bowl. "Any more dust? Looks like too much water."

Laurel said, "It'll evaporate. Might even have to add more after it sits."

"I know. When I make cookies, I always have to add more milk. I use cream if I have it. It's thicker." Zoë hopped down, landing on her toes and bouncing.

"How do you suck those things into the can? They look like spikes. How do they fit?"

"It's attached to some nerves and tendons and muscles inside my arm. When I think in a certain way, a tiny battery runs an electric motor that makes the shafts move."

"Can you feel anything in the hand? I mean, can Glinda?"

"Sometimes she can. A little hum. It tickles." Laurel turned her back to Zoë and leaned over the sink.

"I like my uncle now. He's okay now. Takes me out to dinner when he has money. Never tries to do anything."

Waiting for Laurel to finish rinsing her mixing shafts, Zoë scooped up a brown blob of mud. When Laurel turned around, Zoë aimed it toward her lips and slowly inserted it, closing her bared teeth around it. She agitated her wrist as if scraping off the ball of goo stuck on her finger.

As soon as Laurel grabbed her arm, Zoë's mouth popped open and she pulled the finger out, mud gob attached.

"Yuck. You're not supposed to eat that," Laurel said. "It might have some kind of bacteria or poison it it. Could make you sick."

"Poshents can't make you sick. They're magic. Like Glinda." Zoë wiped her finger on the rim of the bowl and washed it off under the faucet. "Poison...?"

"Poison. Like what we saw inside the mountain."

The toilet flushed in the other room and Devan poked his head out of the bedroom. "Josh's gonna get the stuff. Said he can get it in Rapid City."

"Good," Laurel said, removing the mixing plate from her steel rod finger.

"Nothing like a cold shower," Devan said. "I'm gonna call Matt now."

"Take your time. Zoë and I are talking." Laurel sat down on a metal kitchen chair and composed herself, then turned toward the bedroom. "You sure you don't want me to look at those cuts again?"

"I'm cool," Devan called.

A gust whacked the trailer door against the wall, clanking the thin metal eaves outside. They looked up. Zoë stepped to the window and sniffed. She said, "I'll bring in the crickets pretty soon. Rain's coming close."

"First, tell me," Laurel said. "The fire."

Zoë stared at her for a moment. Only a few people knew the whole story about the fire and her uncle. Then she nodded.

"What about the poison? You promise to tell me?"

"Promise."

"You can't tell anybody. It's private."

Laurel crossed her heart and sealed her lips.

Zoë reconsidered, then said. "It hurt a lot, but it's okay now. If my uncle didn't burn me, I wouldn't have my crickets." Zoë filled the teapot. "I like making poshents and pies. Shall we have tea now? Devan likes peppermint. Want some?"

Laurel stared at Zoë, not replying.

Zoë insisted. "Do you?"

"Sure. I like peppermint, too."

Zoë stared at the ceiling, thinking. Laurel was nice, but snoopy. California people ask too many questions. Sensing her opportunity to learn the secret of Anpetu, Zoë said, "Okay."

"Want honey?" Zoë offered, pointing to a jar. "Mrs. Krochek gave me a honeycomb from her hive. Clover. Smells good."

"I'd love it," Laurel said.

She's worried, Zoë thought. Devan didn't tell her all about me, so she thinks I'm trouble or crazy or something.

"Augie – he's my uncle – he had fat cattle, but he was a drunk. It was after Ruthie died. Bonnie told me to stay away from Augie and my daddy. I can't help it, they're my family."

"You have to respect your family."

"I don't respect them one bit." She paused, placing her chin in both hands and holding her cheeks and settled her chin on her crossed fingers and thumbs.

"Did Devan tell you about my daddy?" If he did, I won't say a thing."

"Not much. Only that you lost your mother and your father spends most of his time drinking."

Zoë sat down in the chair across from Laurel. She leaned forward, reaching to touch the base of Laurel's prosthesis. As she spoke, she traced the outlines of the shimmery moons and stars.

"Right. Except when Ruthie – my mom? – when she was alive and I was little, Bruce and Augie did gross things to me when she was gone. When I told her, Ruthie stopped them."

"You must love your mom a lot."

Zoë wrinkled her nose at Laurel, irritated when somebody said the obvious. Of course she loved Ruthie. Ruthie loved her more than anybody, too.

"Anyway, it was a while after Ruthie went to Heaven, and Augie had been really nice to me. Took me to movies and things. I liked him. So when he said let's go see my steers, I said fine.

"He drove his pickup into the field where he kept his steers, nine of them, just like I was nine years old. We sat there, he tried to kiss me like he always did and I let him – on my cheek, like I always did. He was drunk that day and he was wearing his shiny red and gold cowboy shirt. It was stained so I knew he was real drunk because he never let that shirt get dirty."

Zoë sat back and fiddled with her jacket, jamming her hand in a pocket and flipping the coat back and forth. Little Limbo banged against her knee and she smiled to herself, remembering Mr. J. Ever since she caught his Great Soul, it seemed like her life had speeded up.

"It's really old, the fire. I forget most of it."

"Tell me, anyway, honey. I want to hear all about your crickets."

"You know Ruthie. Arthur and Bonnie and Devan are my Earth family. I haven't seen my dad for a long time."

"I'm sorry," Laurel said, extending her hand.

Zoë brightened but didn't take Laurel's hand. "I'm not. Do you like this tablecloth?"

"It's pretty," Laurel sat back in her chair.

"Well, Augie wanted to play a game. Blind man's bluff. I said you'll never catch me. You're drunk. He said let's see if you can catch me. You gotta give me a minute cuz I'm drunk. That's what I said, I said."

The teakettle whistled and Zoë opened the lid and dropped in an aromatic bouquet of peppermint. Laurel sat at the kitchen table, listening, resting her chin in her palm. She'd detached her prosthesis and it lay on the tablecloth to dry.

Zoë sat down and caressed the rods. She continued, not looking at Laurel. "He said let's make it saint's blind man's bluff. What do you mean? I said. You'll see, he said. He tied a bandana around my eyes. Don't peek. I said no way. He said you might. I tried to pull it down and he said, See, you're trying. I started to cry. I wanted to get out of there."

Zoë stood up again and leaned over the teakettle, sniffing the spicy steam.

"Smells delicious," Laurel said.

"Wait'll you taste it with honeycomb." Zoë lowered her spoon into the honey pot. "Anyway, I stood there in the middle of the field, couldn't see a thing. My head ached. I said Augie stop it. He said let's play. I don't like this I said. I'm getting mad. If Arthur knew about this."

"Devan's dad," Laurel interjected, knowing.

"Devan was gone with his class or something to Omaha or someplace."

Zoë scowled. She scrutinized Laurel, whose eyes had gone dry as autumn oak leaves. "I'm hopping up and down and pretty soon I smell gas. Augie's laughing and then it gets real hot and I smell smoke and then I feel fire nipping my legs.

"I scream Augie! Stop it! I start to run and I fall down and I get up and run, but I hear crackling and smell smoke everywhere. My ankles sting cuz my pants catch fire. I know I'm supposed to lay down and roll but if I do, I'll catch my hair on fire."

"My God, Zoë. Where's he now?"

"I don't know. He disappears and then comes back. A lot. I finally jumped past the fire and rolled on the ground. Good thing Augie was drunk because the bandana came off pretty easy. I saw his pickup bumping away across the field. Once I heard Devan tell Arthur they should string him up. He was in jail for quite a while."

Laurel reached out to hug her and Zoë let herself tuck into Laurel's soft arms. She lay her face on Laurel's breast and let her cheek jostle against it. Laurel nuzzled the top of Zoë's head and kissed it over and over.

When Zoë pulled back and looked up, a tear dripped off Laurel's nose and dropped on the bridge of Zoë's. It tickled. "I'm okay. Really."

If Laurel couldn't take a story about a stupid thing from a long time ago without bawling her eyes out, Zoë doubted she would last long with Devan.

Zoë eased away from Laurel and picked up the kettle and filled two cups with steaming tea, handing one to Laurel. "Feel how it's cooling off outside?" She tipped her chin toward the door.

Laurel nodded.

"Gonna rain pretty soon." Zoë inhaled and raised her cup to her lips. "Ahhhh. My favorite."

Laurel spooned a chunk of honeycomb into her tea and stirred. She sipped and smiled at Zoë. "How long did you stay in the hospital."

Zoë set her cup down. "No hospital. I stayed by the stream. That's when the crickets came. They were my nurses."

"But didn't somebody find you? Take care of you?"

"Yes. But I got well fast. Especially after the crickets put their medicine on my legs."

"Special crickets."

"No. Regular."

Laurel and Zoë sat down next to each other. Zoë continued. "I shucked my pants off. My sleeves were smoking, too, but I slapped them out. Good thing Augie was drunk. You know what he meant by saint's blind man's bluff, right?"

"I don't think so, honey. This sounds like Devil's blind man's bluff."

Zoë laughed. "No. It's Saint's. Like Joan of Arc and the good witches they burned. They were really medicine women. You heard of them?"

"Yes, a lot of people know about them nowadays."

"I guess Augie thought I was one of them. I wasn't then, but maybe I am now." Zoë cackled as she poured another cup of tea and spooned comb into her cup. "Put a lot of comb in, drink it fast. Chew it so the honey squooshes out all over your tongue. Feels like hot ice cream."

Sadness swelled in Zoë's throat. The memory of the fire, combined with her awareness that she had to leave Devan and her whole family for Heaven, brought tears to her eyes. She exhaled slowly, but the melancholy sunk down into her stomach.

Then an idea popped into her head. Maybe the poshent will bring two angels! One for her, one for Devan. She almost hopped into a jiggy two-step. Inky must have put that idea into her head.

Then she became realistic. If I don't attract two angels, only one – mine – I'll come back sooner than I planned. I'll hang out with Ruthie and Inky and Kateri for a few days, get to know my way around, then I'll come back in time to hear Laurel sing in the club and watch Devan act.

I'll go faster than light so time will slow down and they'll barely miss me before I return. We'll go out with Devan, have a picnic. I'll tell them everything about Heaven. That will change their minds about coming with me when I go back again. I know they'll think I'm crazy but when they see me back from Heaven, it won't matter what anybody thinks.

Zoë glanced at Laurel, who shrugged her shoulders and wiggled her fingers, signaling for her to keep talking. Her empty arm lay silent, the dragon's eyes watching as if it had already heard everything and nothing could surprise it now. "I know it's hard to talk about, honey."

"It's not," she said, hardening her voice. "Not as hard as you telling me about the poison." She waited for Laurel.

"If you don't...." Zoë knew she didn't need to threaten Laurel, because she'd find out from Devan, sooner or later. "You promised."

"I did," Laurel said, a weak smile on her lips.

Zoë continued. "I watched the fire crawl across the field, but I was so tired, I fell asleep." She paused, then went on with more animation in her voice than she felt. "When I woke up, the fire was out and about a million crickets were tickling my legs, hopping like black popcorns. At first I brushed them off, but it hurt to move my legs, so I let them crawl back."

Laurel put her arm around Zoë's shoulder and lay her head against Zoë's. "You smell like a sweet flower I never smelled before," Zoë said. "Does your tribe smell that way? Or just the women? Most men I know smell sour."

Laurel sat up, chuckling. "You have a lot of ideas, Zoë. I don't know if we all smell like this. It must be the smell of love."

"I believe it."

Squeezing Zoë closer, Laurel said, "That's it with the fire and crickets?"

"Almost. I stayed there a couple of days. Bonnie and Arthur freaked out when I came back all smudged two days later. They thought I ran away or something. A few years later, when I started living on my own, the crickets found me again. I gave them a home in my coat."

"Do they have names?"

Zoë pretended to glower at Laurel, but good humor shone in her eyes and ticced at the corners of her lips. She said, with a lilt in her voice belying her indignation, "I don't know. I don't speak cricket."

They laughed, then sat silently, sipping the last of their lukewarm tea.

Zoë carried their empty cups to the sink. "Laurel, do you know what scares crickets most? I mean, two things?"

"One of them wouldn't be getting stuffed into your pockets with everything else and getting all crushed?"

"No way." How could she think I'd smash my crickets? "It's lawn mowers. Then, thunderstorms. When the lawn mowers come they have to burrow down to the bottom of the grass – crickets hope the mowers cut high. When the storms come they have to shinny up the grass and hang on till the flood passes. They lose a lot of babies and old people to lawn mowers and floods."

Laurel shook her head. "I bet you know more about crickets than anybody alive. When do you have to go get them? Now you mentioned it, I can smell the rain coming, too."

"We have time. Crickets don't live natural in my coat, y'know. I mean, now they do, but they have things to do in the fields."

Devan's voice boomed as he emerged from the bedroom wearing a black pullover and clean blue jeans. "I smell my favorite tea. Did you save any for me?" Even standing in his stocking feet, his head nearly touched the ceiling.

Zoë looked up at him with a mock-troubled expression. "Sorry, we drank it all."

"Don't you love me any more?" he said, pretending hurt.

"No. I forgot all about you, you stayed away so long," Zoë teased. "Since we're not gonna see each other again for a while, let's celebrate! I'll make a fresh pot of tea, all for you."

Devan grinned at Zoë.

"Laurel's gonna tell me about what happened to you at Anpetu. The toxic poison. The bones. Everything."

Devan glanced at Laurel who nodded.

"She promised. You can't get mad," Zoë said.

"Oh, Zoë. I'm not mad. A lot of stuff is going on is all." He fingered a hunk of comb into his mouth, dripping honey onto his chin and licking his fingers.

"It's all set," Devan said to Laurel. "Matt's going to jump on it first thing tomorrow. He gets the dish from Josh then meets us at Anpetu. He already knows where he can get the radiation protection suits and the cameras. And the other things."

Devan sounded excited, so Zoë fell quiet and listened, trying to understand.

"I called James Little Creek on Pine Ridge. He's putting up a website and he'll start the phone tree and set up the links to Facebook and YouTube and all the others. Once we get inside, he'll start tweeting like crazy. Top 50 environmenal bloggers. They'll get the news out to everybody." He smiled at Laurel. "We leave at dawn. Have the whole thing done by noon."

"What thing?" Zoë asked. "James Little Creek? You mean Takenheka? The genius computer guy?"

"Yeah. Nothing for you to bother about, sweetie." He dodged her glare. "How about some tea? It's just a trip Laurel and I have to take. For our jobs. Rehearsal for the Passion Play."

Zoë fumed, pursing her lips and staring icicles at Devan. She poured tea into his cup, purposely sloshing it over the side. "Sure. Like Judas wears a radiation suit. It's about the old Hunkpapa man. I know. I never lie to you. Why do you lie to me? Radiation suits?"

Devan glanced at Laurel, raising his eyebrows. "Okay. There's some fucked-up things going on. I don't want you involved. If anybody found out you knew something, you'd be in danger."

"You have to tell me. Laurel promised."

Devan tousled her hair, like he used to do when she was little. Zoë shook off his hand and glared at him.

A sprinkle of rain spattered the roof in an uneven rhythm as if warning the residents of its arrival with deceptive tenderness. All three glanced up, then stared at each other. Chilly air blasted through the front windows, dropping the temperature by five degrees.

Zoë lifted her eyebrows and shrugged. "Here it comes," she said, accustomed to cloud busters ripping through the county in minutes and downpours lasting hours. It wouldn't rain tonight, she knew. The sky was always promising rain but the only promise it kept was staying blue every day.

Laurel stepped closer to Devan who put his arm around her saying, "We could ride out Noah's flood in this trailer."

Nodding at Zoë, he said, "Right? Tight as a battleship in here." Then, kissing Laurel on the forehead, he said, "We'll be nice and cozy."

"Doesn't Zoë sleep in your bed?" Laurel said, pushing his hands away.

"What do you say, Zoë?" Devan asked, a false grin splattered across his lips. The crescent tips of his mustache curled up and out. They twittered like sparrows, but Zoë was in no mood to laugh.

"Stop acting on me. I can take care of myself."

"Oh, Zoë." Laurel knelt beside her.

"I'm not mad at you, just him. Besides, when the rain's about to break, I get sad, that's all."

"Why don't you sleep on the couch, Zo? It's plenty big." Devan plumped the couch pillows. "Wanna read or play cards or something?"

"Don't worry about me. I'll go to bed whenever I'm ready. I've slept under the trees during a gullywasher and woke up fresh and dry the next day."

Turning away, she dug into her jeans pocket and found the folded page from *Cooking with Herbs*. Her ticket to Heaven. She kneaded the recipe between her fingers and thumb.

"You just put on your radiation suits and go eat some toxic poison. Me and my crickets will go sleep alone. Just like always."

She'd never felt angrier at Devan. Some luck he was.

"You never told me about the poison."

"Tomorrow, okay? It's just some old oil tanks, or something."

"Sure," Zoë said, slamming the screen door shut behind her. She retrieved her jacket and the crickets before the clouds let loose.

Tonight she might have to throw her foam mattress and sleeping bag into the back of Devan's pickup.

"Hey, Devan," she shouted back into the trailer. "Does your camper roof leak?"

"No way. It's brand new. Sleep well."

Zoë picked up her jacket and felt inside to make sure her poshent sack was secure. She found it and shook it, reassured by the soft crinkling of her poshent sack of angel bait.

She took her sack of poshent ingredients into the pickup bed and left her jacket on the front steps of the trailer where, just in case he needed it, even the oldest, most confused cricket could find it.

Seventeen

ANPETU'S SECRET

The rising sun ironed a black velvet collar of ridges across the pale eastern sky. As usual this year, last night's clouds had lied. No rain had fallen and a warm breeze promised a hot dusty day.

Sitting on the top step in the lacy shadows cast across the yard by Devan's peach trees, Zoë watched him and Laurel load the pickup. She spooned oatmeal from her third bowl that morning. She could eat anything, anytime, and twice as much as anybody else twice her size.

A full stomach after a good night's sleep under the trees put her in a happy mood.

"I can help, Devan," she said between gulps.

He ignored her, so she laughed. "You have to take it easy on your bruised butt. It's a hard drive to Anpetu."

Crouching under the camper cap over the pickup bed, he replied, mumbling into a heap of gear, "Mighty kind, Zoë, but I'm good as new. Thanks to that magic mud."

At least he's lightened up, Zoë thought.

He tossed their luggage around as he repacked the truck bed with the backpacks and cases they'd unloaded yesterday, adding new boxes and sports bags.

"Tell you what. We make it back from this little trip, I'm gonna put that Minneconjou Mud on the market. We'll go on the rodeo circuit and make a mint curing the busted heads and butts of sorry cowboys."

She considered his idea, taking it seriously. Holding her spoon in mid-air, she said, "You gonna make the ads with pictures of your own behind?"

Devan poked his head out from under the cap. "Me? Nobody'd take a second look. I thought Laurel would be our advertising lady."

"Don't you talk about my bottom that way," Laurel called from the cab. "That's private."

Zoë laughed. "Hers is prettier than yours, Devan. It's not as big either."

He looked squarely into Zoë's face. "If she won't do it, there's only one other person around here who qualifies. Her name starts with 'Z'. Know who I mean?"

Zoë flicked a spoonful of oatmeal at him. "No way," she said. "Like she said, that's private property."

Devan said from under the camper cap, "It's gonna be big huge private property if you keep eating so much."

"So what. Laurel's isn't really that small," Zoë said, "and you think she's beautiful."

"She is," he said. "And it's not just her face."

Laurel called, "It better not be."

Their teasing made Zoë flinch. They're too cute with each other, she thought. Must be love. Not her kind, but Devan was sure crazy for this woman. We'll see how long it lasts, she thought.

"Devan," she said, perking up, "you won't tell me why we're going to Anpetu, but I know the real reason – you're taking me to my angel."

"Don't start that, Zoë. You can't come with us. We're putting you on the bus to Las Vegas to meet our folks. They don't serve food on the Greyhound. I called Bonnie and Arthur and they're excited you're coming."

Zoë stood up and opened her mouth to protest. "My angel."

Devan shook his head, growling, "Goddammit, Zoë. Would you cut loose of that angel crap?"

Zoë recoiled. She felt her cheeks folding up from her lips and her eyes squinting. He'd never said anything like that before.

"Devan," Laurel cautioned him.

"It's a little kid's fantasy. She should grow up. Nobody's gonna fly up in the air and land in Heaven. Think about it."

"It's harmless," Laurel said. "Leave her alone."

He glared at Zoë. "You say you're gonna take off. Sounds like suicide talk. That's what worries me. You're gonna do something really stupid. You think nothing matters in the whole world except you flying off to Heaven."

Zoë twisted around on the step, her legs under her, and faced him. "I'm not stupid. You think I can't take care of myself? No way I'm gonna kill myself," she said, about as angry with him as she'd ever been. "I told you I'm living forever. You know that."

"He's worried, honey," Laurel touched Zoë on the cheek with her stump. "Lots on his mind. He doesn't mean it."

Zoë slapped Laurel's arm away. Was Devan pretending or was he really mad at her?

"Why are you still mad at me?" she said. No use fighting him. He was so upset she'd never get through to him. She'd have to outsmart him, that's all.

"I'm not mad. Just grow up. You're distracting me."

Trying to joke with him would only make him angrier so Zoë decided to stay quiet. He wouldn't tell her why they were going or why she couldn't come along. They weren't going to play rehearsal, she knew that much. He was lying and he hardly ever lied.

When Devan lied, he usually had a good reason, like the time he told his cousin Matt that Zoë might be 'on the spectrum' because she didn't relate to people the same as everybody else.

Zoë related to people just fine, and she related to crickets and burros and snakes better than most people did. She could relate to people better than most people. Period. Whenever she wanted to. She just didn't need to waste her time chitchatting or gossiping or talking about boys like most of the girls she knew. She had better things to do. Like work and catch souls and get to Heaven. Now she couldn't even talk to Devan about it.

She'd looked up 'on the spectrum.' It seemed like it was some kind of DNA thing, except not simple like black hair or green eyes. She had a long talk about it with Bonnie and Arthur. Maybe she'd learn to talk to horses like some people on the spectrum did. She couldn't draw or play the piano, but she could add and subtract like a bandit. Bonnie told her she had the highest I.Q. in her class and not to worry – she wasn't on any spectrum.

After talking with Bonnie, Zoë speculated if Devan had some of his own spectrum, he'd understand better why she had to go to Heaven.

Laurel sat on the pickup's tailgate, without her prosthesis in sight. "You make me nervous, Devan," she snapped. "Carry that pistol – you attract violence."

Devan palmed a small black handgun, hefting it. His voice hard, he said, "Don't be naive," and shoved the gun into his back pocket. "Anybody who risks the lives of millions of people like that? They'll be armed. They might be waiting for us. What if they had some recorders that got us when we were shouting up and down that landslide?"

Zoë edged forward on the step. Landslide? Millions of people? Maybe it *is* a movie he's starring in, she thought, relaxing. Maybe he's telling the truth. Devan must have stage fright. He'd told her he never got stage fright from plays, only movies.

"I'm scared, too," Laurel said.

"As far as we know, we have the advantage. If we're lucky, they don't know we're coming. If they don't review their video clips all the time. Give them another day or two to investigate, who knows? They could get troops up there."

Zoë spoke up from the step, "You don't need a gun, Devan. You've got me. I'm your luck."

"We need a lot of luck, honey."

"I could talk to Inky," Zoë offered.

"Go ahead, sweetie," Devan nodded, "but I wouldn't count on him."

"I talked to Inky about your bruises and sore ribs and you feel fine today. Think about it."

It wasn't just the healing mud that healed him. Sometimes Devan didn't use his head. Still, he looked so handsome in his blue-and-white checked cowboy shirt taut across his wide shoulders, his perfect ears holding his palomino mane back from his serious face.

"Inky and a half a bottle of ibuprofen," Devan said, crawling back under the truck canopy.

A hot gust rose off the field, whirling around the trailer and up into the cottonwoods, snapping a few small branches. It died away just as quickly as it came and the arid silence of the foothills settled around them.

Zoë looked off to the west, watching the gray sky turn blue, wondering why Devan argued with her so much now. If they fought before, it was always playful. Was it Laurel that made him so ornery? He'd never made fun of Inky until she came around.

She could calm him down if she didn't take him too seriously. She'd treat him as if he was acting - he could be. Everybody said he was a good actor. That article in the San Francisco paper he sent home said he had 'comic potential.'

Muffled scraping and banging came from the truck as Devan rearranged the bags and suitcases. Zoë raised her voice. "Remember the time the rattlesnake bit you? Your leg turned green and they almost cut it off?" If Devan spent more time with her, he might even learn to see into Inky's world. Inky had taught her a Lakota snakebite remedy she used to stop the venom from spreading.

After a minute, Devan's garbled voice came out of the camper. "Yeah. That and the three spikes of antivenom they shot into it."

The morning was too beautiful to argue with Devan. The sun sending golden rays through the branches, the sunrise breezes delicate on her face, the smell of worms fresh on the air.

"What about that TV show? They turned you down and I asked Inky and the next day you called and said they hired you? Tell me that was some doctor's medicine."

"Long time ago. They hired Hugh Jackman for the lead. I got the sidekick role. Lot of good my episodes of *Mad Men* and *Night Power* did for me. *The Famished* helped a bit. I just don't like those zombie roles." He leapt off the truck's tailgate and baring his teeth, he lunged at her.

Zoë reared back, widening her eyes and tucking her head down into the collar of her jacket while making a cross with her finger and her spoon.

Laurel smiled at Zoë and shrugged. "He's worried."

Zoë rolled her eyes. "He's grumpy," she said, swallowing another delicious lump of oatmeal before it got cold. Devan had brought her some special chocolate chips from San Francisco, enough to top off her oatmeal and to bake cookies, only she hadn't had time to bake cookies.

All she'd done yesterday was to gather most of the poshent ingredients and come home from work. Oh, yeah, she captured her last soul. The great geranium soul of Mr. J. Well, she'd set him and the others free as soon as her angel fetched her.

Zoë had stuffed the herbs and everything she'd collected into a paper bag and stored them in the pock next to her heart. Won't hurt to keep it warm with my love, she thought.

Setting her empty oatmeal bowl down, Zoë found her favorite pair of socks at the bottom of her clean clothes pouch. They were Devan's Christmas present last year – a multi-colored cotton pair that sizzled on her feet – and she rolled them up to her shins. Too bad she didn't have transparent boots so people could see them.

"I'm going with you, Devan. I don't care what you say about Inky. You need me, you need us, more than a gun." And I need you. She almost said that out loud, but Devan was too cranky. "But who cares if you take a gun." To Laurel, "Everybody around here has guns."

Devan walked to the trailer steps and looked down at Zoë, his eyes weary. In a tired voice, he said, "The bus leaves at 6:17. You'll be on it. Bonnie's all set to meet you when it gets into Vegas at midnight."

Zoë stood up on the top step, her eyes even with his. "You can't make me," she said, sensing she could oppose him until he gave in. "I'll get off and hitchhike back. I'll catch up with you." If he didn't give in and drive her to Anpetu, she'd find him anyway. She had to.

Laurel hugged Zoë and said, "Honey, this is the scariest thing I've ever done. You can't come with us. I can't let you get hurt."

Retreating, she said, "I won't get hurt. Inky will – "

"Forget Inky," Devan snapped. "You're on the bus and staying on it."

Zoë raised her hand to her forehead, angling it like a small awning against the horizontal sunbeams that shot through the peach branches. The sleeve of her jacket slipped down her arm, exposing pale skin etched with rusty freckles. She narrowed her eyes and scowled. "I'm coming back from Heaven to see you both. You know that, don't you?"

"We don't mean that," Laurel said.

"You guys are too serious," Zoë said. "That almost scares me. You need me around."

"We're not acting. It's a bad thing that happened. Maybe the worst."

The worst thing? The worst thing that ever happened was Ruthie. "Who died?"

"Nobody we know of. Yet." Devan lifted Zoë off his lap and set her next to Laurel. Devan stood up and paced, restless as a pit bull. "Listen. Yesterday we found a cavern full of nuclear waste tanks."

"What's that?" Zoë asked.

Laurel's body stiffened against Zoë's legs.

"The poison. Radiation. Nuclear radiation. I told you we'd tell you," Devan snapped. "They use it to make electricity. This is the leftovers. It stays poison for thousands of years. If it gets into your body, you die from cancer. It eats you from the inside out."

Zoë stared at him, then nodded. For the last few years, she'd made dying of any kind her specialty.

"I know about that kind of dying. Mr. Ellis over at the Home where I work? He died from getting eaten from the inside. Only the doctors called it pear sites. He got it on a vacation. You shoulda seen him before he died. All bones and papery green skin. We named him 'The Mummy.'"

A thin smile crossed Devan's mouth. "It's like that, but radiation is the worst poison in the world. Imagine a million green papery people. There's so much poison in those tanks inside Anpetu – "

Zoë jumped up from the step, jabbing Laurel in the forehead with her elbow. "Oh, sorry," she said, rubbing Laurel's head absently. "Anpetu?"

"In a huge cave, inside the mountain."

"I hiked all over Anpetu and I never saw nuclears." This was terrible news. Zoë had planned to release her souls from Anpetu because, on its granite peak, Zoë had felt closest to Heaven.

Her thoughts raced. "Where is it?"

"You can't see it from outside," Devan said. "They hid it way down deep under the earth."

"Who did?" Zoë tried to understand. Why would anyone fill up a mountain with poison? Where would they find so much poison? It had to come from a city. Omaha. Denver. They had to use poison all the time for their rats and cockroaches. They should use traps like Arthur did for prairie dogs.

"We might as well tell her everything," Devan said to Laurel. "She'll try to make her way up there unless...."

"Unless what?" This was Devan's secret, and now she had to know everything, but his nervousness confused her.

Why didn't Inky tell her about this nuclear? He must have known all about the poison inside Anpetu. He sees everything. He probably didn't want to frighten her, or maybe it didn't matter since she was going to Heaven anyway. But when she came back, she didn't want to return to a world flowing with poison rivers, all the fish suffocating and birds flopping on the ground and people turning into green ashes and dying everywhere.

All the tourists in the Black Hills – they'd drive up in their big, farty RV's to see the Presidents. They'd take a sip of water at one of the fountains, and pass out in the parking lot and turn crispy from the inside out.

You'd see all the gamblers and drinkers sprawled on the bars and sawdust floors, money blowing in the poison breezes rising off the mountain.

What about all the little kids on the pony rides on the trails? She couldn't bear the image of children and ponies lying in the woods, their bodies rotting into mummies.

A Rapture might save them, but if they didn't go to church, they'd lie forgotten and dead forever.

What about the coyotes and rabbits? Pictured in her mind, a thousand birds plummeted from the trees, tangling in branches as their bodies dropped under a shower of feathers into the silent pines.

"Everybody's going to die?" Zoë collapsed into Laurel's arms, tears welling over her eyelids.

"Not if we can help it, baby," Laurel said, snuggling Zoë under her handless arm. "That's where we're going. We have to try to stop it."

Zoë sniffled. Confused, she honed in on Laurel's dragon tattoo, caressing it, folding and unfolding the loose skin under the dragon's jaws.

"If we don't stop it, who knows what will happen? We have to try." Devan sat Zoë beside him on the step and said, with the first optimism he'd shown since he came home. "But you know what? Even if we don't stop it, if we play it right, we have a chance to change a lot of things for us. Good things."

Laurel removed her arm from Zoë's dawdling fingers and sat up. "How? What do you mean?"

"Think about it," Devan grinned, standing up, holding his arms out with his palms vertical, as if framing his body for a camera shot. "The guy who exposed the Anpetu Mountain affair," he bowed his head and grinned wider, "his face will be plastered all over the Internet, on every news show in the world. You think a hero like that won't pack every movie theater anywhere? HBO's nothing. This is global."

"I knew it. Like I said. You guys are acting," Zoë said, pouting but almost relieved. They were the best actors she knew. Lots better than anybody on TV. She folded her hands behind her head, observing.

"God, Devan, so this is why you're so eager to climb back down into that radiation pit?" Laurel stood up and faced Devan. "To get famous? You are nuts. It's not worth it."

"It's not just me," he said, stepping in close and taking her chin gently in his fingers. "The woman who exposed Anpetu." He backed away and bowed his upper torso to her, flourishing his arm in a melodramatic spiral "Any album she cuts goes double platinum before it hits the stores." He raised his eyebrows and tilted his face away, cupping his ear toward her.

Laurel sat up. "We're really gonna do this?"

"Yeah. We got a plan. We'll just, you know, implement. We'll be in Wyoming before James opens the website and starts broadcasting the images." He shrugged.

"Maybe Matt should hold off on the tweets, too. You know Twitter's just an excuse for Homeland Security to keep track of everybody." She looked away.

"You think we have to be that paranoid?" Laurel said. "Let's send out normal tweets so they don't suspect anything, even if they can track us."

"Cool," Devan said. "James's building the website now and Matt's calling every environmental group he can think of, Sierra Club, Black Hills Preservation, High Prairie Restoration to give them heads up about something big coming down."

"Can we get Ducks Unlimited on our side? They're totally mainstream."

"They'll be on our side, once they see the facts. If we get into the right blogs, by news time tonight, the whole country will be on our side. Devan Jamming and Laurel Azumaya will be more famous than...Elvis ever was!" Devan waved his arm and grinned.

Zoë chimed in. "More famous than Mickey and Minnie Mouse!"

Devan groaned. "We don't want to be cartoons."

"They're the most famous people in the world. If you're famous, you might as well be famous as them. I'll be famous, too. For a different reason."

Zoë stared at both of them. Devan pulled on one side of his mustache and gazed at the brightening sky. Laurel loved Devan, that was obvious. He loved her, too, but he acted so edgy. Did radiation already get into him? She closed her eyes and prayed. Inky, no radiation. No toxic poison. Keep Devan healthy.

She opened her eyes and stared at Devan, looking for signs of poison.

Everybody rotting from the inside out.

I'll stay just a little while, she thought. Fly faster than light so time doesn't run backwards on me and I'm too late to help stop the radiation.

If anybody could stop the radiation, it would be her, once she'd risen to Heaven.

Ruthie and Inky and Kateri would gather their friends together. With all that Heaven energy, they'd take care of the radiation before one more person caught the sickness.

Then Laurel smiled – a forced smile, Zoë noticed – and hugged Devan. With her cheek against his, Laurel said, "If fame is your carrot, hey, go for it. I don't blame you."

"Not a carrot," he said, pulling away. "It's the chance of a lifetime. To do something real, do it right. If you don't see it that way, might as well call in the government." His eyes locked into Laurel's.

Disturbed by the pinched way they looked at each other, Zoë stood up and joined their hug, her arms barely able to span to the middle of their backs. "If you guys want carrots, I can pack some Peter Rabbit organic baby carrots. I always take them when I go for a long hike."

She turned and started for the trailer, then stopped. "What about the dead tourists and kids and everything? The poison. That's not true, is it? It's part of the movie."

Devan and Laurel dropped their arms and faced Zoë.

"It will be a hell of a movie," Devan said, his lips tight. "Let's hope about three billion people see it by this time tomorrow."

Laurel said, "It's a movie about hell, made in hell."

"Hell? I don't believe in hell," Zoë said.

"We didn't either, till we saw it."

"Is it hot? Hotter than July?"

"No, it's cold. Icy. Sterile. Steel vats lined up in a warehouse like missiles."

"I don't like to go to war movies."

"That's what I like to hear," Devan said. "Because you're going to a place some people call America's Paradise: Las Vegas."

Zoë stared at him.

"Pair a Dice. Get it?

Zoë shook her hed, her lips pursed in disgust. "Everybody gets it, Devan." She didn't want to argue with Devan about hell or Las Vegas. "I'll get the carrots."

Back inside the trailer, she knelt in front of the open refrigerator door, rousting around in the vegetable bin for the carrots, thinking about hell.

She'd never believed in hell – it was something adults used to scare kids. In the church library, she'd seen pictures of hell people standing in orange flames that, she'd heard, burned their skin but never burned them to death. She'd already felt that, on her legs. She didn't understand why Devan called the icy room inside Anpetu hell.

Putting the carrots down, she opened the oatmeal pot on the stove inhaling the sweet aroma. The oats had melted into gray goo, just the way she loved it: hot and slippery. She dipped her spoon in and lifted it overhead, spilling the gummy oats into her mouth.

Wasn't hell supposed to have an angel for its king? The smartest angel, one even smarter than God? He wanted to be God. Only, God was older, older than anything, and He didn't want a partner. He said one King of Heaven was enough and he didn't need somebody smarter than him telling him what to do.

What was his name? Zoë trickled the last of the chocolate chips into the gunky cereal and stirred them in, marbling it with rich brown swirls. Lucifer. She remembered. Satan. Old Beezelbug. Devil. Ha. He had a lot of names. Old Nick. She laughed. Old Nick, Saint Nick... people always got names mixed up.

She'd talk to Devan about it, if he could get his mind off the radiation long enough to have a sit-down and jokey talk.

Eighteen

"I'M THE ONE WHO'S SAFE!"

With their legs swinging back and forth, Devan and Laurel sat on the open gate of the truck bed, sipping coffee while Zoë savored her chocolate-swirl oatmeal, thinking.

Images flashed into her mind of dead kids floating in the motel swimming pools and ponies lying with their stiff legs pointed straight out. She forced the oatmeal down.

She had too much on her mind so she stopped thinking at all. She'd learned how to do that years ago, when her father used to make her sit by herself under the table while he and his friends played cards all night.

She'd shut off her thinking and stay wide awake, alert for a dirty boot toe darting at her head or a grimy hand clawing for her hair.

After sitting cramped for hours, dodging manure-caked boots at the end of stained jeans and ragged work pants, she longed for the fresh air outside, rainy, snowy, dusty, anything outdoors. Before morning light, the men's legs had flopped to the sides and she'd crawl out between chairs and around sprawled bodies. She'd find a soft place in the barn and curl up, breathing hay-sweet air, then, she'd fall asleep.

Devan interrupted her daydream. "You get why you can't go with us?" he said.

Zoë decided she could act as well as Devan. "I know you want me to stay safe."

Zoë picked up her cup of mint tea and held it under her nose, inhaling the spicy chlorophyll, her eyes on the pinkening sky.

Salmony cloud tatters scudded westward before unraveling over the mountains.

She shot a cold look at Devan over the lip of her steaming teacup. "It's too 'risky' for you," Zoë challenged. "I'm the one who's safe."

"Nobody's safe," Laurel said, "as long as those containers are inside the mountain. We think an earthquake struck in the last week or so. If another one hits."

"No, I'm safe," Zoë insisted. She was tired of reminding them that she'd be leaving the Earth as soon as her angel showed up. She straightened her spine and jutted her jaw, nodding her head for emphasis. "You have to take me with you."

At an impasse, nobody moved. It's too quiet, Zoë thought.

The normal cheerful morning sounds of hungry birds and incessant wind scratching through the cottonwoods were absent, as if on alert for a huge change coming from the north, from Anpetu. Rain was due tonight or tomorrow early. Rain was always due until July. Birds knew weather. They were probably sleeping late, saving energy to resist a hailstorm or tornado.

An owl hooted.

That was it: the songbirds were smart, hiding until the daylight blinded the owls. For a moment, the idea relieved Zoë. But why was the owl hunting in the light?

She jumped up, sloshing tea out of the cup onto her hand. It didn't hurt, but someone better clown around before everyone started crying. "Ouch. Hotter'n hell."

Shaking his head, a smile softened Devan's face for the first time that morning,

"It's not funny," she said, pretending to be upset. "I don't want to stain my new blouse." She hadn't worn a new blouse since Bonnie had insisted at her THIRTEENTH birthday party almost three years ago.

Zoë dropped her cup and held her arms out, shaking tea drops off her jacket sleeve. She started to wipe the spilled tea on her jeans until she remembered the sundress she'd substituted for her regular clothes. She looked down but saw no tea blotches on her skirt.

"You sure look pretty today, Zoë," Devan said. "You'll be the prettiest girl on the bus. The beautiful way you colored your hair will make you the prettiest in all Las Vegas. You'll fit right in, too." Devan took Laurel's mug, retrieved Zoë's cup from the grass, and set them with his on the steps.

"I'll be the prettiest *girl* on Anpetu, is what I'll be." Catching Devan's eyes turning toward Laurel, she continued, "Laurel will be the most beautiful *woman*."

Laughing, Laurel stood up. "You two stop your pissiness. We have to do a big thing. Now, Zoë we can't have you around to distract –"

"Distract? Distract? How do you know that? I'm the quickest, most invisible girl you've ever met. I can disappear in a blink. Ask anybody in Spring Creek."

Zoë reached back to bring her long hair over her shoulder. "See this braid? It's French. And Fench people can hide in plain sight. Even if their hair shines like firelight."

Tree shadow had peeled away from the trailer and lay shrinking on the grass. The sun ratcheted up the heat a few notches and silvery cottonwood leaves fluttered, unperturbed by the approach of day's dry winds.

"Getting late," Devan said. Picking up Zoë's backpack, he tossed it into the pickup bed and rammed the gate shut. "Let's go." He offered Laurel one arm and crooked his elbow for Zoë to take the other.

"Do we have enough gas?" Laurel asked.

"I'll fill up at Borman's after we drop Zoë off."

"I'll ride my bike," Zoë said, bending over her Trek and jerking it out of the grass. "I know the way."

Devan squinted at his watch. "It's 5:49. You'll never make it to the bus. Besides, we have to buy the ticket."

"My bike's my ticket. So long," she said, tossing her beskirted leg over the seat. "See you at Anpetu."

"Zoë!" Devan grabbed for the handlebars but she maneuvered past him, laughing. She stopped ten yards away and when he lifted his foot, she crowed and pedaled a few yards.

"You're acting like a puppy. I don't want to play. Get in the truck and let's go." Devan turned and stalked to the driver's door. "C'mon, Laurel." He climbed in, slammed his door, and turned the engine over. In neutral, Devan punched the accelerator, racing the engine, and Zoë's face went blank.

"We'll see you in three days, at most," Laurel pleaded. "Please, go to the bus. Ride as fast as you can."

Zoë called, "It's a long way to Anpetu. You better get going before the poison starts leaking out and making everybody sick. If I was you, I wouldn't want that to happen."

She leaned over and tucked the bottom of her skirt up into her shorts, then she stomped on the pedal and pumped down the lane, her front tire spitting stings of gravel onto her bare shins and knees.

Zoë kicked her bike hard, stirring up a dust cloud behind her to camouflage her flight. Shouting over her shoulder as she passed through the front gate. "I'll see you up on Anpetu."

Nineteen

ANPETU BOUND

Two minutes later, before Zoë arrived at the end of the lane, Devan's pickup pulled alongside.

"You're gonna get a ticket," Devan said out of his window. "Eighteen miles an hour. You're riding on the wrong side, too."

That's the Devan she loved. "So you can talk to me while you drive. Tell me 'Let's go to Anpetu.'"

"Get in the truck, Zoë. Right now. The bus leaves in a few minutes.

Zoë rode on, pedaling harder. "No way."

Calling from behind her now, he said, "I mean it."

In a few seconds, the truck caught up with her and Devan leaned out his window. Zoë's crickets pealed as she locked her eyes onto his narrowed gaze. A wan and empty glow surrounded Devan's body like snowy sky. She hoped he'd prepared his soul well for the trip to Anpetu.

Devan said, "You've got to do what I say. What would I tell Bonnie and Arthur if you get hurt?"

"What about you?" she rejoined. "Would you care if I got hurt?"

"Don't be silly," he grumbled. "I'd hate it."

She felt the love in Devan's voice. It sounded like the lion love St. Augustine showed his orphans. He acted tough with them and made them do whatever he ordered. They all became knights who stole the blood of Jesus from some evil people and gave it, boiling and bubbling inside a crystal bottle, to the Pope. He made them all saints. She wasn't exactly an orphan, but she'd like to see some dead saint's bubbling blood someday.

She didn't want to hurt Devan, but she knew what she had to do.

"Give me the ticket money," she said. "I know a short cut to the bus stop. I'll be there in fourteen minutes."

Devan stared at her. "You mean it?"

"Would I lie to you? I bushwhack the abandoned railroad berm until I get to the cattle trail. It's not muddy today, so I'll be in Spring Creek by the time you're on highway 4."

"Don't fib."

Zoë's face fell. He knew her as well as anybody, better than Bonnie, even better than Inky. "Never," she said, impressed by his sixth sense.

It wasn't really a fib, or anything like that. She'd do everything he wanted, only not just when he said, or how. She grinned and whipped her hair around her head, beaming. Anyway, everything she ever said to him meant "I love you, Devan." So, how could she ever lie to him?

Devan said something to Laurel and slowed the truck and stopped. Zoë braked and coasted to Devan's door. He reached out, waving two bills.

"Two hundred. Oughta cover it. Leave you plenty for pop and lunch."

She took the money and jammed it in her pocket, then stretched over her handlebars and circled Devan's neck with her arm. Laurel slid over to reach around Devan's shoulders and hug Zoë. They held each other for a moment until Devan jerked his head away.

"Get going, Zoë. I'll call you on Bonnie's cell tomorrow morning. I love you, Zo."

"I love you, too, Dev. You guys be careful in that big movie you're making. Don't get poisoned. Nice to meet you, Laurel." Zoë aimed her front wheel toward the side of the road. She bounced across a shallow ditch and pedaled into the field.

"Bye," she called over her shoulder.

Laurel's voice came back. "You forgot your backpack!"

"I got everything I need in my coat," Zoë shouted. She waved her arm over her head, mumbling to herself "and I'll see you in a few minutes but you won't see me."

She stood up, pumping her quadriceps with all the power of a mustang in flight, throwing her feet hard into the pedals, holding her body vertical while the bike frame canted from side to side between her thighs.

Devan didn't know about the bike path she'd worn from his trailer into town. She jolted through the alfalfa a hundred yards until she met her trail, a straight shot between Wendell's Ridge and Devil's Backbone. She'd be out of sight of Devan in three minutes.

Thinking she was heading for the south end of town and the bus stop, Devan would drive east to Borman's to gas up. If she had it timed right, she'd arrive just before he did.

She counted on one bit of luck: They'd both have to go to the bathrooms to unload all the coffee they drank before they took the bumpy road to Anpetu. When they did, she'd sneak into the truckbed and hide under the blankets and tarp.

Inky make their bladders ache.

Exulting in the clear sun, oxygen flooding her cells, Zoë hollered out loud. "All right! Yooooooo!"

The only animal she knew could outrun her and her bike on a normal day was an antelope. Today, she would race an antelope and win. She drove ahead, gaining traction with every switch up through all twenty-one gears, never looking behind, forcing air out of her lungs with every right-side down-pedal.

She glanced back. Devan's pickup had disappeared, so she bore down on the pedals. Sweat broke out on her chest and she unzipped her jacket to let the soft breeze pour over her chest and stomach in her favorite caress in the world.

In fact, when she cruised her bike like this, all her pains disappeared, even the ankle ache she got from fending off Ketchup yesterday. She might as well be in Heaven. Except for Ruthie.

Zoë came to the gravel road two miles from the bus stop. She turned and stomped down, the bike's chain whistling as it whirled over the sprockets.

She sped across the gravel, standing up the last quick mile to town. As she sailed down the long slope toward Spring Creek, she sat, waved both hands over her head, and whooped again.

Leaving the road, she sped into the ramshackle neighborhood where most of the off-rez Lakota lived. She knew every back alley and secret path between houses and stores and all the empty garages and barns in town.

She raced down a narrow alley, heading toward the paved street, her jacket flying out like an eagle's tail, her bike skidding on the grass.

If anybody saw her, they'd wonder how a girl could ride as fast as a lightning bolt.

Back on smooth Highway 131, Spring Creek's main street, Zoë felt familiar chills run up and down her legs, spiraling over her arms and back, as she anticipated the total freedom she knew was Heaven's greatest gift. Flying to Heaven at warp speed might be the only thing more thrilling than gliding on her bike no-hands down the middle of a newly paved empty road with a wind at her back.

Pumping so hard in top gear that the pedals spun by themselves, Zoë leaned and turned left at the glittering pyramid of rose quartz chunks that marked the town limits. Gliding down the empty street behind Borman's store and gas station, she pulled a wheeley and slammed on her rear brakes, skidding into the parking lot. Zoë dragged one foot on the gravel and let her bike drift a hundred eighty degrees around until she came to a stop.

She hopped off and ran skipping beside her bike the few yards to the storage shed. It was usually locked because any time they tried to keep beer or pop in it, it disappeared.

Her luck held. The shed's metal door was bent but Zoë pulled it open and rolled her bike inside. She'd pick it up when she came back from Heaven. Even when she could fly, she'd always love to ride.

She peeked around the corner of the building and there was Devan's truck twenty yards away, parked facing away.

Perfect.

She'd sneak up and jump in under the canopy.

Edging around the dumpster to get a clearer look, she noticed that she had to pee. Too much mint tea. She was tempted to squat, but she saw that the truck was empty. She didn't have time to do anything but dash and jump.

She took one last look and fled from her hiding place. At the truck, ignoring her sore knee, she flopped over the tail gate like a high jumper.

Scrambling under the blue tarp Devan used to protect his bags from dust, she condensed her body behind Devan's seat. He'd never see her, and if Laurel looked back, what was another lump in the corner?

Snuggled into Devan's down sleeping bag, Zoë tented a corner of the tarp into a breathing hole. She aimed it toward the window so she could watch the sky.

She heard their voices approach.

"Sure you got everything?" Laurel.

"Extra water. Four power bars. Gum. Got you for luck. All I need."

What? Zoë stopped herself from shouting "I'm your luck. Not her!" She grit her teeth and held her body still, quivering.

Devan had lost his senses. Must be poison running through his blood, confusing him. Laurel's his bad luck. He'll see who his good luck is.

The truck doors slammed, rocking the bed. Zoë settled herself for the long ride. The truck bounced out of the pitted gravel lot and turned onto the asphalt. Zoë kept her ears peeled, but she could only hear the hum of the tires and the scraping of wind through the canopy.

To amuse herself, Zoë studied the blue shadows on the underside of the tarp. Six inches from her face they undulated, obscuring the light in a web of crumpled waves.

This is how a fish sees the sky, she thought, like a rough ceiling. If you were a fish, you'd have to be brave to leap through it after bugs. Well, if you were hungry and a fly tempted you, you'd jump. Close your gills, thrust your fins against the water, and fly. You'd slice through the ceiling into endless air. You couldn't breathe.

Zoë shivered. Her eyes darted to the spy hole where she could see high cirrus patrolling the robin's egg blue sky.

I wonder if they have air in Heaven? They must. If they didn't, why would Inky encourage me to go someplace I couldn't breathe? I better ask him. He doesn't tell me things unless I ask the right question. He should have told me about the nuclear toxic.

She crossed her arms.

If worse comes to worst, they'll have to teach me to spirit-breathe. They want me in Heaven, so they'll help. Too late to worry about anything now.

Relaxed again, she settled back to watch the clouds.

Zoë loved riding in Devan's pickup bed. She usually sat up, swooping through the air with the back and side windows open. As far as she knew, everybody loved riding in cars and trucks, zipping through the air in metal boxes, cruising like angels a few feet above the Earth.

Now huddled under the tarp, cuddled in a sleeping bag, she touched the poshent sack through her jacket. Out the window, the morning star perched right above the hilltops.

A few miles into the journey, the wind turned warm and she began to sweat. A fountain of heat rose from it into her throat and poured down her chest onto her belly. It oozed over her hips and thighs like warm baby oil, taking her breath away.

The risen sun had staked out the eastern sky as its turf. The west, where Zoë watched, was somewhat under the spell of the soft edge of night. The exposed granite of the foothills glowed in brass and fuschia. The wind lay low, stirring small flurries of topsoil, gathering them up to form the coming day's veil of dust.

A gust of wind struck the cab on the driver's side forcing the truck to swerve, rocking Zoë sideways, back and forth. The creaking of the truck springs and the wind whining through the window the only sound.

The truck climbed for miles through sparsely treed canyons, following the road's swells along curves meandering toward the steep mountain grades. Zoë noticed a few small herds of buffalo wandering across dry pastures, nosing the earth for the volunteer wheatgrass and the native sedge.

Zoë edged deeper into the corner and carefully propped herself up, still cloaked by the tarp. Hot wind stabbed through the window and whipped against her cheeks. She gripped the tarp around her face so that it wouldn't flap, and attract curious eyes from the cab.

She used to sit like that, on her mother's lap, when she and Ruthie took bus trips to Rapid City or Scotts Bluff. She tucked herself under Ruthie's chin, the knot of her mother's scarf brushing her cheeks, both of their faces almost hanging out the bus window. They rode for hours, watching the mountains and the canyons and the cattle, never talking, never moving, even to pee.

Demvan's truck hit a pothole, throwing Zoë so high her head bumped the tarp. She laughed at the weightless tickle in her stomach and nearly peed her pants.

Ruthie had prepared Zoë well for her long journey to infinity. Because of the good training Ruthie gave her on the buses, Zoë figured she could fly to Heaven, and hold her pee until she arrived, no matter how far it was. In fact she had to pee right then, but she could hold it. Anpetu wasn't so far away.

THE CLIMB

Twenty

WAKANDA

The lower branches of the firs surrounding the Anpetu parking area sagged under a thick buff of dust. It was only June, but with the years of drought and little rain this spring, a blanket of powder lay on everything.

Zoë pulled her skirt down and stepped back from the stream she'd made in the dust, amazed at how much pee she could hold. Birdsong pealed through the aspens woven into the firs circling the graveled clearing.

Across the parking lot, a wizened man sat against a lone lodgepole pine tree, looking up into the branches. He wore faded dungarees and a denim jacket with frayed sleeves. His silver hair ended in a blunt cut behind his neck.

"Listen," he said to Zoë as she approached.

She stopped and cocked her ears. The wind swung aspen branches against each other, rattling them like chicken bones clacking in a mobile.

"Pretty," she said.

"Wind talks in so many tongues you can't understand them all," the man said. "What do you think it's saying now?"

Examining his dark, creased face for signs of angelic or saintly virtue, Zoë said, "Some kind of song." She propped a hand behind her ear and closed her eyes. "I hear it now – it's my mother's song: 'Breezes high, zephyrs low, wind in the trees, hear it blow.'"

The old man eased himself up. His hands hung at his sides, motionless, reaching nearly to his knees. Even in his boots, he stood only an inch taller than Zoë.

"Same song I hear," the man said. His coffee-colored eyes sunk into his face under white eyebrows that nearly met over the bridge of his nose.

She liked him, but he wasn't her angel. Not big enough to carry her through the universe without dropping her. But what did she know about angels' muscles? They could make miracles so what difference did the size of his body make?

"You're the one showed Devan and Laurel the bones?"

"That's my family up there." He nodded his chin up toward the mountain, his voice hard and quiet. "Did you tell anyone?"

Taken aback, Zoë said, "No. Why?"

He stared at her as if she was about to betray him and his entire family.

Unfazed, she said, "Are they cursed?"

He turned his head, gazing up at the mountain. "Could be," the old man said. He tilted his head as he turned and peered at her with his nostrils slightly flared, his eyebrows quivering.

"You don't mess with people's bones in case the family put a curse on them. Everybody knows that. Devan said you showed them the bones and he fell down a landslide into a radiation place."

His face flattened. He looked at her with disinterest, neither acknowledging what she said, nor ignoring it.

"Your mother's up there?" Zoë asked.

Sounding friendlier, he said, "Yes. Others, too."

Finally, Zoë thought.

It wasn't only the fact that he honored his mother's bones or that the narrow bridge of his nose reminded her of Kateri's long nose. She liked him because she could tell he didn't care about anything except doing what he had to do. Like her. She wanted him to trust her.

"I want to show you something, but you can't tell anybody. Nobody," Zoë said.

"If you want."

"You won't tell?" she asked as she placed her hand inside her jacket and rummaged in a pocket near her heart.

"Nobody to tell," he said.

Zoë took hold of Ruthie's rib bone and wiggled it out of its lodging in her most secret pocket. She'd clutched and rubbed and wrung it so much in her hands that her palms had worn a saddle in the bone near the fractured, but thanks to Zoë's strokes and kisses, smooth tip.

Sensing someone watching, Zoë backed further behind the tree trunk and peeked around. Devan had unpacked almost everything from the truck and Laurel was out of sight.

Zoë turned to the severe but somehow warm old man, and motioned for him to come closer. She held Ruthie's bone on her palm. It was the color of chalk and the size of a small baton. She'd shown only one other person: Lakshmi Parker, before she moved to Omaha last year.

"My mother's rib."

The old man's eyes narrowed but he didn't move.

"I dug up her coffin a few years ago. It took me a month, I had to be careful. Every night, slice up the sod, dig deeper. The casket was metal, but I got the lid off."

Zoë stopped and wiped her eyes. "Nothing but bones and her red silk dress torn into pieces." She glanced around the tree, but Devan and Laurel had gone somewhere. "I took her head. Still have it in a secret place. But I wanted to have her with me. So I broke off her heart rib. It snapped easy."

Zoë pointed out the clefts cutting up from the large end of the bone. "I carry it next to my heart. My mother's Ruthie. It's gonna be strange when I see her in person and show her this bone."

The old man motioned for Zoë to sit beside him.

She replaced her mother's rib and squatted at his feet, saying, "I can't stay too long. I have things I have to find in the woods." She nodded toward the stream that trickled out of a culvert, disappearing under the carpet of rounded boulders and dusty foliage. "Things that grow by the water."

She had everything she needed for her poshent except fresh crawdaddies and leek rootlets. Wild leeks and ramps grew everywhere in these high mountains and the narrow green banks of the struggling rivulet looked like good leek hunting grounds.

She'd use the stinky dead crawdaddies she captured the other day if she had to, but she expected fresh would make a more powerful poshent. She'd seen tiny crawdaddies in thin Anpetu streams last summer, so with luck, she'd find a couple today.

She was glad the old Indian knew her secret about Ruthie's bone. It was only fair because she was about to learn his. Maybe if his parent's grave was dry and nobody else knew about it, she'd move Ruthie's skull up here. When she returned from Heaven, she reminded herself.

"Hey, Leo, you asleep?" Devan's voice crackled in the mountain silence.

"Is that your name?" Zoë asked.

"Yeah."

"Mine's Zoë. Ehawee's my other name."

The old man stretched his arm out to Zoë. "Leo Pace," he said. "Wakanda."

"Hello, Wakanda." They touched fingertips in a gesture unfamiliar to Zoë. He'd cut his long nails into rounded caps. "Oglalla, right? Man of power and magic."

"Hunkpapa. More like Man who don't screw up too bad, be okay."

The man's flabless jowls quivered when he sat up and shouted to Devan. "I'm awake."

"I've got a pack for you," Devan called. "Not too heavy. Some ropes and walkie-talkies."

"Sure," Wakanda said. "You ready to go?" His voice carried an air of patience and calm.

Zoë watched this exchange, pleased that Wakanda was relaxed, unlike Devan. She'd watched from behind the ferns beside the parking lot as his mood had darkened even further.

"Few more minutes. My cousin's almost here with the Hazmat suits."

She couldn't see him but his voice, hoarse as if he'd been shouting, or crying, his voice edged closer to Zoë and the Hunkpapa.

Puzzled, she looked at Wakanda. He knew more than she did about Devan's plans. Maybe he'd tell her something. In a low voice, she whispered, "Hazmat suits?"

Wakanda shrugged, his walnut-brown palms up. "I told 'em they don't need 'em."

More curious, she asked, "But it's toxic poison, right?"

"Could be. I don't think we have to worry. The tanks looked new."

She wanted to sit down with him and get the whole story, but impatient as ever, Devan called, "Leo, come on."

She shrugged and Wakanda shrugged back. As she turned, he reached into his chest pocket and pulled out an orange plastic prescription bottle. Unscrewing the lid, he tapped three white capsules into his palm, popped them into his mouth and gulped.

Zoë knit her eyebrows and plumbed her lips.

He said, "Oxycodone. Painkiller. Feel like I'm sixty again."

"You swallow without water?"

"Why not?"

"You can call me Ehawee, if you want. My old boss at the Home called me that. It means Laughing Girl."

The old man nodded. "I say that Hyaa-whey." He growled the Hunkpapa pronunciation, pleasing Zoë.

"They don't know I'm here. Don't tell, okay?"

Leo shrugged. Zoë whispered, "Thank you." Smiling, she spun on the ball of her foot in the one ballet turn she knew and loved - a pas de deux.

A dozen black and gold butterflies fluttered around Zoë's head as if guiding her eyes toward the truck. She peeked around the tree again. Laurel appeared from the cab wearing her prosthesis with its Glinda wands at full extension. They gleamed like polished knives in the sunlight.

Laurel said to Devan, "I'll carry Leo's pack. He got awful tired when we climbed up the other day."

"He made it back up the landslide about as well as I did. He can handle a twenty-five pound pack. Besides," Devan continued, "you have to carry your suit, the Geiger counter, and one of the ropes."

"That leaves one suit, one rope, a couple of lights. Not much for you."

"Why are you so protective of the old man? He can handle a small pack."

"I guess I'm getting nervous again," Laurel said.

The rods on Laurel's prosthesis began to slide back into their housing. The machine whined its resistance, and the rods reasserted themselves, as if they couldn't make up their minds.

Devan said, "I have to carry the pistol, my 30.06, the oxygen tanks, another rope, our water."

"What about Matt? He can carry some. We'll need him even if Leo hauls up one pack."

Zoë bent low and eased away from the tree. She climbed down the parking lot embankment and bent over, she shuffled back toward the truck. She knelt at the edge of the lot, peering through the uncut weeds and budded raspberry canes.

The coast was clear. Devan's back was turned and Laurel was in the stinky outhouse.

Zoë dashed to the pickup, boosted herself up on the tailgate and scooted under the camper lid, out of the sun. She noticed Wakanda slumped against the tree again. The butterflies had abandoned Zoë and bobbed in demented circles and figure eights around the old man's drowsing head.

The sound of tires crunching the parking lot gravel drew Zoë's attention. From her seat inside the camper, she saw only a large shadow pull up beside Devan's truck. Careful to stay out of sight, she climbed through the window and peaked around the fender. Devan and Laurel had already reached the door of a dusty blue SUV with half a dozen long antennas quivering on the roof.

"Matt. You made it," Devan said. "Got everything?"

"No problem, dude. We're slammin." Matt's voice sounded like a mixture of a girl's and a TV newsman's, giddy and bossy at the same time. "You must be Laurel."

"Hi, Matt. Thanks for your help. We couldn't do it without you," she said.

"Don't I know it." He laughed, then wrinkling his forehead, Matt said, "How're you doin'?"

"We're cool."

Matt threw up his hands and grinned. "Let's do it, dude," he said, climbing out of his SUV and walking with Devan to the rear.

"You sure changed your attitude about me being wigged out," Devan said.

"You are wigged out, man. Look at your woman's face. She's inside out. I'm upside down. Listen, I thought it over. Just by being here, the nukes have clusterfucked the Hills. We might as well raise hell and get the fuck outta here as soon as we can. We're done here, I'm off for Ontario. Way up."

"Damn, Matt."

"Let's do it, bro."

"Did you bring the web cams?"

"I got everything. Take me half an hour to set up."

"Everything? The .38?"

"No. Like I said, I needed another day, unless you wanted me to boost one. You didn't, so I didn't."

They walked behind Matt's SUV and Zoë heard them mumbling about 'phones' and 'rigs.' When Laurel followed them, Zoë jumped down from the tailgate, walking backwards arcing across the lot until she came to the shade of Wakanda's tree. She plunked herself down beside him out of sight of Laurel and Devan and inspected the wrinkled sleeping face.

One of his eyes popped open, then the other. Zoë started, then chuckled. "You weren't sleeping!"

"I was dreaming about my dog," the old man said, coming fully awake. "He was barking at a black sun."

Zoë considered the meaning of the dream, then said, smiling, "If I was a dog, I'd bark at a black sun, too."

Wakanda chuckled. "Guess I would, too." A cell phone blurted. Wakanda reached into his pants pocket and extracted his phone. After the second bleat, he said, "Leo."

Zoë heard a tiny voice squeaking out.

"Just about," he said. "Come to the west parking lot in, say, two three hours."

The other voice squawked something.

Wakanda replied, "No. Latest, be here in three. You wait for me I ain't back.

Opening his eyes again, he said, "I need some water."

Zoë dug into her jacket and brought out her stainless pint bottle.

He swallowed and said, "Thanks. Problem is, this earthquake. Wrecked the burial chamber. Cracked the wall and the bag fell down the landslide. Buried under the rock. Lucky if I find it."

Zoë connected Wakanda's word 'landslide' with the landslide inside the mountain that bruised Devan's ribs and butt. She sipped some water and nodded, feeling she understood almost the whole story now. "Did you fall down the landslide, too? Like Devan?"

Shaking his head, the old man said, "I rode it down. He fell through the hole in the wall. That's how we saw the tanks."

"What bag?"

"Just a bag."

"Sure."

"Well, you keep quiet and I will. It's my family's old things. Lots of memories there. Gold from the Spanish. Way back before anybody's time."

"Oh. What about the toxic poison?"

"I ain't worried about radiation. I'm way too old."

Zoë estimated that Wakanda was at least seventy, maybe seventy three. "You're not that old," she said. "I know old people, real old. They couldn't climb a mountain. I bet you're only seventy or seventy three."

He groaned. "I pass a hundred first, before I see my seventies again. Now, let me rest. Remember, stay out of my way, Ehawee." His head fell to the side and he snorted.

Zoë grinned. Just like the old guys at the Home.

Twenty-one

SPYING

Hunkering beside Devan's truck, Zoë listened to Laurel and Devan quibble.

"Devan, this isn't like you. Take it easy."

Zoë stood up and spied through the dusty windows of the camper cap.

Devan checked his watch. "We're going to make this as fast as we can. Shoot some video and pics, get em onto the website. Facebook it into the hands of news channels all over the world. Matt's going to start tweeting as soon as we get him some video. He'll upload it and in a minute, the video will be playing on a billion phones. Everywhere."

Matt swung a rope over his head. "Yep," he said.

"We're leaving the state as soon as we get out," Devan said to him. "Got room to take you with us to Wyoming, if you want."

"I like Ontario," Matt said. "Third cousin up there. Lives on a lake. Plenty of fish. No more snow than here."

"We'll have to move fast. They'll chopper troops in as soon as my video comes up on their YouTube monitors and they figure out where we are. Better dismantle your antennas."

"Soon as I broadcast. No antennae, no streaming. Don't worry. I run, only spike you'll see will be Saint Christopher on my dashboard."

"I thought they ditched him," Laurel said. "Too many accidents or something."

"That's Italy. He's always done right by me," Matt said. He heaved a bag onto the ground, then gently placed a machine on it. "Okay.

Let's do the check-off. Fuckin' Guard was good for something other than getting my ass shot in Kabul."

Zoë crawled under the SUV, squirming over pebbles until she found a perfect spot to watch from, beside the rear wheel. She wiped dust from her eyes and squeezed her nose against a sneeze.

Matt began calling out names like an auctioneer at the Shannon County fair horse auction.

"Two Hazmat radiation protection suits. One a uranium mine inspector outfit with soft helmet. One full containment suit with oxygen tank, soft helmet, radiation sensor embedded in the visor, built-in radio transmitter-receiver."

The tan legs of the suits dangled flat and empty a few feet from Zoë's nose. The booties attached to the legs reminded her of the jammies she wore so long Bonnie had to cut off the bottoms and sew socks onto them so she could keep her feet warm on winter nights.

"How much did that cost?"

"That one? Half the cash you gave me, bro."

"My month's advance for the Judas job. Good use for those 30 pieces of silver."

Matt continued, flinging out names while he tossed objects into the open gym bags that lay on the gravel. "Two fifty foot classic hemp ro-de-o lariats. Two polypro extra long sleeve shirts. Sorry, Laurel. They didn't have mediums or smalls."

"Gets damn cold underground," Devan said. A package landed in the bag.

"Wish you'd bought some fashion colors," Laurel said. "I like scarlet blush."

Matt droned on. "One black extra large polypro long johns. One medium. Take the rest of this stuff, Laurel. Gently."

Laurel stood a few feet from Zoë's face. Rips in Laurel's cross trainers revealing buttery little toes with violet nails.

"Three WalMart special Maglite flashlights."

"I can see what you've got, Matt," Devan interjected. "We better get going."

"Don't blame you, bro. Cut me a smidge'a slack, hey?"

Devan bent down and zipped one of the gym bags, his broad butt facing Zoë.

"Okay, here's the heart of the matter," Matt said. "One Sony digital dual vid and webcam, infrared, 360 minutes battery life, five waterproof vid cubes, one indestructible titanium case. Headband one. Headband two."

"Two?"

"For your phone, dude. Backup. We're all about backup here."

"Did you check the camera?" Devan asked.

"It works, sarge." Matt laughed. "Not only that, I found a mini Konica 35 millimeter dig-cube video camera with infrared lens attached. Zoom to 150. Back up. You're set, bro."

"What's this?" Laurel nodded at the rifle Matt propped against the truck.

"That's one sweet tool. My own personal field-proofed Remington 30.06."

"A pistol's not enough?" she said.

"Gotta be prepared," Devan said. "You don't know these people."

"Might be bears or lions up there," Matt said. "Mountain lions are coming back to the Hills big time. Killed a tourist last summer. No big loss, but still...."

Zoë had seen mountain lions every year since she lived on her own. She would sit for hours in the foothills, watching boulders change color under the moving clouds and sun, waiting for animals to appear.

Three times in three different places, always in the evening of a summer day, a mountain lion strolled by her. Zoë held her breath, barely moving her awed eyes to follow the lions. They moved silently, all muscle and tawny fur rippling, shadows the color of slanted light. After they passed and she let herself inhale, their tangy musk floated in the air for a whole minute.

Once she crept after a lion, foolish, she thought, but she wanted to let his smell soak into her skin and hair. She found his den and sat in it for ten minutes, her teeth chattering. For days afterward, dogs and horses fled when she came close.

Matt jumped down from his truck, his boot heels striking the gravel and sending two clusters of dust spinning toward Zoë's face. She recoiled, banging the back of her head on the axle.

"Oh." She clapped her hand over her mouth and ducked, gritting her teeth.

Matt's enthusiastic voice covered the sound of Zoë's exclamation. "Here's the capper, kids. Bullet proof vests."

Zoë rubbed her hair, then examined her fingers. Grease.

"Good going, Matt."

"Army Navy Surplus. Rapid City's finest department store."

"It fits," Laurel said. "How does it work?"

"Mine, too," Devan said. "Little tight in the pecs...."

Laurel's feet turned toward Devan's and lifted on their toes. Was she kissing him?

Devan and Laurel made small grunting sounds, then Zoë heard the crackle of Velcro closing.

"You're crooked. Let me help." Matt's knees nearly touched Devan's.

The dull shriek of Velcro tearing loose, then the tiny snippy snapping of its closing.

"Now you're half bionic, like me," Laurel said.

"Almost state of the art Kevlar," Matt announced. "Five years old but better'n we had in Baghdad in '06. Good as what we had in Kandahar. Guaranteed to stop a .44 slug from twenty feet. Don't get any closer, kids. Special carbon thread woven in to protect our men and women in close quarters combat. Saving lives as we speak in the hidden quarters of the empire."

"Killer," Devan said.

Laurel flinched.

"Still, we need these vests ... we're in more trouble than I want to handle." Devan zipped shut and picked up the other bag. "Let's go. Get this thing done."

A few feet from Zoë's nose, the bag rose up from the ground like an oblong black thundercloud.

Devan's feet pivoted and started off. With her temple flat on the ground, Zoë could see a thin green line of color from the bushes across the lot filling the space between Devan's boot and the gravel.

Matt called, "Dev, you wanna get this thing on half the phones in the world, right? CNN by news time tonight?"

"Of course."

"Now, don't take this the wrong way. If I lead with a topless shot of your lady. Better, if I take her pulling one of those suits on over the buff, you know, maybe show some nipple."

Devan coughed. "Stop playing around, Matt. We gotta go."

Laurel said, "Sex sells. We wanna get those googlin' geeks watching and forwarding like madmen, don't we?" She sounded giddy.

"The tanks will be enough." Devan had reached the front of the truck. Underneath, Zoë squirmed around to see everything she could.

"Nobody will notice old gray tanks," Matt claimed. "Should I wear my hat?" Laurel tipped her new white Stetson back and tilted her hip. She wiggled her shoulders and flashed a wide-open smile toward the men.

Devan said, "Sun's pretty much gone from this side of the valley, but, hey, wear anything you want."

"Come on, Matt," Laurel said. Her prosthesis whined as the rods emerged and clicked when Laurel locked them down.

"Geeks see metal and plastic all day long. You think they want to look at your hand?"

Devan grunted. "You two stop fooling around. We gotta get up there. You're gonna have to run back, Matt. Save your energy."

"Lighten up, Dev," Laurel said. "It's only life and death." She giggled. To Zoë her voice sounded weak and tiny – she was scared.

"I am serious, cuz," Matt said. "Dead serious. You want millions to check out the video? A little teaser with Laurel will slam the server down in Spring Creek. That's the kind of attention we want."

"Forget it. Let's just get going." Devan set his bag down and walked back to Laurel. "Best thing of all, I got my bionic babe," he said, pulling her to him.

She pushed him back but held his hands. "When we first met you told me you were a mountain lion, with nine lives. Seems like you have at least eight left."

"Seven, if you count the coma for two months when I was seven with that mold allergy. Six, if you count the time they gave me CPR in Oregon when I had that compound fracture of my arm."

"I don't buy it. You still have at least eight."

"Did I tell you about the time I fell off the tractor?"

"Always been one of those kids who loved danger?"

Devan took a deep breath. "You think I can do this, don't you?"

"I know you can."

His face went blank and he stared off into the trees. "I'm thinking of those weird noises I heard down in the mountain." Sighing. "Maybe it's my imagination." He paused. Tossing his shoulders, Devan hitched his pack into place. "Onward Christian Soldiers," he said.

As they marched off, Zoë stood in the shade of the truck sipping water, observing a buzzard sailing thermal drafts up into a silvery swath of sky. For an instant, she recalled the morning she lost her mother in the car crash.

Six years old, unsure if she was asleep or awake, one minute Zoë was laughing at something Ruthie said, the next minute she had wakened on her back, staring straight up from the bottom of a green well formed by leafy alfalfa plants under a dazzling white sky. As she blinked dizziness back from behind her eyes, she tried to focus on a black dot circling the rim of the well she lay in. It circled closer and closer until she noticed it had a body and wings, wide wings bent at the tips and a reddish pouch under a hooked beak.

She rolled over and stumbled through the uncut hay, calling for Ruthie, falling and picking herself up, aware only of a putrid odor dropping on her from overhead and the thud of her knees when she tripped. Zoë never saw her mother alive again.

 Devan found her and scooped her up into her new life, a life filled with his and Bonnie and Arthur's love, but that would never feel as safe as her mother's love.

Almost ten years ago Ruthie's soul flew up to Heaven from that dry pasture. In a matter of hours now, Zoë knew they'd be kissing and crying and hugging and forgetting everything that happened to rip them apart.

Across the valley, Anpetu Mountain cast a shadow onto the trees. It was hot, but for some reason, Zoë shivered.

An hour later, Leo still napped and Zoë sat on a rock watching him, waiting for Devan to return from his reconnaissance up the mountain. She planned to follow him up the mountain to Wakanda's parents' cave. When Devan saw her, she expected him to be angry. But he wouldn't do anything to her because he had to carry out his plans. Devan always did what he said he would do.

As soon as she heard their voices in the woods, Zoë retreated to cover behind dense bushes. She watched them emerge onto the lot.

Matt said, "That fence and sign up there gave me a real bad feeling." He tossed his pack down and removed a small gray box. He puttered with some dials or buttons, then set it on top of the camper roof. "Good spot. It'll catch anything you send down."

"All we need," Devan replied.

"That and my 30.06," Matt said, raising his hand into a sunbeam threading through the aspens.

Devan caromed his fist off Matt's before interlacing their fingers and shaking their hands back and forth, up and down. They grunted and looked up at the branches latticed in the morning sun, murmuring words Zoë couldn't make out.

Matt raised his voice. "You're sure nobody's inside the mountain?"

"Just Leo's dead old folks up there. Crumbling away. Harmless."

"I don't mean them. I mean living, breathing creatures."

"We didn't see any fresh tracks," Devan said.

Matt shrugged.

While Laurel struggled into a pack, Devan reached under the camper canopy and retrieved the Winchester.

Zoë slipped across the streambed, her eyes absorbing Anpetu's green radiance. Starting uphill, she glanced back to make sure she had them in a line of sight that obscured her. A chickadee hopped from branch to branch, from inside the cover of a leafy bush, following her. With its unblinking eye, the bird watched over its shoulder as she moved. Zoë clicked her tongue to reassure it but it darted off into the branches.

From far down the valley, a truck's transmission coughed and groaned as it began its long climb up the grade. Zoë lay on her stomach in the woods, watching and listening.

Zoë smiled as Devan and Laurel, like ordinary day-hikers, entered the woods. Wakanda, wide awake now, followed silently, while Matt sat on the tailgate of his SUV in the parking lot, swinging his leg, scuffing his boot heels in the gravel.

With a curtain of dense aspens and a dark veil of pines between her and them, Zoë began the final stage of her trek toward her angel's arms.

Twenty-two

SCALING ANPETU

Wakanda hiked in front and Devan brought up the rear as they bush-whacked along a narrow ridge. On the other side of the valley, Zoë had covered her hair with her camouflage bandana so she could stay within shouting distance of them without being noticed, her jacket and bandana blending into the colors of the trees and bushes.

She climbed a hundred yards ahead, traversing the mountain above Devan and Laurel. She intended to arrive before they did. While they stopped on a plateau to her north, Zoë edged ahead, assuming she'd find a Lakota trail through the glittering jumble granite and talus beautiful Anpetu wore like necklaces.

Broken spears of branches that stuck out of the pine trunks forced her to stoop and duck-walk in the dim woods. The dense growth made it impossible to avoid the fallen boughs and branches that lurked under a blanket of pine needles, ready to explode under her boot.

She came to a small clearing. Looking back, she saw that Laurel had reached a line of young fir growing on the edge of a talus slope below the next ridge.

Embracing a tree with two surrogate fingers, Laurel swung her hand of flesh and her feet up to the next tree. She locked her arm around it before throwing her hand into place beside her bionic hand, and tugged herself forward and up.

Devan followed close behind Laurel, climbing bowlegged, either because he wanted to catch her if she fell, Zoë guessed, or he forgot how to billygoat up these hills since he became a city man.

Zoë plucked a stalk of wild mint growing in the shade and stuffed it in her mouth. Spreading her arms, she inhaled the spice, clearing her head, and started back into the woods. A warm wind rattled branches, loosing a shower of pine needles on her head.

Some needles skittered past her cheeks, landing on her nose, pricking as they bounced, ricocheting off her jacket. She closed her eyes and listened. Unlike the chafing cottonwoods or murmuring apple trees, pinewoods sizzled when the wind pushed through.

Before long, she'd outstripped Devan and Laurel, and stood at the head of the ridge, watching them work their way up. Her view north through a low pass revealed a hazy image of the Crazy Horse monument in the distance. A dark sphere jutted off the distant cliff, as if in headlong flight away from the rock, with no shape of man or horse visible.

Maybe they'll finish the Crazy Horse statue by the time I come back from Heaven, she thought. A wonderful idea came to her as she considered the generations-long task of sculpting faces and horses from the mountains. When I come back, I'll find somebody to carve Inky and Kateri on some mountain. Maybe Anpetu. They'll be signs for other people like me who want to ascend body and soul.

Entranced with her vision of the granite heads of Inky and Kateri, American natives who faced the gun-toting conquerors with love and peace, and still they died. Zoë climbed mindlessly, plunging into a pile of scree at the foot of a sheer wall. She twisted her ankle and fell to her knees on the stones.

She tried to stand and snagged her skirt under her toe, ripping a hole in it a few inches above the hem.

"They say you shouldn't climb mountains in dresses. Even if you have a good jacket to protect it," she mumbled, amused and irritated at the same time. "Unless you're getting ready to fly away." Her kneecap throbbed from her encounter with Ketchup yesterday so she sat down on a sparkly boulder to rest.

A few crickets protested that it was too early to wake up, then relaxed into the silence of their mid-day naps.

Zoë rested her foot, assessing the climb ahead, seeking a silent path past the scree, praying Devan and Laurel were talking when she fell, as they usually were, so they wouldn't hear the mini-slide she'd set off.

Bird calls spangled from a stand of oaks and aspens interspersed among the pine and spruce and just then, Laurel's voice rose above the low hum of the breezy woods. Zoë judged she was close, about fifty yards away, on the other side of the canyon.

Laurel sang a few notes.

She sang again, this time a run of high notes flowing up and back and up again.

Awed, Zoë sat unmoving, in the open. She's singing to the birds.

The birds didn't answer. Laurel tried again, this time raising her voice in a soprano cooing and mewling.

A bird, or two, or three, chirped several bars that flowed into each other after intervals of a few seconds.

Laurel laughed and sang again. The birds sang back. Then the mountain silence surrounded the rocks and tree and Zoë got up, having spotted a way up that avoided the scree.

Overhead, Anpetu Mountain extruded a long, haphazard ridge with sharp smooth spires, an enormous stone comb with missing teeth and random roots and plant growth caught like hair in the spaces.

Forty yards away and twenty yards below a massive rock wedged itself into a V formed by granite outcroppings. Uphill, a boulder had broken loose and rolled downhill, bludgeoning a fresh channel through the forest, leaving a path of mashed and split tree trunks leveled to the earth.

Zoë observed the damage. Looks like a pig, she thought. Beady eyes. A green wig of trees sticking out all over its head. In groves along the mountainside, pines leaned into each other, victims of a greedy beetle.

"Leo, check it out, out-ow-ow." Devan's voice echoed across the hill.

Zoë spotted Wakanda standing a hundred yards ahead on a flat outcropping, his tiny body silhouetted against the sky. He waved and hurried on, picking his way effortless as a ram.

Deciding to copy his gait, she maneuvered uphill, scrambling, hopping from boulder to boulder across a narrow swale. She passed through a treacherous talus bed poised to slide down the canyon. Plumes of dust drifted out from under her boots. She stopped to let the dust settle, hoping Devan hadn't noticed.

Leaving the talus, Zoë found herself on a stony, overgrown two-track road. Puzzled, she guessed it was an old Forest Service road, maybe built on a miner's route that probably followed an ancient Lakota trading trail, she stepped onto it and noticed human boot tracks in the dirt.

In all her years wandering around the Shannon County hills and mountains, Zoë had seen only a few hikers. The medium-sized boot-tracks belonged to a solitary man and dust had drifted into the sole treads and the wind had almost flattened them into invisibility. She followed them as the trail hairpinned uphill.

At the top of the rise, she wiped sweat from her eyes and surveyed the terrain. Ten yards ahead a sagging chain link fence emerged from the long grass. It stretched as far as she could see in either direction along a plateau until it disappeared around the mountain's shoulder. Three lines of barbed wire ran through brown ceramic knobs like the ones farmers used on their electric fences. The fence sagged and vibrated in the stiff wind, a futile noose around Anpetu's thick neck.

Zoë followed the trail along the shoulder of the mountain until she came to a dented, rusty sign attached to one of the fence poles. One corner of the twisted metal plate lay folded over like a book page mark and the rest was pocked with ragged bullet holes. At first, Zoë couldn't make out the words because big islands of paint had flaked off and a mountain marksman had peppered the sign with holes.

KE   O T

F   r l F l ny

Tr s   ss rs Will B Pr s cut

T Th   F l Ext nt f   L w

<u>wnstr m Un er r un M n g m nt Pr j ct</u>

Puzzling out the words, it dawned on her that the shooter had used the vowels and letters with loops in them as bulls' eyes. She got the 'Keep Out' and most other words except 'F   r l F l ny.' When she noticed that most of the holes looked fresh, a creepy feeling forced her to hunch her shoulders and look around. She listened. She looked up. A few dark dots fluttered against the pale blue sky.

Buzzards? No. Too high. Couple of eagles, maybe. Planes don't fly that close to each other. Something else?

Billy Kimball once took her to the fields out behind the football field where he showed her the spy drone he'd built. He got the kit from a website and was practicing to become a spy pilot. He flew the drone so high they could barely see them.

Billy was a stupid kid about most things – he sure didn't know how to talk to girls – but if he could build drones to spy on people, she was glad she lived under the trees or in the trailer outside of town.

While Zoë scanned the sky, the specks overhead disappeared. She rubbed her eyes, listening to a faint sizzle.

Nothing but wind in the grass.

The fence loomed a few yards above her. A wren balancing on the wire hopped off and fluttered away as she passed.

Near the tree line, a few stands of fir and pine clustered randomly on the mountain. Scant juniper bushes and dense grasses covered the trail almost completely at this elevation, but a path following one of the wheel ruts lay crushed through the weeds by human steps.

She walked, half in the daydream walking alone in high mountain silence always put her in. When her chin fell to her chest, she jerked awake. The tracks that guided her had ended, so she doubled back until she found them again.

Beside the trail, someone – Devan? – had laid two heavy pine branches across the fence, depressing it for an easy step over. She hopped over and spotted the tracks again, climbing straight up.

Three turkey vultures drifted up from below to investigate her sounds. Discovering only a living human, they soared off toward the firs, leaving their shadows flickering on the granite at Zoë's feet. For the second time that hot afternoon, she shivered.

The peak of the mountain was near, but invisible overhead, behind sheer cliff faces and eroded crags. She followed the tracks up less than a hundred feet when she saw a narrow path leading along a horizontal cleft in the rock.

She hiked along the path, holding her body close to the mountain wall until she saw an outcropping ahead descending in a half arch. Beneath it, a ledge jutted out of the granite and hung over the cliff. From Zoë's angle, the shapes formed the open beak of a giant eagle. She smiled to herself, delighted with the mountain's mimicry of the winged life it was home to.

She approached the ledge and pulled herself up onto it and there was Wakanda, resting in the shade of an overhang. A breeze stuttered across the bald rock, sweetening the air with sage.

Zoë fanned her cheeks with a stalk of fern she'd plucked. Glad that she barely sweat no matter how hard she worked, she opened her jacket and waved it back and forth, cooling off her stomach.

"Good tracker," Wakanda said, motioning for her to sit next to him. "I led the others up here the other day, but you've never been here."

"Couldn't miss the trail." She walked back and forth on the broad ledge, looking behind a few rocks crouching next to the mountain face like watchdogs. "Is this the graveyard?"

"Inside." He waved toward the far edge of their perch. "Behind the sumac."

Zoë immediately crossed to the tall bushes and probed into them, pulling back leaves and branches, looking for the entry.

"I found it," she mumbled, her shoulder and leg still inside the foliage.

Wakanda nodded.

"Cool breeze coming out." She stepped back and shrugged her coat off her shoulders. Standing a few inches back from the sumac, she closed her eyes and exposed her throat and chest to the mountain's cool breath, savoring its slight bitter taste as she inhaled.

Cooled off, Zoë ducked her head and pushed between the leaves. The broken tips of some branches scraped at her, catching her jacket by a pocket. She slowed, edging carefully between the branches, using her hands as antennae to sense the opening in the mountain.

She stepped through the sumac into a slit in the stone that spread twice as wide as her shoulders and closed far above. Pale green light filtered through the sumac behind her lighting the smooth gray walls of a tunnel.

Ever prepared, Zoë pulled her flashlight out and shined it into the cave. At first, the walls reared back as if attacked by the sharp ivory beam, then they bounced back into place, enormous security doors guarding a secret Lakota passage into the underworld.

She took a few steps through the sumac into the cave, crunching small stones or bones underfoot. She shined the light at her feet then back along the tunnel floor. Several sets of footprints had scoured a trail in a light dust.

A few small animal bones, none larger than a rabbit or a small coyote, lay against the wall near the entrance. She peered at the prints, but all were boots or shoes, none paws.

She couldn't see much further than a few feet because the walls tilted to one side and the path angled down and away to the left. The ceiling was about as high as any normal hallway in a house.

She took another step forward, shut off her light and listened. Only the brushing of the mountain breeze against sumac leaves and a distant crow caw from down the mountain. Zoë decided to return to Wakanda.

She dropped down beside the old man, easing the bottom of her jacket up and leaning back on the ledge with only her skirt between the cool stone and the backs of her stretched legs.

"Good idea to wait," Wakanda said. "No use rushing. Your friends would worry about you if you started exploring by yourself."

"They think I'm on a bus," she said. She picked at coppery patches of lichen that polka-dotted the shady side of the boulder beside her. "Your parents," she said, "I mean, they're inside, right?"

"Their bones," Wakanda said. "Some things to help them on the journey to the next life."

"I like bones." She grinned, patting her side pocket where she kept Ruthie's rib. "Up in the Rapid City cathedral they have saint bones, only a piece of a finger and a chunk of a skull, but they're cool. Old as Jesus, I hear."

On the next ridge over, granite pinnacles reflected a soft glow over the early afternoon.

Zoë offered Wakanda a protein bar. He shook his head. "How about an apple?"

He looked away.

Sometimes, when she didn't eat, Zoë felt like a breeze could knock her over, so she bit into the apple and peeled the wrappers from two protein bars, one for lunch, one for dessert.

"How long do bones last? Do they ever melt or crumble?"

Shifting his body so that he could look at her face, Wakanda said, "Mold on my father's ribs. My mother's skull has stains on it, bacteria eating it."

"Ruthie's skull has black marks on it. Every year the eyes – where the eyes were? – they get wider." Death's ways fascinated her. When she came against it, she knew it was as complicated as the living world.

As she tucked her feet under her legs, Little Limbo patted her thigh, as if the souls wanted her attention. Reaching inside her coat, she clasped the bottle in her fingers and pulled it out. Checking the lid, she set Little Limbo down to cool the souls off. They needed a good rest before they rocketed through the stars with her and their angels, or whatever they did.

She once thought she would turn invisible like the angel and rise to Heaven in an instant until Inky said she'd need a strong angel to carry her all the way. She could see that, since her soul would still be in her heavy body. Not really *heavy* heavy. She was still only about ninety pounds with her coat on. Well, heavier than nothing, like a soul. Was a soul nothing?

Zoë caressed her cricket pocket and jiggled the coat. A few cricket chirps bubbled out, but they were still too sleepy to harmonize. Touching her palm to the leather, she felt them bouncing weakly against the soft pocket walls.

They'd climbed at least two miles from the road and more than a thousand feet up the valley's eastern slope. The peak of the mountain lay at least a thousand feet above them.

From their ledge, she watched a bevy of small cumulus in the south beginning to merge into what might become a thunderhead by evening.

"Looks like rain over Spring Creek. That'd be good for the peaches."

"We've seen the last rain in the Hills for a while," Wakanda said, eyes still shut, but breathing easier.

"How do you know?" She knelt up, eager for Lakota lore. "What signs tell you that?"

His eyes cracked open and a smile quivered the corners of his mouth. "I call it The Weather Channel. Watched it this morning. All the signs say dry."

Zoë laughed. He was funny when he tried to be so serious, like other old men she'd met. Wakanda knew medicine, she was sure. How else could such an old man climb Anpetu faster than Devan?

"Do you have any poshents?"

"What?"

"You know. Magic things to eat or drink. Or put on sores. Like that healing dirt you gave Devan. He could hardly walk before we smeared it on his sores."

Wakanda squatted, wrapping his arms around his legs and holding himself by his upper arms, he said, "That dirt. My niece gave it to him. I know stories is all."

"What stories?" Listening to stories made Zoë happier than almost anything. Almost as much as riding her bike or camping at the lake.

"I'll tell you. After."

"I can't wait. I love stories. What about just a little one now, before they get here?"

All trace of smiles and friendliness faded from Wakanda's face. "Not now. I'm concentrating."

"On what? Your family?"

"Yeah." He sat down off his haunches and leaned against the stone. Wakanda tapped a capsule into his hand and tossed it into his mouth. He closed his eyes.

That's his magic, Zoë thought. Old people in the Home had a lot of pills, too.

Zoë observed him, his slow breathing, his flickering eyelids, the way he crossed his legs. His jeans had holes in the knees and a fringe of short threads dangled from the frayed hem of his jacket sleeves.

She turned away from him and went to the verge of the platform. She sat on her hands, dangling her feet over the emptiness. She spotted Devan and Laurel a hundred yards below, hiking up, side by side. They were so focused on their conversation they didn't look up to see her.

Good, Zoë thought. Better to surprise them. She gazed out over the slopes of Anpetu, forming a telescope with her fingers and aiming it southeast, toward the Badlands, but she couldn't see through the mountains.

She marveled at hundreds of miles of beautiful forests and gleaming granite peaks spread out before her. Sprawled in an abundance of light and shadow, some had eroded into peaceful domes, others wore into long serrated ridges, and others weathered into vast needles and pillars, all reaching straight up, signposts to another world.

Soon, she'd look down on the Badlands and the whole world, the way Inky did, watching everybody.

Twenty-three

EVERYBODY NEEDS SOME LUCK

Devan and Laurel pitched their packs onto the ledge and started to clamber up.

Zoë had it planned. She stretched her hand out to Devan. When his mouth dropped open and he took it, she said, "Should I let go?"

"What are you doing here? How did you get here? I told you to get on the bus!"

"I snuck into the back of your truck." She grinned and laughed, hoping to soften his anger. His grip tightened. She slapped his hand and jerked free, backing away.

"Christ almighty. You don't know what you're into here."

Devan glowered, then he glanced at Wakanda. The Hunkpapa stared back, umoving.

Devan turned to Zoë. He dropped his pack and lunged, shooting his hand toward her.

She danced further back. "Don't be mad," Zoë said. "I have to be here. You know why."

Then, reaching into her jacket and pulling out a soggy paper bag, she showed him what she'd found in the woods. "Look," she said, pulling two languid crawfish out of a jacket pocket and dangling them in front of Laurel. Laurel stared at her, saying nothing.

Zoë reached into a jacket pocket and pulled out a clump of mud with a half dozen roots. "I looked in the cave. I know I'll find my angel down there. Remember how Jesus did it? First he was in a tomb and an angel came and rolled the rock away and then Jesus went to Heaven."

"Goddam it. Hold it," he barked, standing up straight and glaring at her. "Now you're Jesus? Laurel, take her back to the truck. Stay with her and send Matt up."

Laurel said, "No. I'm staying with you."

Devan snapped, "Do it. Get her out of here." He swung his arm around in disgust and kicked a stone off the ledge. "I don't want to see her."

Laurel nodded. Passing by him, she placed her hand on his back for an instant. He didn't respond and Laurel spun around and dived for Zoë.

"Ha! You can't catch me!" Her coat flapping, Zoë ran to the far side of the ledge and shouted. "Devan, I'm your luck. You need me here."

Devan threw his bag down. The end of a rope fell out. Picking it up and starting toward Zoë, he said, "You're not thinking straight, Zoë. Even in your world, angels don't live in caves. They live in Heaven."

Zoë eyed the rope. "Don't be stupid, Devan."

"The whole fuckin world's gone crazy," Devan said as he sidled across the front of the ledge, blocking Zoë's escape.

"Laurel, call Matt. Tell him you're bringing Zoë. Tell him to show you how to set up the transmitter."

"For all of us, Zoë," Laurel said, "come with me. You can still give Devan all the luck you've got. Please. Come."

Zoë stared back, first at Laurel, then she narrowed her eyes at Devan, half-smiling, feeling like a mother who'd given up on trying to make her children understand.

Wakanda watched the exchange of Devan's pointed words and ominous looks and said to Zoë, "Stay out of my way, Ehawee." Nodding toward Devan, he added, "Your friend shouldn't worry."

"Wakanda, you need luck, too. I have so much luck today my toes are tingling." Zoë toe-pointed and pirouetted, spinning close to the front of the ledge. If Devan lunged for her, she'd drop down to the outcropping below.

Devan grabbed her by the coattail. To Wakanda, he said, "She'll get in everybody's way."

Reeling Zoë toward him, Devan said, "You're going back, if I have to drag you."

Zoë's face fell. She squirmed and clawed at his hand, glancing quickly at Laurel and Wakanda.

Devan circled her upper arm with his fingers. "Come on."

"We're here," Wakanda said, pointing to a tall sumac bush at the end of the ledge. "It's getting late." Though his wizened body reached only to Laurel's shoulders, Wakanda's baritone took on a note of calm command. "Why not tie her up and leave her here till we come back."

Devan nodded. "I want her down below. Laurel, hold her while I get this rope around her waist."

Sensing that she had, max, ten seconds of freedom before Devan captured and tied her, she said, "Okay. Okay. I'll do what you say."

Devan glanced at her, continuing to uncoil the rope.

"Hold her."

Laurel approached and Zoë screamed as loud as she could.

It worked. Devan dropped her arm. Laurel stopped.

Zoë turned and ran to the clump of sumac in front of the cave opening. She took her flashlight from her coat and wrapping one of her sleeves around the handle, she waved it like a torch. "Laurel, here's my prothesis. Can't stir flour but it sees in the dark." Zoë giggled at her joke.

Devan and Laurel looked at other.

Wakanda moved toward the ferns beside Zoë. "I'm going in. You do what you want," he said to Devan.

Devan spread his legs and his arms, taking up so much space in front of Zoë, she had only one direction she could go. His voice cracking with anxiety, he said, "Please. Zoë. Do what I say. It's the only way you'll get to Heaven."

For a moment, nobody spoke. Black Hills spruce dozed alongside the ledge, their tips still as the early afternoon shadows. A stand of quaking aspen encroached on a meadow to the south and dry oak spread lordly boughs over the broad knoll below them.

Devan broke the silence. "Ruthie wouldn't want you going in there."

Zoë heard a catch in Devan's voice, as if he were about to cry. Or scream at her.

Wakanda stuffed his shaggy gray hair under his watch cap and pulling his collar around his neck, picked up a bag and moved off. He tugged the cap down and, without glancing back, disappeared behind Zoë into the sumac.

As Wakanda passed her in the cave opening, Zoë waved her light at Devan. "It's time," she said. "Wakanda," she called. "Wait for me."

Devan lunged for her but she dived through the sumac, laughing as she scrambled into the mouth of the cave.

HEAVEN'S CAVE

Twenty-four

LIQUID DARK

A little way inside the slit in the rock, Zoë saw Wakanda's shadow. Cupping her mouth, she called, "Wakanda. Wa-kaaan-da. Wait up."

He didn't answer.

Behind her she heard the sumac rustling. Devan would be right behind her.

"Leo!" Devan shouted, "Zoë's coming. Stop her at the door."

Moving fast to stay ahead of Devan, Zoë scuttled along the tunnel wall, aiming her light a few feet ahead, following Wakanda as he curved one way, then the other. Wakanda's light disappeared and Zoë picked up her pace.

Almost jogging, she nearly passed the opening to the grave. A flicker of dim light stopped her and she spun into the chamber. She shined her light across a dusty chamber the size of Bonnie's living room. The floor sloped away toward a floor-to-ceiling gash in the drab walls. A steady flow of cool air blew out of the opening, past their faces, carrying a musty odor.

Wakanda aimed his penlight at the slash in the far wall. The globe of light hung on an opening onto nothing but a black surface spangled with drifting flecks. Then, he trained his light on a low scaffolding made of sticks. Bones.

Zoë shined her light on the crack in the wall and nodded. "Is that where Devan fell down the mountain?"

"Yeah. That's where the big tanks are, in a room somebody built. My family gold's down at the end of the tunnel."

"Oh, good. Now I know why I'm here." Satisfied that she knew where her angel was waiting, Zoë honed her light in on a diorama of human and animal bones and skulls posed on a heap of skins and sticks and pots. "Cool," she said.

Wakanda nodded. "My parents."

The tableau of bones and skins vibrated under Zoë's light. A small human skeleton, with no left hand, garbed in frayed buckskin, sprawled against the chest of a huge bison skeleton. The relics of another small human, with two tiny hands, dangled from the bison's neck, a bone necklace or a child-sized amulet.

Dark leather scraps encircled many of the skeletons' joints, as if leather splinted the joints, supporting the bones against gravity. The bison's legs had collapsed and its head tilted, but the barrel of its ribs supported a heavy skull and horns. All the bones glowed dull as bark.

"Wow!" Zoë's light spread across the assembly of relics. Then, opening her jaws until they hurt, she put the flashlight between her lips and bit down on the handle. The light wobbling, she shuffled up to the horned bison skull at the center of the arrangement.

"Inky should see this," she mumbled. Touching one finger to the tip of a horn and the other to its cracked forehead, she closed her eyes, sensing its massive size and strength.

Zoë's hand wandered inside her coat on the side where she kept Little Limbo and Ruthie's rib bone. She patted the bottle and fingered the bone, slipping it up and down each finger, catching it in the webs above her knuckle joints and squeezing until her finger bones ached.

"Is this your mother?" she asked, tapping on the skull of a larger human skeleton in the shredded leather wrapping. Wakanda nodded.

Letting go of her mother's rib, she measured the small Indian skull between her palms then holding her hands apart, she raised them to her temples.

"Perfect fit! She's my size." Zoë stepped back, crunching some beads or shells that had fallen from the woman's shredded robe.

His eyes wide in the glow from the flashlights, Wakanda said, "My mother was never big. She shrunk when she got old."

"I'm bigger than she is," Zoë said, straightening up, comparing her height to the sagging bones.

Stepping toward a taller skeleton leaning against the wall, Leo said, "Meet my grandmother. Avoca Latayeha. She scared me when I was little with her fake hand."

Zoë scrambled over. "No way. She has both hands. You said your grandmother was a one-hand."

"Look close," he replied, grinning. He lifted the flashlight as high as he could. Zoë bent to inspect the hands. The left hand bones were neatly carved, polished, deep brown, made of fine-grained wood.

"Her grandmother was a one-handed woman, too," Leo expanded. "And her grandmother. Hand goes from one generation t' the next. We say whoever wears the hand can dream dreams to find things. Make sick people well. Tell the future."

Leo set the lantern down on an upturned wheelbarrow. He reached behind his back into his belt and withdrew a small blade the size of a paring knife, then cut the rotting leather strap holding the wooden hand onto his grandmother's radius and ulna bones.

Holding the hand between his fingers and top of its palm, he turned to Zoë. The polished wood fingers dangled and shook like pike lures just dropped into dark water, enticingly amber.

Wide-eyed, Zoë stepped back, then laughed.

"Yeah, she used to shake her wooden bones at us kids and we'd all run screaming. She'd shout Spider hand! Spider hand gonna getchoo! That's why I brought your friends here. Laurel's no hand."

"She's all right," Zoë said. "Her fake hand's pretty cool, but I never heard she could fortune tell."

"Who knows. She's a strong lady, looks like my family, too. Maybe she can help me find something."

Nodding her understanding of the connection between the two women with missing left hands, she pointed to a small skeleton sprawled on the pelvis of the Zoë-sized skeleton, "Who's the little one?"

"My twin. My sister." He squatted in front of his sibling and caressed the tiny forehead with his knuckle. "She died a few weeks after we were born."

Zoë hunkered down beside him. "When did your mother die?"

"Long time ago. I was grown up, though."

Zoë's fingertips scraped an arc of dust free of the flowstone. "I wish my mother had a grave like this. She's in Heaven, but all that's left of her body's in the ground back in Spring Creek."

Wakanda tilted his head and nodded toward her jacket.

"Most of it," Zoë said, a grin on her face, Zoë rested her hand on his arm. "Is your mother in Heaven?"

"Could be." Wakanda stood up and exhaled.

Fascinated by the bones, Zoë circled the main structure. Strangely comforted by the moldering bones Wakanda had tended with no apparent desire to follow their souls into the afterlife, Zoë fingered Ruthie's rib. Her hand felt swollen, as if her hand bones, too, wanted to shed their flesh and join Wakanda's monument in eternal peace.

Inching her eyes across the pale statuary, she noticed a knobbed bone as thick as a lamp post, four or five feet long, propped against the wall, throbbing in the dusty glow.

"What's that? Dinosaur?"

"Mastadon," Wakanda said. "My people say it's been with them since the beginning. I don't know."

Zoë shook her head and jutted her chin toward the shadows. "Look at those giant horse heads. Those guys must be bigger than Budweiser horses."

Two immense horse skulls buttressed the ends of the skeleton diorama.

"Them?" Wakanda said. "Grandmother's last horses."

Wakanda's devotion to his dead was deep and older than Zoë could imagine. He was already so wrinkled and skinny, if he lay down, he'd fit right in with his ancestors.

Zoë shuffled to the other side of the diorama. She poked her flashlight into a pile of rags and bowls and small tools that lay next to the bones. A pair of long spiraling horns caught her attention.

"Can I pick these up?"

Wakanda said, "Sure. Family's animal. They believed the ram connected them with their ancestors. Hold it and you could talk with them."

Zoë smiled. Like Ruthie's rib. What if she could speak with Wakanda's people? Her hand darted toward the horns. She didn't sense an angel here, or any saints, but Wakanda's dead people had made their home inside the mountain for so many years, their guardian spirits hovered over the bones, only she couldn't see them.

Beside them a triangular pole frame tied with leather straps leaned against the ceiling like an open lodge with one end collapsed and dangling into the fissure in the wall.

A bow, several knives, sticks with oval eyes running along the stems, a few small hoops, two rusted and pitted officer's swords and a bayonet slumped together against a blackened metal helmet.

Responding to Zoë's raised eyebrows, Wakanda said, "Battle trophies." Sitting down on a low pile of hides, he coughed, waving dust away from his face.

Zoë pulled a small bottle from one of her pockets. "Water?"

Wakanda accepted the canteen and slugged down half the water and passed it back.

She tipped her head back and drank, swinging her eyes around the walls and the ceiling. An erratic net of cracks outlined a gray-on-black shadow mosaic, random three-dimensional pictographs. She strained to interpret the vague images of four-legged animals and teepees and rivers and hints of two-legged figures scratched higgeldy-piggeldy into the granite.

Glancing at Wakanda with a request for his explanation on the tip of her tongue, she noticed him deep in concentration on the bones, so she shrugged and set the water down beside a cluster of costumes. A rusty shield embossed with a crest, a pile of crumpled sacks the size of shopping bags. A pair of tri-corn hats, each with a ragged feather, drooped from the bars of the frame.

She raised her flashlight to illuminate the rest of the cave. Constellations of mica or quartz flashed and sparkled in the volcanic rock.

Zoë's mouth fell open. "Stars inside the Earth?"

"Mica," Wakanda said. "More mica flakes inside Anpetu than stars in the sky."

Just as Zoë thought, Anpetu was closer to Heaven than any place in Shannon County, maybe it was the first level. Lakota called this place holy, and though she felt its holiness for all her years of roaming these foothills, the glittering ceiling proved the Indians' wisdom.

"Leo, do you have her?" Devan's voice came from just outside the chamber. "Hold on to her."

Thanks, Inky, Zoë muttered.

Devan and Laurel edged into the cave and dropped their packs. Laurel set a camping lantern in the center of the chamber and lit it and they switched off their headlamps.

Devan stood over Zoë and groaned. "Jesus, Zoë. You're screwing this whole thing up."

Zoë turned and opened her eyes, the bloom of ivory light nearly blinding her. She covered her face with her hand, peeking through her fingers until her eyes adjusted.

"Hi, Devan. Hi, Laurel." Giving them her pixie smile, she returned to examining Wakanda's parents.

"Careful, Zoë," Laurel said. "Leo – Wakanda – wants to save these for a museum."

"No he doesn't."

Zoë glanced up at Laurel and saw disapproval. Devan wanted Laurel to be Zoë's jailer, so she couldn't trust her, but no use making her madder. Anyway, Zoë would talk to Wakanda's people in person before long.

"You're going back," Devan said.

Without turning away from his family shrine, Wakanda said in a deep, calm baritone, "Everybody drink some water'n sit for a few minutes. Then we'll get going."

Zoë slid closer to Laurel, touching her prosthesis. "Laurel, can you tell the future?"

"What?"

"Or make sick people well?"

"Not that I know of, honey. Where did you get those ideas?"

"Zoë, get out of here," Devan said. "You know the way back." He scowled again, this time at Wakanda. "I'm ready."

Zoë's stomach muscles tightened. She was ready, too. She expected Devan to approach her, but he just stared with a wrinkle deep between his eyebrows.

Under the harsh light from Devan's lantern, the walls and floor surrounding them shone velvety black. The skeletons floated in the darkness.

"You didn't tell me about the buffalo," Zoë turned, speaking to Wakanda, while keeping her distance from Devan. "How did everybody get here?"

The old man sat down, humped forward as if he couldn't hold his spine straight. "It's what they did," he said. "My family."

At that point, Devan leapt the six feet between him and Zoë, pinned her to him and said, "This is it. I can't trust you any more." He picked her up, circling her waist with one arm. Her head bobbed two feet off the ground. Their scuffling splattered dust into her face. She sneezed.

Zoë wriggled and kicked, bucking against him. Devan had locked her against his hip.

"Let me go." She kicked harder, banging her head into his ribs. "Laurel, tell him his future so he'll let me go."

Devan clutched her tighter. "Laurel, get me the rope."

Laurel stirred around in one of the bags, then turned with the coarse lariat coiled in her prosthesis.

Inky, what should I do?

Zoë looked toward Wakanda for help, but he was turned to his family, pondering. Ignoring Zoë.

"You're hurting me," she moaned. "I can't breathe."

Devan loosened his grip, still keeping her immobile against him.

A shadow veiled his face, except for the glints from his eyes. Devan spoke quietly. "I have to go film those toxic tanks and I don't want to have to think about you. You're going to stay here with the bones. You love bones."

Sensing her chance. "Good. I don't mind. I can give you my luck to take with you, like a kiss. Like Laurel said."

"I'll put you down and you give me your hands so I can tie them."

"No way."

Devan shifted her body and turned her around. "In that case, I'll just tie you to one of these stalagmites."

"Okay, okay. I'll do it."

Devan dropped Zoë into a heap at his feet.

"I'm sorry, Zoë. It's not your fault."

Devan sounded so mad that Zoë turned around to hug them. She buried her face in her hands, a lump forming in her throat. A tear threatened to flow over the edge of her eyelid.

Running his fingers through Zoë's hair, Devan said, gently, "Trouble is, we'd need a whole flock of angels to handle this. Give me your hand."

Zoë complied, offering her hand to Devan. "Just say 'Inky, We need your help' and everything will be fine."

Devan pulled her up and knuckled the top of her head. "That's a good prayer, honey. Say it for us."

"I'll just stay here and pray for you," she said.

"How can I trust you after all the sneaky things you did today?"

"I'm here. You're here. My angel will come. All I have to do is wait. It's better I pray for you if it's so dangerous."

"All right with you, Laurel? Watch Zoë?"

"I think you better tie her up," Laurel said. Her Glinda rods slithered in and out of the base.

Watching the sinister rods, Zoë said, "Please, no."

"You're right, Laurel," Devan said. "I'll do it in a second. Let's get ready for my descent."

Laurel unzipped the bags and pulled out the Hazmat suits and a small square machine. She placed the machine at the door and spoke into her walkie-talkie.

"Matt, calling Matt. This is Laurel of the Mountain. Do you receive?"

"Sounding good." Matt's scratchy voice filled the chamber. "You guys gonna do it, or what? I'm getting hungry and I forgot my pizza."

Devan took the handset. "Nice job with the relays, buddy," he said. "I'm going down in a few minutes."

"See you when, say, O sunset thirty?"

"Before that. Stay cool. Any cars come, pretend you're taking a nap."

"That's about how exciting it is down here in the old parking lot."

Zoë took Laurel's wrist in her hand and pulled the handset to her mouth. "This is Zoë. Over and out. See you later, Matt."

"Zoë? What the hell?"

"Don't worry, Matt. We have her under control."

Devan pulled off his sweat-stained T-shirt and asked Laurel to hand him the Kevlar vest. He slipped his arms into it and she sealed the Velcro and buckled the leather straps in the back.

The long blonde hair on his arms looked black and furry in the gloomy light, but his winged 'Z' tattoo glowed like an iridescent bird in flight.

Devan stepped into the floppy Hazmat suit, pulled it up and over his limbs, zipped and snapped it shut, and strapped a holster around his waist. Laurel helped him hoist a small oxygen tank onto his back. He cinched its straps around his chest and pulled on a soft, transparent plastic helmet.

"I'll be back up here before you can say rock n' roll."

Zoë edged toward him and touched the oxygen tank, quickly pulling her hands back from the chilly metal.

Wakanda picked up a rope from a pile of relics and strung it over his shoulder. The loops hung to his knees. "I have my work to do," he said. "I showed you this place. I trusted you." He tipped his chin up. "You have to trust me."

"Leo, the radiation – ." Laurel objected but Wakanda interrupted.

"I'm old, older'n you guess. I have one more thing to do. If I do it'n live, I'm happy. If I do it'n die, I'm happy. If I don't do it, I can't live. I can't die. I'm not happy."

"You're on your own, old man," Devan said. "I knew you'd do whatever you wanted."

"I have to find the bag. It's worth a lot to my family." Wakanda adjusted the rope and worked a stick loose from the burial midden. "Not just money."

"You expect to find it under a hundred tons of rock?" Devan asked.

"I don't know," he admitted. "I'll listen to what the bones tell me."

"You listen to the bones, I'll listen to the walkie- talkie," Devan said, as he tied a yellow plastic rope around the base of a plump stalagmite that sat near the fissure. "You hear anything, let me know right away."

Glancing at Devan, Laurel said, "If he thinks it's in the cavern, it must be. I used to find four-leaf clovers, but not much else."

"See, you can find things. At least you'll be here. that's what matters. You'll find your gold, Wakanda. Don't worry."

Wakanda tested Devan's knot and tugged the rope. "Good," he said. "When I find the bag, you can have some gold coins to help you with your problem."

"Sure," Devan said. "We get outta here, we'll need gold. All the gold we can get." He turned to Laurel and inspected the closures on her miner's suit. "Wish you had a better suit," he said. "But it oughtta be fine up here."

Laurel removed her prosthesis and let it swing from her arm. She held Zoë's hand in her dry palm and lay her nubbed arm across Devan's shoulder.

Zoë looked up at Laurel. "Why did you take it off? Will you put your hand back on? Please. I'd like to see it glow."

Laurel grimaced. "In a little while. We have to get Devan on his way."

"Right now? In the shadow? You arm kinda looks like one of those tan potatoes."

Shaking his head, Devan scowled at Zoë, then, unable to keep his mouth hard, he let a smile pluck at the corners of his lips. "You. I love you so much, and here you are, no suit, no protection."

"Wakanda doesn't have any."

"He's old. You heard him. Even if he gets radiation, he'll die before the cancer grows."

"I'm fine. I'm fifteen and way more than a half. You'll be surprised how fine I'll be." She grinned, excited. Finally, Devan would take her to the angel, whether he knew it now or not. Hey, she thought to herself, I can tell the future. She almost giggled.

Devan shook his head, then addressed Wakanda. "I won't have any time to help you down there. Once I finish and come back to the bones, we're outta here. You're not with us, we have to leave you. I'm sorry."

"My nephew's coming to pick me up at sundown. Either I have the bag, or I don't."

A faint breeze rose through the gash in the wall moistening their cheeks. As the others mumbled to each other, Zoë heard something else from the invisible cave below, a faint rhythmic click underscored by an electronic hum.

"Listen, everybody," she commanded. "Hold your breath." They went still.

"I hear something strange. Fans? Sounds like water."

"There's water down there. A lot of it," Wakanda said. "Moisture's rotting my family to nothing. It used to be dry in here, until something broke the wall. Might have been a few quakes over the years."

Indistinct odors and faint sounds churned into the chamber. A lemony fragrance quivered at the edge of Zoë's nostrils and a meaty iron scent from below rode the air.

"Smell that?" she asked.

"Yeah. Smells like we're in a machine shop," Devan said.

Laurel shook her head and sniffed. Sniffed again. "I don't smell anything."

"You have dust in your nose," Devan said.

Zoë concentrated her listening as Wakanda shifted on his pile of hides, crunching tiny animal bones under his thighs. A low note pulsed, then fell silent. Then a distant creaking, like a metal spring bending.

"I-beams shifting. I noticed one was bent when were down there the other day. There's that underground river, too." Wakanda swung his penlight toward the sagging reliquary.

"Could be an underground channel of the Cheyenne," Devan said. "When I was a guide at Wind Cave, we told tourists the fact there's more water under the Black Hills than in the Amazon River."

Thrusting his shoulders up and down to settle his load, Devan stepped toward Laurel and pecked her on the lips, then drew away. "Give me your arm, Zoë."

She had no choice, so she lifted her arm up to his chest. Zoë grimaced. "This is stupid."

"I don't think so. I hate to waste the rope."

Zoë arranged her sleeve so that when he wrapped the rope around her wrist, she could try to squirm out. Inside the sleeve, she made a fist.

Devan circled the sleeve twice, tied the rope with a bulky rope, and handed the loose end to Laurel. She wound it a few times around a three-foot high stalagmite and dropped it.

Laurel reached into one of the bags and turned to Devan. "Don't forget this," she said, draping a lanyard around his neck. A disc the size of a saucer hung over his sternum.

Pointing, Zoë asked, "What's that?"

"It's a RadAlert. A Mini-Geiger counter. Tells me to run like hell if there's too much radiation."

Orange numbers blinked on the round face of the alarm. Reading them slowly, as if counting down to an unknown endpoint. "One point zero. One point three. One point two five."

Zoë's eyes followed the blinking digits. "Why do they switch back and forth?"

"Background. That's all. But if it reads anything close to ten, I'm outta there, video or no."

Wrapping a length of rope around his forearm, Devan said, "No pain, no gain. Landslide, here I come." He pulled the rope tight, jerked it twice. The soft plastic facemask distorted his face, bulging his cheeks and shortening his chin as in an amusement park mirror.

Zoë giggled and said, "See you."

"One small step." He saluted them and backed into the blackness.

The other three crowded into the narrow opening as he descended, stepping down sideways across a steep granite surface, then entering a shambles of broken stones and sharp boulders, the rope taut and vibrating. Devan skidded, disappearing into an opaque bloom of dust.

His muffled voice came through the walkie-talkie stuck in Laurel's pocket. She took it out and laid it on the pile of bison fur.

Devan's words echoed in the chamber. "Leo, when you come down, watch you don't snag the rope on the rocks."

"Devan sounds like a girl," Zoë said, nodding at the handset.

Damp air from the cavern boiled up with the dust Devan had roused from the talus.

Devan shined his headlamp toward the opening above him. Faint light drifted across the scorched caramel color of the chute. Half-buried, cracked and tilted pillars of granite rose diagonally twenty feet up one side of the passage. Wide fractures zigzagged through the walls and ceiling of the rift, some gathering along one wall and broadening into a welter of veins that threatened to shatter at any moment.

"Okay, I'm at the wall. C'mon down, Leo." Devan's voice came through loud and calm, his headlamp now shrunk to the size of a flashlight beam.

Laurel picked up the handset. "See anybody or anything?"

They waited. "Some kind of light in the room. It's still dark, but there's a blue glow to the place. It wasn't here before."

Angel color, Zoë thought. Blue and white and gold. Wakanda's gold. She shook the rope but the knot didn't budge.

The old man secured his rope to the same stalagmite as Devan's. Wakanda wrapped the rope around his waist and climbed into the crevasse. Devan's headlamp shined a dim path up through the dust for the old man.

Soon the ropes fell slack and Zoë realized that they'd dropped them. "They're in the cavern now," Laurel said to her. Into the hand-set, "You in?"

"I'm in, honey. Man, you can't believe these vats. Must be a thousand."

"Hurry back," Laurel said. She sat down next to the rifle and lay her head back against the wall.

Laurel smiled at Zoë and closed her eyes. After waiting a few seconds, Zoë stepped back and flattened her fist and stomped on the rope on the floor. She twisted her arm back and forth, yanking at the rope. Gritting her teeth against the burning as she tugged, she slid her hand out from the knot and, with her other hand, slipped the rope off her empty sleeve.

Laurel lunged at Zoë. The prosthesis blades, back on the end of Laurel's arm, grazed then hooked the corner of a jacket pocket but Zoë spun away, ripping the pocket.

Snapping her flashlight on and brandishing it over her shoulder at Laurel to blind her for a moment, Zoë hopped over the jagged lip of the opening. Gripping one of the men's belaying ropes in her other hand, she stepped onto a shattered ramp of stone, veering down what felt to her like a sled path.

Her boots collided with the pile of shards at the bottom of the slippery granite sending rock tumbling further down the shaft. Dust billowed around her head and her weak flashlight made out fleeting animal shapes of outcroppings and broken granite chunks. The snap of stones bounding off stone crackled through the chute.

"Zoë!" Laurel screamed from above. "She got away! Zoë!"

The rope singed Zoë's palms, but she almost danced when she dropped the rope and slid down the talus slope at the bottom of the chute.

"Laurel! Laurel!" Zoë shouted up the tunnel, singing the name with the enthusiasm of a cheerleader. The yellow egg of Laurel's light glimmered from the slanted opening above, winking through the folds of dust spiraling behind her. "I'm fine." Her voice echoed. "Don't worry. I'll find my angel now."

Twenty-five

ANGEL?

A jumble of broken wall and thick hunks of concrete spiked with iron rods and bent and torn sheets of steel sprawled down the slope in front of her. Dusky violet haze shaded the cavern as if the collapsing wall had pummeled and bruised the air itself.

Zoë squinted. Beyond the rubble on the cavern floor, hundreds of cylindrical stainless steel tanks stood in perfect rank and file like giant old people's medicine capsules lined up on a table the size of a football field.

Awed by the immensity of the room and vast numbers of tanks it contained, Zoë waved her flashlight across the sides of the tanks. Focused on one vat, the scribbling on the side revealed itself as precise black letters stenciled written from end to end.

Downstream Underground Management Project
Millennial Energy**: A Joint Venture**
U.S.D.O.D. • U.S.D.O.E.
General Energetics • Bickstal • Hully & Bernard
Caution: Radioactive Materials

Zoë recognized the black tri-petalled symbols, the same emblems of nuclear radiation danger Devan had drawn on a napkin to give her an idea of what was inside the mountain.

Zoë's heart dropped into her stomach and sprung back into her throat on a spurt of bile. The vats held the poison that would melt everybody's flesh if it got loose. She played the light along the edges of the white pallets the tanks sat on, searching for puddles or any signs of leakage. The floor looked dry, but maybe something had leaked and evaporated.

What a strange place for an angel. If he knew she was coming, wouldn't he have waited for her outside, near Anpetu's peak where Earth and Heaven meet?

Far into the field of tanks, Zoë saw Devan's bright headlamp following a straight channel between tanks. It bobbed along through a yolky halo reflected off the silver tanks and dissolved in a grape-colored haze.

At the base of the rampart of shattered concrete and twisted hanks of steel rods, Wakanda's tiny flashlight weaved back and forth. Unaware of Zoë, he moved his legs in a marching-in-place step while he muttered to himself in a rhythm that matched his steps.

Zoë picked a path down the collapsed wall, testing, tip-toeing, using the jutting iron rods as hand grips, leaping, knocking only a few rocks loose. When stones showered onto the floor near Wakanda, he glanced up, shined his light toward her, then ducked his head and continued his search.

Zoë panned the wall with her flashlight. Close to her, a row of massive steel posts bent taut as drawn bows supported rusty beams on the ceiling. She admired their powerful resistance to the weight of the mountain.

Thanks to Ruthie, Zoë wasn't afraid. Her mother had taken her to the amusement park in Rapid City the same summer she died. The first time they rode the tram into "Satan's Dungeon" Zoë had screamed, burying her head under her laughing mother's arm. Zoë hated the noises and the jerky car and the creatures diving at them, but Ruthie ignored her complaints. They rode five more times. By the last ride, Zoë was sticking her tongue out at the devils and the snarling dragons that bounced off the walls a few inches from her face.

Grateful for her mother's foresight in forcing her to ride until she overcame her fear, Zoë tap-danced on a flat chunk of concrete, celebrating her mother. It was as if Ruthie knew the future and had prepared her for this trip into another "Dungeon" that was not half as scary as the first few rides in the amusement park.

A loose curtain made of hundreds of chains hung from the darkness above, ending about a foot above each tank. She shined her light on the closest chain, tracing it link by football-sized link upwards until the murk swallowed it up in a great yawn.

She descended another dozen steps into an ooze of chilly air that seemed to issue from the tanks themselves. Her teeth clicked, shivers dancing across her shoulders and pricking the hairs on the back of her head.

As she stared out over the field of tanks, a single long bank of fluorescent lights blinked on in a far corner across the hall. In the shock of light, some of the chains flashed like frozen lightning.

A sharp white beacon emerged from the darkness at the other end of the cavern, a hundred yards away, cutting through the dim blue gloom. The beam swiveled from one side to the other and back, then it slowly jerked its way down the wall, as if whoever carried it was stumbling.

Could the lights be angel signals?

She quickened her descent, picking her way down treacherous rubble through cooler and cooler temperature zones. When she stepped onto the cavern floor, she buttoned her coat halfway. Her breath formed a thin cloud in front of her face.

Collar turned up, she scouted out into the labyrinth of tall tanks.

The further she penetrated, the more amazed she grew at the enormity of the cavern and the height of the towering tanks. I'm a midget in a nuclear city, she thought. Skyscrapers, without a sky.

The breeze she'd felt up in Wakanda's family tomb had disappeared, replaced now by a mantle of cold. Her ears were used to constant Dakota wind rushing past and now, isolated five feet down in the silent arroyo between vats, she sensed a fierce tumult approaching. Yet, knowing she was immune from danger as long as she focused on finding her angel, Zoë accepted whatever was about to happen as little more than a normal, if vexing, change in weather.

Curious as usual and always scientific in her explorations, she slapped a tank as close to the center as she could. Her palm clapped right on the letter D. She jerked it back before it froze to the metal and sprung back, wincing. She withdrew her hand into her sleeve and rapped on the tank with her knuckles. The tank thudded and her knocks plonked and died as she pounded on solid metal or something frozen solid.

She whisked her hands against each other and brought the warm palms to her cheeks, then squatted and brought one hand close to the floor. She waved her fingers a few inches above blueberry-colored concrete, as if dousing, then she touched the floor.

A thin coating of frost stung her lacerated fingertips. Satisfied she'd found the source of the chill, she stood up and buttoned her coat to her neck.

Zoë shaped her lips into a whistling 'O' but before she blew, she heard sharp barking or quacking coming from where she'd seen the beam at the end of the cavern. Hurrying but barely breathing so whoever held the light wouldn't hear her or see the clouds of her breath, she counted five tanks forward, then five to the left, then five more forward. She zigzagged until she heard the voice off to her right shouting, "What in God's kingdom have you gotten me into?"

'God's kingdom?' Who would talk about God's kingdom down in this frozen, steely, poison place? She answered herself: Angel. It had to be.

She tiptoed back to keep two or three tanks between her and the being at the end of the cavern and sidled toward the voice.

Zoë eased one of her coat buttons open to access the poshent bag. Clutching it, she shook it to hear the reassuring brushing of leaves and claws and crushed pills together. A pungent wild leek odor rose from the lining of her coat.

She only needed two more ingredients: some water and, well, for the last ingredient, her body would have to provide it. No matter when, she could always pee, no matter where or how cold.

Hiding behind the edge of a tank, gripping her lapels tight against her neck, Zoë could see a heap of shattered concrete chunks under the missing wall at the end of the cavern, but the being with the light was invisible. Maybe it was a spirit without a shape.

The voice cried out. Sharp words careened off the tanks, bouncing back and forth, echoing around Zoë. The voice shouted at some invisible listener. "Lamb, you tricked me. This is no computer warehouse. Son of a bitch! I shoulda known you'd lie. I want outta here."

Zoë thought, Lamb? Lamb of God? Who else was he talking to but Jesus? Inky always said that Jesus and everybody could hoodwink you to make sure you had the gumption in your mind and the love in your heart to deserve Heaven.

She knelt on the freezing floor and, withdrawing her hands into sleeves, she put them on the floor, too, then bent low to observe the speaker, secretly, from under the tank. Was this her angel?

Shaped like a man? Dressed like a man?

"Where are you, kid?" the speaker said, swinging a powerful beacon back and forth. "I know you're in here. I saw you from over there."

How could a man know she was in the cave? Maybe those *were* drones she saw in the sky. Or, maybe, maybe, could he be her angel?

He shined his beam behind him, revealing another cleft in the cavern wall. Her attention drawn to the tumbled wall, Zoë heard a river rushing.

"You were over there, but I know you were coming my way," he said.

Of course he knew. The angel looked like an ordinary Spring Creek man wearing a blue ski jacket and a red-checked hunting cap. When he walked, his boots squished, the way Zoë's shoes did after she wore them in streams hunting crawdaddies or watercress.

He made tracks on the floor, leaving outlines of his soles frozen in place as soon as he lifted his foot.

For some reason, he wore a telephone headset and mumbled into it. Then, the angel ripped off the headset and let it hang down from his neck. In the cavern's immense silence, Zoë heard tinny braying come from the headset.

Angel looked strong enough to carry her up through the empty spaces, but he was acting confused, whipping his light between rows of tanks, shining it up to the ceiling, then running it across the jumble of rock he'd just climbed down.

"Kid, c'mon. Don't play games. I only wanna help you."

I know, Zoë thought, unable to move.

She shook her head and shoulders, stood up and took a full, deep breath, all the way from her nose down to the bottom of her stomach. The frigid air sent prickles over her scalp when it sliced into her sinuses. She exhaled, and a hot surge of energy flickered under her skin.

Amazing. A miracle. I knew he was coming, but still. A miracle the angel's here.

"It's just me, Reverend Roy. Reverend Roy Kassup from Spring Creek? We gotta get outta here. It's no place for a kid." He tilted his head back and rolled his eyes up, as if expecting someone to jump over a tank. Mumbling. "No place for anybody."

Not able to understand his mumbles, Zoë's feet glided ahead and she rounded the tank and, standing not ten feet from him, said "Hello, Angel." Her face split into a grin so wide her front teeth ached.

He jumped back, dropping his beacon. "Shit. Wait a minute." He bent over to pick up the lantern. He raised it and aimed it at Zoë, the light crashing into her eyes before she ducked her head.

He said, "Lamb, it's a girl. I'll grab her then I'm comin' out. Open the goddam door."

Her back to the harsh light, Zoë peeked at the angel out of the corner of her eye. She thought she heard "Motherfuckin' asshole" and some other swear words coming out of the earphones, but she must have misheard.

"Angel," she said, her voice trembling, "don't blind me. I want to see you."

Angel lowered the beam to her stomach and started toward her. His boot sole stuck to the concrete and he lost his footing and stumbled, falling onto the floor at the edge of the scree fan. He flung the lantern straight up and as it arced and fell, it washed the tanks with lemon glaze.

He cussed again and rolled to his knees.

"Oh, Angel! Can I help you?" Zoë leapt toward him, reaching out with both hands. "Get up. We can go to Heaven now."

The angel picked up his lantern. The lens had cracked into a web of lines, distorting the powerful full spectrum beacon into a rainbow eye. Pointing the lantern toward her face, he growled, "How did you get in here?"

She drew back toward the tanks, blinking, her thin body vibrating inside her coat. That smell. She knew it, too well.

"Hey, you're my little Rapture girl! Zoë." He choked out a sinister laugh. "We seen each other twice in two days. How did you get in here? That's what I call ordinated by the Good Lord!"

He laughed, almost braying, and washed the light over her coat, down to her shoes, then up, flashing it past her eyes, finally focusing it on face. "You won't get away from me this time."

He sounded like Ketchup. She thought she could smell him, stinky like Ketchup. But she couldn't identify him as long as he held the light in her eyes. Why would Ketchup be in the cave? No way Ketchup was an angel.

"How'd you get here? Is there anybody with you?" he asked, without lowering the lantern.

"Angel, take the light out of my eyes. You know what I look like now. Let me see your wings."

"Don't flirt with me unless you mean it. I ain't forgot for one minute who bit my nose off!" The beam sunk slowly away from Zoë's head. Then bringing it up, he whipped it under his chin. His face became a jack-o-lantern mask of lines and shadows and fiery eyes. The light sank into a dark round smudge in the center of his porky face.

It was him. Ketchup. How?

He bared his teeth and sprung toward her, shouting a hoarse "Boo!"

"Stop! Stay away," Zoë cried. She giggled nervously and inched back, holding her arm across her face in case he shot the light toward her head again.

Somebody was playing tricks on her. Or was she wrong back in the Little White Church? He was mean and ugly, and angels were beautiful and kind. Could Ketchup be an angel? If he was, he was a fallen angel. But he couldn't be a devil, even if he acted like it sometimes. He was just testing her to see if she was pure enough to go to Heaven. That's it.

Ketchup's light drove against her, laying on her as heavy as Minister Ketchup when he pinned her down on the altar those years ago. Her knees went loose and her head began to swim.

The man let the light fall, focusing its rainbows on the floor between them. Softening his voice, he said, "I'm sorry, kid. I was just playin'. Angels play all the time, you know. I just want to play. Shall we play?"

"Why are you here?"

"Like I said, me and you are ordinated by the Big Guy himself." He raised a small metal bottle to his lips and gulped.

Zoë touched Little Limbo through her coat. All quiet.

She recognized Ketchup's bottle as a hunter's flask like the ones she'd found on deer runs during hunting season. They always held whiskey. Zoë noted that if it was whiskey in his flask and Ketchup drank too much, maybe that was good. Maybe he'd fall asleep. She shuddered when she imagined him any closer to her.

She cast her eyes up, toward the infinitely distant ceiling. Inky, what should I do? She waited. Behind her, she heard Ketchup's boots scuffling toward her. She couldn't wait for Inky to wake up.

She turned to Ketchup, backed up a step and asked, in a small, respectful voice, tricking him into thinking she might do what he wanted. "What did you say your angel name was?" She almost said "I don't know" but she swallowed her tongue.

"Like I fuckin' said, what's his name? Roy? Like me?" He slurred his words.

Angels wouldn't swear. Having had experience with mollifying and deluding drunks, Zoë sweetened her tone. "That's a funny name for an angel," she said. Usually angels had magnificent names like Raphael or Gabriel or powerful names like Michael, but Roy?

"Let's play hide 'n seek," she said. "I'll hide first. You find me."

Frightened of Ketchup, but confused, too, because why would he be here where her Angel was waiting? Zoë spun into the gloom. The tanks now looked like wingless bodies of planes abandoned on a twilight field. She sneaked a glance back, waiting, showing herself, expecting him to loft his body over the tanks to land in front of her.

Lunging toward her, Ketchup called, "Zoë, come back. I don't like hide 'n seek. I won't bite." He hooted.

Retreating into the shifting shadows his lantern cast behind the tanks, Zoë stopped to get her bearings. She'd lead him to Devan so he could find out what he was doing here. He knew all about Ketchup. He hated him.

"Here I am, Angel. Come and get me." She waited for him to follow but Angel was spraying his light everywhere again, under the tanks, up to the ceiling. What did he think, she had wings?

She listened. All she heard was his boots cracking loose from the icey floor, stomping, crackling. Zoë raced on her toes toward the far side of the room and Devan.

Before she put the distance of two tanks between them, she heard Ketchup shout, "Fuck. Little bitch's gone. Goddamit. Don't sweat it, Lamb. I'll get her."

Inky stayed silent. He wasn't making this easy for her. Zoë was on her own.

Twenty-six

DOWN THE STAIRS

Zoë bounded from between a row of tanks. Devan had reached the cavern wall and turned around, raising his lights and camera toward the room.

"Devan! Devan! Help! There's somebody after me!" She leapt into him, jabbing her shoulder into the edge of the RadAlert on his chest. Her head jerked back and she dropped her flashlight.

"Zoë! Christ." Devan pushed her back, shaking his head. He spoke into the transmitter in his helmet. "Laurel, I got her. Yeah." He let his light sink toward their feet. "At least I didn't have to run all over this pit looking for you." He reached for her shoulder. His voice, muffled by the helmet, softened. "Stay right beside me. We head back in two minutes."

"He's coming!" In her shock, Zoë twirled around, shaking. "I saw him! He's looking for me!"

She ran a circle around Devan, then, shouting, she jumped onto his back, ratcheting her arm around his neck. She threw her other arm around his visor and dug her toes into the backs of his knees, monkeying up his back.

Devan stumbled, caught himself, reached around with one arm to brace her bottom and clamp her body against his. Using his arm as a stair, she raised her knee to push herself up. Every time he shuffled one way to balance them, she scrambled toward his other side. She clutched her hands together, pressing her palms against his throat and pulled him backwards.

Their silent dance ended with him tipping to the side, losing his footing, twisting to avoid crushing her when he fell. They clattered to the floor at the moment the overhead lights dimmed, then fell dark completely.

Devan swung his flashlight toward the ceiling and ran the wide beam across the dull metal wall ten yards away.

"That must be him," Zoë panted, extricating herself from Devan's baggy suit and jumping up.

A pale streak of light shone toward them from twenty yards down the wall. It widened and cast ashy light over them as a door opened. The lanky silhouette of a man appeared in the center of a rectangular violet aura. Zoë squinted, but she didn't see wings and he wasn't wearing white robes like in the church paintings. Now she knew you couldn't tell them by their clothes.

Devan grabbed Zoë's ankle and lifted his head, nodding toward the open door. "Is that him?

"I don't know," Zoë replied, more confused than she'd ever been. Zoë shook off Devan's hand and sprang up as the figure slipped back into the brightly lit doorway. A few overhead lights flickered on.

"Zoë! Wait!" Devan rushed after her. He caught her sleeve as he spoke into the microphone in his helmet, his voice dulled by the plastic. "She's chasing some guy. Went through a door in the wall. I'm going after her."

"Hey Laurel," Zoë called back, hoping Devan's microphone would transmit her voice. "I think I found my Angel."

Zoë dashed through the door as fast as a swift hunting in a night barn. "Come on, Devan."

Devan shouted into his helmet, "Laurel, stay there."

Relieved by her escape from Ketchup and thrilled to find what must be her Angel, Zoë laughed and stepped inside the doorway. A spiral staircase descended into a steel-walled cylinder through pale turquoise light. Behind her, Devan's Geiger counter squawked like a hoarse goose.

Devan caught her by the collar and lifted his Geiger counter to check the readout. "Look at this," he said. "We got a problem. A huge problem."

The display had cracked. Green numbers tumbled and dove across the fractured display.

"That's strange. My visor sensor shows 0," he said.

"What's wrong?"

Devan dropped her arm. "Radiation. Radiation means cancer. We have to get out of here now."

"Okay. Let's go. Down the stairs."

"Laurel, the RadAlert's gone nuts. Reads between 0 and 999. Can't tell for sure, but it looks like we've got radiation." He waited. "Can you hear me? Are you there? Laurel?" Static buzzed from the helmet receivers. His wounded machine whined as shrill as a morning alarm.

"Laurel. Laurel. Damn." He gasped, his breathing out of control. Zoë took the Geiger counter in one hand and pounded it with the palm of the other. The screeching stopped. He stared at Zoë.

"It's okay, Devan. See? No radiation. It broke when we fell down. I'm sorry." She lifted her shoulders and said, "I'm going."

Devan rushed toward her but she turned and balancing on one arm, she launched her body over a round steel banister. A strange odor wafted up the stairs. At first, she suspected it was her own body revealing its nervousness, but soon she identified the sweet, pungent fragrance of curry.

She descended a full flight of metal steps, her boots ringing as she stomped down on every other step. Behind her she heard Devan swearing. "O my God."

She noted, not for the first time, how cussing often sounded like prayers.

Still in the cavern behind her, Devan shouted to Laurel that Zoë'd broken his Rad. Devan was so upset about radiation, he'd forgotten all about Angel. He was more scared by blinking green numbers than she'd seen him in her whole life.

She was upset, but more excited than she'd been ever since she learned about the Rapture. Besides, if there was radiation, and if the being was her Angel – and he must be – he'd cancel the radiation. Nobody had to worry about cancer. Why didn't Devan just pay attention to what was really happening?

Without warning, her body staggered, her heart racing and her lungs pumping out of control. She tried to slow her breathing down by grabbing onto the handrail and letting the jolt of cold stop the plunging of her chest. She clenched the railing, bracing herself for the last few steps.

Laurel's voice, blotchy with static, scratched the air as it followed Zoë down the spiral staircase. Devan was coming.

Devan's radio squacked. "…hear you. Devan…going…."

Zoë saw Devan's black boots on the landing half a flight of steps above. He shouted again, panic in his voice. "Laurel, you're breaking up. Stay there till I call you. We don't need everybody to get radiated."

A grinding, metallic caterwaul reached Zoë's ears from the cavern, the screeching a rusty overhead door makes when it opens. Where? A random series of flat gongs thudded from the cavern overhead, as if someone struck the tanks with wood, beating out a clunky music.

She glanced up again, curious, but not too surprised at the noises, especially since Angel had arrived. His presence would make even radiation tanks try to dance. Satisfied that Devan was following, she stepped off the last step and passed into a blast of air so hot her cheeks burned.

This angel looked like a man standing in the middle of a large kitchen with white tile walls and stainless steel tables and stoves and navy blue cupboards. Behind him, a window as wide as the wall framed his long blue body and smiling brown face and long ebony hair.

This must be a true angel body in the flesh. He was more beautiful than she'd ever imagined.

"Hello," he said. "Welcome to my home. I am Vikram J. Kapoor, PhD, MD, JD. We're quite informal here, so why don't you call me Veejay."

His words caressed her ears with the lilt of a flute and the sweetness of a mother cat's purr. His magnificent real name resonated with the same power as Ink'p'du'da and Kateri Tekawitha. Veejaykapoor.

Dumbfounded by his presence, her heart throbbing in her eyes, the angel's body pulsated. He looked younger than Devan, but not too much. Zoë was good at math and guessing how old people were, so she estimated his age in a flash. Devan was about thirty, so Veejay must be about twenty-six and a quarter or a half, approximately. His face was lovely and kind. He *could be* her Angel. Yes!

Maybe this was an Inky trick. He always played games with her. He didn't want her to waltz into the cave and jump on a some creature who was hiding underground, waiting for her to climb aboard the shuttle to Heaven.

Angel held his hands out toward Zoë, welcoming her. He said, "Who might you be, my dear?"

Her mouth went dry, but Zoë, ardent seeker and determined daughter of Ruthie, rolled her tongue twelve times each way between her teeth and lips, a Lakota trick for wetting her mouth. Then, swallowing, she said, "Zoë. Zoë Rarefield."

Her hand reached out and Angel stepped forward, his teeth gleaming from abundant, open lips, his arm long as a featherless wing outstretched toward her.

Their fingertips touched and Zoë felt the blood rush from her head down her arms and into her fingers where Angel clasped her hand. She sank toward him and he caught her in both arms, gathering her with no more strain than a zephyr lifts up a fallen leaf.

As she closed her eyes in certainy she mumbled, "Veejay. Angel Veejaykapoor. My strong Angel."

Twenty-seven

DIRECTOR, R.I.P.

Zoë woke up sitting in a leather desk chair, her feet folded under her, her eyes immediately finding the dark chocolate eyes of her angel staring into hers. Her coat was bunched up under her bottom. She shifted and smoothed it across her knees.

Offering her a glass of water, Angel said, "Are you all right, Zoë Rarefield?"

"I am unbelievable wonderful." She took the glass and swallowed her first divine water other than the holy water she always sipped out of the baptismal font when she visited Catholic churches. "It's stuffy in here, is all."

Easing out of the chair, she grinned and backed across the room so she could keep her eyes on him while she explored his kitchen.

A long spigot arced up out of a dazzling chrome sink. He'd have plenty of water. Glancing into every corner of the room, she noticed a microwave oven high up near the ceiling. Angel was so tall, he could probably reach it without leaving the ground.

Angel stepped closer and stared at her face, frowning. "Are your eyes all right? They're wobbling."

"Yes, yes." She blinked hard. "They're just happy to see you."

"Should I dim the lights? Your lenses may need time to adjust after the twilight upstairs."

"No." She held her eyes on him. He glowed. Whose eyes wouldn't wobble when they looked at an angel?

"I wondered if you would find me before that hunter caught you," Angel said. His lips twisted and he wrinkled his forehead again, looking over his shoulder at the door. "Your friend will be here soon."

Devan's anxious voice drifted into the room from outside the open door. He must have stopped to talk with Laurel on the walkie-talkie.

"What hunter?" Zoë said.

"That one." He nodded toward a screen the size of an entire entertainment center. Somebody was wandering the maze of tanks, stumbling, bouncing off them and tripping, picking himself up and staggering on. Shadows filled the screen, so at first, Zoë couldn't identify the person.

He had a puffy body, like the down jacket she'd seen on Ketchup, and he wore a cap. When he waved its flashlight rainbows splattered on the sides of the tanks. It was Ketchup.

Zoë fondled Ruthie's rib, muttering to herself, "Is Vejaykapoor him, mama? He looks strong enough. Tall, too. You always said angels were tall as the ceiling. Remember?"

Angel opened his arms as if to embrace Zoë again. She danced toward him, forgetting the thing on the screen, laughing. She'd found her Angel, he wanted her. Maybe she didn't even need the poshent.

Angel pulled back before she could touch him. Opening his arms wide, raising them, he pivoted his body stiffly in a half circle, imitating her twirls. His white sneakers gleamed against the white tile floor and his jeans clung to thin but muscular thighs.

"Welcome to Research International Project Worldwide, known affectionately as R.I.P. Our motto: *We create the future out of the poison of the past.*"

Zoë stared. She folded her arms and then propped her chin on one fist, holding her body in concentrate-and-study position.

"Let me explain. R.I.P. is my tongue-in-cheek name. You see, we all want peace but I'm afraid humans will never find it."

He spoke in a bass voice, trilling clipped r's and enunciating his words in a new accent, one she'd never heard before. It wasn't Spanish. A bit like Ahmad Khan, the Pakistani who ran the Kum 'n Go convenience store in Spring Creek.

She gazed into his sunken black eyes, the rhythm of his words delicate as a quail's calling to her hidden chicks.

"So I say, let us Rest In Peace even here, this storehouse of the vilest means of destruction humans have ever created."

Yes, Zoë thought, humans can only rest in the peace of Heaven. Zoë's eyes followed his amber fingers and chambray sleeves as he waved his arms, lecturing about his angel work.

"But here is my secret, my victory. I have found a way to bring peace to anybody who wants it. Out of the most fearful garbage on the planet, I've made fertility, peace, prosperity – above all, endless health."

His fingers gestured, drifting across the screens and windows, the cupboards, a wake of nearly visible feathers rippling across his arms as they swept through the air.

Around the room, silvery screens displayed bananas and pink worms and bright green pickles twisting and braiding into each other. On the ceiling, whole galaxies of stars and suns and comets sprawled over the black universe. Rising from one wall, a sun brightened the edge of the sky.

For sure, she thought, he's my Angel. He's here, inside the ground, but his head almost touches Heaven. This is a miracle place. It must be the foyer inside the Heavenly mansion's front door.

Stainless steel countertops and sinks shone like ice puddles under streetlights. Glass boxes built into the wall reflected powdery blue bulbs and rainbows of color and little people twirling and dancing. Soft string and drum music played, comforting Zoë. Already she felt at home, almost as much at ease as in Devan's trailer

"My dervishes," Veejay said, pointing at paintings on one wall. "Do you like them? They come in all the way from India, whenever I call them."

Zoë's glance locked onto a painting of women robed in scarlet and gold and floating above a wavy, blue lake. In her lap, she held a white flower with a hundred petals.

"Are they angels, too?".

"A saint. Radha is her name."

"Like Kateri." Zoë bit her lower lip in astonished relief.

"You might say they're people that somebody let loose into space."

Like me, pretty soon, Zoë thought.

She stared at the constellations creeping along over her head. She didn't recognize any of the shapes. She must be seeing them from above, looking down from outside the atmosphere.

"You like my sky?"

"It's nice. Isn't it usually way farther overhead?" Her face parallel with the ceiling, her mouth open, Zoë turned around in a slow circle, astonished, a few feet from the stars. She stretched her arms up, wiggling her fingers to sense the temperature of the tiny lights. Her hands reached only as high as her Angel's eyes.

Preening before her, he pressed a button on the counter and the sun blazed and said, "Down here, I control the weather. Some days I make sunny and," he tapped his fingers "some nights I make cloudy."

The night sky returned with wisps of stratus flooding across the ceiling, obscuring the stars. "My computers don't like rain, so I keep it dry. And the wind? Out here in South Dakota, the wind blows so hard dust that my computers couldn't imitate it." He laughed and brought up an azure daylight sky.

He finished his guided tour and sat on a stool, scrutinizing Zoë with one eye, watching the monitors with the other.

Without thinking, Zoë came up on her toes and pirouetted, lifting her arms, twirling, slowly at first, then faster. Her boot soles tapped a jig on the floor and her coat flapped and her hair rayed out like flames, she hoped.

In her flowered shirt, feeling as serene as Angel's cloudless sky, her long colorful skirt blending with his Heavenly aura, she twirled, dizzying herself as she always did when absolute happiness seized her. A half dozen crickets launched out of her pockets, landing on the floor in a tumult of crawling and hopping.

Zoë danced, circling closer to her Angel with every leap until she brushed against his knees and swooned like an accomplished diva into his arms, the way she always fell into her mother's arms when she spun herself to the point of throwing up when she was a little kid.

This dizziness felt different, less in her head and more in her lower body, her legs, up into her breasts.

She leaned into Angel, panting. Clinging to his stomach, her head full of light, her heart pounding with joy, ready to lift off.

Leaning down from a celestial height even greater than Devan's, the slender director of R.I.P. held her in large, formal hands. Oiled black hair with the sheen of crow's feathers draped his long face, tickling Zoë's forehead as she lay against him, trusting as if he were a long lost friend.

He inhaled deeply. She felt his warm breath in her hair. He inhaled again.

"You smell like Mother Earth herself," he said. "Spicy as ferns." He pushed her away, holding her at arms' length. "Who are you, girl? Are you a clown? A dervish? Why have you come here? It's not proper to sneak around mountaincaves, you know. Bad things lurk in the shadows."

"You know why I'm here," she said, ready for another test. Angels always tested people because they had to be sure you believed in them. Lots of people didn't. "I came so you can take me to Heaven."

Boots clanged down the staircase outside the open door.

Hastily, Veejay said, "We must get ready for your friend."

Releasing her while extracting a card from his pocket, Veejay aimed it toward a bank of switches and buttons.

The sound of a door slamming shut echoed into the room from behind Devan at the instant he appeared in the open laboratory door dressed in his moon suit, pointing his pistol at Veejay's stomach.

Holding the pistol steady, Devan stepped into the room. He stopped and swung his helmeted head around, noting the monitors and lights.

"You don't need that silly suit you're wearing, you know," Angel declared. "There's no radiation danger here. Do you think I'd risk my life?"

Zoë knew that. If only Devan didn't take his machines so seriously. He was about to learn that he was safe, Laurel was safe. All he had to do was to ask Angel to clean up the radiation pots and he and Laurel could go home and go back to their acting and singing while she and Angel drank the poshent and disappeared into the sky.

Zoë grinned at Devan. "What took you so long? At least it's nice and warm."

The RadAlert spasmed numbers across Devan's chest.

"Except for that little gun, you look like a typical war journalist out for an afternoon of tragedy," Angel said.

Devan turned to Zoë and asked in a quiet voice, "Zoë, you okay?"

"Devan, I'm happy now." Her grin hadn't left her face since her beloved brother arrived to meet her beloved angel. Her voice trembling and liquid, she said, "Devan meet my Angel. Veejay meet my brother."

Neither man nor angel moved.

Angel's dark face was smooth but a few whiskers shadowed his cheeks and chin. He stared coolly at the armed interloper as Devan edged toward Zoë.

Unvelcroing his helmet with one hand and pushing it back, Devan spoke to Zoë while glaring at Veejay. "We gotta go now." To Angel, he snapped, "You the watchman? Janitor? Somebody sweeps around those tanks?"

He moved toward Zoë, reaching for her with one arm while aiming the pistol with his other hand. "We have to leave. Come on." He beckoned with gloved fingers. "You can give your angel your address."

"No, Devan. You know what's happening. I'm going with him now."

"Young lady," the angel sounded offended. "I can't take you anywhere."

"She doesn't know what she's saying," Devan said. "She's confused right now."

"Who isn't these days?" Veejay replied, thick black eyebrows scrawling low on his forehead, nearly meeting between his eyes.

"What I mean is, she doesn't know what she's got herself into here and she thinks you're the answer to her prayers. I'm taking her."

Devan moved next to Zoë, but she slipped behind Angel.

"Where are the others? I know you're a terrorist." Devan demanded, stealing closer to Zoë but stopping short of grabbing her. He faced the door to the stairwell and noticed that it had shut. "Trapping me? What do you think you're doing? What is this place?" His words seethed.

"You can go whenever you want. I'm no terrorist. I'm a working man. Only, I'm keeping everybody safe."

"Open the door. We're outta here."

"All right. But first, let me tell you what we're doing here," Veejay offered. "It won't matter if you take the pictures of the warehouse back to show them around, even if you put them in the hands of the most radical journalists. Nobody wants to know about this place." He shrugged. "Everybody will have to deny that it exists. Nobody will allow themselves to believe anything you say or show them."

"I see." Stretching his free hand toward Zoë, Devan said, "I'll shoot if you try to pull a gun on me."

Ignoring Devan's hand, Zoë giggled to herself. Only Devan would have the courage to complain about things to an angel.

Veejay addressed him. "But you don't see," he said. Angel's voice rose and his mouth filled with the clitter-clatter of pebbles like the stones she collected and polished in her tumbler. "This is Research International Program, division of Downstream Underground Management Project, supervised by Your Electronic Security and Surveillance System, division of Practical Links Urgent Technologies Operation, division of countless divisions of those in control."

Devan dropped his hand. "Who's in control? What do you research anyway?" Now Devan sounded interested. "You probably won't mind if I take your picture, then? What did you say your name was?"

"I didn't say. I am Vikram Jiddha Kapoor. Yes, you may take my picture. Record everything."

Zoë emerged from behind Angel. He placed his hands on her shoulders sending shivers down her arms.

Devan softened his voice and aimed the camera, holding it two feet in front of his face, glancing back and forth between the camera and his subjects. He said. "What do you do here, Mr. Kapoor?"

"I watch, I wait. I experiment."

"I'd like to see some of those experiments," Devan said.

"Would you like to take pictures of them, too?"

Devan considered Angel's good will offer. She smiled when he answered with respect.

"If you don't mind, Mr. Kapoor."

Zoë sensed that Devan was practicing his acting. Otherwise, why would he point a gun at an angel? He probably had blanks in the gun the way he did when he played Wild Bill Hickock in Deadwood.

"It's *Doctor* Kapoor, but why don't you call me Veejay, like she does? What should I call you?" he asked politely as a divine ambassador.

"Call me Devan. She's my little sister."

"Of course. I like Zoë. She shocked me somewhat, but I am fascinated by her hair."

"Do you like it?" Zoë said. "I colored it for you, so you'd see me from a long way."

"Lovely. Especially the blue and yellow tips."

"It's a fire."

Veejay nodded and glanced at the video monitors. "No, I don't mind if you take photos. I don't mind if you take Zoë, too." He paused. "Do you want to know why I don't mind?"

"I hope it's not because you think you'll get my camera or drives?" Devan waved the pistol.

"I don't want anything of yours. They don't matter. In fact, I wish you could take them out of here and publish them. I deserve publicity. My work is some of the most important work on the planet today, if not the most."

"What work is that?"

Their talk started to bore Zoë.

"I will tell you, but first, please make sure your video and audio recorders are in order. I want you to get everything I say."

"No. Download everything to a flash, no, make that two. I'll take them now."

Veejay threw up his arms and said, sadness in his voice, "Either way, it's no use."

"Why not?" Devan sauntered around the room examining the equipment, still aiming his gun at Veejay. "Pretty tight space," he said. "They give the janitor here a decent-sized living area? This is smaller than my trailer house."

Devan the joker had come back. Zoë expected him to put the gun back in his holster, but gripping the camera in his left hand, he filmed from the hip.

Veejay said, "If you give the drives to anybody, you might as well give them your heart on a platter. Give it to them warm and still beating. That will be less painful than what you'll get from my captors when they find you."

"Captors?" Devan's voice hardened.

Captors? Some kind of a raptor, like a hawk or eagle? Maybe an owl. They see in dark places like the tank room. Zoë interrupted. "Do you mean dinosaurs like T Rex? Or birds, like owls." Angels live forever, so she guessed that he saw dinosaurs when they lived in South Dakota a million years ago. "You can time travel, can't you?"

Veejay stared at Zoë and, pursing his lips, he smiled weakly at Devan. "Time travel is impossible, my dear."

"I mean, as an angel."

"As an angel, naturally."

Nodding her head proudly, she knew it.

Veejay said to Devan, "You might like to know what I do here. I think you'll begin to understand the misery you and your baby sister and your friends will walk in the rest of your lives. You made a huge mistake coming here."

"I'll decide that." He held the gun steady but his voice quavered.

"Perhaps you'd like to sit," Veejay said, pulling a stool out from under a table and pointing, "while I enlighten you on the true facts of life in the twenty-first century."

"I'll stand." He turned to Zoë. "Sweetie, at least hold my hand. I thought I lost you in the cave."

"You found me, Devan. You always find me. You're my luck, too." She took his hand and kissed his palm. Holding it to her cheek, she said, "I told you my Angel was inside Anpetu."

He squeezed her hand and stroked her head, then sat down on the stool. Pretty soon, Devan and Veejay would make friends. Veejay had already calmed Devan down more than he'd been since they arrived this morning. She jumped up on Devan's lap, still her favorite place on Earth.

Twenty-eight

ANTHROPOLOGIST
OF THE FUTURE

Veejay touched the pad on the wall beside a bank of screens.

"What we have here is a museum of alternate futures. In 5,000 years, people, or what people become." He paused, smiling to nobody, "They will tour the Black Hills to look at remnants of ancient civilization just like tourists traipse around today looking for arrowheads and watching staged gunfights."

The views on the screens displayed pink and peach images of parked trucks and cars, a crane and boom, rooms full of household furniture. Four screens showed long-range views of the warehouse above with the cylinders with the rows of stainless steel medicine capsules.

"Is this a video?" Zoë asked.

Veejay shook his head and chuckled. "It's live, or should I say, half-live?" He stepped between the tables and desks. His voice turned teacherly, authoritative. "You might say that not only am I an inimitable scientist and inventor, but I am an anthropologist of the future."

Zoë listened closely, concentrating. If she'd stayed in school, maybe she'd understand him better, but what would you need school for in Heaven, anyway? As soon as you got there, you became a genius, like Veejay.

"Each object you see, except the outer tank walls, is highly radioactive, stored in a vacuum. Radioactivity preserves these artifacts indefinitely in a vacuum."

Not understanding Angel's rambling words, but amazed at the number of radioactive objects stored inside Anpetu Mountain, Zoë jumped down from Devan's lap.

"Devan says radioactive means cancer."

"Yes, it causes cancer. It poisons anything it touches. First it weakens you, then you lose your hair, then you die."

"Not angels," Zoë said. "You're alive. I feel perfect."

She'd observed how some young animals, especially coyotes, got thin and weak and their fur fell out. They would lay in the arroyos exposed to the sun, waiting for their coyote angels. Was that radioactive cancer? Her vision of the woods overflowing with dead and rotting animals flashed across her imagination and snatched her breath away.

"We don't let radioactivity near us," Veejay said. "I wouldn't allow depraved gamma rays to vandalize my neighborhood."

Devan stood and paced silently, glancing into screen after screen, his face as drawn and sad as when his dog Falstaff died. His shoulders sagged and his gun drooped.

"Where did this garbage come from, Kapoor? Where is it now? This stuff can't be here," Devan demanded in a voice as morose as Angel's was boastful.

"It's leftovers, my friend," he answered, his tone as bland as boiled squash. "And yes. This 'stuff' is here. One hundred feet below where we're standing. It came from 'accidents' like Chernobyl, Three Mile Island. From calculated risks like Hanneford, Johannesburg. From sabotage. From weapons caches. All over the world." Veejay cast his gaze over both of their faces.

When his eyes lit on hers, she felt her nose go numb.

"Don't tell me you don't know we've got bombs and reactors and ovens and engines planted like weeds that grow anywhere? Underwater. Inside mountains. In the sky. Under our cities."

Zoë had never seen a bomb or an oven in the sky, unless the clouds hid them. She hoped not, because a thunderstorm from a radiation cloud would make everybody it rained on sick. The radiation must be up near the sun, or past it, out in the dark matter.

After Zoë and George had fooled around in The Good Food Store back room, George had told her about the dark matter and the dark energy, the invisible world under our noses. Not spirits but, he said, stuff in the universe that dripped onto our heads every minute and we couldn't feel it. We only guessed it was there. Nobody had proved it yet.

Once Zoë knew something was true, proof never mattered to her.

If the dark stuff held all the radiation, that was another good reason she needed a strong angel to fly her through, to dodge the hidden poison asteroids and intergalactic dust, another fact George had taught her about.

Zoë regarded Veejay, appreciating her incredible luck – thank Inky – for having found an angel with a body powerful enough to free her from this creepy cancery universe.

Caught between Veejay's lecture and Devan's gloom and her sudden understanding of the absolute danger of being alive, Zoë's head filled with cotton and the roots of tears began to tickle her throat.

Now Veejay sounded angry. "Everybody knows we've got stock-piles of gamma and beta dumped around the planet like manure around a barn."

Devan glared at Veejay, his gun still pointing down.

"Everybody's asleep out there, aren't they? Nobody knows a thing. You have millions of sources of radiation perched across your country like vultures waiting for fresh cadavers. Every hospital, every major construction site, every university research center, factories, food irradiation centers, smoke detectors."

A sad smile settled on Veejay's face as he watched Devan's reaction.

"If you just look, you can find sites like this one in every country. Half the countries in Africa beg to sell their caves and mountains to the major governments. Isotopes are today's diamonds and gold."

Devan pointed his gun toward the ceiling. "What about the tanks up there? What's in them? Can it blow up?"

"Don't worry. Despite all the bad news, we're creating a beautiful future. The best future we can, given our humanity."

When he said the word "our," Zoë pricked up her hearing, setting her ears to fine-tune. The word reminded her that angels grew human bodies so they could help people. At the same time, they'd get to feel what it's like to have a body. According to Inky, most of them didn't stay in a body for very long – too much pain for a spirit person to bear.

"We don't have time for lectures, Kapoor." Devan took a deep breath, edging closer.

"You're right, we don't. But rushing to your death won't make it any more memorable or pleasant. Once you see what we create here, you'll feel a lot better. After all, you're safer here than you will be at the top of those stairs."

"My safety doesn't matter, Kapoor."

"Ah. I am sorry to hear that. Carelessness is the ultimate danger."

The exchange between Devan and Angel flustered her. With every word they said, they befuddled her worse.

Angel had come a long way to fetch her, and she liked him. But Devan was the finest man, the handsomest, the funnest she could ever meet and he was determined to take her with him.

She'd loved Devan longer than she loved anybody except Ruthie. The haze settled in her head while her stomach knotted with doubt. If only Inky would show up and give me the words to make Devan and Veejay friends.

The scientist angel droned on. "You're thinking of the others. That heroic, self-sacrificing spirit of yours that some of my colleagues advocate preserving in the new creatures they're developing. I'm not sure it's advisable."

"Creatures." Devan scowled.

"Billions of people already sacrifice themselves and their descendants because they think a hero will come and save them. Christ didn't. Mohammed didn't. Marx didn't. Jefferson didn't. Buddha didn't. Human life is soap opera, that's all."

As Veejay fingered the remote, the screens changing images again, Devan watched the door.

Rapt with his own speech, Veejay went on, "My job is complex, but I love the challenge. I really couldn't be any happier in my work. Of course, I prefer sky overhead rather than granite, but circumstances change. How old are you, about 30?"

"About." Taking the bait, Devan said "How old are you?"

"Chronologically? Forty-three. Do I look it?" he retorted. "I look like my pictures from my mid-twenties. I am probably intellectually still an adolescent. Physically? I can run the mile in four minutes and thirty seven seconds." He pointed to a treadmill standing in the corner.

Devan grit his teeth, clenching his jaw so hard a vein bulged on his temple. In an animated blue tattoo, blood pulsed across his head in a vein from in front of his ear, straight up at first, then zigzagging down toward his eye.

Veejay signaled for Devan to sit beside him on a stool. "As I said, I am a museum director. An anthropologist. Today, your Black Hills cave guide. That is just the surface, the epidermis of my life. Look closely at the center screen and you'll see my real job."

The video camera scanned ranks of green metal lockers, close enough for Zoë to see the printed labels.

Veejay read the names aloud in a small voice. "Sergie Romanov, left kidney, Chernobyl. Carol Brockton, heart, Yankee Rowe. Captain Vladimir Krushnic, liver, Riga. Gary McCarthy, pancreas, White Sands."

Zoë's crickets punctuated Veejay's litany, a small chirping choir practicing for a Requiem mass. Zoë hummed with them while the man and the angel developed their friendship.

"Jean Paul, eyes, Cherbourg. Wilhelm Meistersohn, eyes, testicles, Chernobyl. Tonumo Morinaka, adrenals, Tokyo C. Aisha Khaleel, left ovary, Jerusalem 1-B."

"There must be hundreds of lockers," Devan said. The dull shock in his voice alerted Zoë to new danger. Her hand in her pocket circling Little Limbo, she pressed her face close to the screen. Did Veejay use those school lockers to keep souls the way she used Little Limbo? She focused on the labels. Eyes, kidneys, brains.

She'd heard that some people believed that souls live in different organs – mostly the heart or the stomach – but she knew her soul lived in every cell of her body, like water soaked into a shirt in the rain.

Devan aimed his camera at the screen. "What is this?"

"Martyrs for future generations, you might say. Their unwitting sacrifice allows us to explore all kinds of possibilities for healing. We've already concluded hundreds of experiments on their organ tissues." Veejay sounded excited. "Watch closely now." He indicated the next screen higher up.

"This is unbelievable." Bravura barely covered the tremor in Devan's voice. "Why don't you give me a flash of this so I can show it to people outside?"

"I'd be glad to – when we're ready. I have several colleagues whose work depends on my conclusions. My colleagues need to refine our conclusions before we feel it's safe to inform the public. We have publicity plans. The timing is soon, but not just yet."

If Devan just went back up the stairs and out of the cave, back to Laurel, it would be time for her and Veejay to drink the poshent and fly. How could she convince him to go back now? As usual, Devan could read her mind.

"We think now's the time," Devan said.

Veejay objected. "No, you don't understand."

Yes, Zoë thought. He wants to keep me with him.

"The audience has to be ready. We can make the world a wonderful place, but if the wrong people find out too soon, well, you know the plutocrats." His voice trailed off, letting the silence underline the risk.

"I'm ready. Show me what you're up to. Quick. Zoë and I have about thirty seconds to get out of here."

No. Zoë backed away.

"I can be quick. It's simple. I bind tiny mutated organ DNA into crystals at the quantum level. Call it crystobiology, or biocrystography. We're inventing the whole discipline. All our research is networked through your old Star Wars satellites all the politicians pretended were worthless. You thought they canceled Star Wars thirty years ago?" Veejay said. "By the time they made it public, you had a web of satellites over northern Europe as far east as Siberia and North Korea."

Devan's eyebrows quivered as he said, with disgust in his voice, "Star Wars, nukes, mutations, mad scientists. What else?"

"Those we will offer the results of our study will be the new leaders of humanity: they will live for hundreds of years."

Zoë pushed a stool over the sink. She climbed up and turned on a faucet, washing her hands in a cool trickle and filling her palms for a drink.

"If you want drinking water, it's in the refrigerator," Veejay said.

Devan pointed the pistol steady. He checked the RadAlert – blinking. He glanced at his watch.

"But," Veejay persisted, "we finished the first three phases of our research in record time. I shipped my final results to Horst Kreppel, a thousand kilometers down inside the Laurentians outside Montreal. Kreppel is the real genius. The rest of us so-called super-intellects are slime mold compared to his brain."

"The Hawkings and the Nyanas get the money and the fame." Caustic anger edged Veejay's voice. "If anyone knows the truth about the universe, if anyone saves the human race, it will be Horst Kreppel with V. J. Kapoor at his side."

"You're disgusting," spat Devan. "Tell me how you're going to eliminate that nuke waste you have stored upstairs and I won't shoot you. How'd you like that?"

"If you shoot me, you'll upset your lovely little friend, but my work would go on. We have five other organ banks. No, you won't kill me. You think I'm all the enemies you ever had wrapped into one, but in the long term, I might be your best friend"

Veejay turned back to the mosaic of monitors. He punched another code in the keypad, manipulating the focus dials.

"If I weren't already your ally, would I show this to you?" Veejay said, indicating numbered monitors on the laboratory's rear wall. "We can see the entire warehouse from here. Watch number 6 and number 11."

In number 6, a man dressed in a bulky winter coat, carried a large lantern shining kaleidoscopic colors around him. He made his way among the tanks.

In number 11, another man, this one wearing a cowboy hat and a sheepskin vest strode along carrying a wide-beamed light in one hand and a sawed-off shotgun or short, thick rifle in the other. He walked along the aisle between the wall and the end of the tank rows.

"Who are those guys?" Devan jerked his gun hand toward the screens. "What are they doing here?"

"Look at this picture. This is right outside the upstairs door I locked behind you to protect your friend and you."

Veejay pointed to monitor 7.

Wakanda crouched in the shadow of the tank across the end aisle right outside of Veejay's door. He looked asleep.

So many people were roaming around the tanks, Zoë expected to see Laurel next.

Reading her mind again, Devan said, "Pan the whole cave. Is anybody else in there?"

The cameras moved. Tanks and shadows.

The camera zoomed in on the rubble beneath the cloven wall where Devan, Zoë, and Wakanda had all climbed through. "Is that who you're looking for?"

Behind a cone of weak light aimed into the pulverized concrete, Laurel stood in a uranium miner's suit, staring into the warehouse gloom, a coil of rope hanging from her fully extended Glinda, waiting for her chance to perform along with everyone else.

Zoë smiled. They didn't know it yet, and she hadn't expected it. All Angel Veejay had to do was to make the guns disappear and her beloveds would throw her the happiest going away party any ascending girl could imagine.

Twenty-nine

IN HER HEART, ZOË KNOWS

As the two men approached the door across from Wakanda, Zoë watched him turtle deeper into the shadows.

"Why are they coming this way?" Devan demanded. "One of them has a gun."

"He's Wink Lamb, the boss of Y.E.S.S.S. He's my keeper. I don't know the other. No doubt he's Lamb's toady."

Roy Ketchup was a toad? Zoë knew every fairy tale about princesses and frogs and toads. She used to think Ketchup looked like a pig, but today he did look like a toad. She chuckled to herself then lost interest in the monitors. Everything was in Angel's hands now, though she was surprised angel talk bored her so easily. She relaxed a little, expecting Devan and Angel to become friendly once they got to know each other.

A couple of crickets called, distracting her from a budding drowsiness. She isolated the song of the one she'd named Charger, counting the notes. During the past summer, she had perfected her cricket song weather forecasting technique. By adding 40 to the number of nighttime chirps she counted in 14 seconds, she could predict tomorrow's afternoon temperature reading on the Shannon County Savings Bank time and temperature sign.

Tomorrow, she calculated, she and Angel would soar up from the Earth in perfect 75-degree weather.

Zoë wandered among the tables and counters and odd machines in Angel's kitchen while the he and the Devan discussed their business. She kept half an ear peeled to them, but focused on finding a pan to boil water for the poshent. If she and Angel drank poshent while Devan watched, he could witness her ascension. Then, when he went back to Spring Creek, he could tell Bonnie and Arthur and everyone so they wouldn't worry.

If they wanted to find her, they could pray and she'd come to them the way Inky found her. First she'd show up in their dreams, then she'd come in the spirit world of day dreams. When the right time came, she'd drop into their homes in the very flesh and blood that she lived in now.

She imagined herself sitting down to a spaghetti dinner with Bonnie and Arthur after she'd spent a while in Heaven, astounding them with her stories about Ruthie and the saints and angels. If they asked her about God, she'd say, He comes later, when I get to know my way around.

Zoë didn't trust God. He stole her mother. First thing, in Heaven, she had to make sure Ruthie was all right, hear it in her own words, see her face to face. If she wasn't, no way Zoë wanted to meet God. She'd have to figure some way to get Ruthie back to Earth, or to some other place where they could be safe.

Veejay interrupted her reveries. "Lamb's boss is a someone in Washington, or London. Maybe even Beijing," he said. "He's on assignment here. Lamb is king of what's called D.U.M.P. Downstream Underground Management Project. This whole underground storage area and the communications enclave his on the west side of the mountain. Your friend in the warehouse and that other man heading toward him will not survive their encounter with Lamb."

Having pocketed his gun and raised his camera, Devan glared at the screen while he filmed it. He said, "Hey, I recognize that guy. Lives in Spring Creek. A jerk. Zoë, come here. Look at him."

She skipped over to the monitor. Arching her neck, she squinted at the screen as if peering through a smudged window.

"At first, I thought *he* was my Angel," Zoë said, pointing the figure in screen 6. "*He's* only Ketchup," she said, glancing away from the monitor and smiling at Veejay.

He smiled back, studying her.

"You know him?" Veejay asked Devan.

"That guy?" Devan cut in. "He's trash. A fake preacher. Don't you remember, Zoë? He's the one whose nose you bit off."

Zoë beamed.

"Oh, my," Veejay said. "She *is* the rare one."

Devan slumped against the counter, continuing to stare at the screen. "I should have called in Greenpeace," he muttered.

"What good would they do?" Veejay answered. "Lamb and his men have Federal authority. He's an idiot. He should have mobilized the National Guard the minute the mountain shook. But now you're here, I'm glad he didn't."

In the bright fluorescent light, Devan's face looked gray as a mouse's coat. Zoë pitied him. If he waited patiently and got to know Veejay better, he'd soon understand, as she did already, that Veejay was the answer to all their problems.

Devan banged his fist on the table. The steel rang and Zoë flinched.

"Goddamit," he said aloud. "I'm not done yet." He stuffed his camera into a pocket, pulled out the gun and aimed it at Veejay's forehead. "I guess we'll all have to go upstairs, Dr. Kapoor." Devan motioned toward the door.

Veejay shook his head. "That is a bad idea. Very bad."

"We don't have any other choice," Devan said. "You're our ticket back to the outside world."

"You really don't understand. He will kill me, you, all of us. He doesn't care about my work. He's my jailer. To him, I'm a criminal. I'm an Indian nuclear scientist, trained in North Korea, then rented to Tehran for their 'secret' program, now on loan to the US military. Lamb's my commander. If he decides I'm the enemy, I'm dead. If he finds me with an intruder, he will believe I invited you here."

Devan spread his legs, ready to fight. "If you were worth anything to our government, they'd make sure you were safe. Your bluff won't work." He tugged the scientist's arm but Zoë tore at his hand where he held Veejay.

Veejay disregarded his Zoë. "Lamb has this chamber and my apartment piped for gas. If he wants to get rid of me for any reason, he simply turns a gauge in his office and odorless natural gas out and the crazy scientist dies. Officially, a heart attack."

"Prove it," Devan said, letting the man's arm go and aiming the gun at his chest.

Veejay opened a door under the sink. Zoë and Devan bent to examine the pipes. Behind the U-drain, a small nipple protruded from the wall. Then Veejay pulled a chair over to the counter and motioned for Devan to look. Devan disdained the chair but he looked up. Zoë climbed onto the chair then stood on the counter. In both corners of the room, hidden beside the screws that held the light track to the ceiling were buttons the size of blueberries.

"There are two more in here, several in my bedroom and living room, two in my bathroom and three placed vertically in the stairwell. But don't worry."

"Why should I worry? He's out there. Up there. He can't turn on the gas from the warehouse. Can he?" Devan asked, his voice shaky.

"He can never turn it on."

"What?" Devan's tough cowboy voice came back.

"I mean he can't, period. Quite simple: I control his computer. I control his alarms. His heat sensors and his motion detectors. I decide what he knows about this little estate and wgat he doesn't know it. As far as he knows, it's always business as usual. Calm, cool and quiet in the warehouse." Veejay grinned, his teeth large and glistening.

Relieved, Devan said, "Well, we don't have a thing to worry about then, do we?" as he signaled again toward the door.

"Well, maybe one small thing."

Devan and Zoë waited silently. In the faint turquoise light, the screens and walls and Veejay himself seemed as immovable as boulders heaped at the bottom of a canyon.

Veejay took a small cube the size of a Wal-Mart jewelry box from a cabinet and inserted it into a slot under a screen. "I recorded this a little while ago. You'll hear the two men you see on the screens."

Zoë crawled up on a table and scooted back against the wall. The long drive from Spring Creek and the effort of her zealous search for Angel and the heat in the kitchen made her sleepy. She rolled her eyes part of the way back into her skull, stuffed her hands in her pockets, pulled her knees into her chest, and rested. Angel and she would leave soon, she felt it. She would take a short nap now to refresh herself for their flight beyond time where she'd never feel sleepy again.

The voices she heard from the recording Veejay played mesmerized her. She drifted into one of her favorite dreams, the dream she let herself see whenever she wanted to nap for just a few minutes.

She lay on a cloud as big as a house, swaying across an endless lake. Warm light poured over her face and body. White birds perched on soft peaks of the cloud chirping hosannas. Zoë felt Angel holding her body in his gentle, muscular arms. She sank into her warm cloud dream and she lost contact with the bright, shimmery room until a scratchy tenor voice laughed out of the speakers.

Instantly alert, she opened her eyes, half-expecting Angel to have done something scientific, like starting an experiment on the table.

"There she is, Roy," the high voice came from one of Veejay's monitors. The screen was dark, the voice sharp. "The beginning of the Devil's Boulevard. That's your personal Highway to Hell."

"That's Lamb," Veejay said. "You'll hear the man you recognize in a minute."

The other voice whined, "What's my job, really, Wink?"

"That's the fake preacher, all right. He whines like someone's going to whip him," Devan said.

"Jesus. Tell me the truth."

"Like I told you, you make me money. Do that, then your boss and my good buddy Winston Lockhart makes his big. And you get your big, too. Get it?"

"I mean the task. My action plan. Why put my ass in a wringer?"

"Shut up. Your ass all about that half mill you're about to earn. Follow this road down into the mountain, find the boulder that's blocking the river. You set the C-4 and the caps and wires. They're in your pack. Anybody could do it. When you're done, you get your puny ass out and I blow it. Nothing to it. We're all rich."

"Why don't you handle this yourself? You're the pro."

"Royboy, you forget one thing. Somebody's got to place the rig and a professional's got to blow it. I could do both, but I can't be in two places at once. And we do have a time line."

Devan groaned. "Oh my God! They're setting off explosives!" Appalled, he looked to Veejay, who nodded and fast-forwarded the tape.

This time, Lamb's near falsetto told Roy he was coming down to the warehouse.

"Why would they blow up the tanks?" Devan asked.

"It's not the tanks. It's the boulders that fell into the river."

"What river?"

"A river flows under the warehouse and keeps it cool. A quarter degree Celsius above freezing."

"I don't get it," Devan said.

"Lamb's involved with a local man, Lockhart. A businessman."

"I heard of him. Guy from Utah built a factory outside Spring Creek." Devan lowered the gun again.

"It's supposedly a water bottling company. He built a series of underground hydroelectric generators south of here. It's on the same river that flows under Spring Creek."

Devan glanced at Zoë who was playing with the torn pocket of her coat, folding it and refolding it with her head down. She seemed to be listening to them, but he couldn't tell.

Veejay went on. "They have millions of Department of Energy and Department of Defense money and who knows from where else. PhilaPharm. PetroEmir. Qingdao Industries. Some consortium. The public deal was, they'd get the government money to build their water business in exchange for watching over the cavern. Lamb told me he's the eyeballs the Department of Defense hired."

"Who hired you?"

"I might as well be a slave. But I'm here only until we can make sure our families are safe."

"Yeah? What about the millions of families you're putting in danger with this nuclear dump?"

"I'm making sure this 'nuclear dump' becomes a resource for all human families."

"Sure. Now they're going to blow it up?" Devan took a step toward Zoë and opened his free palm, never taking his eyes off Veejay. "Idiotic."

When Veejay remained silent.

Devan said, "Goddamit. I'm not gonna let them come and save you, so stop wasting time."

"They won't come to save me. Didn't you hear? They'll do anything to make their money."

"What money? I don't get it."

Veejay threw his hand up as if the answer should be obvious. "The earthquake. A chunk of mountain crashed into the river. It blocks the flow. Lockhart – the guy who owns the water business – he can't start up his turbines. I don't believe for one minute he's running a water bottling company.

Those turbines are meant to provide electricity for half the country. Whoever owns them, will own the U.S."

"So they blow up the rocks and risk poisoning the whole watershed? Idiots. Why don't they just call in the engineers?"

Veejay gazed at Devan. "Maybe they did. Maybe they don't think they'll blow up the cavern. Lamb's a demolitions expert. Besides, maybe radiated water will conceal their real plans. I don't know. I can't read such devious minds."

Devan stalked around the room to look in the other monitors. Zoë noticed that Laurel no longer stood on the hill of debris. Zoë's eyes followed Devan's to another screen where Wakanda squatted in the shadows, hugging himself.

"Look," she said. "Wakanda."

Devan examined the screen Zoë pointed at, then inspected the other monitors. "See Laurel anywhere, Zoë?"

Zoë jumped as high as she could in front of each screen, then found a stool to climb on. She peered into the monitors from six inches away.

"No. She must be walking around in the tanks."

"No doubt," Veejay said. "We could make an infrared scan, but it's slow. She'll be all right, if she stays away from Lamb. I'll be all right if you put your gun away. I'm no danger to you."

Ignoring him, Devan said, "If she gets too close, there must be some way to warn her."

Veejay shrugged. He picked up a glass of water and sipped. "You forget," Veejay said. "This whole warehouse is a secret. Lamb worked for the National Security Agency. I assume Lockhart is tied in to the politicians behind this."

Concentrating and pacing furiously with the gun dropped to his side, Devan fired questions at Veejay the way the middle school principal used to browbeat Zoë when she came back to school after she took a few days off to camp out.

"How far away is this blockage? What happens to the tanks if they blow it? What about the river?"

Veejay smiled. "I made some quick calculations when I first intercepted a phone call between Lamb and Lockhart. I'm only a little worried."

"Right. Unless they're the greediest assholes in the world, why the hell would they take the risk to blow this place up?"

"Don't be such an innocent. People will do anything for enough money. Lockhart makes megabucks and his lackeys get rich, too."

"It's suicidal."

"It depends on where they set the explosives. How far downstream from the warehouse the explosion is. How much they use. How stable the overhead granite is. How much abuse the tanks can absorb before they crack. There is some evidence that the older tank walls have thinned."

"Great. One of those tanks collapses, the river's contaminated, right? What a mess."

"Again, it depends." Veejay now paced, his hands clasped behind his waist, his head nodding as he answered. "First of all, the warehouse walls are four feet thick, reinforced with steel plates. The ceiling is a reinforced geodesic dome, most efficient load-carrying structure ever designed."

Devan interrupted. "You saw those bent beams and columns. Just minor design flaws." He drenched his voice with as much sarcasm as he could.

"You couldn't see them," Veejay said, "but six hundred twenty-four-inch titanium I-beams, cross-braced and strutted, can hold up three mountains."

"Right," Devan grunted. "Like they can stop earthquakes."

"It all depends."

"I'm bored with *all depends*." Devan growled.

"It's complicated. How far the river carries any toxic leakage," Veejay said. "It runs as far south as Texas. A branch leads toward Denver, another toward Omaha, another straight south into the Oglalla Aquifer."

"I know, I know. I grew up here. The Oglalla Aquifer is the largest source of fresh water in the country, outside the Great Lakes." Devan sighed. "Zoë, we're outta here. We have a chance to stop the worst thing that could ever happen to South Dakota and maybe the whole country."

Looking past the pistol, Veejay said, "I'm positive that we won't have an explosion in the storage area itself, unless someone bombs the cave on purpose. If it weren't so cold in the storehouse, then we might worry about the ferrocyanide in the tanks detonating."

"Oh, just a baby nuke explosion. Nothing to worry about." Devan's jaws clenched and unclenched and clenched again. A blue vein in his forehead bulged.

"They built this warehouse here because we're standing on a four-mile deep, three-mile wide basolith, a hunk of granite embedded in the Earth like an upside down mountain. Only, it never erodes, never moves."

"What about the earthquake?" Devan chewed the tip of his mustache.

"Superficial slippage. Didn't even register on the Denver seismograph. No, the worst that can happen is the tanks leak and the aquifer becomes contaminated." Veejay paused, returning Devan's horrified glare with a mild smile. "You cowboys would have to import bottled water for a few thousand years."

At that moment, Zoë feared that Devan would smash the pistol into Veejay's face. Instead, containing his anger, he gripped the countertop and growled.

"You're as bad as the rest of them. Without you scientists we wouldn't have to deal with millions of years of nuclear garbage."

"I am not responsible for the 'garbage.' It is true that my Soviet colleagues perfected the art of low-cost mass production of nuclear warheads." The pitch of his voice began to rise. "But food companies and Big Pharma take the prize for mass production of carcinogens that are much more efficient than radiation." Louder. "It's you American people who want everything nice and easy and cheap. And you don't care about the consequences. You don't want to know."

Devan shouted at him. "Are you going to help or not?"

Veejay shrugged. "I told you, I'm trying to solve the whole problem. That's my vocation."

"Forget your vocation. We have to get out of here."

"What do you think I can do?" Veejay asked.

Devan thought. "Can you jam the transmission from his detonator?"

"I can try, but I don't know. Some of my relays were damaged by the same rock slide that led you here."

"Can you find out?"

"I already set my computer to interrupt every signal he sends, but we won't know if I'm successful until he tries to detonate the explosives."

"Shit," Devan said, shaking his head. "Zoë, let's go."

"You don't have to go up there." Veejay held up his palm. "It's safe here. I can pressurize the stair well, slide two more four-inch thick steel doors into place. No explosion can touch us."

Devan looked up. "Your ceiling can collapse."

"I have another room beyond this one," Veejay said, a smile flattening across his jaw. "And," he looked back over his shoulder, "I have an escape route out of this mountain that nobody else knows about."

"Sure. If you have a secret escape hatch, why are you here? I believe you think you have a way out, but I can't trust it to be any use to me."

Devan lay his camera on the stool. Opening one end, he plucked the data cartridge out and, holding the gun in one hand and the cartridge in the other, he unzipped his Hazmat suit. Working his vest up to his stomach, he pushed the cartridge into a back pocket, watching Angel and talking all the while.

"I've got to get Zoë out of here, stop Lamb, do something with the preacher, pick up Leo and Laurel, and get this cartridge to the transmitter. That's a lot of shit to handle all at once."

Zoë said, "You can do it. Don't worry."

Devan held his hand out, palm up to Veejay. "What about those flash drives?"

"If you weren't in such a rush, I could make you another copy." Veejay dropped a cube into Devan's palm.

"You can't help me, so let us out. We're leaving."

Devan stuffed the cube into his inside. He said, "We gotta go," and he squeezed Zoë's shoulder and shook her.

Zoë cringed. "Angel? Angel?"

"Angel doesn't want you, Zoë," Devan said. "We're in big danger if we don't get out of here right now. The whole Black Hills has no chance unless we get out of here."

Devan grabbed her arm and pulled her off the table. Zoë landed heavily, striking the back of her head against his stomach. She struggled, kicking and biting at his hand. He ignored her and kept the gun aimed at Veejay who managed a flat smile, shaking his head like a disappointed teacher.

"I agree with you," Veejay said calmly. "You should go. Try to disable Lamb. Kill him. You'll have to kill him if you want to return alive to your friends. Even with Lamb dead, you may spend the rest of your life on the run."

"Do I have a choice?" Devan asked.

"Leave the girl."

She knew it. Angel wanted her to stay, of course. Now if only Devan would figure out what was really going on. She thrashed in

Devan's arms, stamping on his feet. Good thing he wore steel-toed boots.

"If you take her, you sacrifice her. If you leave her, I will sneak her out my back door."

Devan held her around the chest. She stopped resisting when it registered that Veejay had a secret route out of the mountain, into the clear air. Of course. A secret path to Heaven.

Devan dropped his arm from Zoë's coat. "Here's what we do. I go up the stairs. Watch me on your monitors. Keep the doors open. Once I handle Lamb and his creep, you bring her upstairs. We'll all leave together."

"You know, the Indian army trained me."

This revelation surprised Zoë. He's a Lakota warrior?

"If I have any problems, you slam the doors and run. Get Zoë to Spring Creek. Safe and sound."

Veejay angled his arm slowly behind his back, feeling along the panel. "There," he said. The door slid open.

Devan's voice broke. "Zoë, you can stay with Angel, but listen." Taking her by the shoulder again, gently now, he turned her to face him. "If he has to, he'll take you out by his secret passage. You know how to get home from here." He narrowed his eyes and nodded with his teeth biting his lower lip like he was telling her a secret message.

Zoë hugged him. She was almost home already.

"You still love me, Zoë?"

"I love you always. Here. In Heaven. Everywhere."

"Enough to come with me?"

"Just talk to Inky. He'll take care of you, too." She hugged him again and pulled his face to hers. Her chapped lips puckered and smacked against his full mouth. His rough moustache tickled the side of her nostril.

Zoë's eyes overflowed with tears. "Good bye, Devan. Thank you for bringing me to my Angel. Don't worry. Pray to me in Heaven and I'll be with you. You always have my good luck. I know we'll meet in Heaven if I don't get back to Earth before you die."

Shaking his head, tears ran down his cheeks. Devan squeezed Zoë, then pushed her gently toward Veejay, and backed to the door with his eyes on the scientist. "You touch one hair on her head, I'll hunt you down."

Devan stopped at the monitors to examine the images. "Better give me all the luck you've got, Zoë. Laurel, too. We need it. Throw in some prayers to Inky." He set his shoulders and strode toward the staircase.

He entered the stairwell and Zoë watched his legs and then his boots taking two steps at a time, climbing into his mission at the top of the stairs. She heard the upper door slide open, then clang shut again.

Take care of him, Inky. I promised to come back to see him. He has to stop the explosion. Help him.

Confident of Devan's safety, Zoë turned to Veejay, thrilled to finally be alone with him. "Angel, we need some water. Where do you keep your pots? Do you have one of those hidden stoves? A microwave will do fine. Only, I'm not sure how many minutes it will take. I make tea at home in sixty-three seconds. But we have to boil it before we pour it over the other ingredients. Let's say, three minutes? So, get ready!"

КН3О

Thirty

WATER EATERS

"Water." Veejay toothed a soap opera grin. "I'll show you the purest water on the planet. All the water you can eat!"

Zoë gazed into his eyes in complete adoration. She didn't understand how anyone ate water, but she didn't expect to understand an angel's thoughts. They were strange as God's, she knew, and just as smart, only without memories of time before light.

"It won't be long now," she whispered to the crickets in her jacket. She caressed her pockets with wake-up strokes.

"No. Not long now." His eyes on a panel of monitors and keyboards, he said, "First, I'll send word to Kreppel," he said, "before Lamb can terminates my access. Then we're off to Lake Sunrise. It's the water that guarantees tomorrow. Our only guarantee of tomorrow."

Crickets burrowed in the arroyos of Zoë's pockets chirped feebly. "What's the matter," she said into her coat. "I'm sorry. I'm so happy I almost forgot about you." They might still be cold from the cavern. She chafed the leather to warm her flock.

She shook both pockets gently, hoping to excite her crickets to low peals, at least. When she needed the crickets to warm her or sing a beat for her to dance to or even improvise a bedtime story, she scuffed her pockets until they responded.

Something was terribly wrong. She rubbed back and forth, up and down, slow, slow, fast, fast, slow fast slow. She jiggled her pockets with the vigor she usually reserved for celebration times when her jacket would erupt in chorus like St. John the Baptist church choir.

She twisted her waist back and forth, flapping her unzipped jacket so breeze could wake the slumbering acolytes.

"What are you doing, my dear?" Veejay asked with more curiosity than care. Answering his own question, as any all-knowing angel might, dropping his voice to a soothing pitch. "Oh, you're excited."

Focusing again on the monitor, he continued, "You know, we're about to take an adventure Carlos Slim would give his whole fortune for. I'll show you something," he said intently, his long fingers snapping the keys. "I'll show you something bigger than Einstein, bigger than Buddha, bigger than Shiva's lingam!"

Veejay's eyebrows quivered. "Let's go," he said, tensing. "Kreppel's got my code. Wink Lamb's bosses will have to change their Armani underpants when they see how their meek Veejay demolished their little plan to use him and his brilliant colleagues to help them blackmail the people of the West. It's time for rogues to run free. You're going with me."

He pushed the louvered pine doors closed over the monitors, then took Zoë's hand. The doors yawned, swinging open on their finely milled brass hinges. "Oh, well, we might not be able to stop them from ruining the aquifer. We'll see."

Zoë began to cry. As she leaned against the stainless steel table, whole, single tears bubbled from her eyes, rolled off her cheeks and splattered on the floor.

"If you really cared about me," she sniffled, "you'd care about my crickets. They're sick. We can't go until you help them."

As if he didn't understand, he narrowed his eyes and pursed his lips. The overhead light glinted on his shiny forehead. "Tears? Why? What did I do? Oh, you miss your Devan. Well, he's doing what he can to save the world. He's a courageous one. It's too bad."

Zoë felt a mask of misery melting her face.

"Somehow you bring out tenderness in me," he said. "Maybe because I have no children? I've never had a chance. Always working. You know, you remind me of the betrothed virgins in my father's town in the country – sweet, pure, delicious in their eagerness."

Veejay bent to pull Zoë to her feet. His hands slid gently from her shoulders under her arms. He scooped her up and held her in front of him.

"It's all right," he repeated, "we're much safer than your friend upstairs."

Smiling through a spate of tears, in her stomach she felt Devan's safety, no matter where he wandered. Her faith in him assured her that they'd meet in Heaven. If not there, they'd hug again when she returned with the magic secret of how her loved ones could fly with her in their bodies and souls to wherever they wanted.

Veejay set her down, still gently gripping her shoulders as he surveyed the monitors. The drum and string music in the background came up for a moment, then fell silent. Smiling to herself in the quiet, Zoë expected her crickets' twitter to signal their happiness that they'd soon be leaving with Zoë.

The long silence shamed Zoë for her indulgence in dreaming while her crickets languished. Zoë straightened in Veejay's arms, her back and neck gone rigid. Angel released her and she leapt away. She had to stop feeling sorry for herself and take care of her crickets.

She dug into both pockets, carefully raking a cluster of insects into her fists. Cupping her palms together, she raised them to Veejay, offering him the chitinous mass of nearly inert bugs. A few sluggish antennae vibrated. A flat note burped out of the heap.

Peering into her hands, Veejay thrust his face toward the ebony clump of bugs. One of Zoë's tears landed on the back of his neck and followed a crease around his throat and ran under his shirt. The skin on his neck twitched and his shoulders jerked.

Catching his breath, he bent lower, his long nose a few inches from Zoë's trembling fingers. Another tear splashed from her chin. Another. Zoë watched them follow the course of her first tear, circling Veejay's neck, then rolling down and vanishing under his loose collar.

"I see," he said, reaching a slender finger and pointed thumb into the cluster of bugs. Veejay gently extricated a rigid cricket. Its legs bent, its antennae stiff, it showed no signs of life.

"Come," he beckoned, indicating the counter where she'd napped earlier. He placed the cricket in a petri dish and set it on the viewing plate of a microscope, saying, "Look."

Squinting, Zoë saw the cricket lying paralyzed on its back, his horned antennae drooping inside green fungus sheaths. Sharp pebbles of dust jammed his leg joints and crumbs as big as bushes stuck to his carapace. The cricket's wings sagged under a gray blanket of fuzz.

"Dirty," she mumbled. The lump in her throat choked out the word "Dead." She jerked her head away from the insect fatality scene.

In a panic, she blew warm breath into the lump of ashen cricket corpses that lay in her palms.

"Excellent," Veejay said, glancing into the microscope, grinning. "I'm amazed how fate provides me with opportunities to practice." He patted her head with formal affection. "Don't fret. They're only sleeping."

Zoë had seen more than enough deaths to know the difference between asleep and dead. Tears teemed in her eyes and overflowed onto her cheeks and dripped off her chin.

Veejay reached into his shirt pocket, taking out a flat brown vial the size of an eye wash bottle. "See this? Dr. Veejay's Fountain of Youth. Let's see what happens when we treat your bug with a drop of Dr. Veejay's medicine."

He brought an index finger and long pointed thumb toward the round dropper bulb. The dropper reminded Zoë of a miniature soul syringe. She grinned at the reminder of the community of souls she'd assembled. She remembered the other souls she'd garthered. The souls were still safe in Little Limbo in her pocket.

Then, fearing that Veejay would remove the souls from her crickets, before she carried them with her to Heaven, she said, "Careful!"

"It's all right. It's medicine."

"Leave their souls alone," she whimpered. "Don't suck them out."

"I'm making their souls happy. Watch."

Veejay pinched the bulb with the tube inside the bottle, then released it. Slowly, aqua-silver liquid rose up the tube.

"Look in the microscope. You'll see what a miracle I have developed. Quick, we have do this fast. We have only a few minutes."

"A miracle? For my crickets?" He loved her enough to perform a miracle already. Zoë stuffed an eye into one lens cup and squeezed the other shut.

The dropper tube briefly obliterated the cricket's image like mist hiding a duck on the lake. When Veejay pulled it away, a gelatinous globe flattened across the bug's exoskeleton. Zoë waited, staring, warming her other crickets in her tightly sealed palms.

Under the microscope, the cricket's antennae began to vibrate. Its body quaked and its legs unkinked, snapping and kicking, jogging upside down on air.

The miracle didn't surprise Zoë. She actually felt at home with miracles. She'd witnessed at least one every year since she was six, but she'd never had a miracle performed just for her.

When the cricket's wings shot out sideways, rotating on their thin stalks, she let her breath out. She closed her eyes, praying a devout thanks to St. Nancy, patron of insects, and St. Jude, patron of lost causes. She smiled to herself and whispered aloud, "Inky, you're always right. Me and the crickets are where we're supposed to be."

When she opened her eyes again, the smile crept toward her ears. Her cricket had rolled over, squatted, and began preening. Fresh tears, now of joy, streamed down her salt-runnelled cheeks.

With its paps, the cricket bowed each antenna into his mouth, slipping it back and forth like a licorice stick. The antennae popped back into place, flexible and sensitive again. He flapped and shook his wings to dust off his carapace. Suddenly, just as joy bulged in Zoë's chest, the cricket stopped, tipped over, and curled his body into a dark larval crescent.

"Oh no!" she gasped. "He died again." Wide-eyed, unable to bear the cruelty of a false miracle, she pleaded with Veejay.

He tugged her away from the microscope, taking her place at the view. He smiled immediately, saying, "Look again, cricket girl."

She pushed her eye into the viewer. The cricket snapped his body erect and shuddered forth a wake-up warble. The healed cricket hopped down from the petri dish and crawled casually across the steel tabletop, punctuating his voyage with a few staccato chirps.

"Oh, Angel, it's true," she whispered, awed. "Fix them too?" She presented him with the crisp heap of carcasses remaining in her hands.

"Lay them down. Dr. Veejay will resurrect your sleeping beauties."

He sprinkled liquid over the brittle bodies. In a few minutes, they all repeated the same grooming and snapping, shakes and flutters. The pile of bugs exploded into a slippery, jangly chorus. They chirped and crawled and leapt and flew in a lively squall all over the lab.

"What if I told you I had enough of this water to keep us alive for a thousand years? Ten thousand?" Veejay's wide teeth shone, tiny smile wrinkles raying out from his eyes like alfalfa petals. "I can heal anyone who's sick. I can stop cancer. I can turn white hair black."

He paced, his words almost singing elated harmonies with the cricket mob. "I used to be going bald. Bald. I'm forty-three by the calendar. I look twenty-five. I don't know for sure, but in a few months,

I'll look almost your age." He thrust his hand toward Zoë's face, wiggling his fingers. "I can regrow lost fingers, hands, legs."

Veejay's expostulations rose toward hysteria.

"What's AIDS?" he called, raising his face toward the ceiling.

Zoë followed his glance, noticing the stars twinkling in approval.

"Nothing more than a weekend flu." Again he called, "What's a brain tumor? A minor headache. Girl, guess this. What's that old demon called nuclear radioactivity? Is it still toxic? No. Not with Dr. Veejay and his water on the loose. But is it still dangerous? Yes. More dangerous than ever because nuclear radioactivity, my life's work, my life's passion, is our savior."

Savior? He must be one of the top angels in Heaven. A rill of pride poured through her whole body. She didn't deserve such an important angel, she just needed a strong fast one. Inky must be a powerful saint to have this much pull with the Heavenly choir.

"I bring forth the new savior to life here in our little manger, attended by bugs, buried in a cave under millions of tons of rock. Only in America, my dear, only in America."

He paused in his fulminations, waving the bottle around like a stubby baton keeping the beat to the cricket song.

"This simple liquid is KH3O. Kapoor H Three O. I made it. It has three ingredients: water from Lake Sunrise – where we're going – archaea, the soil from the tunnels below where infinite potential lives, and the genius touch – a matrix of radiated microcrystalline calcium and pseudomonas aeruginosa, the same bacteria that gives you pimples. It can adapt to any environment. KH3O is the most powerful rejuvenator the world has ever known."

Loosed into full oratorical abandon, he stopped in front of Zoë. Awed by his reckless strutting and shouting, she almost cowered before such power.

"Ten thousand times more powerful than that Human Growth Hormone. Ten million times better than the tonics you buy in pharmacies or health food stores. Adaptable to every human gene and expressible as life force itself."

Angel took a breath, and now, with a lilt of calm in his voice, he said, "You're looking at the world's richest man. Mine will dwarf the plutocrats' paltry billions. The internet billionaires, the entire WalMart family, all the sheiks. The Chinese and Russian thieves. For one liter of

KH3O, they'd give every jewel, stock, bond, all their islands, factories, political power, everything."

Nervously, Zoë reached inside one of her deepest pockets and rubbed Little Limbo. The thermos bottle felt cold so she circled it in her hand. She decided to take the faithful souls with her, especially since Angel had so much influence. The souls would thank her for introducing them to one of Heaven's most important angels. It always helped to know somebody when you go to a new place. He could show them around, find their families in an instant. She was lucky she already knew lots of Heaven people: Ruthie, Inky, Kateri. Their friends would soon be her friends.

"They'll beg for one treatment with my microcrystalline Archaea-potentiated radiobiological Water of New Life." Angel's deep voice rose and he crowed. "Inside this mountain, down below, I have millions of gallons of KH3O! Countless millions!"

He marched around the lab toting the eye drop bottle like a stubby flagpole without a flag.

His confidence relaxed Zoë, now she was only a few minutes away from Heaven. She'd adjusted to the truth that she'd never fully understand Angel's endless talking. Didn't matter. Her crickets pranced around the lab chortling songs she'd never heard, happy as on an August night. If Angel could dribble that water on sick people and make them well, what about the people in the Home? Would they get young again?

"We've got to leave now, girl," a suddenly sober Veejay ordered, "before Wink Lamb tries to turn this sleepy old mountain into a volcano." He opened a white enameled locker door, motioning for the girl to step inside.

"Just a minute, Angel," she said, sitting down on the floor and spreading her legs into a wide vee. She rolled her tongue into a pink channel, and blew a moist trill between pursed lips.

"Come on," Angel urged. "I have to leave now. If you want to come with me, hurry up."

"I listened to you, now you can wait for my crickets. They go where I go. You know that." Zoë learned devotion from crickets long before she had her own to offer Angel.

Dozens of crickets emerged from behind computers, squeezed out of closed counter doors, dropped off ceiling lights, fluttering like maple seeds testing the breeze. An ebony flurry landed on Zoë's welcoming thighs.

"Last call." Angel partially closed the locker door as if he would leave her behind.

As the crickets mounted Zoë's jacket and squirmed into the pockets, their chirping receded.

"I want you with me, Zoë," Angel said, "but if we don't go now...." He pointed to the monitors across the room. Her eyes followed his finger.

In one of them, Ketchup and Lamb stood arguing. Roy twirled his flashlight around while Lamb pointed a shotgun toward the camera, as if sending them a warning.

"Just a minute. A few more crickets." She continued her patient trilling.

"We can't wait. Your crickets will be all right."

"Oh look," she said happily. "You have crickets, too."

A silent swarm of translucent and ivory insects skittered across the floor. Zoë opened her palms toward them and the pale bugs crawled over and under her legs, flowing into her hands.

"Can't you sing?" she asked them, a pencil-thin worry line slanting between her eyebrows. "Sing. Angel crickets. You must know some Heaven songs."

Veejay's jaw dropped. "Cockroaches. Albino cockroaches! Of course. Where you find humans and water, you find cockroaches. In Mumbai, we call these pests 'water-eaters.'"

The cockroaches crept into Zoë's clothes, vanishing among the wrinkles and pockets. "Listen," she admonished the newcomers, brushing into her side pockets the few roaches stuck like moist grains of rice to the leather. "My darlings will teach you to sing."

She rose and approached Veejay. "Let's go, Angel," she said, rousing him toward her seraphic destiny. "We need some water now. And one little pot to boil in.

Thirty-one

TACKLING LAMB

The instant Zoë stepped through the locker doorway into the Veejay's secret escape route, two muffled thunder cracks rumbled into the lab from the cavern above. Then, three more, followed by two massive booms and a volley of thunderballs.

She jumped back and ran to the laboratory door. It had no handle so she pushed with her hands and shoulder. Then she kicked it. "Veejay, let me out. They did the bomb. Devan and Laurel are in trouble."

"Wait. It's all right. Look."

She whirled and followed his finger to a monitor. Clouds of blue smoke rolled over the tanks. Her false angel Ketchup and the man with the guns sprawled on the floor, the gun man on his stomach aiming his rifle. Beside him, Ketchup lay curled up, his legs flopping.

She ran half a dozen steps to Veejay. "Where's Devan?"

Veejay fingered some buttons and switches and the scene on the monitor changed. First, it panned across the whole cavern. Movement in the middle of the hall showed Laurel darting from tank to tank, waving a long needle of white light before her. Behind the spike of light her hand glowed orange. The light bounced between the tanks, illuminating a zigzag path before her.

The camera tilted and stopped and Zoë bent her head to right the sideways view. Pressed against one of the tanks, his head at the level of the nuclear flower, Wakanda stared up into the thin smoke.

Zoë's hands flew to her mouth. "Oh no."

Devan sprawled on his back on the floor. A narrow dark trail of what had to be blood ran from his leg. "He's hurt. I have to help him."

"You can't. Lamb – the guy with the rifle – he'll shoot you. I promised Devan we'd escape. Let's go now."

Zoë slapped him on the stomach. "Veejay. What do you mean? Angels help people. Let's go help. We can do it."

"Haven't you figured it out? I'm a man. A scientist. I'm not an angel."

Zoë ignored his protests. How an angel could suddenly be so weak and stupid and not want to help? He wasn't her Angel. She didn't want one like that. "Veejay." She stamped her feet and ran back to the door.

She raised her fist to pound when she remembered: he'd saved her crickets. He could revive Devan no matter how bad he was hurt. She ran back to him and scrabbled her hands into his pockets, searching for the KH3O bottle.

"Stop it. What do you want?"

"Water. Your miracle water. That's what he needs."

Pushing her back, he fished in a pocket and pulled out the bottle. "This? This should help but it may not be enough. Devan's a big man."

Zoë snatched the bottle from his hand and jammed it into her chest pocket. She ran back to the door, pushing and yelling. "Let me out. If you won't come, I'll do it. I have to give him my luck." She slapped the door with her palm and when it didn't move, she stared over her shoulder at Veejay. "Hurry up."

The door didn't budge.

Zoë rammed her shoulder against the door. "Let me out!"

"All right," Veejay said. "Go on."

The door slid back and Zoë's knees buckled in the open space and she stumbled into hallway. She found her balance, raced up the stairs, arriving at the top landing as the upper doors crawled open. Right outside the door, ten feet away, Wakanda stood pressed against the shadow side of a tank.

He spotted her at the same time and lifted both hands palms out, mouthing "Stop."

She almost tripped over her toes into the cavern, but caught herself by the doorjamb. Nodding to Wakanda, she peeked around the edge of the door.

Ketchup lay about thirty feet away, groaning. "I'm shot. Get me a doctor. Oooo...oooooo."

Zoë didn't see the other man, Lamb, so she dived across the open space to the shadows.

Behind her, the door clicked shut. She looked back, expecting to see Veejay by the wall, on alert, ready to help. The doorway stood empty. Realist that she was, not wasting a second wishing for an angel's help that wasn't coming or regretting that Veejay had let her go because how could she think of leaving for Heaven while her beloved Devan lay bleeding on the floor, she jumped up and pivoted across the aisle landing on Wakanda's back. It was harder than she thought it could be, he was so old.

He twisted aroundas fast as a cat and one of his arms reached to cover her mouth, the other pulled her deeper into the shadows.

She whispered, "Where's Devan?" She tried to disentgangle herself from the scrawny Hunkpapa, but she was stuck to him. Then he dropped his arms from her but quickly placed one of his hands over her mouth, covering her nose.

She widened her eyes and jerked her head up and down, understanding the need for silence. He let her go and her deflated lungs heaved. Acrid smoke from the gunshots drifted over her face, gagging her.

She jammed her face under the lapel of her coat and sucked in her own rancid sweat odor mixed with the aromatic peppermint and fresh leek scent of the poshent ingredients tarrying in her pocket. The heady mint settled in her nose and cleared her sinuses.

"I'm going after him," she mouthed to Wakanda, exaggerating the shapes of the words, spreading her lips and inclining her jaw nearly to her chest after each word.

He shook his head violently and balled his fist and pointed his index finger at her face, snapping the hand and recoiling it.

She crossed her arms over her chest and pursed her lips, then shaped "Ye-es," her chin dipping on the second syllable.

Zoë closed her eyes and Wakanda's arms went around her. They stood delicate cheek to grizzled jaw for a few seconds until he let her go and clapped his hands on the sides of her head. She smiled and ducked to the freezing floor. The icy cement stung her fingers.

Devan lay three rows over, his arms stretched out like a Jesus, still as a dead man. A dark stream of blood trickled out and pooled under one leg. Zoë skirted two tanks so she could come around behind him. She didn't have a plan other than to approach silent as a fox and do whatever she could to drag him out.

A shadow flitting inside the shadows, she slid to the tank next to Devan's body. Dozens of tiny holes had sprayed the abdomen of his radiation containment suit. His helmet lay a few feet away, crumpled like a scrap plastic bag.

The puddle of blood barely moved but it seemed to grow thicker as she watched. Devan lay motionless, eyes open, ragged holes peppered across his chest and leg.

Shotgun. Shot him with a shotgun. Inky, stop the bleeding. Let him live. I'll do anything.

A few feet away, Lamb stalked over to Devan's body. "Asshole," he said.

Zoë flattened herself on the frigid concrete, halfway under the tank, far enough back that he wouldn't see her, she hoped.

Black cowboy boots with silver tooling up the sides poised beside Devan. With one silver-tipped toe, Lamb pushed the body away from the tank, then he hauled back and kicked him in the stomach. Devan didn't flinch.

Lamb bent down and ripped Devan's cameras off the lanyards around his neck. He snickered and stood up and stepped across the body to where Devan's .22 dammed a rivulet of blood as it seeped away.

"Idiot." Kicking the gun across the smooth tiled floor. he muttered. "Shit, shit, shit!" It crashed into one of the steel pallets the tanks sat on and ricocheted across the aisle, slamming into another pallet, before it stopped, silent and harmless.

Picking up Devan's floppy helmet, he flung it over the tanks, into the murk. "Fuck! Fuck! Fuck! God fucking dam!"

His hysterical falsetto echoed around the cavern like a squad of angry starlings battering a thieving crow.

Zoë crawled back into the open aisle and sprung to her feet, edging around the nose of the tank behind Lamb.

Lamb wiped blood from his boot on Devan's arm, the way somebody scrapes mud off on a mat. Then he raised his gun and aimed it at Devan's head.

Feeling as sleek as a bobcat, Zoë shot out from under the tank. Growling like a mountain lion, she slammed her shoulders into the soft backs of Lamb's knees. His body jackknifed and fell back on top of her.

"Leave him alone." She clawed his puffy face with her fingernails, striking his cheeks and gouging at his eyes.

He grunted and rolled off, catching her in the stomach with his elbow, driving her back. He knelt on all fours panting, shaking his drooping head.

Zoë leapt on his back and dug her fingers into his ears, ripping. He slapped at her and stood up with her sharp knees pounding his kidneys and one hand now yanking at his nose and the other tearing at his hair. He stumbled backwards, twisting like a baby bull in a rodeo, until he reached the oblate wall of a nuclear waste tank. He heaved his body up to raise her high near his shoulders, then he fell back, crushing Zoë against the unyielding metal.

She lost her breath and couldn't get it back. He rocked his curly head back and forth, attempting to butt her in the nose. Breathless but still quicker than his head's turkey-jerking at her, she dodged and continued kicking his thighs and flailing at his face. He caught both of her hands in one of his and hollered, "Roy, get the fuck over here."

Woozy, about to pass out, Ketchup moaned, "Don't let me die."

Zoë took a shallow breath and deployed her most savage and dependable weapon – her teeth – biting Lamb's sweating neck while kicking at the back of his knees again. She tasted rancid hair and blood and he screamed and jumped away from the tank, dropping her to the floor.

He swung around and she leapt up, her teeth bared to the gums, snarling. Her whole body pulsed with fire. He punched at her face, but she bobbed and, seeing her chance, she drove the top of her head into his crotch.

He crumpled taking her with him to the floor. He finally dropped his gun and with both hands he grabbed her head and pulled it out of his crotch and squashed her temples between his palms. She flailed at his wrists while swinging her knees at his balls, connecting once. He recoiled, then a black cloud settled over her head and she felt herself falling.

Zoë landed on her side, her forehead smacking into the concrete. The cloud evaporated in a burst of light, but she couldn't move.

For a long moment, the cavern fell silent, as if preparing to absorb all the noise and death Lamb could muster. Veils of smoke fluttered down the sides of the tanks. Inhaling the biting smoke, Zoë hacked. Wires of pain shot across her skull and into her neck again and down through her shoulders.

When she opened his eyes, she saw the profile of his face a few inches away. He lay on his back, his pistol arm folded over his stomach, catching his breath and keeping his body still.

A long bent nose rose off a flat face. If she could only get her teeth on that thing, she'd rip it off his head and drag his brains out the hole. Blood welled into his slack curls from an egg-sized patch of scalp.

She wiggled her fingers, feeling gooey strands of hair stuck between them. If she could only raise her hand to wipe it clean.

The man sat up and Zoë squinted her eyes, leaving a slit so she could observe him. The light was so dim, everything looked gray and dimmed out as moon shadows a week after a full moon.

"Wilder'n a slope bitch," he muttered, holding the back of his head in one hand. He looked at his palm and wiped it on his jeans. Then he reached out with the same hand and dragged his shotgun over to him. He took it by the barrel and holding it, he dropped his knees onto her chest.

Sour liquid rose into her throat and she choked. She couldn't move her arms and legs. Little Limbo had lodged against the side of her thigh. The bottle vibrated, massaging her leg. She felt her souls caring for her. She'd never let the demon Lamb take Little Limbo.

A few twitters trickled out of the coat pockets. Then, a sawing clamor of chirps and peeps fountained into the immense silence.

She watched Lamb's head oscillate, his eyes wide. He sat back off of her, then squatted on his heels as a fleet of black bugs boarded his body. He slapped the top of his head and cringed.

The chirring sound increased and, Zoë thought, took on a sinister note. She'd never heard of soldier crickets, but she knew hers could read her mind as well as she could read theirs. Several insects bounced off his face and one lodged in his ear. He shook his head, flapping his arms, then stabbed a finger into his ear.

Lamb wobbled up and limped a few feet away. Raising one of his heavy boots, he aimed it the dark cluster of bugs vibrating on the floor a foot from Zoë's face. He stomped down, crunching carapaces and legs and antennae, smearing them into the concrete. Hundreds of crickets hopped away in ten directions, fleeing his boot. He stamped with his other foot and again with the first until he'd splatted at least fifty bugs. Twice as many escaped into the frigid darkness under the tanks.

A fleet of pale roaches scampered up the sides of a tank, clinging to its bulging overhang and disappearing up and over the top.

Lamb scanned the area and, apparently satisfied he'd eliminated the crickets, he nodded and shook his head again and slipped the pistol into his pocket. Holding the side of his head, he placed his foot on Zoë's sternum and pressed. She softened her spine, curving it as the boot sought to crush her like another cricket.

Under the pressure, the bottle of Angel's miracle water in her pocket shattered against her breast. Broken glass punctured her skin and a gush of warmth spread across her chest. Water or blood, she didn't know and didn't care. She heaved and twisted until Lamb reduced the pressure. Staggering off balance, he jerked his boot off Zoë's chest and fell back, bent over, and held his knees, breathing hard.

Zoë opened her eyes then narrowed them, watching him through her lashes as he peered into her face. His sour fried onion breath almost gagged her as badly as any dying old man's at the Home, but she stiffened her stomach and clenched her eyes until he stood up and shouted, "Roy. C'mere. I got a job for ya."

From the stench of his breath, Zoë knew Lamb was not long for the Earth. Let him die right now. She sharpened her ears to listen for the sound of angel wings buzzing but Ketchup lumbered into sight, muttering. Zoë opened her eyes wide.

"You bastard. I'm hit."

"Jesus Christ, Roy. Lockhart picked a wimp for this gig. Fuckin' .22 couldn't cripple a rabbit."

Bracing himself on the tank, Roy muttered something to himself. Then, noticing Zoë, "Whatja do to the kid?"

Stepping away, Lamb pulled Ketchup's hand away from his head and examined the wound.

"It's nothing, Royboy," he said. "Your head's still got brains, all the good that does you."

Ketchup groaned.

"You're one lucky asshole," Lamb said. "Maybe I'll keep you around for my good luck charm." He pushed the sagging man against a tank. "I'm gonna give you this gun and you're gonna pay me back for saving your life."

"Mmm gghh wha?"

"She saw you. She knows who you are. You know what that means. Shoot her in the head." He handed Ketchup the gun who took it in both hands, aimed it toward Zoë. His arms wobbled and he staggered, the gun swinging around to point at Lamb.

"Not me!" Lamb shouted and slapped Ketchup's hands away. The gun pointed straight up and fired. The concussion and recoil knocked his feet out from under him and Ketchup plopped down hard, dropping the gun, grasping the sides of his head.

"Jesus, Roy. You're a headcase," Lamb said.

Zoë felt her blood and anger return, boiling and bulging thoughout her body. She shook her head and worked her feet. She rolled over and opened her eyes wide, fumbling toward Lamb, screaming, "Killer. There's a hell! You're going to it!"

Lamb dug the toe of his boot into Zoë's stomach. "Shut up or I'll nail you to my boot." He pressed down.

She stared at him, hardening her eyes, puffing her cheeks, ready to scream again, but she held her tongue and exhaled, saving energy.

"That's right. You be quiet, maybe you'll live a while longer."

She tossed her head back and forth, eyes darting into the shadows, her mouth closed tight. She grabbed his ankle and tried to push the boot away.

He snapped, "Leave the tooling alone, kid. You scratch the leather and it's the last thing you'll do." He raised his foot, shaking her hands off, then dropped the whole boot, sharp heel and steel-clipped toe, back onto her sternum. She kicked and rocked sideways, jamming her hand into her coat.

"I've had enough." Lamb raised the shotgun and waved the butt at her head. She went still with her forearm hidden inside a leather lapel.

"That's better," he snarled. Turning to his wounded accomplice, he said, "Roy, go back to the main door and wait for me. I'll fix your little head wound in a minute."

"Wink, I'm dizzy."

"Stay close to the wall and keep walking. I'll be right there."

Lamb shoved his pistol into his pocket and dropped to his knee and reached around Zoë's stomach to pick her up.

She twisted out of his grip and raised her arm over her head, holding Ruthie's rib bone like a knife. She clasped it in both hands and, grunting, drove it at Lamb's wide eyes.

At the last second, he jerked back and the bone nicked his shoulder. Dragging the bone down, Zoë gouged a trail across his boot. Her swing propelled her over onto her stomach and Ruthie's rib slammed into the floor, shattering and crumbling in Zoë's fist.

Lamb dropped to his knees, then sat on her back. "What the fuck is this?" Bending her wrist back, he forced her to drop the tip of the bone. "Goddam cow bone. Piece of shit." He slapped the back of her head, smashing her cheek against the concrete. She lay quiet. Little Limbo had slipped deeper into her pocket. It had stopped vibrating.

"Tricky little bitch. You try anything else...."

Taking her by the coat collar and her skirt waist, he jerked her up and settled her on his hip, squeezing her head between his arm and his ribs. Zoë flailed and kicked and freed her head, while nearly slipping down his side.

"De vaaan. De vaaan. Don't goooooo."

Lamb stopped, let Zoë fall face-first onto the floor and knelt with his knee in her back. Flopping, she twisted her face back to watch him. As he whipped his belt off and prepared to strap it around her, he loosened his grip for an instant and she rolled away, lashing at his leg. He lost his balance and fell onto his back.

Edging away, Zoë pirouetted on her toes, ready to run into the dark maze of tanks. If she could draw Lamb away from Devan, maybe Wakanda or Laurel could pull him to safety while she lost Lamb somewhere in the room. They could all climb back to Wakanda's parents and get away down the mountain to the truck. If he tried to follow, she and Laurel would pick up some of the rocks and smash them onto Lamb's head.

She inhaled and stopped short. Fragments of the broken magic water bottle burned into her breast with each breath. She opened her jacket to unbutton her beautiful blouse that was ruined now, not that she cared, Angel had already seen her and he loved her so she didn't need any pretty clothes for him. If he really was her Angel.... She doubted it since her real Angel could have knocked out the gunman with the flick of a wing, if he really cared.

Zoë glanced down and in the drab light she saw a dark red string of drying blood running through the daisy petals on her blouse. She reached inside the blouse and flicked the glass debris from the top of her breast, shuddering when she brushed against one piece buried too deep to remove with only her fingertips.

She peered at her breast, her grimace morphing into a weak smile when she saw smooth, unscabbed skin. The miracle water, of course, the flesh smooth and pale over the fragment buried inside. But when she moved her shoulders, the glass shard sank deeper, searing, inflaming the nerves in her entire breast, but she didn't have time to wait for the water to heal the pain.

Gritting her teeth, she sidled toward the shadow, determined to escape when Lamb seized her hair and twisted it in his fist. She swooned and fell, conscious but stunned, and lay at the foot of the tank.

Lamb twisted her arms behind her and wrapped the belt tight around her middle, cramping her crossed hands against her back.

Zoë screamed as loud as she could, rocking up and down on the icy floor, kicking her heels at his arms, managing to face him.

He gripped her neck and yanked her head sideways. At the same time, he covered her mouth with his hand. Laying his gun down, he dragged her to where Ketchup sagged against a tank, holding his head, blood streaming through his hands.

"Gimme something to gag her," he said.

Ketchup blubbered, showing no awareness of Lamb or Zoë. Lamb jerked Ketchup's coat zipper down. He reached inside the coat and felt in the pockets. A grin tore across his face when he extracted a small knife.

He pried the knife open and carved a crescent out of Ketchup's coat. Ketchup slid down the side of the tank, so Lamb pulled his legs out straight, flipped his torn coat open and punched at Ketchup's stomach.

"Suck it in," Lamb ordered. He grabbed Ketchup's belt buckle, unhooked it, and heaved, tearing the belt out of Ketchup's pants. Then Lamb bent one leg to the floor, as if genuflecting, and sliced into the knots in both of Roy's leather bootstrings, tugging and ripping them out and shaking them like snakes.

Turning to his captive, he sat her up and clamped her head between his fingers, forcing her mouth open. He stuffed the shredded coat into her mouth and looped Ketchup's belt around her head twice, then buckled it and set her on the floor, flipping her around.

"I don't care who hears you or who else is in the cavern. Your screeching annoys the hell out of me."

Lamb proceeded to wind Ketchup's bootstrings around Zoë's bound wrists, wrenching the leather so tight, her palms swelled. She'd seen a veterinarian tie off tumors on a goat's stomach and let the poisonous flesh dry up and fall off. Her fingers went numb.

Picking Zoë up by the belt around her middle with one hand and grabbing his shotgun in the other, Lamb said to Ketchup, "Get your miserable ass off the floor. We got to finish what we started." He probed Ketchup's chest with the shotgun.

Ketchup rolled over to his stomach then propped himself up on his knees, floundering and sagging against Lamb who shoved him ahead.

At the wall at the end of the row, Lamb said, "Wait here."

Ketchup wobbled and stopped, swaying back and forth like a sapling in a breeze.

Dropping Zoë, Lamb whirled away and stomped toward Veejay's door. Pounding his fists, he yelled, "Kapoor! Kapoor! Open up! You know what's going on! Open the goddam door now! Or you'll never open it again!"

He hammered the door with his shotgun butt, dull notes clanging without echoes into the cavern.

"This is my house, Kapoor. My goddam house. I'm the one who decides what to do. You'll be sorry, you son of a bitch. I won't get you out of that Israeli prison next time. You'll be lucky they don't hang you by your balls."

Lamb banged on the door a final time and strode back toward Ketchup. Passing Devan's inert body, he glanced at it, and stopped to kick it again, planting his toe directly into the ribs. The body jerked but didn't recoil as a living body would, then it resettled into morbid inertia.

Lamb found Ketchup collapsed against the wall, angled sideways over Zoë. "Don't you make a cute couple."

Her eyes flashed at Lamb and she kicked out as he came close. He picked her up and threw her over his shoulder, head down.

Dragging Ketchup by the arm toward the exit, Lamb lugged Zoë over his shoulder toward the lights beyond the docile rows of radioactive sludge. Zoë drilled at his back with her chin, almost the only moveable part of her body, but he ignored her.

"C'mon, Roy."

The wounded man had slipped behind Lamb and Zoë. Leaning against the wall, he raised his hand and pointed at the tanks. "Missiles?"

"Just big old milk tanks filled with water. A few little isotopes here and there nobody else wants. We store 'em and make a mint. We're landlords, you know."

Zoë listened close, trying to understand. Who was this man? Did he own this cave?

"The Feds insisted on a long-term lease, so we gave 'em a million years, with an option to renew for five." Lamb laughed, then jerked Ketchup away from the wall, pushing him ahead.

Pulsing blood filled Zoë's head, aching behind her eyes and casting a pink glow over the blue concrete floor. Her chin banged every other step against Lamb's lower back, jolting the pain that had settled into her jaw after the voracious bite she'd taken from his scalp.

Inky, where are you? What am I supposed to do now?

She closed her eyes and listened but heard only Ketchup's random moans and Lamb's toe and heel clips' rhythmic clicking as if he was warming up for a swing dance routine.

Thirty-two

FOR LUCK

Lamb shoved Ketchup through a door wide and high enough to handle road graders and tractors. They entered a corridor lit by a few round globes high on the wall. A few yards inside the passage, Lamb turned and pulled the faltering man after him down a gravel slope.

Tossing Zoë up and adjusting her stomach across his shoulder, he descended. Zoë's chin whacked into his back again and again as he drove his boot heels into the ground. His shoulders punched her in the stomach with every step he took. Clouds of pale pink breath spread out from her nose.

"Hey, Roy, we're almost there. The scene of the crime."

"Get me a doctor. I'm gonna faint."

"Shut up. I'll take care of you and your little bitch girlfriend."

Zoë kicked, flailing. She was nobody's girlfriend.

Laughing, Lamb flipped Zoë off his shoulder and dropped her onto the road. She landed on her bottom and, tucking her knees, she rolled over on a sheet of ice and wiggled, tried to stand up.

"Stay here, Roy. I'll get the girl inside."

Towing Zoë by her collar, Lamb sent her skidding under a half-raised door into a lightless chamber where she lay shivering and immobile, stiffening her neck to hold her head off the ice. A hideous roar filled the darkness.

Unable to maintain her pose, she let her head sink to the floor so that only the tip of her skull at the back of her head rested on the ice. A dull yellow gleam flowed into the chamber from a spotty row of overhead lights illuminating a wide platform. Nothing but concrete and chunks of rock beside it squatting like massive dogs.

A few minutes later, a flashlight beam wandered across the room as Ketchup shambled past Zoë with Lamb directing him with his fist in the center of his back. Then Lamb returned and hoisted Zoë over his shoulder again.

"You're a pain in the ass," he said, dumping her beside the wounded Ketchup.

Another light came on, shining a beacon across Ketchup's body into the emptiness behind Zoë's head. "Fuckin' A, Roy. Good thing your light still works. Keep it here beside you while I go check your placements. You'll be my lighthouse when I come back from the river." Lamb coughed and gagged in a harsh laugh.

Ketchup groaned. "I set 'em right."

The ice under Zoë's bottom had completely driven the grogginess from her head. She observed Ketchup, slouched against the grooves in the sides a short fluted stalagmite. He stared up at Lamb out of white agate eyes that reminded her of a blind collie she used to feed.

Her hands felt painless and free, but when she tried to wiggle her fingers, she felt the same empty feeling like the time she nearly frost-bit them and her legs and feet when she tried to pull a calf out of a December lake. Her hands had entered a void place, the first parts of her to leave Earth.

Lamb bent into the ivory beam of Ketchup's light, glancing at Zoë, his pupils contracted. He jabbed his finger at Ketchup's chest. "You keep your girlfriend company till I get back." He nudged Zoë who, fully alert, kicked at him.

Squatting in front of Zoë, he said, "Think you can get away? You hear that noise? That's the deepest, fastest river east of the Rockies." He snorted. "You want to jump in? Float you all the way to Phoenix. You'd freeze or drown in about ten seconds."

Zoë grunted, straining against the belts.

"Okay. You'll drown first then freeze. Up to you."

Lamb surveyed the concrete platform, empty but for a few rocks and a film of ice. Turning his shadow-twisted face toward Zoë, his narrow eyes glinted in Ketchup's light. One of his eyeteeth hung down like a stalactite between his lips.

"I gotta go check Roy's plastique," he said. "Time to clear a boulder dam upstream so my business partner downstream can run his factory. Too bad you dropped in today, girl. This just ain't your day. But I'm having a good time."

Zoë pushed at the gag with her tongue, working her jaws in a painful ellipse the way she'd seen ponies resist the bit. The belt had slipped a little and she'd be able to push the cloth out in a few minutes, once he left them alone.

"I bet you got something in that coat I can use." Lamb stuck his hands inside Zoë's coat and rummaged in the upper pockets. He pulled out several T-shirts and a few pair of underpants. Then he ran his hand across her chest.

She flinched when he touched the breast with its embedded glass shard. The inflammation had faded, but his probing fingers shot a dagger into her chest.

"Ha. Sweet little titties." He palmed her breast until he found her nipple, then pinched. She winced and kicked. The pain in her breast, lessening but still sharp, forced her to breathe slowly through her nose. She chomped at the gag in her mouth.

"I like you, kid. You're spunky. If I had time…. Forget it. It's too goddam cold in here anyway." Lamb took a pair of underpants and forced her feet into them and twisted them tight around her knees. He added another pair and tied them around her ankles. Then he took the last pair and stuffed it in his pocket.

"For luck," he said, winking at her. He stood up and said to Ketchup, "I'm gonna make sure we can blow this right," he cackled. "We go home like every other work day. Happy Hour, here we come."

"You can't…." Ketchup's head lurched as he attempted to sit up.

"Leave it to Wink. I can lay C-4 so fine it'll shave a crow's tail feathers and leave its wings alone. Besides, I'll be fifty miles away when this baby goes."

Lamb hunkered down next to Ketchup and pointed his flashlight upstream.

"I've changed my life more times than a snake sheds skin. By this time tomorrow, old Wink Lamb will be a virtual trail blowing in the wilderness of the cloud."

Boasting done, Lamb stood up. "Stay cool. I've got my Glock here and, see this?" He held up a thin black case the width of a cell phone with a three-inch antennae. "See? The detonator's right here." He buttoned the detonator into his vest pocket. "Don't go 'way now."

Lamb faded slowly into the heap of boulders at the river edge of the platform where Zoë lay beside Ketchup, huddled into herself, stiffening inside her damp clothes.

Zoë had stopped struggling against her bonds and Roy turned toward her but his head fell onto his chest before she could catch his eye. His breathing deepened and stabilized and he passed out.

Zoë inhaled carefully, expecting Ketchup's foul breathing on her from a few inches away to nauseate her. She smelled nothing, so she risked a sniff. This time, she sensed a faint odor of apple blossoms.

"Oh," she mumbled. "He's going."

The rushing river a few yards away churned and gurgled, lifting Zoë's spirits for the first time since she'd seen Devan lying on the warehouse floor. Her breast throbbed, but as she relaxed against the dying man, warmth rose up her legs and pacified her so that she felt like sleeping, too.

Inky taught me to be patient until I found Veejay, she thought. Where is he now?

She raised her head to search for him, but the yellow light had faded to the strength of a night light in a bathroom with the door half closed.

She knew he wanted to take her with him but he was so patient and caring, too. He showed her what was happening to Devan and he opened the door so she could give him the luck to get away.

Zoë tried to speak telepathically with her Angel, the way she and Inky talked. Veejay, come here. Bring special water.

No answer.

Flopping her body like a fish, she urged herself up, angling her side across Ketchup's trunk and legs, wincing when her breast rubbed against his stomach. Letting her head drop onto his chest, she rested. A finger of warmth slithered down her cheek to the sensitive corner of her lip, tickling her. A whiff of rust invaded her nose and she sneezed.

Ketchup's bleeding on me.

She scraped her cheek across Ketchup's parka and scrutinized his face. Crusty scabs covered his ear, but a fan of blood dribbled out of the wound, darkening his neck and coat collar. Cherry lumps had formed on his jacket where the blood had cooled and begun to freeze.

It's just blood but it's already turning to red ice. That won't bother Veejay. Lots of souls get liberated by bloody accidents but I'll have to take a bath before we go to Heaven. It's getting cold.

At first the cloth in my mouth tasted like old work gloves. Now, it tastes salty like moldy old jerky. I bit my tongue or cut my mouth when he knocked me out. My head still feels like he's driving nails in.

Ketchup's blood leaked across her chin and she closed her eyes.

Don't go to sleep, Zoë.

What? Veejay?

Don't worry about Lamb. He's no problem.

Inky? Is that you?

I'm always with you, Zoë. Except when I have to drum for the Chorus of Angels or go on a hunting party for souls.

Where's Veejay?

He's on his way. You have to stay awake until he gets here.

I'll try. Inky, my head hurts worse than the time Harold Gone Away's pony kicked me.

Only a bit longer, little one. Soon, you won't feel any pain, only happiness. Ruthie's baking a cake for you.

I knew it. What kind? Lemon? Chocolate fudge?

Both.

I'm not hungry right now. Getting sleepy again.

Ketchup mumbled and shifted. He sagged further aslant the rock and threw his arms around Zoë. She cringed, her shoulders aching and her legs numb.

Inky?

He didn't answer.

I can't see you, Inky. She tossed her head around, looking for her guide and accidentally brushed her eyelashes against the crimson rivulet on Ketchup's chest and absorbed a drop of blood into her eye. She squeezed her eyes shut then opened them, blinking hard against the briny sting. The blood spread across her eyeball, smearing her sight into a pink blur. She sighed, unable to struggle any more.

Ketchup snorted, then an explosion went off beside Zoë's ear. She started, expecting the mountain walls to collapse. Then another boom erupted from Ketchup's throat. He was snoring.

She closed her eyes again and relaxed. Inky? Are you still here? Please?

I'm here. I'm always here, even when you can't see me. You just have to relax.

That's easy for you to say. Just try getting tied up and all bloody in your eye and see if you can relax.

If Inky worried about her getting mad at him, he might as well go back to wait for her in Heaven. He couldn't help her right now anyway. She drowsed again, losing consciousness as Ketchup's chest rose and fell, peacefully rocking.

At least Inky could keep me company.

She'd give him one more try. Devan! Is he all right? Where is he?

Inky answered, Devan's okay. He's coming.

No. He can't come here. Lamb wants to blow up the mountain.

Laurel and Wakanda will take care of him. Besides, you came here to give him your luck.

I hope I have some luck left for me. Does Veejay need luck, too?

Angels always need luck, Inky said.

Soon as he comes, I'll give him more of mine.

Don't worry. You have enough luck to last for eternity.

Thirty-three

THE ROCK AIN'T FROZE

A stone bounced off Ketchup's chest, pinging onto Zoë's neck.

He woke up and pushed Zoë off his legs. "Hey."

She rolled onto her side while Ketchup, grinding his body against the rock at his back, swiveled away from her. The river slithered and splashed against the rocks sending a fine mist into Zoë's face.

The wizened, hairless Wakanda entered the amber light thrown by Ketchup's lantern beacon.

"Goddam," Ketchup said. "Everything hurts."

"You okay, Ehawee?" Wakanda asked.

She nodded and groaned, shaking her head to say yes and to show him the gag.

Wakanda wore only long johns and a ripped shirt, no shoes. In one hand he gripped the neck of a large brown bag, dragging it behind him. In the other he held a pistol pointed at Ketchup's face whose eyes widened.

Wakanda lay his sack down and wrangled Zoë's body away from Ketchup. Setting the gun down on the floor, he worked the belt down from Zoë's mouth and extracted the cloth from between her lips.

"Gaaah." She spit. Coughed. "Water?"

Wakanda shrugged and shined his light into Ketchup's eyes. "Have any water?"

Head lolling, his eyes glazed and blinking, he seemed to nod toward his lap.

"You awake?"

Wakanda searched Ketchup's jacket pockets, coming up with a small bottle of water. He uncapped it and tipped it to Zoë's lips. "There."

She swallowed the entire contents.

Wakanda rifled through Ketchup's pockets again and came up with a flask. He unscrewed the lid, sniffed, and poured the whiskey into his mouth. A smokey tang wafted over Zoë's face as Wakanda glugged the whiskey.

"My scotch." Ketchup rasped, "Give me...."

Ignoring Ketchup, Wakanda coughed and said to Zoë, "Can you talk?" He squatted and tugged at her bonds helplessly.

"Lamb's gone to blow up the river. I think he wants to throw us in."

"It's all right, Ehawee. We're going out the road over there. Don't know about this guy. Think we should leave him?"

"Untie me, Wakanda. I gotta find Veejay before Lamb blows everything up."

The Hunkpapa retrieved Ketchup's lantern and shined it directly on Zoë's bonds. He tugged the underpants bond down off her legs and said, "Laurel's bringing Devan. We found the way outta here."

"Oh, thank Inky. I knew it."

"I can't untie this mule twine. Too tight. Belt's stuck or froze."

"I can hop." Zoë clambered to her knees while Wakanda turned to Ketchup.

"I know mountains, friend," he said to the seated man, his voice veiled by the river's wash. "I know rock. How it looks froze, but it ain't."

His eyes paralyzed as if in a vision, Ketchup disregarded the threat of a gun a few inches from the black tip of his nose.

"The rock ain't froze," the old man continued in a slow, deep voice, waving the gun at the surrounding darkness, sending the slumping man's eyes into a wide-awake trance. "All rocks move sometime. Rock stands like a heron on one leg. Still. Invisible to fish. Wind shifts. Heron dives. Water splashes. He eats. Something changes."

"He's a bad man," Zoë said.

Wakanda glanced at Zoë, then focused on Ketchup. "When your friend blows these boulders, you know everything's gonna fall."

Wakanda activated the pistol's safety, turned it around, and placed the gun in his lap.

"Maybe you can help," he said to the wounded man who lay, exhausted, nodding his head.

Wakanda's voice rumbled like small river inside the blocked, roaring one. Gripping his scored leather bag in one hand and offering the other to Zoë, he said, "Let's go."

Unable to stand, even with his hand under her arm, she stumbled and fell, twisting sideways to avoid slamming her aching head against the floor. The old man dropped his bag and levered his hands between her sides and her biceps, and lifted. She managed to get to her feet, but as soon as he let her go, she tottered and fell, catching herself on her knees.

"Wait," he said, picking up the bag and nearly skating across the platform in the direction of the door.

"What about me?" Ketchup swayed trying to throw himself to his feet. "I'm hurt."

Zoë looked at him and nodded. Somehow she pitied him, but she'd never help him. "You're uglier than a pig and a toad together. It's all your fault."

To Wakanda, she said, "If Veejay doesn't come soon, we're both in trouble."

Ketchup stopped swaying and slumped against the rock. "Lamb's crazy. He won't let anybody go. We're dead." He stared up into the dark stone, unaware of Zoë and Wakanda. The gun lay untouched. "Half a million bucks. Who gives a shit...half a million bucks. Tell my wife I said good-bye. I used to love her." He giggled. "Who loves me now?"

The smell of cinnamon and oatmeal surrounded Zoë and she felt herself lifted into Laurel's arms. "Oh my god,' Laurel cried. "What did we get you into?"

Laurel kissed Zoë all over her face and neck and hugged her so tight Zoë groaned. Her shoulders and breast burned a little and Laurel knocked her breath out when she pressed into her back with the base of her prosthesis.

"Laurel," Zoë gasped. "Where's Devan?"

"Just over there."

Zoë couldn't see him. "Is he okay?"

"Alive. Hurting."

A sob of relief burst out and Zoë lay her head on Laurel's shoulder. Like you said, Inky. Tears rolled off Zoë's cheeks, pooling in a crease in Laurel's prospector suit, then fading into stain.

"Hold her, Leo," Laurel said. "We gotta get these belts off. Look at her hands. They're blue."

Laurel sat Zoë down on the floor, and the ice felt warm on her bottom and thighs. Wakanda crouched beside her, balancing her while Laurel manipulated the panel on her bionic arm.

"I'll slice this off in two seconds."

A blade slide out of Glinda's body and Laurel turned Zoë around to get at the bonds.

An electric buzzing coming from behind her back, comforted Zoë as much as Inky's voice ever did. The belt fell away and her shoulders rolled forward, back home in their sockets. In an instant, her arms dropped to her sides and she attempted to raise them to hug Laurel. They wouldn't budge and Zoë looked down. Laurel's hands were as filthy as if she'd been gardening all day.

"Come here." Thin trails of tears ran through dust smudges on Laurel's cheeks and chin.

"Bastard." Laurel said. "Are you all right?"

"My hands hurt is all. I want to see Devan."

"Here drink some water."

Zoë glugged.

"Let's get going." Laurel pulled Zoë to her feet and with her natural hand pulled her into her hip. Leaning into her and using Laurel's leg as a crutch, Zoë hobbled, gaining strength with every step.

With a quick glance back into the shadows at Ketchup lying half-conscious against the icy chunk of limestone, Zoë called back, "You should have stayed away from me."

"Keep moving," Wakanda said from ahead. "The other one will be back any minute."

"What about Ketchup?" Zoë asked.

"Ketchup?"

"Him. The one who's hurt."

Wakanda looked back. "Leave him."

"He's bleeding bad."

"He's got what he needs. He takes care of the other guy, we'll all be okay."

"I bit his nose off," Zoë said. "He deserved it."

"We gotta move," Laurel said, clutching Zoë by the shoulder.

They ducked under the partly opened overhead door and Wakanda pointed up the gravel passage leading away from Lamb and Ketchup. "That way."

The road curved and followed a shallow incline through a tunnel. His bag thrown over his shoulder, Wakanda led them toward the pale light glowing from ahead.

Now that she could make out chiseled walls no more than ten feet away in the gloom on either side, and maybe four times higher than the top of her head, for the first time, the weight of the mountain bore down on Zoë. The murk and the dust surrounding them carried a threat of eternal imprisonment inside suffocating earth, Zoë's greatest fear.

She clung to Laurel's shirt. "Where's Devan?"

"Not far." Laurel stretched her legs, forcing Zoë to hop and stumble as she took two steps for every one of Laurel's slow long strides. "He's around the curve. We left him out of the way, in case."

Her legs regaining strength from the hopping, Zoë separated and walked alone beside Laurel, though she still clung to her sleeve. With her other hand, she dug into her Little Limbo pocket, caressed the humming bottle.

"Don't worry," Zoë muttered, patting Little Limbo a few times. After a few strokes, the bottle quieted down.

Laurel mistook Zoë's comment. "Way too late to worry now. We just have to move." She tugged at Zoë's sleeve.

Flexing stiffness out of her fingers, Zoë shrugged her shoulders and rotated them, detecting her energy and enthusiasm returning. She was weaker than before she tangled with Lamb, still a little achey in her breast, but she was free and starting to feel better. Maybe Veejay's water is working?

"Can you run?" Laurel pulled ahead, her long arm tugging Zoë uphill. "Jog a little? Devan needs a doctor."

Zoë unhitched Laurel's arm from her sleeve. Devan was alive, that's what mattered. "Hurry up. I can only walk fast." He needed a doctor, Ketchup needed a doctor. Pretty soon the mountain would need a doctor. Thank Kateri, she didn't need a doctor, she needed Veejay.

As she ran, granite dust swirling up as the floppy pant legs of her prospector suit swept the road, Laurel passed Wakanda and vanished into an eclipse the tunnel wall formed on the hazy light.

Zoë was a girl made to move and with every step, she recovered more of her normal spring. She bounced a little on her toes and scuffed after Wakanda, swinging her arms as she matched his pace, smiling. "Come on. Devan needs a doctor."

"Gave him these pills. He won't feel a thing," Wakanda said. He handed his vial of painkillers to her, then he trudged on, listing as he hauled the bag full of his family treasures over his shoulder.

When she rounded the sharp curve, bright light almost blinded Zoë.

She thought they'd emerged from the mountain, into the late afternoon. A large lit globe hung on the wall a few feet overhead, deceptive as a sunset casting its mesmerizing glow onto a restful twilight. As Zoë's vision adjusted to the light, she saw a cluster of people twenty steps ahead shifting and shuffling through the dusty shaft.

Pressing her fist to chest to hold her tender breast still, she ran. "It's them. Wakanda. Hurry up." Skidding to a stop in billowing dust, she nearly tripped over Devan's legs and pitched headlong into his face.

Laurel reached up from her kneeling position with a flattened palm to stop Zoë, and at the same time, a strong arm caught her around the stomach and lifted her off the ground.

"Slow down. Everybody's fine." Veejay's clipped baritone sang in Zoë's ears.

Angel was here and soon they'd be gone. She almost laughed but she saw Devan's face over Veejay's shoulder, paler and grayer than the rock he lay by. She kicked and flailed. "Let me down, Angel. We can go in a minute."

Veejay set her on her feet next to Laurel who was pulling Devan's containment suit off his shoulders.

"Hey, Zoë." Devan's voice wheezed as if he had asthma. "I'm okay." He struggled to sit and, taking Veejay's hand, he pulled himself upright. "Good thing I still have your luck."

Laurel slipped the suit off his trunk and he lay back down while she lifted his legs and eased them out of the bulky cloth. From the knee down, one of the pants legs was streaked maroon and purple – blood, fresh and clotted.

Zoë knelt and took Devan's hand. She leaned her face into his and sniffed and smiled at him. He smiled back and pursed his lips, then smacked the air like a cork popping. Zoë smacked back and then they both giggled and smacked again, a play ritual they hadn't practiced since his last time home.

Raising up, she said, "You okay?"

Devan grunted. "I'll make it."

Taking charge, Laurel said, "Zoë, get up. We have to get out of here." Laurel took her by the arms and boosted her to a sitting position beside her brother. To Devan she said, "Let me help you get that vest off."

He turned to his side while she unsnapped and unvelcroed and unbuttoned the Kevlar vest. "Thank God you're smarter than me," she said, tossing it to the ground.

"If I wasn't, I'd be dead." He coughed. "Good thing that idiot couldn't hit anything with his shotgun."

Zoë picked up the tan vest. Dozens of holes pocked the heavy material. In some places, tiny pellets protruded like peppercorns on a broiled fish filet.

"Laurel says you saved me, Zoë. Twice."

"Our luck." Her voice quavered. "We always save each other."

"First you tackled him, then, look here." He pointed to a soggy tourniquet tied just below his knee. "His shot caught me there. Recognize the handkerchief?"

Of course she did. It was his good luck bandana. She'd given it to him when he left to act in the movies out West. She made him agree to keep it with him all the time.

"Good thing you keep your promises, Dev. If you didn't, you wouldn't have my luck."

"Thank God you're all right," he said. "He could have killed you, too."

"He wanted to, but I wasn't worried."

Devan snorted. "You ought to worry sometimes."

"They both have the rottenest breath I've every smelled. That means they're almost dead. That's why I didn't worry about them." She pouted. "I worried about you." Tears brimmed in her eyes.

"I'm sorry, Zoë. I didn't mean it. Bad breath? Help me up, Laurel, before this terrorist here decides to assassinate us because his boss couldn't."

Veejay stood back, shaking his head. "Go," he said. "In a quarter mile, you'll find the entrance to the tunnel. Another quarter, take the path up. It ends at Lamb's cabin."

On his feet, propped against Laurel's shoulder, Devan said, "We'll make it. Come on." He limped away, leaning on Laurel while bracing one arm against the wall.

Veejay took a step after them. "Don't follow the road around the mountain. It'll take you over the top. You don't want to be there if Lamb blows it."

Already ten yards up hill, dragging his bag through the gravel, Wakanda stopped and turned back. "Ehawee, you come with me."

She looked at Veejay. "If Angel comes along?"

"No, I'll go a different way. Hurry. I think Lamb's about ready to detonate the charges. Do you want to come with me, little one?"

"Can we all come your way?" Zoë asked, almost pleading.

"Not enough time. This way out is closer for them." He nodded toward Devan.

Ignoring Veejay, Laurel bent her knees and widened her stance, to bear Devan's weight. "Zoë, hurry up," she snapped. "Need your help with Devan."

Reflexively, Zoë ran toward them and ducked under Devan's arm. "Lean on me, too. It's not far."

Devan grunted and staggered, still braced against the wall. He stumbled and tipped sideways, ramming Zoë into the granite. She dropped back and ran around in front of the hobbled pair of lovers.

"I want to help you, Devan. How can I?" She glanced behind Laurel as Veejay began to ease his way back down the slope, sliding into the darkness. He stopped and waved Zoë toward him. When she didn't

She darted into the center of the road and called to him. "Angel. Where are you going?"

"I have to go. I have to do some things, then I'll climb out the back way. It's too steep for him," he said, nodding toward Devan. "You can come with me...if you want...."

Laurel and Devan trudged on while, standing under one of the lights on the wall, Wakanda waited, his bag at his feet, watching Zoë.

She looked toward him and he gestured with his chin, "Come."

"Come with us," Laurel said. "Devan needs a doctor. You can help."

Panic filled Zoë's chest. How could she get Devan to the doctor and come back to drink poshent with Angel if that stinking Lamb blew up the mountain?

"Who's that guy? He's not our friend." Laurel said.

Zoë's body stiffened. "He's more than a friend."

"Is he a doctor? We need a doctor."

"I can't. He's my Angel. Dev found him for me. I have to go with him. He'll take care of me."

Laurel stopped. "Dev, hang on a second." He slumped against the wall as she reached for Zoë, who flinched, then smiled when Laurel brushed her cheek and knelt down to look her in the eye.

"Honey, we don't have time. Tell your friend to call you when he gets out. I'll give him my number." She squeezed Zoë's shoulder. "My magic hand might not be strong enough to help Devan by herself." Laurel held Zoë's eyes in hers.

Tears of frustration bubbled onto Zoë's cheeks and a sob broke from her throat. She smeared the tears away and took Laurel's hand and kissed it on the palm and, mashing it into her nose and cheeks, she pressed the scraped knuckles to her lips.

Zoë dropped Laurel's hand and the exhausted woman's face folded in on itself. At the wall, Devan struggled to push himself onto his feet. He nodded toward Zoë and turned uphill, shambling on.

She went to him. "I love you. You can make it. Here." She dug into her coat and pulled out a red scrap of cloth. "This is my best of all luck." She stuffed it into Devan's pocket, saying, "It's part of Ruthie's dress. She'll take care of you."

Afraid she'd tip him over if she hugged him, Zoë kissed her fingers and reached up, touching them to his chin. She smiled, "See you soon," backed away from him and Laurel, and ran down the road, shouting to the small shape plodding along, "Wakanda. Wakanda. Good bye. I'll tell Kateri about you. Hope you got a lot of gold."

"Ehawee." His voice drifted back, followed by a faint echo, then another.

Her throat swollen and her face awash with tears, Zoë waved to Wakanda and backed downhill. "I love you Laurel. I love you Devan. You'll be fine. Ruthie knows where you are."

She whirled and waved her hand up and down in front of her face, as if brushing a mirror clean of dust. With her head held high, she sprinted back through the dust toward the nightmarish heart of the mountain. If only she could catch Veejay before he flew off to the place no bomb could touch.

"Angel, wait. Veejay, I'm coming."

Dust clogged her nose and scratched at her throat but she hurried on, knowing Veejay was close by. He had to be. He had to be close and he had to be her Angel. He had to be.Inky, she prayed. Take care of Laurel and Devan. Wakanda, too.

She ran all the way back to the wide door where Lamb had taken her. Still no Veejay. Gathering her wits, she squatted and peered at the ground, looking for his tracks among a crowd of footprints pointing in every direction. Frustration competed with panic.

"Zoë, over here. I'm waiting for you.

"Veejay, I'm almost there. I'm going with you." She ran, back into the cavern with the tanks, still focused on the path in front of her feet. As she entered the warehouse, its vague lavender light glimmered off the row of tanks in front of her.

She looked up and there he was, waiting for her, smiling, his tall shadowed silhouette like the first time she saw him hours ago. No minutes ago. No, right now. He's telling me it's always right now. She rushed up to him and foundered against his legs. "I'm so tired."

Veejay bent over and took her face in his hands. He touched the welts on her cheeks and wiped at blood caked at the corners of her lips. "The bastard."

They smiled at each other for a moment until Zoë said, "Let's find some water. Now it's time, isn't it?"

Thirty-four

GOD'S SPERM BANK

Veejay scooped Zoë up and sat her bottom on his forearm, carrying her in both arms like a bride. He loped along the corridor between the files of tanks and the cavern wall as she lay with her head on his shoulder, head bouncing, eyes open, scanning the warehouse.

She stiffened and arched back to look into Veejay's face. "Devan and Laurel will be okay, right?"

"If they hurry."

Thin lines crossed her forehead. "Are you sure?"

He patted her on the back and said, "Would I lie?" He laughed.

Zoë relaxed, Angel's warm chest rubbing up and down against her stomach as he trotted. She let her arms and hands fall and lay her cheek against his neck.

She sat up. "Why don't you fly, Angel? I can hang on."

They arrived at the door to his quarters and started down the stairs. He hugged her close as they descended and passed through the lab.

Stopping before a wide steel door, he set her down and held her hand while she balanced herself. "Can you stand?"

"My head feels better. I can walk," she said. "I like it better when you carry me."

"We have to hike down a steep ledge. We'll be safer if you walk."

"Wait a minute then." She dug into a pocket and came up with her last protein bar. She chewed.

"Hurry. Lamb won't wait while you eat lunch."

Zoë gnawed off a chunk of the bar and stuffed the rest into a pocked. "Water," she mumbled, savoring the bar like a delicate pastry.

Veejay dashed to the refrigerator and brought back a full beaker. "This will revive you."

Zoë swallowed half the water in the beaker and he grabbed the beaker and set it on the counter.

Veejay opened the door and pushed her through into an unlit room. When he closed the door behind them and total darkness surrounded her, Zoë sucked in her breath, felt herself falling, dropping into bottomless night. She blinked several times, attempting to banish the fear from her chest, but her body expanded into the emptiness. Her arms flew up, seeking contact with anything.

The feeling passed and she relaxed, sensing she'd soon see as well as she could in night barns when she searched for someplace to sleep on stormy nights.

Then Veejay clicked a switch, illuminating a line of ping pong bulbs that curled away along a narrow cleft.

"I don't mind the dark," Zoë said. "If you take my hand, you can turn out the lights."

He took her hand but left the lights on and she felt at home again.

"It's steep," Veejay said, "watch where you're going." With every step they took, Anpetu imposed its protective bulk between them and the waste storage cavern. The trail ended in a circular landing under a bright bulb. Veejay dropped Zoë's hand, then picked her up and tossed her around onto his back, placing her hands around his neck. "I'll give you a ride.". She clutched his head in one hand, laying her cheek against fine hairs that fell across his shoulder.

"Let's go, Angel!" Cicking her tongue, she slapped him on his hip and rocked up and down. "You're my pony to Heaven." Her knees jabbed into his ribs, and he staggered.

"Calm down. We're still in danger."

Zoë shifted Little Limbo from her thigh to the front of her left hip. It poked Veejay in his kidney and he jerked again, raising Zoë higher.

With Zoë attached to his back, Veejay reached overhead and pulled a metal sheet down from a shelf in the rock and inserted it into grooves in the rock wall. Maneuvering thick chains that hung from metal bars sunk into a low ceiling, he lowered two more thick plates, fixing them into a steel threshold bolted to the floor. "Better safe than sorry." Veejay barred all three doors, then crisscrossing them with narrow steel I-beams, he bolted them together.

Then he rappelled slowly down a wide chute, passing random fluorescent tubes, his breathing shallow and quick while Zoë clung tight.

"This is sort of flying," she said, as her hair swished and flopped with each jerk of his shoulders.

"We're almost there," he said. His feet pounded into the ground, nearly shaking Zoë loose. Huffing under Zoë's ninety pounds, Veejay dropped the rope, bent over and shrugged. She landed on her feet and he slammed another hatch door shut over their heads. "This way."

Zoë didn't need directions. She smelled the water Angel had promised her. Yellow light rose around them and sharp stones crunched under their urgent steps.

She copied Angel's movements, bowing, twisting, striding, though unlike him, Zoë had no trouble squeezing between the corridor's walls as they angled closer together. Eventually, Veejay stopped, hunkering down against the wall.

Zoë sat beside him, sifting dust through her fingers. She picked up some of the crumbled stone and examined it in the dim light.

Raising a dust-tipped pinky to her mouth, she tasted buttery batter, rich as a pound cake. She licked her other fingers clean, then, while they were damp, combed them through the powder near her feet. With a sudden inspiration, she fumbled in her pocket and opening her angel poshent bag, she scooped up and drizzled into the bag a few pinches of mountain flour.

"Here's the real secret," Veejay said, still breathing hard. "Where human genius blossomed."

He stood up and tapped a sulfur lamp lodged between rocks. Its blinding beacon spread across a chamber that slanted away from them in all directions. They stared out into the view like tourists overlooking a scenic gorge.

"It's Cambrian rock. Old lady Gaia, Mother Earth." He nearly chanted.

She'd been waiting for him to show his happiness and now he couldn't stop talking. She relaxed her shoulders and honed her hearing to his rapid-fire words, not understanding their meaning, but feeling their truth in his excitement.

"She was untouched and innocent billions of years ago. Right here! We all started here! These rocks are saturated with the pre-organic bacteria that created DNA! Archaea! Primeval goo."

She rubbed her palm across the wall. It felt like a calf's skull, all wiry fur and bony.

"Here it is," Veejay said, scraping a fingernail along a wide vein in the wall. He waved it under Zoë's nose. "It's not a rock. Not a bug. Not a plant. Not even alive! But it's the mother of all life."

Zoë sniffed the goo: her favorite perfume – lilies. The scent reminded her of the oils and herbs aisle of George One Cloud's health food store.

"Do you know where we are? We're sitting in the middle of God's sperm bank! God passed through and spilled enough ur-seed to keep Lady Gaia pregnant until the sun burns out. Thirty-six species of Archaea inside the Earth! Now, I've created one more."

Zoë frowned, fearing she had to learn something too hard for her before she'd qualify for Heaven. She examined his face, imagining his disappointment that she didn't understand, but he grinned his assurance that it didn't matter.

"The true Garden of Eden!" he shouted, waving his lantern like a conductor with a baton, the word "Eden" reverberating and chiming off the walls and ceiling.

Astounded by their return to Eden, even if it wasn't a jungle with apple trees or sheep and lions roaming around, Zoë fell to her knees.

Veejay's lantern lit the chamber like the dome of the Rapid City cathedral. A vision of saints and martyrs she'd never imagined emerged from the walls and ceilings everywhere she looked. As a child, she'd visited the cathedral where, inside that vast and fragrant building, she'd almost fainted when she felt her soul drawn up and out of her body into the soaring nave.

Now with Angel at her side, blissful tears wet Zoë's face, rising from hidden springs of loss and loneliness that merged at the axis of her life. In this mountain cathedral she felt at home in a way she'd never felt since Ruthie left.

She saw images of her true sister, the Blessed Virgin. The wise dreamer, St. Joseph of Egypt, whose multicolored cape sparkled in a constellation of rose and aqua and flamingo crystal. The other St. Joseph with a hammer sat proudly beside the Mother of God, whose beatific face shined out from the stone ceiling.

Was that St. Agnes standing straight with flowers sprouting from her delicate feet? Black vipers and boa constrictors coiled everywhere among the sculptured saints.

"Oh, it *is* the Garden," she whispered. "Is that Kateri?" she asked, pointing across the broad nave into the heart of the beacon. "Oh sweet Inkp'du'da, it is! Kateri Tekakwitha! My heart's desire. My suffering saint. Inky, you came with me. Thank you!"

"I tell you," Veejay raved on as they trotted deeper into the mountain. "If the human race decides to wipe itself out, who cares? We're sitting in the middle of a bio-mass potential vast enough for ten new human races."

Of course, Angel knows all about creating human races. That's one of the main jobs angels take care of, all over the universe. Maybe after we hang out with Ruthie and Inky, Veejay will fly me around the different suns and planets so I can meet the other kinds of people out there.

"With this Archaea and my irradiated Lake Sunrise water, I can make a new race!" He stopped, raised his index finger, posturing like a TV preacher. "I have no doubt that my water will force evolution to speed up."

Still slightly breathless, he hooted until his voice forced a high peal from crystal knives sprouting from the walls. A delicate soprano note Zoë recognized from piano lessons, high C above high C, echoed harmonies with itself.

Angel made music with the mountain as his piano, music for her, under earth, the music of stone singing with an angel.

Veejay glanced at the girl, then at his watch.

Zoë, transported by the music, gazed through him, listening, at last understanding what he meant by his unstoppable waterfalls of words.

"Eleven minutes since we left your friends. They should be out of the tunnel. You and I have only fifty meters more, straight down."

Still in a fugue state brought on by the miraculous sculptures and the entrancing music and her bruises and wounds, Zoë didn't move.

"What is it? Do you need some of my water? Stand up. We're almost at my lakeshore home. You can rest then." Veejay wrapped both of his arms around her shoulders.

She peeled her eyes away from the holy frescoes and paintings that adorned Angel's cathedral.

"Angel, it smells like Easter lilies in here," she said. "Is this your church?"

"No, girl," he said smiling. "It's not lilies, but it does smell nice. Never noticed before. Probably the Archaea."

"Are we closer to Heaven?"

"I'm taking you to my heated pool at the heart of the Earth."

"You're funny, Angel. We don't need a whole pool for the poshent." She ran ahead.

Zoë's jacket exhaled a chord of determined cricket chirps. Miniature echoes sawed into the tunnel, testing the adamant underground spaces for the presence of any new cricket lovers.

"Do you hear my crickets tinkle, Angel?" Zoë called from the shadows. "Like jingle bells at Christmas."

ASCENSION

Thirty-five

THIS MUST BE LIMBO

They squeezed between limestone columns shaped like massive melted candles. Veejay stopped and set the lantern beside a wall of rose quartz that bellied outward over the trail. A spangled rainbow filled the passageway.

"Angel," Zoë squealed, "you made Christmas lights with your flashlight!"

All business, Veejay said, "Behind you, in the band of light on the floor, do you see a handle on a round trap door?"

Zoë nodded.

"Pick up the handle and wait for me. Don't try to go down because there are no stairs."

Carrying a rope ladder, he approached Zoë as she peered into the hole. She climbed on and, clinging to his back as if she'd been riding him for years, crimping her body between his bony shoulder blades, she floated down thirty yards to a rough ledge. Warm, misty air immediately dampened her face. Light poured down from the lantern abandoned above, flushing their skin with a rosy glow.

"Here it is, Zoë," Veejay said, waving his arm, pointing across a dark, still pond that stretched into obscurity. Black water barely moved against smooth flowstone walls at her feet.

"It's so hot, Angel," she said, taking off her coat, tying its arms around her waist. She dug into a pocket to secure the rumpled paper bag with her cherished poshent ingredients. She settled Little Limbo against her hip. "Smells like sour milk."

"Bacteria. It's a hot springs. No common Thermopolis or Devil's Cauldron. This is the tip of mother Earth's arteries," he said. "Hundreds of kilometers below us this water is a thousand degrees Celsius. And it doesn't boil."

Ever the alert chef with her mind on the delicious beverage she'd soon concoct, Zoë asked, "Do you have a pan, Angel? Or a cup? We have to boil something."

She darted around the ledge looking for a path down to the pond. Veejay pointed out the path down a natural stairway and she skipped down before him.

In the pink glow from the light he'd left on the chamber overhead, the rocks seemed to tremble. Veejay pulled a small rubber raft from a mooring a few feet off the smooth stone shore. When Zoë hopped in, he held the sides of the boat still against her squirming until she settled in.

Veejay raised his arms, spreading them toward the invisible reaches, a proud king revealing his secret cornucopia of power and wealth. "Lake Sunrise."

Pleased that Veejay controlled places inside the Earth as well as beyond the stars, Zoë rocked back and forth, tipping the boat. Veejay grabbed both sides and extended his legs to balance their weight. Zoë shifted around, rocking the raft, bouncing in her seat, looking for signs of morning sun. "Still night. When does the sun come up?"

"It's always night. Lake Sunrise is just a name. This is where I get my healing water. Mix it with Archaea and a touch of beta-decay, and magic. Water to heal everything."

Zoë's hand pressed her chest, then mashed her breast flat and rotated her palm. "It healed me. Your bottle broke when I tackled Lamb. For a while, my breast burned and ached. Now, I can feel the glass inside, but it only prickles now."

Zoë harrowed her fingers through the surface of the water, stirring up a fine steam that enveloped the boat. The sour, fermented odor floated into her nostrils and mouth. She inhaled tentatively.

"Stinky. It's a rotten smell," she said. "Hot to touch, Angel. I'll have to boil this water for our drink."

"The water - it's electric. Its colloidal properties guarantee you absorb 99.9% of its nutrients. With my radiated Archaea treatment, you absorb ... 1,000%!" Pulling hard on the oars, he said, "You won't have to boil it."

Veejay removed his shirt, exposing wide shoulders and a long rib cage. His skin glistened like dark polished oak.

"Archaea, similar to what you ate, gobbled up the steel in the Titanic on the bottom of the Atlantic. It's the fuel of the future, once my colleagues work out the details of the ribosome."

Zoë ignored Angel's teacher talk. His firm muscles and smooth stomach fascinated her. Without his shirt, the curly hair on his chest made him more beautiful than any angel Zoë had imagined. But something was missing.

"Where's your wings, Angel? I thought you hid them under your shirt?"

"We fly with mind power."

"I never thought of that." Zoë slapped the water, splashing her face with peppery drops. "Strange, like, I'm inside a mountain, not on top, and I'm going to fly to Heaven."

Zoë held the light steady and Veejay rowed fast, aiming toward the shore.

He climbed out and lashed the boat to a rock. Helping Zoë onto a ledge, he announced, "Welcome, Zoë, cricket girl. On the shores of Lake Sunrise, we can be our own natural selves. No danger, no social posturing, no clothes," he proclaimed, removing his shoes and pants.

"But how do we fly out of here, Angel? Do we have to break through the mountain?" She giggled.

He switched on another lantern that cast daylight around them. "My real home," he said. Behind a curving Plexiglas wall, he'd furnished a rambling room with a bed, table, chairs, couches, rugs, kitchen furniture. Blue and maroon and gold Persian and Chinese rugs decorated floors and walls.

An array of monitors, processors, wires, spools, assorted computer and telecommunications hardware sat stacked on shelves near the rear wall. Laden with green fruit, banana palms and dwarf papaya trees sprouted from a narrow trough that separated the bedroom from the work area.

"Like the Caribbean, isn't it?" he said, shining his light through the transparent front wall. It rose at least twenty feet to a granite ceiling and ran a hundred feet along a steep bank.

"Angel?" Her nose a few inches from Plexiglass, she said, "How do the bananas get sun?" Noticing no bathroom, she asked, "Where do you poop? Do angels poop? Do you have a shower? Where do you cook? Do you eat? Do you drink? I never saw you drink … I hope you drink!"

Veejay laughed. "Of course I drink. I eat. I excrete. See that dooe in the corner? Behind it is the composting toilet. When it cures, I toss it into the lake and hungry microbes gobble it up."

Zoë wrinkled her nose. Did he poop in something like a cat box? "Yuck. What are mikerodes? You didn't tell me Lake Sunrise has piranhas!"

"No. No piranhas," he laughed. "Microbes. They're invisible. Except when they transform human organic matter into Lake Sunrise organic matter in about thirty seconds."

Believing him, but not fully understanding, she accepted that the water was safe. She nodded and examined the filthy glass wall between the water and his room.

"What's this?" She scraped her fingernails into a streak of the black slime on the Plexiglas. Sniffing it first, she touched it to her tongue. Her nose wrinkled. "It's spicy. Can I eat this?"

Veejay shouted, "No!" Then, he mumbled, "It's all an experiment." He narrowed his eyes. "Go ahead."

She gave him a flirty look and licked the Plexiglass. "Mmmmm. It tastes like the floury stuff I tasted back there," nodding toward their passage through the mountain.

The time to drink the poshent was now. They might as well go ahead and take off to Heaven, before Lamb or Ketchup made their crazy mischief in Anpetu. Her lips open, her eyes wide, she smiled at Veejay with the most persuasive smile she could form.

"Do you have a pan inside? I have to make our poshent now." She felt along the window, probing for a door.

A panel opened in front of her. She stepped into the room and a lamp blinked on beside the bed and some machine hummed like an old fridge. Veejay followed her inside.

"Aren't you hot, Zoë?" He checked his watch again. "Twenty-three minutes. You'd think Lamb would have detonated by now. Maybe he had to set more blasing caps. That dunce he had with him probably screwed things up. The good news is your friends have had time to reach Lamb's cabin, half a mile away from the peak when it goes."

"I *am* hot, Angel." She stared into his chocolate eyes. "I have to make our poshent. Where's a pan?"

"We'll find one," he said. "One of the reasons I like it here is the heat and humidity remind me of home." He stepped out of his briefs and tossed them toward the inner wall. "We can be our true selves. Do you mind?"

Zoë had seen plenty of undressed men and boys in her life, beginning with her father a long time ago. Devan, too. Without their clothes on, below their necks, they mostly looked alike to her. Some had more muscles, some were skinnier. She liked naked fat guys – they jiggled when they walked and made her giggle.

Veejay had a lovely willy. Longer than George's, caramel-colored like his, Veejay's dangled from a bush even darker than his shiny ebony hair. Her eyes moved up to his face, then back down. His willy quivered when she stared at it.

As she pondered his nakedness, it dawned on her that angels wouldn't bother with clothes. For one thing, they couldn't get cold, for another, flying through the sky with clothes would slow them down. Not only that, they'd rocket through space so fast their clothes would burn off. So, why bother?

"Will this do?" Veejay turned to a stainless steel counter like the one in his office upstairs and picked up a glass beaker. "It's all I have. Mix my magic things up in a glass and drink."

"I thought you'd know all about poshents." His angelic nature confirmed once more, she accepted the beaker and dumped the contents of the paper bag into it.

"I'll be right back," she said, cantering through the door, jumping down the stone incline to the water. Zoë stopped at the bottom of the ramp to gaze across the turbid, misty water.

Thank you, Inky. I have the poshent, the water, my Angel's waiting.

Now, for my special ingredient.

"Don't watch, Angel." She wasn't a saint yet, so she needed her clothes, even if he was an angel. Lifting her skirt and pulling down her tights, she squeezed out a dribble of urine into the beaker, and pulled the tights back up.

Immersing the bottom of the beaker, she tipped the lip under the water, watching the dark liquid wet the poshent powders. When water reached the beaker's neck, she pulled it out and swirled the mixture until dissolved into a loose, murky soup. She felt like she'd been working over a cooking fire all afternoon. "It's so hot beside the lake."

She slipped off her boots and socks and dipped her toes into the water and jerked them right out. "That stings." Wrapping the beaker in her socks, she bounded, slipping once, up the ramp.

"I think it's ready. The recipe said I should boil it?" she asked, showing Veejay the blend.

"It's at least seventy five Celsius. Too hot to drink right away. Let it cool while we talk. I want to tell you what you ate off my front door and what's in your potion."

"I know what's in my poshent," she insisted. "I made it. I'll drink first. Don't worry, Angel. It's good for both of us."

In the excitement of the final stages of her first and final seduction, Zoë revealed the true purpose of the poshent, its primitive drive. Winking, she said, "We're going to fly, Angel."

"I can't wait, but first I just want to tell you what the slime is."

Uh oh. Did she make a mistake by tasting the window goo? It wasn't slimy. "It's okay, isn't it? It's yours, so it's all right? It's not mud or anything."

"It's not mine, but it is all right. If it's anybody's, it's everybody's."

His acknowledgment of the commonness of the goop on the glass sent a rill of pleasure through her whole body. She grinned, feeling his approval and she relaxed.

""I know you don't care, and I don't either. I am curious to see what happens. You've just eaten Archaea."

"Like Noah's Ark?" she asked, trying to grasp Angel's meaning. He wanted her to understand his wisdom about the world and his mind and everything. His teacherness inspired Zoë to be a diligent student. It was strange now, when she listened to him, she almost understood most things he said. Not in words, but in the music of his words.

""Yes," his voice lifted. "Remember I told you about God's sperm? It's not just God's sperm. It's really his first creature on Earth. It lives inside Mars and Venus and the moon and the asteroids, too."

"I'm not surprised," Zoë said. "You're God's right-handed man. You know everything about the moon and the stars and creatures. I feel like your house is the front door to Heaven."

"Not yet, little one. Wink Lamb and his detonator are still roaming around inside the other part of the mountain. Where he is, Heaven's not."

"If we're not in Heaven, are we in some limbo?" Hearing herself, she touched her Little Limbo through her jacket pocket. "I can't wait to go, Angel. Is now a good time?"

Veejay stared at her, shaking his head.

Zoë raised the beaker to her lips, held it there a second while she hailed Ink'p'du'da, then, sniffing rotten eggs, she tossed her head back and gulped. Her eyes widened as the poshent scalded her tongue. She swallowed and blew to cool the inside of her mouth. Her cheeks reddened and a triumphant smile lit her face. Shyly, she handed the beaker to her Angel.

"Drink. It's time to soar way up into eternal bliss."

Thirty-six

IN FLIGHT

Sitting on the edge of a platform that was covered with a green India-print bedspread and several pillows, Veejay accepted the beaker with one hand, while picking up a vial from a wooden bedside table with the other.

"If we're going to Heaven, you'll be my Gopi girl. Yes?"

Zoë nodded an eager yes.

"We don't have any controls here, but let's see. Two drops of my water mixed into one half liter of your hot poshent."

Veejay pinched the rubber bulb of the dropper and swirled the drink between his palms.

Angel squeezes water into the cup, the opposite of me when I catch a soul.

He sniffed its bouquet. His chest expanded with a deep breath, then deflated. A globe of sweat trickled from under his chin down into the hair on his chest.

"Sweet Radha, this is strong drink." Gesturing with both hands, he said, "Sit down."

Zoë was too excited to sit down, but she climbed up on the bed and stood, bouncing, beside him.

"Like my bed? It's built on a stalactite I sawed in half." He looked up.

She followed his eyes. Directly overhead, a limestone moon protruded from the ceiling. She bent her knees and sprang up, stretching her arm as high as she could. On her first leap, she tapped the rock with her fingertips, brushing something oily.

"It's leaking." She jumped again, this time sliding her whole palm across the rock. She landed and peered into her hand. Sticky glop of some kind. She showed Veejay.

"Once a stalactite, always a stalactite." He chuckled. "That's Anpetu's blood smeared on your hand."

He dodged when she threatened to wipe her hand on his cheek, so she cleaned it on her skirt. Then Zoë held on to his hand while she hopped from one leg to the other and back, springing up and down.

"Angel, this is the bounciest bed I ever jumped on! Watch me!"

She leapt up, twirled and flipped, landing on her fingertips and bouncing on all fours. She popped into standing position, vaulting off the bed onto Veejay's colorful rug. She somersaulted across the rug and skated on her bare feet across the floor, coasting the flowstone.

Curtsying and bowing, she grinned at the amazement on his face. Angel hadn't watched over her long enough to see her acrobatics, and she was happy she'd performed for him before they got to Heaven where seeing Ruthie and everybody might be too serious for fooling around, for a while.

Moving to the front of the bed, Veejay said, "I think we can go to Heaven. If that's what happens to me with this drink, Let's step into the shower. We have to be fresh and new when we rise into heaven."

Angel knows more than me about how to get into Heaven. "Yes!" Zoë said. "I feel grungy, and look at you – you do smell like old garlic."

"Angels need showers, too. It's sweaty work being here on Earth."

They crossed the room to an alcove where a wide showerhead began spraying both of them with hot but just the right temperature water as soon as they stepped over the threshold. Zoë hopped back and said, "Don't look," as she stripped her shirt and jeans off. They stood side-by-side, she in her panties and a t-shirt, Veejay naked, while Zoë shook her hair and watched the water swirl down the drain.

"I'm clean," she said, reaching for towels. She plucked two of them from their hangers, handing one to him, and quickly rubbing her hair and drying her skin. She noticed the pain was gone from her breast where the bottle had broken.

As he toweled off, Veejay sauntered back to the bed and sat on the edge. "I'm ready for you." Then speaking to her as if she were princess, with all the respect and honor she deserved, he said, "Please, come here and bring the beaker."

Ever the polite, respectful girl, she offered it to him saying, "Your turn. I already had some."

"Promise to take another drink after me? I want you to taste it with a KH3O in it."

"It's not in the recipe." She flushed.

"Zoë, I'm a scientist. I invented everything you see here. We can change one ingredient in a recipe. It's an experiment."

She pondered his argument. It made sense, but an experiment could weaken the poshent's power. Still, Angel was a scientist.

"You drink first."

"A natural diplomat. They should have had you at the table in Jerusalem."

"I've lived my whole life to drink poshent with you."

She jumped onto the bed behind Veejay and settled into the creases between silky pillows. She caressed the cloth and rubbed the cool green cases against her cheek. Then she heaped the pillows on her stomach, flopped, and bucked them off. Water stains streaked the sheets and the pillowcases.

"Does this concoction have a name? I like to know what I'm drinking before I swallow it."

"*Angel poshent.* What else?" she said. Zoë crossed her legs and leaned forward, balancing her chin in her hands. "Go ahead. Take a nice big drink." She put her hand to her ear. "My voice sounds like it's a mile away. Something's tickling. My ears are on fire."

Veejay sipped the warm brew, his tongue flicking at the liquid.

"More," Zoë said. "A good swallow."

He gulped and his Adam's apple bobbed twice.

Zoë nodded and clapped her hands.

He swigged, then poured down a steady flow. "I've taken poshents before," he said.

Her mouth dropped open.

"I make my own energy drink. Some chemicals like amphetamines. Black Mollies are the most effective when I blend them with coffee. Get a lot of work done."

He unscrewed the cap from his KH3O vial and poured a teaspoonful into the liquid remaining into beaker, then offered the drink to Zoë.

She immediately guzzled as much as she could funnel down her throat and gasped. Her eyes teared, her face burned. She wanted to take hold of his hands and pull his long, beautiful brown body into hers. She tensed her muscles, holding back.

"You know," he said, a catch in his throat, "if we want to go to Heaven, maybe we both should have our clothes off. We'll fly through the atmosphere so swiftly our clothes would burn off. We don't need them in Heaven anyway."

She knew that. Now, it was like he could read her mind, like a best friend, but better than Carrie Smith Fingers, like the eternal best friend she always wanted to meet but never expected to find anywhere in the Black Hills.

"Just a minute." Zoë crossed the room to where she'd dropped her coat, picked it up and folded it, careful to pleat it at the lapels so her remaining crickets could breathe. She unpacked her blouse and skirt that she'd planned to wear when she made her triumphant entry into Heaven like a princess bedecked in all her raiment.

She doubted if Heaven had any thrift stores, but once there, she'd imagine the most gorgeous blouse and skirt and as soon as she said the word, the clothes would appear on her the way sunrise shined colors onto the early morning.

She loved her coat so much, she wanted to beg Veejay to let her wear it to Heaven, otherwise, how could the crickets travel? Could Angel pour his water over the coat to protect it from outer space?

As she smoothed a lump out of one corner, the rigid metal of Little Limbo jutted into her palm.

Little Limbo! She loved Mr. J and the other souls she'd safeguarded for years. Now, she was a few minutes away from her ascension, and they lay stuck in a cold steel cup. She had to take them with her somehow.

Should she let them out, right now? No. Dozens of angels would come swarming after them - too much confusion. They'd distract Veejay. What if he was the guardian angel for one of her captive souls? He'd have to rise up with both of them, and Zoë didn't want to share her ride. He could always come back if he had to. Why not ask him? A best friend would tell you the truth, even if you didn't want to hear it. It was the least she could do for her souls. She owed them that.

Turning her head but not looking directly at him, she said, "Have you been looking for any other soul to take to Heaven?"

The bed groaned but he stayed still.

"Well?" If he didn't answer, she'd know.

"No. No. Only you." When he spoke, his voice trembled.

Jealous? Was she jealous? Maybe she was a little jealous, but she didn't have to be jealous of a flock of wrinkly old souls who were so slow they let themselves get caught.

She picked up Little Limbo and shook it. A soft rattling like sand brushing the metal answered her, the contented sound the souls always made.

The perfect plan formed in her mind: She'd loosen the thermos lid the instant before she and Veejay left the ground, then she'd kick Little Limbo over, releasing the souls to their reward in Heaven.

Setting Little Limbo on the floor beside her jacket, she knelt and pried the cap up on one side and wiggled it free without raising it off the lip. She patted it. "Not long now for you either. Mr. J, I'll see you soon."

She shimmied out of her panties and pulled her t-shirt over head her head.

Standing naked with her back to Angel, preparing to turn and run to him, her eyes fell on her trustworthy coat again. Her crickets. He'd already said they couldn't bring their clothes, but maybe she could let them ride in her hair or on her arms. She wouldn't tell him, but when she knocked over Little Limbo at the last minute, she'd shake the crickets out her jacket pockets onto her body.

Zoë giggled when she thought how she would be the crickets' angel. They were so small, they only needed her to carry them through space.

With her plans for her crickets and her souls in place, Zoë took a deep breath and, with the toes of one foot bent behind the other in spin position, she swung around to face him in her birthday suit.

A gasp broke from Veejay's mouth.

"Too bad the lake's so hot," she couldn't help grinning. "We could go skinny dipping." She looked into his eyes and skipped to the bed. He scooted back to give her plenty of room, not that she needed it now, and she hopped up.

His eyes aimed at her belly, Veejay said, "I see you have naturally scarlet hair."

"Not really," she said. "I dyed it for you."

Veejay shook his head and sighed.

They sat cross-legged, facing each other on a bed soft enough for a princess. Veejay bent toward her, his hands flickering toward her trembling shoulders and puckered nipples.

"When do we leave, Angel?" Impulsively springing up. "It feels like a warm wind from Heaven is blowing inside my bones." She bounced and twirled her body around him, pinwheeling her arms.

Twisting to keep her in clear view, Veejay gyrated his body, copying her antics with his head swinging back and forth. Laughing while she pranced, he lurched to tackle her.

"Come here, Zoë. Drink this now."

She accepted the beaker and gulped. The room brightened as Veejay lay back on the pillows, his eyes darting around the room.

Across the room, the stack of electronic gear and lab equipment shuddered, rocking slowly. The bank of screens and doors and buttons yawned. A huge flat-nosed face emerged, smiling wickedly.

The placid crickets, still huddled in the jacket, chirped in a lackadaisical but rolling cadence.

"You're beautiful." Veejay's words clacked like pebbles in his throat.

Her body glowed, pulsing in rhythm with the crickets as she sipped and offered him the beaker. "More poshent, Angel?"

Kindness brimmed from her heart. Waves of cool breeze washed over her skin alternating with warmth as delicate as cricket breath.

"You might need some more. You don't look like you're ready to go yet." She raised her eyebrows into the arc she'd learned from Bonnie when she disapproved of something Zoë did.

He followed her glances at his erection then he raised his eyes to hers. His face gleamed with lilac-hued drops of sweat reflecting the computer monitor screens.

"You don't want any more?" She couldn't tell if the poshent worked or not. She felt happy and peaceful, but Veejay didn't seem eager to go anywhere. A shudder of disappointment crept down her back. "Can we go now? It's so hot in here so why am I'm shivering?"

"Come here, little Gopi. I'll warm you up. We can go now."

Without the beaker, she knelt on the bed. "What about my crickets? They go with me everywhere."

Her eyes drilled into his, testing his powers over nature. Her will to rise bodily into divine ecstasy matched her uninhibited love for the loyal bugs. What if they couldn't come along? "They're part of me."

She could sneak them in, but, the more she thought about it, having his agreement would protect the crickets from any mean Heaven people. Just because somebody made it to the afterlife didn't guarantee they liked bugs, not matter how holy and good they were. She didn't really know anyone who liked bugs. If Veejay said to bring them along, everyone in Heaven would welcome the bugs as the saints they were.

"We can come back for them later," he assured her.

Like she thought. That's the perfect, blessed answer. They'll wait a little while is all, and then, when Inky and Ruthie and everybody say it's time to bring the crickets, we'll drop back down and pick them up.

"Sit on my lap now and we'll fly to Heaven."

Veejay's tumescent erection stretched away from his stomach. It reminded her of George's. Pretty much the same color and shape, only Veejay's was wider, not so wide she couldn't get her hand around it, though.

Veejay's undeniably human male attribute worried her. It was almost too beautiful. She took his long fingers in both of her little palms. "I can't sit on that! Angel, I don't want to hurt you. Besides, it might hurt me."

"I'll never hurt you," he said. "How could I ever hurt you? In my country we have many names for that thing in my lap." Nodding toward his erection, he declaimed, "Sapling of Joy. Vishnu's Wand. Spirit's Wing."

He has names for his willy like I have for my cottonwoods.

"How about Barkless Tree Trunk?" she said, joining in the game. "Shorty Stalagmite?" She laughed.

"That's it," he said. "My tree trunk. This is how we worship God in my country."

"Everything in Heaven is God-worship."

"Some of greatest saints in India have called this the Horse of Heaven. We can ride it to the front gate of God's palace. Come. Jump in the saddle."

Unfolding her legs and kneeling up, her back straight and her shoulders squared, Zoë said, "I don't want to ride. It might burn. Let's fly on your wings, please? Make wings on your mind, can't you?" Her voice rippled.

She sat back on her heels, waiting.

Under Zoë's harsh gaze, his erection dwindled and a russet shine crept down his thighs. With his scientist eyes narrowed and his lips pursed, Veejay watched the wick in his lap as it sputtered and shrank.

"Let's try some more poshent," he said, timbre returned to his voice. "Maybe we didn't drink enough. I'll just mix in a few more drops of my KH3O. Then we'll leave."

"You drink. I had enough. I'm sweating. Look. My skin is so wet, like I never dried off after the shower."

Veejay swilled the rest of the irradiated aphrodisiac and his stomach spasmed, his face flushed. He raised his arms toward the girl, opening his palms upward in supplication.

"I'll fly with you now," she said. "Your little breanch can't hurt me," she giggled, peering closely at his harmless crotch. "It's time."

Glancing down, Veejay smiled the most angelic smile Zoë had seen on his face. Light sparkled in his eyes, his plump lips revealed gleaming teeth shining, tiny laugh wrinkles raying beside his eyes. "Let's make wings."

Zoë leaned toward him, her hand cupping her ear because he sounded like he had a mouth full of peanut butter and crackers. As she listened, along the entire front of her body, all skin exposed to Veejay's consuming gaze, from thigh to cheek, her flesh swelled. Inside, where her heart and stomach and her organs belonged, a fearsome silent void.

At the same time, a painful desire, so intense it was a kind of fulfillment in itself, flooded up from her groin to the prickly roots of her hair.

Zoë leapt into Veejay's arms, hugged her naked body to his and clenching her eyes tightly shut, she burrowed her head into his muscular chest.

"Oh, I feel smoke on my cheek," she said, squeezing her legs around his waist. She blended into his body, her heart pounding in rhythm with the thudding of his. His powerful hug forced a deep sigh that rose all the way from her toes.

Rocking together, gaining momentum, their limbs ribboned into each other's in velvety bows and knots and her hips bored into his belly, seeking an anchor in the storm of her desire.

Moans escaped her lips and percolated into her ears. They rocked slowly as the inside of her head began to fizz.

"Oh Angel! We're taking off. I feel wings starting to grow all over my body. Bumps of wings are jumping in my skin, everywhere. My legs. My back. My tummy...."

The flesh on Veejay's inner thighs began to shake. He snorted, his legs twitching, his neck bobbing, tension in his vertebrae popping like buttons snapped off. His pelvis vibrated. His whole body fluttered. Convulsions raked his diaphragm, chopping his breath into panting while, from his groin, his Sapling of Joy inflated against Zoë's stomach.

At that moment, the first wave of earthquake that Wink Lamb's C-4 thrust into the mountain poured through the rock and slammed into Veejay's secret lair.

The bed tilted and swerved on its foundation. The floor and walls emitted horrible groans. Cracks scored the Plexiglas wall and Lake Sunrise sloshed against the window, seeping into the room. Bananas and papayas tipped, splattering fruit onto the floor.

Zoë screamed into the tumult, "Angel, hold me tight! Tighter!" She tried to shed her body and immerse herself into Veejay's flesh. Her heels dug into his kidneys, while her fingernails carved into his shoulder blades.

Oddly, the deeper Zoë drove her nails into his back, the more relaxed his body felt under her hands. She opened her eyes. The light was changing from chartreuse to aquamarine. Some of the computer monitors blazed blue distress signals, then tumbled onto the floor.

Veejay unglued Zoë from his sweating abdomen and lifted her by the armpits, raising her until her thighs grazed the revived tip of his Wand of Vishnu. He arched his hips toward her, waiting, letting her slip down, breath by breath.

He held Zoë in midair, as if he didn't know whether to throw her into the sky and follow her or to cover her with his flesh to protect her while they flew. For a moment, she felt her spine and arm bones and leg bones go rigid with fear.

Her breath hitched in her throat while a rough ache of desire twisted through her belly. Everything depended on what she did now. Zoë faced the most momentous choice of her life.

Her body, all feeling, demanded the relief of sinking into Veejay for the pure consuming sensation of it and she resisted, bracing herself, his palms scorching inside her armpits, his long fingers throbbing on her shoulder blades.

Never a gambler but always game for meeting the unknown, she was willing to risk anything when she had to, whether it was a visiting old Ketchup's church that time, or the most enormous risk she could imagine right now, because, if she took it and if everything worked out the way she expected, she would be dancing beside Ruthie in a few minutes.

If she wasn't the second virgin ever to enter Heaven, Inky and Ruthie would be disappointed, but they loved her and they'd want her with them no matter what. A true virgin was somebody who'd never been married, but to make sure she had all her bases covered, she'd never taken a man or boy inside her, only George in her hand a few times, and that was nothing.

Besides, Veejay was an angel. They couldn't take your virginity any more than a man in a dream could, and she'd had a lot of dream lovers, especially when she slept in the cottonwood grove.

She made up her mind and opened her eyes. His were two blurry inches away and she nodded and closed her eyes.

He eased her down.

"Oooooooo," she moaned and he joined in her cries.

Zoë slid down Veejay's Sapling of Joy at the same time the fragrance of a garden of tuberroses and gardenias and sage exploded into her nose.

"My souls," she said.

A dense cloud of geranium enveloped her head, then dispersed as Mr. J signaled his gratitude as he departed for Heaven, the unmistakeable sign of Zoë's correct choice.

She murmured, "I'm right behind you, Great Soul," and settled on Angel's lap, her legs encircled his lower belly and spread as wide as she could. Accepting him, urging him, grinding into him grinding back. Clasping her hands around his neck, she pushed up, helping gravity to lock her body down into his.

He groaned and she opened her eyes and saw Veejay's closed above his wide, open-mouthed, angelic smile. Her eyes half-closed, she swung, slow as a baby, back and forth, inhaling and exhaling together with him, gathering force, listening to him hum the sweetest song she'd ever heard.

A window of silence fell open around them, as the floor canted and water rose. Before reaching the bed's surface, the water gurgled back through the doorway as the room returned to its original plane.

Zoë clung to Veejay as the one safe harbor for the most precious cargo in the world, her body and soul. She threw her head back, beaming when he lowered his face as if to nuzzle her nose. Instead, she reached around his neck and pulled his head down. She opened her mouth, mashing his lips into hers, focusing all her muscle and drive into absorbing his hungry mouth.

All the forms of love Zoë had ever felt – her consuming desire for union with the divine, her motherly affection for her insects, her abiding care of her souls, her daughterly adoration of Ruthie, her gratitude to Bonnie, her devotion to Devan, now this longing for Veejay inside her – all the love she could feel eddied and swam around the hot juicy mouth she shared with Veejay.

Then, a crash of thunder blasted Zoë out of her euphoria. The second wave of mountain quake rolled through thirty million-year-old stone, Wink Lamb's explosion transforming Anpetu Mountain forever.

The collapsing mountain crushed electrical service boxes and severed the tangled cables that served Veejay's hideout. A sheet of blue flame raged in the lake water on the floor, sparking and crackling and dancing across Zoë's shoulders and scalp. She laughed and screamed, "Angel, this is what I wanted. More, more!"

Another howl shattered the network of computers igniting them into a mantle of violet streaks. The overhead lights clashed and strobed. Veejay's body began to spasm in time to the waves of the quake and a stream of heart-breaking pleasure swelled in Zoë's belly and gushed up into her heart.

Her taut body shivered and flopped like a puppy's shaking off water. She clutched his neck tighter and butterfly-soft wings caressed her shoulders. Shivers and tickles flooded down from her throat to her stomach and legs into her soles.

Spiny scarlet nodes of flame arced around the room's surfaces tagging the ceiling, the equipment, the bed, darting around like a panicked school of tropical fish floundering into the bubbling shallows on the floor.

A fiery node englobed their bodies in a saffron cone the shape of a miniature rocket. Zoë's skin sizzled and she smelled the acrid scent of burning hair.

Distracted from her physical pleasure by the odor, she pulled back from their kiss and opened her eyes. A crown of gold corkscrewed out of Veejay's head toward the darkness above. His eyes popped open, dark embers flashing among tongues of blue licking at his face and body.

"Your hair's on fire," Veejay said.

"For real?" Zoë said. "It doesn't hurt."

"No," he groaned.

"Oh, we're glory." She eased herself up and let herself down again, faster than before. "It's so hot."

They reached up at the same time to brush the other's lit hair. The painless flames whipped around them in a tornado of rainbow light, burning without smoke.

Sensing a prickling on her stomach, Zoë glanced down. A fountain of silver specks flowed up from the crease where their bodies touched at their breasts. Tiny and swift as the starry flecks erupting from Fourth of July sparklers, they twinkled and disappeared in the sheen of sweat on her skin. Zoë rode her bounding angel through galaxy after galaxy far beyond the familiar moon and stars.

"We must be almost there." She began to pant, and aware of the only way she could breathe freely while they galloped through the far reaches of the known universe, she pulled Veejay's lips to hers and sucked in his breath that tasted faintly now of curry and garlic and ashes.

The electric flame encircled their mouths, darting at her cheeks and tickling the inside of her nose. Clinging to his lips, she followed his mouth as it opened and drew in an icy current of air.

Zoë lost her breath and inhaled again and when she let go, the wind dragged her soul up from her belly into her lungs and out through her lips into Veejay's mouth and across his slippery tongue. There, in the moist cave, more flame crackled and she merged with the radiant center of his soul.

Now, an exploding nova that was their commingled souls drew them through Veejay's fontanel, speeding them toward a crack in the ceiling. They raced up a dusty mound of fresh scree cloven in the mountain's viscera by Lamb's madness.

Shuddering through the mountain's ruptured granite, Lamb's detonation flung the two souls past the calamity of their individual desires and cast them into fusion in flight. Shed of skin and bones, lost in union, Zoë surrendered to the beckoning sapphire sky.

A hundred feet above the mountainside, Zoë spotted a red-tailed hawk, coasting on thermal updrafts in the evening sun, poised to drive his talons toward a careless creature in the darkening sea of grass below. The mated souls rushed past the hawk, singeing his wing feathers, searing his beak, dragging him in their wake thousands of feet away from his prey.

Five thousand feet over the imploding peak of Anpetu Mountain, the lovers slowed and stopped. The stunned hawk dropped away from their magnetic field and tumbled, its feathers smoking.

Drifting in ivory sunbeams that angled skyward from the setting sun, Zoë discovered Veejay immersed in her mind, in the sky, in the wind they'd become, her true soul mate.

Serene and safe in Angel's swift arms, fulfilled in her mission, moored in the heart that beat as one for her and Veejay, she regained some presence of mind and glanced around the sky with her new vision, scanning for Inkp'du'da himself.

She looked east toward the creeping twilight. In the distance, the Badlands basked on their haunches in the setting sun. Those eroded hills, amphitheater to millions of angelic powers, robed in burnt orange vestments of stone, shimmered and bowed toward the liberated souls floating over them. Lined up like fenceposts along the border of the Badlands, tiny crows perched. "Little peckers," Zoë thought, smiling to herself.

Beyond time, she and Veejay rambled among the peaceful foothills of Heaven. They spoke endearments to each other in humid pulses of insight and question. She dawdled in the spirit world, trying out the new wings of her mind, patiently anticipating her body's arrival.

Scents of rose and geranium and other vague floral fragrances teased her nostrils. Searching all six directions for signs of her old souls without spotting them, she wished they could see her flying with Veejay. She sighed.

The Badlands drew night's velvet gown up their legs, over their bodies, veiling their faces with evening's sable shadows. In the west, the sun, no larger than normal at this divine elevation, had banished the clouds and hung like a melting scoop of orange sherbet in the evening sky.

They lolled in the sky well below Heaven's highest reaches, basking in the tranquil scent of the empyrean until black shreds of smoke drifted past their beatified bodies. Curious, Zoë tried to look down, but she was still attached at the mouth to Veejay. She tipped her shoulders back and kicked her knees the way she did when backflipping off a diving board and nudged him with her knees. She lay on her back with Veejay resting on her body, glued to her.

Then she tilted her shoulder and turned them all the way over, so she lay on top, cushioned not by his flesh, but by an invisible pillow of air.

She tipped her shoulder the other way and they reversed direction, spinning over and over in slow barrel rolls, watching the piney Earth brighten into pale violet sky that soon faded into dusk dulling further into the gray-brown of cottonwood bark.

As the sky acrobats rotated, the fluid nature of the universe, in its swaths of light and dark, wheeled around Zoë and Veejay.

They turned over and over, as if anchored in one place. Used to the vertigo caused by spinning and downhill-rolling, Zoë became a little impatient with her clear head until the bands of bright sky dimmed and the charred scent distracted her.

Veejay nuzzled at her lips, nipping at her tongue, apparently unaware of the burn fumes from below. She snuggled into him and, using the tips of her elbows as wings, she stopped their spin and settled with him under her. Zoë stared straight through his eyes, sending her awareness out the back of his head toward the Earth.

Anpetu had collapsed. The whole mountain had fallen in on itself, like an exploded volcano. Spires of dense smoke gyred up out of a vast pit where the majestic turrets and golden castle battlements used to rise, leaving behind a massive caldera. Thousands of acres of uprooted trees lay fallen, their green needles and russet branches and trunks seething in shadow and smoke.

As Zoë examined the disaster, the chaos of the toppled forest formed itself into a pattern. Straight pine and fir trunks with exposed, dirt-globbed roots lay stacked on each other, pointing toward the center of the caldera in the shape of a decaying sunflower head.

Instantaneously, Zoë opened shocked eyes into Veejay's stunned face.

Their bodies lay curled together back inside Veejay's hideaway, their open lips glued to each other's. She pulled back and shook her head to free herself of the vision of Anpetu's destruction but it shimmered like a mirage fused in her mind.

She opened her eyes and, in mild shock, looked around the room. Machines, plants, furniture, clothes lay exhausted in the aftermath of Lamb's strike at the heart of Anpetu. A few crickets sawed a weak harmony. All else had fallen quiet except Lake Sunrise's froth washing against the Plexiglass wall.

Unwilling to abandon Heaven to a memory, Zoë closed her eyes and submerged her being in Veejay's arms. She whimpered as her deepest, unspoken fear broke into her serenity: that she'd been expelled from Heaven for her pride in believing she, of all people, could be the second virgin to ascend into Heaven.

She burrowed her face against Angel's damp chest. Holding Zoë in quivering arms, humming and moaning, Veejay caressed the back of her neck and nuzzled the top of her head.

United with her body again but returned to boring old Earth, separating from Angel in a rapidly fading memory of total union, body, mind, and soul, Zoë squeezed her eyes tight and refused to allow herself to split off from his soul.

Thirty-seven

I MUST BE A LITTLE BIT GOOD

Finally, Zoë untangled herself from Veejay's arms. A lump of despair in her throat, she said, "Angel, this isn't Heaven, is it?"

Veejay squeezed her arm and pulled her toward him. "No, but we're safe. My back-up generators will keep the lights on and the air fresh."

She resisted, then she kissed him quickly and drew back.

"Where did the seraphim go? I saw them, heard their choir. I thought I became you for a minute. I felt like an angel myself." Dazed, she look around. "This is your house. We're still inside Anpetu. Am I such a sinner?" She began to weep.

"If that wasn't Heaven, what was it?"

"That was Heaven?"

"We're still quite close. What was in that drink you gave me?"

"I didn't see Inky. Kateri didn't show up. I thought you were taking me to Ruthie."

"I've never been closer to Heaven," Veejay said, pushing himself up and sliding off the bed. He took a step and slipped, sitting back down. "This floor's soaked. Thank Krishna we didn't get electrocuted."

Zoë stood up and paced around the bed's damp margins. "Can we go back again?" She sat and hung her feet down, dragging her toes back and forth in a small puddle.

Veejay surveyed the room. "I'm a little tired right now. Why don't we clean up a bit before we go?"

"Can we stay longer this time? Can we go all the way? Ruthie's expecting me."

"I don't know." He stood and planted one foot, then the next, making his way toward an upturned table. He braced himself on it while he palmed a circle in the moisture on the Plexiglas wall. "We could try the drink and see how far it takes us." He glanced around the room. "No matter if we only get halfway, we have something that will change the world."

Zoë scooted back onto the bed. "I don't want to change the world. Not now. I'll come back later and help you."

"Damn. It's smashed," Veejay said, staring at the debris on the floor. "I was afraid of that."

A half dozen curved pieces of the poshent beaker lay in the middle of the floor next to its whole but jagged neck.

Black specks of herbs and crushed pink crawdaddy legs mingled with the shards.

A few feet away, Zoë's coat dangled from a toppled chair, the tips of the sleeves angled like short, flat shoes on the floor. Next to it, Little Limbo sprawled on its side, wide open as an empty grave, the cup's black lid nowhere in sight. Mr. J had stayed with her for the whole journey into the mountain. Now, he was in Heaven.

Hope he gets to know Ruthie and tells her how good I was to him.

She was happy for Mr J, and sad for herself. Now that she'd fallen back to Earth – unless Angel agreed to fly her up again, this time all the way – she might have to start collecting all over. The recipe took her only as far as the lower edge of Heaven. Higher than eagles, maybe, but a long way from the Eternal. She sighed.

Inky, you said I didn't need the souls but I'm still here. Where are you?

Veejay picked up Zoë's coat and offered it to her. Water dripped from the sleeves. "Why don't we make some more of your drink?"

She glanced down at her naked body, then at Veejay's. Streaks of sweat ran off his chin and dripped onto his chest, losing itself between his cinnamony nipples. His body was the most beautiful human she'd ever seen. Zoë wondered how much longer Veejay would stay in the man body. A wave of heat washed over her. She'd love to take a swim in a nice cool lake. "I'm too hot for my coat, Veejay. Put it on the table, please."

Cricket song lilted from the shadows above them. "They're okay. Too smart to drown. I taught them to swim a long time ago." Relieved.

"Besides, they wanted to fly to Heaven with us, but they couldn't get through the ceiling."

Veejay jiggled her coat. "Maybe you have some of your 'poshent' in a pocket."

Why would he want poshent? Zoë was finished with poshent. It worked, but not the way Grandma Esther promised. Had she included all the ingredients? Yes. It must have been the goo on the window. Or, oh no, what if it was Lake Sunrise? Or worse, Angel's special water?

She'd never know. She'd met her Angel and she didn't need poshent any more. Another reassuring thought arose: She wasn't married, so in human life she was still a virgin. But in her soul, she wasn't a virgin – she was a lover. An angel lover. They didn't need poshents.

Veejay smiled at her. "I'll take you back."

"You will?"

"We can stay longer this time."

She bit her upper lip, holding back tears of appreciation. She raised her eyebrows as a new insight struck, evaporating any doubts she had about her virginity. "I must be a little bit good to have my own Angel!" She sighed, pushing off the bed and rising on legs that had forgotten how to stand. "Why didn't we go all the way up? I must be a virgin."

"Forever impetuous." Veejay shrugged. "With more drink, maybe we can go further."

"Did I do something wrong?"

"You did everything right. What else could you do?"

Pleased by Angel's praise, Zoë nodded and tipped her soggy boots upright. When she pushed her feet into them, tepid water sloshed over her toes, sending a cool thrill up her ankles and calves. She poured the water out and set the boots aside.

"Veejay, this is important."

He frowned and pursed his lips. "Yes?"

"My soul flew up with your Angel body but my human body stayed here. Why didn't you take my body, too?"

He looked down and thought for a moment. Stammering, he said, "You need an enormous soul to lift your body up to Heaven with you. Think of a manned balloon."

Piqued at the idea that her body was tethered to her soul like a basket, Zoë demanded, "You could carry me. You're strong."

"I could escort you, but what about after I delivered you to the saints? You wouldn't want your body to slip away and drop back to Earth. Heaven has no gravity, but your body does. That is a fundamental law of physics. A fact of science."

Furious with herself that she didn't know science, she grit her teeth. She should have known she needed a bigger soul, a great soul, like Mr. Johannson.

Instead of collecting old souls for all those years, she should have concentrated on expanding her own soul. If she'd known better, she would have found some living great souls and learned how they became great.

Angry tears cascaded down her face. "I'm not a Great Soul and it's not too late to learn how to be one before I'm sixteen. But I'm a fast learner. Can you teach me?"

Veejay pulled on a pair of soggy slippers and wandered around the disaster of his room, righting chairs and his worktable. He heaved some computers onto the table and found a broom. "It takes time, my dear. Time and suffering."

"I have five months and seven days before I'm sixteen. I can suffer a lot between now and then." She imagined sitting in school with a broken leg and never seeing Bonnie or no longer sleeping out under the cottonwoods with her crickets. She could handle that for five months.

That kind of suffering was nothing compared to what Kateri bore in her last days on Earth. She's a saint and Zoë didn't want to become a saint. She would sacrifice what she loved about Earth, even baking peach pies with Bonnie, but she wouldn't let anybody torture her. Lamb's cruel tenor voice rang in her memory.

After brushing broken glass into a dustpan and disposing it in a trash bucket, Veejay straightened up and interrupted Zoë's torturous ruminations. "We can try it again, Zoë."

"We can?"

"We have to experiment. At this point, I believe our interstellar voyage depends on the interrelationship between your poshent, my water, and the voltage that assailed us as we played."

"What?" Angel language confused her, but he'd raised her hopes.

"We have to reconstruct the ratios between your herbs and my water."

Zoë concentrated.

"How much poshent to how much water."

When Veejay spoke slowly she understood him perfectly. Like when she first learned Spanish from the men who picked peaches, she thought their tongues raced through their words. When she began to hear the meanings of what they said concealed inside their tongues' whirring and slurring, their speaking slowed down almost to South Dakota's easy pace. Now she had a plan for learning to understand and speak Heaven talk.

"But the anomaly: the electricity. How do we measure that?"

"You mean the blue flames and sparkles?"

Veejay had arranged most of the machines on the shelves and he began to untangle wires. "Yes. Good. I'd have to establish how much current we can bear."

"It was like lightning bolts. I want to get struck again like that." She giggled. "It felt good."

Veejay wasn't paying attention to her. He seemed to be thinking hard.

"We'll wait here until the commotion in the cavern dies down. From the looks of it, we might have quite a while before they discover my lab and follow us here."

"It might take that long to grow my soul big enough to go all the way up. Will you help me grow my soul real fast?"

Veejay grinned. "I'll do whatever I can."

"Oooo, what's this?" she said. Shaky, surprised, she reached down to scratch her thigh. She drew her fingers through a milky spoor of goo dribbled on her leg. "It's sticky."

Veejay peered at it. "Don't worry. It's Angel cream. Sometimes, when we go back to Heaven, we leak our joy into this world."

"I know what it is. George One Cloud calls it jiz." Losing interest and rubbing her fingers on the sheet, she said, "Did you see the little soul out there with us?"

"No, I didn't see anyone but us."

Zoë's front teeth bit her lower lip in a shy smile. "There was a little soul out there," she said. "Followed us way up into that part of Heaven we visited."

He said, "I saw a red-tailed hawk flying near us."

"The little soul followed us all the way to Heaven, I'm sure," Zoë insisted. "We flew higher and higher. The seraphim sang and the little soul, she was so happy. I saw her land in your hair. She was pink – a little pink hat on her head. I know she's a girl. Did you see what else she did?"

Zoë pirouetted and danced on her bare toes around the soggy room. Leaving her question unanswered, and peering through the door, she said, "The lake is so quiet now...does it have fish in it? Do you ever go fishing?"

"Be careful," Veejay said, his voice hoarse. "You could cut your feet on broken glass. I still have sweeping to do."

She turned back to Veejay, her mouth wide open. "Angel, did you see what that sweet teeny soul did?"

"I'll guess. He flew all the way up to Heaven."

"No, silly. *She* dived right through the top of your head. Then she peeked out through your belly button. Guess where she is now?" Zoë couldn't stop giggling.

Veejay sat down and stared at his stomach, his forehead grooved and his lips in a pout. "No little soul here."

"Because she's inside my tummy! Another miracle!" Zoë bounded back into his lap, hugging his neck, gnawing at his lips. She tickled him, laughing for him when he didn't respond.

He sat still. "You're far too much for me. You've incinerated my nervous system. I'm exhausted."

"Angel. You should be happy. What's the matter?"

"I'm sure of one thing," he said, hugging her breasts into him. "For the first time in my life, I feel my soul."

"You're all soul. Even your smelly body," she said, tickling him again.

He smiled and, tilting his furrowed face, he asked, "Are you telling me you think you're pregnant?"

"Yes! She's an Angel baby!" Zoë paused, waiting for the answer. A word hovered in the back of her head, then it appeared.

"Angel!" she brightened further. "I know your name. Gabriel! You took me close to God so he could make me a mother. I should have known. That's your job."

"I've been called a lot of names in my life. Who is this Gabriel?"

He was teasing her. "You remember. You came to Mary and told her she'd have God's baby."

"Of course. The New Testament. I studied that in our Christian philosophy requirement."

The realization that she was carrying a baby changed everything. Zoë dropped to her knees and closed her eyes.

Inky, you are the worst tricker I've ever met. Why didn't you tell me I was only going to the foothills of Heaven? I mean, why didn't you tell me I was supposed to have an Angel baby? I know Mary had a God baby and she was a virgin. Am I still a virgin?

She listened but Inky held his tongue. She focused her inner eyes, probing the formless dark. In the silence surrounding her, Lake Sunrise's tiny waves nibbled at the plexiglass wall and two crickets chirped, then fell quiet.

I'm not getting married to anyone, that's for sure. That's the kind of virgin Mary was, too, right? Now, what am I supposed to do?

Inky left her wondering. She hated it when he didn't answer, but now that she knew he'd tricked her into getting pregnant, he was probably laughing his head off with Kateri and Ruthie.

Ruthie was sixteen when she had Zoë and now when Zoë was almost sixteen, she was doing the same thing as Ruthie. But not everything like her mother: she'd never get in a car with a drunk guy, she'd never leave her little girl. In that moment, for the first time, she felt angry with her mother. Ruthie didn't have to get into that car and leave me.

Zoë opened her eyes and got to her feet. Veejay lazed on the bed, leaning back on pillows. Her mind raced. She'd talk with Inky later about this new feeling about Ruthie. Without much time to plan, she'd have to follow the tried and true.

She propped her hands on the bed, staring as hard as she could into Veejay's eyes. "Are you going back to Heaven?"

She didn't give him time to answer, because if he said yes, how could she talk an angel into staying, if he had another important job somewhere else? Inky, help me be as tricky as you.

"Don't leave. Yet. I've got to find a Joseph. You know. Somebody to take care of me for a while. How can I find my Joseph down here?"

Veejay remained as distant and speechless as Inky. Confused, Zoë jumped up and pulled on her drenched underpants and shirt. "Veejay, before you go back to Heaven, you have to take me to Spring Creek. I've got to talk to Bonnie about this baby."

Veejay sat up, his normally radiant face dull, his high cheeks sagging into a ridge of flesh that drooped below the edge his jaws. "Calm down. I won't go back to Heaven yet. We have to stay here for a while together."

"Oh. You'll stay."

"We have all of my KH3O water if we get thirsty or hungry. See the bright lights? I have food. And more miracles."

Grinning with relief and anticipation, Zoë said, "I love your miracles."

"I have five generators. Every one has enough plutonium to run it for a thousand years. I have the best food and thousands of movies and more games than you can imagine. We can have a lot of fun here. When it's time for us to leave, we'll go."

"When is it time?" Zoë picked up her jacket and shook it. The pockets came alive with comforting chirps. "It's too hot in here."

Their eyes locked.

Hesitant, but since Angel knew everything anyway, she admitted, "I'm not sure what to do. I thought you'd take me to Heaven and set me next to Ruthie and Inky and God and everybody. Does he have other plans for me?" Her face brightened. "It's my little girl, isn't it?"

Zoë grasped the divine logic of the tease of her ascension. She had to be physically close to Heaven in order to conceive a divine child.

"He had a Son and now it's time for a Daughter. I was wrong to think I could be the second virgin assumed into Heaven without earning it. My girl's got to grow up and get crucified and resurrect herself. I'll suffer with her, like Mary. That's how my soul will grow Great. I'll love her with all my breaking heart." She began to cry.

As she spoke, slow twinges kneaded Zoë's belly. She couldn't tell whether they hurt or felt good. Fingers she couldn't see stroked her around her waist. Incorporeal petals caressed her back, circling her shoulders, dancing up and down.

She imagined her daughter's future, foreseeing pain far worse than even what Lamb had done to her. At the same time, she thanked Inky for the premonition of the joy such a Heaven child would bring to her mother and to the world.

"I'll help you, little one," Veejay assured her. "And I need you to help me fix this place up again."

Despite the infinite honor of carrying an Angel baby, uncertainty and fear stabbed at her faith. Zoë wasn't ready for this. "Maybe we could have stayed in Heaven if we'd brought my crickets."

"Maybe." Veejay left the bed and wrapped her in his long arms. "I have the finest poshent in the world for pregnant ladies. Think a minute. Would God make you pregnant with his Daughter if he didn't have plans to take care of you?"

"No. I'm still scared. I'm worried about Devan."

"He had plenty of time to get away. We can get out too, whenever we want. I know a lot of tunnels in the mountain – one of them must still be open. If not, we can blast our way out. First, drink a little with me. You'll feel better."

"I already feel better." Flexing her legs. "When can we go find Devan? I want to go now." Pacing. "I'll take the boat. Just tell me where your tunnels are. Maybe Laurel knows about babies. I doubt it. How far is it to Las Vegas? I need to talk to Bonnie."

"Slow down." Veejay's voice turned solemn again. "You can't go out there. We don't know if the explosion released radioactivity. The whole mountain could be contaminated."

Zoë's face twisted up. "You said that wouldn't happen."

"Give me some time to reinstall my communications systems. If I still have satellite access, I'll learn about any danger."

"Hurry." She took his hand and tugged.

"Relax. It's not easy flying to Heaven one minute and coming back inside the Earth the next." Coaxing, he said, "Maybe we can even take another little flight to the foothills of Heaven?"

"Even with the baby?"

He nodded. "We could try."

"But I can't stay there. I've gotta have this baby on Earth."

"It takes nine months. The whole world will change in nine months. We don't have to rush things."

"We can't stay underground very long. Three more days at most."

Zoë always knew what was best for her, so she was surprised when she heard herself say 'three more days.' In her exuberance about the baby, she was ready to travel now. Besides, if she couldn't see sky, she might as well die.

"I have to contact a colleague. Then we'll find my escape tunnel. If it's blocked, we'll find another. Don't worry."

Three more days and they'd be on their way to Bonnie's. In three days, she'd be on the trail to Devan and Laurel. Devan didn't bring her all the way to Anpetu and get shot by Lamb just so he could forget about Zoë. He'd be so excited when he learned he was the uncle of a beautiful little girl.

Zoë placed her hand on Veejay's cool cheek. "Do you love me? I mean, not Heaven love. Your love?"

"Of course I love you. I'm the father of your baby. How could I not love you?" He shook his head. "It's got to be love. I've never experienced anything like this. The water. You. The poshent. My god."

"I knew you loved me but I like hearing you say it. He's your God? I hope he's not that cruel old bearded one."

Zoë picked up Little Limbo and retrieved the lid from under Veejay's clothes. Replacing the lid, she tucked the mug into her coat pocket. Musing, she said, "I can call you Veejay, but that's your human name. Should I call you Veejay or Gabe?"

"You can call me Gabe, but I like Veejay. Do you love me?"

Zoë dropped her coat and turned to face him squarely.

She spread her feet and propped her hands on her hips and said, disbelief rippling through her voice. "Veejay. Are you cuckoo? I love you more than anybody now. Well, maybe this little girl inside me...."

She stepped up to where he sat on the edge of the bed and braced both of her hands and arms on his bony knees. She looked him hard in the eyes. "I always loved you. I just had to find you." She kissed his nose and laughed. "Know what?"

"What?" he said, a grin splashing across his face. He reached out and buried his fingers in her hair. "'If my fingers burn up in your firey hair, I'll cool off in your azure eyes.'"

"Gabe, I mean, Veejay - I like Veejay better - you always talk funny." She shook her head, "But I'm learning Angel language fast."

Zoë lay her head against his chest, listening. His words vibrated in her ear, soothing as the cool evening zephyrs swarming past Devan's trailer on summer nights.

"What I said is from one of our poets I memorized. I feel its beauty in my heart, like you."

"I feel it too."

"My KH3O will make us happy the rest of our long, long lives."

Zoë jumped back onto the bed and bounced a few time. She landed, sitting sprawled on his thighs, her thoughtful face perched a few inches from his.

"So many people love me, here, back in Spring Creek, up in Heaven. I feel my soul growing bigger every minute, just as fast as my baby's growing." Zoë's hand absently circled her stomach. "I know Ruthie's happy for me, too. It's okay we didn't get all the way up to stay with her today. Anyway, we'll all be together in a blink of my eyes. There's no time in Heaven."

Thirty-eight

NEWS FROM OUTSIDE

Veejay slept so long without moving that Zoë poked his ribs to make sure he hadn't left his body and flown his spirit to Heaven without her. He snorted and jerked, keeping his eyes closed. One of his arms flopped out toward Zoë's side of the bed and then he rolled away from her without waking.

Zoë glanced at the digital clock that lay upside down on an upended table by the bed. 17:47. She translated. She'd learned to read Greenwich time when she studied the stars in the early days of her scheming to slip between planets and asteroids and other celestial bodies as she blazed her way to Heaven. 5:47 in the afternoon.

On her knees, she leaned over Veejay's back, her stomach against the roots of his wings – if he'd ever sprout them for her – and peered over his shoulder at his serene face. Satisfied, Zoë lay down with her ear pressed to his back between the shouler blades.

His angel heart thrummed as loud as a Lakota drum. After a few minutes, the sound bored her so she jumped off the bed, nearly losing her footing on the moist floor.

As soon as she stood up straight, a flurry of crickets dropped onto her head and shoulders. Their tiny claws clung to her hair and dug into the flesh on her arms. Shivers scurried from the top of her head into her stomach. "Oh," she giggled, as the crickets migrated to her stomach and clung.

"Get to know her," she murmured. "But you have to wait a long time in cricket time before you can meet her in person." Zoë picked up a ripe papaya and devoured the pungent flesh. Stuffed, she threw the rinds into Lake Sunshine and watched the microbes fizzle around them. Barely able to keep her eyes open, she brushed the crickets onto her jacket, and before crawling back into bed, she tugged on her panties and purple T-shirt and then, slept again.

When she woke, she glanced toward Veejay, but his body was gone. Her eyes caught the time as, wide awake, she scanned the room for Angel. 21:32.

One of the monitors glowed in the dim corner near what used to be a tidy kitchen. Veejay squatted on the floor, wearing a long white robe, fingering something into his mouth and watching the screen.

"Hi, Veejay. I love the papaya. It's juicier than the health food ones George One Cloud gives me." Zoë slid across the floor and bumped into his side. He didn't move. His whole body was like a stalagmite propped in front of a TV.

"Of course, all my fruit is organic," he said. "Look. They're showing the damage." He took her hand and pulled her to the floor beside him. Holding hands, she squatted and looked.

The television camera focused on the head of a pug-nosed, wavy-haired newscaster.

"Good evening. Bob Blackstone with your up-to-the-minute South Dakota, regional, national, and international news. Here it is, the most recent update on the Anpetu Mountain disaster."

The reporter shuffled some papers and peered into the camera, his chin jutting out "Right now, the entire planet wants to know what happened in the fabled Black Hills." The reporter spoke in a dramatic, chesty voice. "Just thirty-two hours ago, human beings caused the most horrific environmental disaster in the history of the West."

The TV showed Anpetu mountain, its towering bare peaks shining gold in the sun.

"Beautiful," Zoë said. "Looks like always."

The camera panned the mountain, taking Zoë on a guided tour of cliffs and crevasses she'd never seen.

"You're looking at Anpetu mountain – yesterday, before it happened," the reporter said, edging his voice with an ominous tone.

Veejay said, "Next, they'll show the chaos."

"Yesterday?" Zoë said. "It's only nine o'clock. We came here about lunchtime. I remember. I was getting hungry and then we drank the poshent."

"We slept all day."

Zoë stared at him, then back at the TV.

The camera closed tight on the announcer's face. He continued. "...anguish to conservationists and people around the world, the Anpetu Mountain disaster. Authorities are searching for a couple they believe are eco-terrorists responsible for the implosion of the mountain's peak.

"What seismologists first assumed was an extraordinary, localized earthquake – one that registered 7.5 on the Richter scale just in the center of the mountain – is now surmised to have been an explosion caused by vast amounts of explosives."

The TV showed an aerial view of the shallow, mile-wide caldera scooped out of the heart of Anpetu Mountain. Smoke from several tree fires gyred toward the viewers.

The announcer's voice-over went on. "The couple have histories of eco-terrorism dating to the mid 80's. According to British Columbia news reports, the couple singlehandedly destroyed Northwest Diamond Company's main logging camp during the clearcutting of the Clayoquat Sound old-growth forest. While the Vancouver Island terrorism caused damage to millions of dollars' worth of logging equipment, no act of eco-terrorism in the history of the U.S., or the world, can compare to the damage done to our Anpetu. In Lakota, 'the Radiant One.' Fortunately, no human deaths have been reported."

As the camera cruised the circular rim of the pit, it zoomed in on thousands of acres of trees uprooted and fallen with most of their tips pointed toward the center of the caldera.

The camera climbed for an overview of the entire depression. As it rose, the chaos of the toppled forest began to form itself into a pattern. The straight pine trunks with their exposed, earth-globbed roots lay stacked on each other, arranged toward a center like ripe seeds of a gigantic sunflower head just like Zoë saw fom the foothills of Heaven.

"The couple apparently survived the catastrophe by driving away before the mountain sank behind them. The man, Devan Jamming of Spring Creek," Blackstone went on, "had landed the role of Judas in next summer's revival of The Passion Play." The announcer harumphed and said, "Sometimes reality is too ironic."

"Devan!" Zoë clutched Veejay's shoulder. "What did he say about Devan? Is he all right?"

"They found out he was inside the mountain. They're blaming him for the explosion."

"It was Lamb! He's lying. Devan tried to stop Lamb."

"It's a TV story, Zoë. They need someone to blame other than the people who really did it."

"He'd never do anything like that. Devan wanted to save the mountain from all the nuclear."

"They covered up Chernobyl and twenty two other smaller disasters, like Hanneford." Veejay stood up. "They would have covered up Fukushima if they could have. It's far worse than they let the public know."

Zoë's hand dropped and she covered her mouth while she watched more TV lies. That's what TV does. She knew it before she was ten. She knew it when she was in the hospital. She could tell by the people's faces. Almost everybody on TV except little kid shows like Sponge Bob Squarepants lied all the time.

People on TV laughed at jokes when nothing was funny. Even the audiences clapped and cheered and all they wanted was somebody to tell them to come back and be in another TV show audience. This announcer obviously lied about Devan.

The announcer concluded his narrative on a factual, dismissive note. "If you're planning a sightseeing tour to the Anpetu area in the next few weeks, you'll have to see it by plane. Better yet, stay glued to your television. Most of the roads will be closed all winter.

"The National Guard will be with us, so don't worry about any criminal elements taking advantage of the chaos." Images of young, laughing men and women in camouflage and with rifles filled the screen.

Blackstone continued. "The new Super FEMA promises to fund any and all efforts required to rebuild the region. Red Cross and other federal disaster relief agencies have been on site since before dawn this morning. Local and state police forces will rotate duty to direct traffic away. Heavy equipment has begun clearing Highway 73A. The Highway Department plans to open the road by Thanksgiving, if the weather holds."

On the screen, images of cranes lifting partially buried cars, earth scrapers with wheels big as boulders, huge double-tandem dump trucks at work hauling away talus and trees.

"Fortunately, we South Dakotans are able to salvage the good in most situations. Tourist business – which the Chamber of Commerce had previously projected at record levels –is now expected to set inconceivable records. We're going to see a lot of federal government spending here. There's always a silver lining in our magnificent South Dakota clouds, eh, folks? There's even a huge new idea floating in state government circles."

Blackstone lowered his voice, inviting the camera closer for a confidential revelation, "The mountain, once it's been reshaped by the earthmovers, might be opened for residential development."

"Ah, very good," said Veejay. "Build houses on a nuclear waste facility. A ruptured one. That's what I like about your country. So practical."

Veejay's disgusted tone troubled Zoë. Angels loved everybody, took care of people and animals and bugs and trees. They don't get angry.

"In related news," the announcer continued, "Roy Kassup, salesman for R.O.I. of Spring Creek and pastor of the Christian Church the Many Paths, has miraculously regained consciousness."

The camera closed in on Blackstone's glossy dental embellishments.

"When Army Engineers attempted to start up their underground turbines on the river forty miles downstream from Anpetu, they found him lodged in the spillway. Kassup apparently fell into the river while photographing the turbines for a sales promotion campaign."

A black and white photo of a grinning Ketchup shaking the hand of a tall smirking cowboy appeared on the screen.

"Medical experts surmise that the cold water lowered his body temperature to less than seventy five degrees Fahrenheit in a matter of minutes. With only a few broken ribs, some scalp wounds, and a minor concussion, Kassup should recover in a few weeks. Maybe there is something truly miraculous in that river water, folks."

Zoë watched Blackstone's lips curl in what he thought was a smile. She saw the real thing: a grimace, the expression of gas pain. More lies, she thought.

"Rumors of a second body found in the spillway above the turbines were dispelled by police today. According to Kassup, admittedly still groggy, he was inside the mountain with six others. One was thought to be the unidentified body that apparently does not exist. Kassup claimed the others were a girl from Spring Creek, the two terrorists, a dwarf Indian, and a mad scientist. It sounds a bit deranged, doesn't it folks?

"No doubt he's still in shock after surviving the explosion and being washed miles downstream. How he survived, well, maybe we'll find out later when Kassup regains full clarity. In the meantime, our own Linda LaCourt is with the FBI and the State Troopers. She'll keep an eye on developing news and we'll break into network programming to bring it to you. Stay with us and we'll be right back. We expect to have an interview with Roy Kassup when he is lucid, that is, wide awake."

Turning to Veejay, Zoë said, "I can't believe Ketchup is all right. He's stupid and wants to baptize everybody – he stinks, too."

"We'll never know." Veejay hit the mute button, letting the TV scroll through its commercials.

Sensing that Veejay had more worldly command of machines than she'd understood until now, she said, a note of desperation in her hushed voice, "I want to talk to Devan."

Zoë never begged for anything from anybody – she prayed and all, but she never wanted anything from anybody so bad she had to lower herself, but she'd never felt so anguished for something she needed.

"Can you call him? Your computers work." She gripped his wrists. "Carrie Fingers talks to our friends on her computer. You can, I know." Her lips twisted down.

Crickets chirped in the near silence while shadowy Lake Sunrise foamed against the transparent wall. Sternly, Veejay took both of Zoë's hands.

"It's dangerous for him. They can trace phone calls. They can trace emails. Devan's smart. He won't answer if he knows they're looking for him."

"Who? Who's looking? Why?" Zoë twisted away, confused. "Lamb's friends. The police, the FBI. Probably the

Army. Green Mountain Group. Air All Over. Exsite. Any number of private military contractos."

"No. Devan's fine. I know it." He had Laurel and Wakanda. I gave him so much luck, he's fine.

Zoë sat down on the damp tile floor, thinking. She closed her eyes, envisioning the gray mist Inky came through. She waited. She breathed deeply and waited longer. Where was he when she needed him? She waited, her eyes riveted on the darkness behind her lids, until her body fell over sideways.

She woke with her head in Veejay's hand. "We have to go right now," she mumbled. "Devan might need help."

Veejay lifted her up and carried her to the bed. "Rest first. Tomorrow, we'll cross the lake to see if my chimney is still open. If it is, we'll pack up and climb out the next day."

"That's good. I know Devan's okay." Giving in to drowsiness, she said. "Besides, we have to stay down here three days. My daughter needs to grow a lot right now. I have to give her all my energy."

As she turned onto her stomach, she mumbled, "Anyway, something in that poshent sure wore me out."

Thirty-nine

EMERGENCE

Sweaty and bedraggled after a two-hour climb up a craggy fault inside the mountain, Zoë emerged from a slit between boulders partway up the side of Anpetu.

For the first time in her life, she had welcomed a leash around her waist, the belaying rope Veejay looped between them and stretched tight as they worked their way up the cramped, crooked fissure.

She followed Veejay until they reached a broad chamber where he insisted they rest before their final escape from the embrace of granite. Zoë spotted pale sky not far overhead and spidered up the smooth wall, leaving him to gather his breath. She didn't know what time of day it was, but it felt like morning outside.

She'd muttered and whispered Inkp'du'da's name a thousand times during the ascent. He spoke to her in calming tones, appearing just ahead of her, behind Veejay, glowing like phosphorous.

You surprised me, Zoë. I knew you were a brave girl. But now you have an angel baby inside.

I know. It's nice, but I'm sad, Inky. Ruthie's gonna be upset.

No, no, no. Ruthie's so happy. Her grandchild will do things in the world nobody ever dreamed of. Everybody in Heaven's telling her how wonderful and courageous her daughter is.

Stretching her legs from ledge to ledge, slithering up smooth boulders as Veejay tightened the rope and pulled, Zoë had little time or breath for talking with Inky.

You sure she's not disappointed? She expected me three days ago.

She's a little sad, like you. But Heaven people don't worry about little things like yesterday and tomorrow. Every minute has every other minute inside it.

This was shocking news to Zoë. They did have time in Heaven, only upside down and inside out.

I'd sure like to see their clocks. She thought a moment. It does make sense. People always look at their phones and clocks, so Heaven would have its own eternal kind of time, wouldn't it?

Zoë grunted and pushed her way past another stone wedge. Inky, please stay with me until I get out of here. But, can you tell Ruthie again how much I love her?"

Inky nodded. Shadows cast by her lamp wavered through his image and he stayed silent for the rest of the climb, probably conserving his energy while he watched over Zoë and, at the same time, he relayed her message to Ruthie.

 Now, at last, clear light and open sky. Her helmeted head peeked over the open lip of the mountain and she moaned aloud, the words thunking off the plastic visor. "Thank you Inky thank you Inky thank you thank you."

Standing outside, she shucked her heavy pack and rose on her toes and sighed. Sluggish and weak in her legs and arms, the open sky beckoned, but she spread her legs to anchor herself to Earth. Frustrated that she couldn't taste the free air and feel it brush her skin, she was tempted to strip off her bulky suit and its foggy helmet.

Veejay had demanded she wear the overalls and braid her hair as a condition of his guiding her up from Lake Sunrise into the unpredictable world of Anpetu's misfortune. The other condition was that she wear a backpack holding two gallon jugs full of KH3O – "For the baby," he'd said.

She also filled Little Limbo with his KH3O elixir and sipped it as she stumbled upwards, scaling the mountain from inside.

Before they left Lake Sunrise, he'd warned her about possible radioactivity they'd face, an insidious killer she wouldn't be able to see or feel before she fell over, retching and clawing at her throat for breath.

She believed her leather coat would protect her from almost anything, but Veejay knew things she would never grasp. So, as sweaty and thirsty as she was, she decided she could handle the claustrophic outfit for a few more minutes until he arrived.

One visible star hovered above the border of night's somber departure. Low in the western sky, the crescent moon drove through veils of sooty vapors spiralling up from the confusion of shapes on Anpetu. Zoë sat on the horizontal trunk of a broken lodgepole pine observing the jagged outlines of wreckage in the dim light.

Widening her eyes and peering through her misted helmet mask, she gaped toward the rim of what used to be Anpetu Mountain. The peak lay sliced flat as flat as the top of a carved pumpkin. Its magnificent turrets and spires were gone and with them the sunrise radiance that had always awed Zoë as much as any miracle she'd ever seen. This morning, the only glow came from a blurry ocher slice of sun rising over Little Anpetu, its tip now higher than its larger namesake's collapsed ridges.

Veejay strode up behind her, his headlamp transforming morning's shadows into towering pine hedges spiked with ripped trunks and ragged branches fallen helter skelter across each other.

Zoë glared at Veejay through her mask, biting her lips as she watched him calibrate the Geiger counter. Lime and lemon flashes reflected off his helmet as he pored over the machine. He might as well have been an astronaut model, his snug suit smudged but almost wrinkle-free, his helmet glistening, a beacon in the early morning shade.

"Nothing," he said.

"Nothing?"

"All clear."

Zoë wriggled out of her backpack and ripped off her helmet. The blue sky poured over her face, cooling her cheeks and filling her lungs with dazzling pine-spicy air.

She unpeeled the suit's velcro bands and unbuttoned the twenty tight snaps and unzipped the two zippers that bound her into the soggy suit.

She dropped it and stepped out, then tossed her jacket aside and pulled her heavy shirt over her head and sent it sailing over in an impulsive fit of joy at standing under an open sky, breathing tangy forest air, buoyant natural light flooding her eyes with its balm.

Zoë shook out her braid and let a breeze sough through her tangled mane, tickle her ears, and drop into her presence like an old friend with important news. The clement wind caressed her face.

As she inhaled nearly invisible smoke, a sharp scent of pine pitch irritated her nose and eyes. With a glance at Veejay, who still wore his helmet and fiddled with his machine, she zippered her coat and bounced up and down, splashing dust. Flapping and punching the air with whirling arms, she shrieked her fierce mountain lion howl at her beloved now-dismembered peaks.

Then her legs buckled and she folded down to her knees. She slumped over and wept into her hands. Sobs racked her narrow back and her moans rung out all the energy remaining in her muscles.

Veejay sat down beside her and put his arm around her. "I thought it would be worse."

She barely felt his presence as she groaned and rocked back and forth, tears dripping on her thighs.

Sobbing and then weeping until her stomach ached, she sniffled and wiped her face with her arm, smearing dust into her eyes, calling forth her final cleansing tears. She laid her head on Veejay's arm and opened her eyes into the sharp glare of the sun.

Jarred by the brilliance, she turned and burrowed her face into the rough fabric of his jacket. Then she opened her stinging eyes into the ivory gleam of his visor, barely breathing as she waited for her daylight eyes to strengthen.

With her eyes closed, her ears revived. A wave of cricket song washed over her head. Her own crickets chimed in and crawled out of her pockets, hopping off the coat and into the bushes. Veejay's albino crickets skittered down and dropped off the hem of the coat, landing beside their larger black cousins and scurrying off like tiny warriors to explore their new world.

Dawn brought restless notes of sparrows and starlings underscored by the hollow calls of mourning doves. Keeping her head pitched low, Zoë glanced at the uprooted forest, thinking she heard an indigo bunting, whose velvety feathers and cheerful song meant summer had arrived and everyone could celebrate.

Instead, she spied a tawny owl perched on a shattered branch, a glint of sun striking its beak as dawn swept down over the headless shoulders of the mountain, banishing shadows, perhaps blinding the bird. It gave a long "ooooo hooooo" and lifted off. Its speckled wings disappeared into the tangle of fir and scrub and lodgepole pine, tracking a clear path through the compressed branches.

The owl was the omen of freedom Zoë didn't know she needed. Her first view of the ravaged forest lying crushed had disheartened her. Hiking down the mountain through the impenetrable ruin would take days, maybe a week.

They carried enough food to last two days and, no matter that Veejay said his KH3O water would give them energy, she knew her baby needed food, and a lot of it. Already she had a taste for a rib eye with french fries and a double hot fudge sundae for dessert, and she never ate meat. She'd never eat steer no matter how many babies she had inside. Maybe she'd try pheasant or some other wild bird. Maybe.

She'd eaten all her energy bars and frankly, she could barely stomach his Lake Sunrise food. She usually loved rice and lentils, but when he mixed in canned spinach, she retched at the odor. She liked his hard India Indian cheese that reminded her of tofu. 'Pin ear' or something like that.

Now the owl's flight revealed that the Dairy Queen and a decent meal might only be a few hours away, if they had luck hitchhiking when they got to the highway.

Veejay had already told her they wouldn't fly. "These cowboys with their shotguns will think we're buzzards and fire away."

No matter what he thought, she'd find the best path downhill through the slaughtered trees.

The raucous cries of a gang of crows declared their scavenging less than fifty yards away. Zoë sat up and barked out a string of caws, her voice as harsh as the carrion birds', as cruel.

"What is it?" Veejay asked.

"Crows. Fighting over dead meat."

Veejay stood up and pulled Zoë to her feet. "They don't need to fight. There will be thousands of dead animals under those trees."

"I know." Her voice fell and she sighed against his hip. "I can smell it."

Inhaling, Veejay said. "Rotten barbecue."

"My nightmare come true. Radiation killing everything."

"No. I'm positive it's not radiation. Most likely the cavern contained it. The worst that could happen was that some amount infiltrated the aquifer. That wouldn't kill animals up here."

Veejay's fingers slipped around her waist and caressed her stomach. No longer bashful in front of him even when they were both naked, right now she was not in the mood for playing, even if Veejay was. As far as she knew, he was always in the mood. He had been for three days straight.

Zoë was usually in that mood, too. She'd lost count of the times they flew when they were underground, soaring in Bliss, without any poshent. Though they didn't reach Heaven's foothills again, they explored regions where she and Veejay always dissolved into one ever-expanding soul. She hoped the effects of Grandma Esther's poshent would last for eternity.

But now the faint stink of flesh rot drifting through the smoke would discourage any human being from being in the mood. She retrieved her coat and slipped it on, saying, "What killed the animals?"

"Trees fell on them. Boulders smashed them. They suffocated."

Tears streamed down her face again. Zoë recognized the benefit of sacrifice, exchanging one's death for another's life: Ruthie for her, Anpetu for all of them. "The trees and animals gave their lives so we didn't have to. Lamb is evil."

"That he is." Veejay opened his pack and offered Zoë a pear.

She bit into it and said, "We gotta get to Spring Creek." She scrounged around in her inner pockets and pulled out her phone. "I plugged it in last night. Hope it's charged."

Veejay reached into his pocket. "If it's not, I have three that are."

She glanced at the gum-pack sized phones in his palm and touched Devan's number on hers. With her eyes closed and face thrown back to the sun, she let it ring.

Veejay leaned against the tree trunk, his suit unzipped and the upper half hung from his waist. Smiling, he chewed a papaya.

She grinned back, more hopeful than she'd been since they returned from Heaven's foothills and learned she was pregnant.

Veejay tore open the wrapping of a protein bar and when she stared at it like it was a hamburger, he offered it to her. Zoë could have eaten fifty and washed them down with ten malted milks and ten sodas. She grabbed the bar and gagged it down.

The phone stopped ringing. Zoë pressed it hard against her ear.

A tentative female voice answered. "Hello?"

"Laurel?" Silence. "Laurel?"

"Zoë. Oh my God. You're alive."

"What did you think? Veejay's here, too."

"Veejay?"

"The Angel. You know."

"What? Where are you?"

"We're on Anpetu. What a mess. Dead animals, trees down everywhere."

"You okay?"

"I'm okay. Guess what?" Zoë raised her eyebrows and nodded at Veejay with a big smile on her face.

"What?"

"Big news."

"What? Are you all right?"

Zoë hesitated, feeling shy because Laurel's voice sounded weak and scared. It wasn't the right time to tell her. "I'm good. What about you guys? Is Devan okay?"

"He's okay. His leg's fractured. He had surgery and everything's gonna be fine."

"I knew it. Can I talk to him?"

"He's out of it right now. Heavy drugs for pain. I'll give him the phone but he might not be able to speak. You have to talk fast and get off the phone."

Zoë heard her say "Devan. Dev. Wake up. Zoë's on the phone. She's okay." Then, mumbling and rustling. Crackling came through the receiver.

"Zoë. You there? Zo?" Devan's voice sounded scratchy and short of breath, like an old dog's bark. Hearing Devan lifted her spirits so high she almost didn't care that she was stranded in the aftermath of Lamb's hateful blast and so hungry she doubted if her stomach was big enough to hold everything she needed to eat. Concentrating on Devan helped her stomach settle down.

"Are you all right?" Zoë asked.

"Yeah. Bum leg. Be outta here soon."

"I knew it. Our luck. Where are you?"

"Don't know." Devan coughed. "We can't really talk. Somebody's probably listening."

"Who?" She turned to Veejay who beetled his eyebrows and nodded, waiting to hear news from the far end of the cell. "He had an operation. Won't tell me where he is."

Veejay ignored her. His eyes were raised toward the ridge. He cupped his ear and said, "Hear that?"

"Devan, hang on a minute." She removed the phone from her ear and closed her eyes, focusing her ears. The distant sniveling of an engine approaching. It came closer, at first a rising whine, then grumbling. Veejay grabbed her and pulled her against the prickly branches of a spruce, a helicopter whupping toward them.

"Hang up the phone," Veejay said. "They might be tracing us by the phone'"

She lifted the phone to her mouth and said, "It's a helicopter."

Withdrawn under dense boughs, she waited to see what the chopper would do. Instead of passing overhead, the helicopter turned down the mountain a hundred yards away. Its rotors splattered their flatulent echoes across the morning before drifting off into into silence. Lighthearted sparrow song and agitated crow disputes rebounded into Zoë's ears.

"It's gone, Dev."

Veejay motioned for her to slide back inside the tree while he scouted for more helicopters.

"We can't talk now. You gotta get off Anpetu," Devan said.

"Geez, Dev, I just climbed out of the cave about a minute ago."

"This is big."

"It's the biggest thing that ever happened to me, that's for sure." She ducked out from under the branch and came back into the sun.

"For all of us," Devan said. "The explosion cracked Mount Rushmore. George Washington's jaw dropped off. Abe Lincoln lost his eyes and nose."

"Yeah. We saw that on TV." She never liked the old Presidents and now with half their faces gone, they'd look even more like Halloween monsters. Nobody would want to visit them anymore. "What about Crazy Horse?"

"Didn't touch him."

"That's good news."

"They say we're terrorists."

"Saw that on TV, too. Lamb was a real terrorist. How's Wakanda?"

"Leo. He's fine. With his nephew."

"He got his gold?" Without Wakanda's leading them into the cave, she would never have found Veejay. Wakanda deserved gold.

"Lots of gold. Other stuff, too." Devan said. "Some ancient Spanish crown. Emeralds."

Devan sounded wasted. He needed to cheer up.

"I have some big news. Bigger than the Lincoln nose." She managed a nervous giggle.

Veejay interrupted. "Tell Devan to meet us as soon as possible. My KH3O water will heal his wounds immediately."

Zoë slashed the air with her free hand, frowning Veejay quiet.

Devan rasped. "No. What is it?"

She couldn't say it aloud.

"I'm fading, Zo. We gotta figure out how to meet up."

"I'm having a baby girl." The phone went dead. Zoë shook it and shouted at it. "Devan? Devan?"

Devan choked out "What did you say?"

Her fingers rose to her lip, thrumming it down as she spoke. "I'm pregnant."

Silence.

Zoë waited for him to absorb the wonderful news of his unclehood.

"You don't know anything about pregnancy," he said.

"Veejay and I flew up to the foothills of Heaven and I came back with a little girl inside me. I know it's a girl. She had on a pink beanie."

"Sure." Devan went silent again.

"Aren't you happy, Devan?"

"Happy. Yeah. I'm really zonked."

Devan's voice sagged and he mumbled something Zoë didn't hear, then he came back, a little stronger. "Sorry I'm so wasted. Glad you're safe. I love you, Zoë. Here's some more luck." He smacked into her ear, then silence.

Zoë sighed, listening to the rustling and groaning in the background, expecting Laurel to come back.

She sipped Veejay's water from Little Limbo. It tasted like late summer lake water, kind of grassy with algae. Probably what made it so powerful, like Veejay said, it was from the new Garden of Eden.

Laurel spoke in her ear. "Zoë, are you alone?"

"No. Veejay's here."

"Do I know Veejay?"

"Did you forget everything? My angel? He used to be Vikram Kapoor. Still is but he's really Veejay. In Heaven they call him Gabriel. I figured that out when I got the baby."

"Whatever. Here's the plan." Brusque. "Get to the place where you and Devan buried Falstaff. Only we three know where that is. Somebody you know will meet you there. Don't leave with anybody you don't know. Don't even let a stranger see you."

"Why there?"

"Don't say it. Just get there as soon as you can."

"If we walk, it'll take a long time."

"I know. Just go. Somebody will be there."

"Is Devan really okay?"

"He's good as he can be."

"Veejay wants him to drink his water. It'll fix him. You should have seen the way it healed my crickets. It mended the cut in my breast. It can heal Devan."

"I love you, Zoë. We're gonna lose our phone. We hope nobody can trace this call, but they'll break through any time."

"I love you, Laurel. I love Devan. I love Veejay. I love my baby. I love Anpetu. I love all the Heaven people. I wish Veejay had enough water to pour on the trees." She listened closely. No sound came from the phone. "Laurel. Laurel?"

Zoë tossed Veejay the phone.

Veejay stamped on in the phone, and peeled the plastic back. He dug out the insides and stomped on them. sun overhead had caused her to sweat and she thought it wouldn't bother the baby, but she didn't want to get overheated so she tied the sleeves of her jacket around her stomach, cinching them tight to dull the hunger pangs.

"We have to go meet somebody where Devan and I buried his dog."

The breeze picked up, swirling wisps of smoke across the plateau. The sky took on a mustardy cast.

Zoë continued. "Three years ago. He was a hundred nineteen. I thought he'd never die, but one day, he laid his head in Devan's lap and fell asleep and never woke up."

"How far is it?" Veejay asked.

"Not far. We came out pretty low on Anpetu." She surveyed the hills and valleys below. "Twenty, thirty miles."

"We have to stay under cover, as much as we can. They'll have battalions surrounding the mountain." Veejay pressed one of his phones to his ear.

"Kreppel. Kapoor here. We have seven seconds." He listened.

"Yes. I'll be there."

Zoë heard a distant buzzing, not like the blatting of helicopters. More like the angel wings that used to hum at the headboards of her old diers in the Home.

Must be animal angels collecting souls to take them to Heaven. Ruthie will love all the new deer and bobwhites and chipmunks arriving in the Heaven woods.

Veejay's voice sharpened. "Four gallons." He glanced at his watch. "Don't worry. It's hidden." He shoved the phone back into his pocket.

"That was lucky," he said. "Got hold of Kreppel before he took off. Now I need twenty-four hours of good luck and KH3O and Veejay Kapoor will become the most famous scientist in history."

Luck, and Inky, had brought them this far, so why wouldn't they make it?

"What are Battalions? Angels? Like Thrones and Dominations?" Veejay shook his head.

"The Seraphims and Cherubims and all?"

"It's real soldiers with real guns."

"Sure," she said, rolling her eyes.

Maybe it was angel talk and Zoë never would get it. Three days and nights with Veejay and now she followed most of what he said, but here in the daylight, he started not to make sense again. Oh well. Two can play goofy talk.

"If the owl can fly, so can I." She giggled at her rhyming, then corrected herself. "If the owl can flee, so can we."

Veejay shot her a perplexed glance, then smiled and said, "If the owl can hoot, we don't need our suits." He stepped out of his Hazmat suit and buried both his and Zoë's under a broad flat rock.

Like everything Veejay said, his poem had at least two meanings. This time, she got both of them. "That's a silly rhyme."

Hoisting his pack, he said, "Can't leave any signs. They'll find the cleft we climbed. If they find Lake Sunrise, kiss KH3O good-bye."

The breeze died and the morning sky took on the amber cast of smoldering wood smoke. In the distance, ripe banana-colored clouds shot with brown streaks bunched up against Anpetu. She sniffed the air. Rain was on the way. That would clear the smoke from the air.

"Follow me, Veejay." She ducked into a passage between a row of fallen lodgepoles and an immense boulder. She stopped and glanced back, staring into his eyes. "We could fly down, you know. Get there quick and have a good lunch. You're sure you won't fly us?"

Spreading his arms wide and rotating his head from horizon to horizon, Veejay said, "It's a beautiful day for a hike."

"You're so stubborn."

Veejay picked up his pace. "Believe me, I'd fly us if I could." He caught up with Zoë and stuck his hand inside her jacket tied at her waist. "You know, flying takes two."

She grinned. "We can fly that way later. Right now, I am so hungry, I'm could become the first vegetarian cannibal."

Reaching behind and grasping his wrist, she spun around, now holding Veejay's hand in both of hers. "You know what I'm starving for right now?" She puckered her lips, darting a minxy glance up at him, and opened his palm to her face.

Raising his hand to her mouth like a plate and holding his dark liquid eyes in hers, she said, "Angel food."

She chomped down.

He screeched in mock pain and ripped his hand away.

Zoë threw her head back and laughed so hard she doubled over and staggered backwards, nearly tripping. Bracing elbows against a chest-high boulder, she stopped herself, clutching her stomach and shaking her head while fat tears flowed down her cheeks.

Watching Veejay flop his arm around, pretending she'd taken a chunk out of his hand, Zoë burst into laughter again. "Don't make me pee my pants."

She finally got her laughing under control and signaled Veejay to follow her uphill.

"Wait." Veejay ran toward her, his pack loaded with the water forcing him into gawky, herky-jerky strides. "Where are you going?"

"We have to go up the mountain to get down to Falstaff's grave," she said, still giggling. "You should know that."

Zoë turned and skipped into the massacre of trees, her laughter echoing off the ancient and tranquil stones of Anpetu Mountain.

Thank you

To Amy Swisher, whose perseverance and humor and clear eye and sharp editing pen filled my grueling, slippery climb with gorgeous vistas and beckoning light.

To David Grant, for his generous partnership along the way up my own Anpetu Mountain of composing and making Zoë's book ready for Ascension.

To Angela Borda, who traveled with me from Zoë's early days on the page through my inconsistencies and dubious notions about girlhood right until Zoë's Emergence into the world.

To Joe Ferrantino, without whose marketing wisdom Zoë would still wander the empty fields of dreams unfulfilled.

To Oona Hart, whose unparalleled cover artistry honors Zoë's courage and vision.

To Susan Cohen for naming Zoë's tale.

To Faith Seddon, whose unflappable patience and focus on page after page ushered Zoë into our tangible world.

To Claude and Shirley, should they ever be able to read it in any of the realms Zoë traverses.